PRAISE FOR *FALL*

'A mesmerising portrait of toxic family relationships: one which perfectly captures a turbulent era in a changing Britain. I was gripped by the way an architect's dream of a better way to live turns into a human tragedy, and the writing is beautiful' Caroline Wyatt

'West Camel's beautiful prose and fascinating characters drew me in and I lost myself in the world he has created in this exquisite book ... *Fall*'s characters will haunt me, its story will stay with me and I will return again and again to the many wonderful lines in this beautifully written book' Katie Allen

'West Camel's empathy with the human condition – male and female – shines from the pages. In much the same way as he did with *Attend*, he embraces a myriad story elements with a lucidity that marks him as a writer to be cherished' Carol Lovekin

'Suspense and twists keep you turning the pages, while the unfolding of complex characters and relationships draws you in' Valeria Vescina

'This is marvellous ... There are a lot of beautifully written characters in this but the main character, Zöe, really personifies an intelligent creative woman having to work around men's prejudices' Mrs Loves To Read

'Told through two timelines, it's a tale of families, greed, tension and determination.' Sally Boocock

'The author's enticing storytelling and intelligent prose is emotionally engaging, stylistically expressive, and has totally, utterly hooked me' The Book Whiskers

'Free will among the concrete blocks. Tolstoy and *Our Friends in the North*. Time-travel. *Fall* has it all. It's an extraordinary read' Richard Fernandez

Attend – SHORT LISTED for The Polari First Book Prize

ZÖE GOLDSWORTHY : ARCHITECT
DEPTFORD STRAND ESTATE

ABOUT THE AUTHOR

Born and bred in south London – and not the Somerset village with which he shares a name – West Camel worked as an editor in higher education and business before turning his attention to the arts and publishing. He has worked as a book and arts journalist, and was editor at Dalkey Archive Press, where he edited the *Best European Fiction 2015* anthology, before moving to new press Orenda Books just after its launch.

He currently combines his work as editorial director at Orenda with editing *The Riveter* magazine and #RivetingReviews for the European Literature Network. He has also written several short scripts, which have been produced in London's fringe theatres, and was longlisted for the Old Vic's 12 Playwrights project.

His debut novel, *Attend*, was published in 2018, and was shortlisted for the Polari First Book Prize and longlisted for the *Guardian* Not the Booker Prize and Waverton Good Read Award. *Fall* is his second novel.

Follow West on Twitter @west_camel and on his website www.westcamel.net.

Also by West Camel and available from Orenda Books:
Attend

Fall

WEST CAMEL

ORENDA BOOKS

Orenda Books
16 Carson Road
West Dulwich
London SE21 8HU
www.orendabooks.co.uk

First published in the United Kingdom by Orenda Books, 2021
Copyright © West Camel, 2021
'Zöe Goldsworthy' illustrations © David F. Ross, 2021

ISBN 978-1-913193-92-8
eISBN 978-1-913193-93-5

Typeset in Garamond by typesetter.org.uk
Printed and bound by CPI Group (UK) Ltd, Croydon CR0 4YY.

For s se contact *info@orendabooks* *uk*

KEY:

KEY:
1. MARLOWE TOWER
2. THE SCHOOL
3. THE HEALTH CENTRE
4. THE TOWN SQUARE
5. THE OUTDOOR THEATRE
6. THE COMMUNITY CENTRE
7. THE POOL
8. THE PARK
9. THE AVENUE
10. THE SHOPS
11. THAMES VIEWING DECK
12. THE SCULPTURE PLATFORM

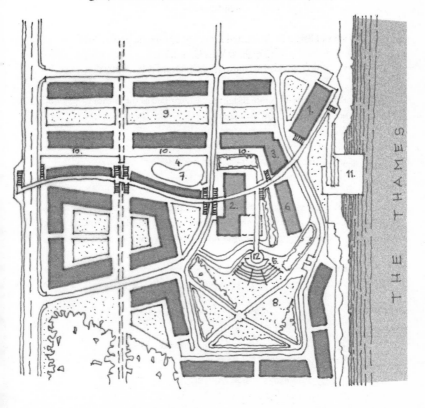

ZÖE GOLDSWORTHY : ARCHITECT
DEPTFORD STRAND ESTATE

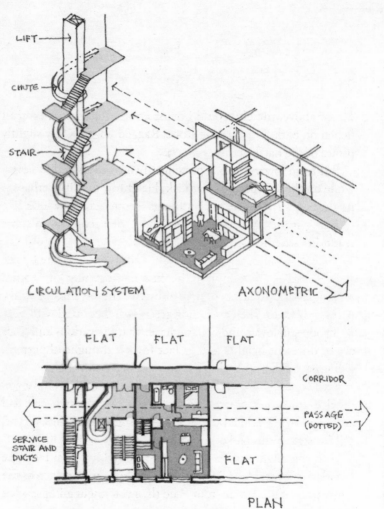

LIFT

CHUTE

STAIR

CIRCULATION SYSTEM

AXONOMETRIC

FLAT   FLAT   FLAT

CORRIDOR

PASSAGE
(DOTTED)

SERVICE
STAIR AND
DUCTS

FLAT

PLAN

ZÖE GOLDSWORTHY : ARCHITECT
MARLOWE TOWER

1

From above, the city could be just another colour. A layer of lichen on bark. On a paving stone. Ragged-edged. Only slightly proud of the Earth's crust.

But from lower down, a passenger bent into a window seat – while on the approach to Gatwick, Heathrow or City perhaps – might begin to see the tall buildings. From here they look like standing stones, arranged in the landscape according to some recondite scheme.

We can drop even lower, though, and now the estate by the river seems to be simply a haphazard grouping of shapes: rectangles and squares connected by the curved slips of roads, paths or bridges. Then a startling green swatch, dotted with pea.

Swoop still lower, and you might see that the various buildings are of different heights and in fact form a thoughtful pattern, giving each other space and meeting at purposeful angles.

And you might, if you trusted your wings enough to take you down even further, notice that the roofs are surprisingly pale and are topped with various boxes – sheds housing water tanks, maybe, or lift mechanisms and other plant.

And you might notice, on top of one building, what look like two dark glyphs; black letters that seem to be moving across the white page of this tower's roof. And then you might glimpse what looks like a face, a grizzled head.

These are women, and one is beckoning to the other. They move to the edge of the page, and lean over the high, concrete balustrade at the top of this epically tall concrete tower, which beetles, in the words whispered by its architect as she bent over her drawing board more than fifty years ago, over the taupe

Thames. You might see that they're standing close together now. And you might even think you notice stress and concern in the tension of their bodies, in the way they're pressed against each other, in the way they crane their necks to stare at something down below.

2

That something is – usefully for the beginning of a story – a someone: Aaron Goldsworthy.

Aaron has forgotten that the elevated walkway that leads from the parade of shops on Evelyn Street to the tower by the river is now partially demolished. The contractor's fence, intended to prevent pedestrians using the walkway, was forced aside long ago, and he has stepped through the gap and reached the centre of the estate without once looking up from the envelope he holds in both hands.

He gasps and sways. Then breathes out in relief. Four more absent-minded steps and he would have fallen – not to his death; the walkway is only a couple of storeys above the ground – but certainly to a broken-legged, fractured-hipped inconvenience. He raises his eyes towards the tower by the river. He thinks of the greyed tarmac at its base, empty and dusty now.

He shakes his head a little. It's lucky he looked up in time. He has no one at home to look after him, so an accident like the one he has just avoided would, no doubt, have led to an extended hospital stay. And in his absence he is sure there would be some form of bricking up, of dismantling, of cutting off of water and electricity. If he were hospitalised, and maybe even sent to some care home or other to recuperate, he may never be back here again, living in Marlowe Tower. With him gone, the last remaining resident of Marlowe, they could get on with redeveloping it.

The evidence of the estate's transformation is all around him – in the half-empty blocks, clothed for the most part in scaffolding; in the chalky scars on the side of the community centre; in the rows of yellow skips that now occupy the school playground. In hospital, he knows he would find it impossible to resist any longer. But he's not. So he can. He will refuse whatever new offer the council makes him. They have made three already.

Aaron pauses for a long time, just a few steps back from the broken edge of the walkway. Below him, in the large open area in front of what once was a parade of shops, a group of teenagers are spread out across the space occupied by the now-dry reflecting pool and the benches that surround it. They hop onto the low walls that form the pool's sides, then push each other off. Shrieks and running. Aaron looks at the envelope again, at his name on the white sticker. Then down at the cracked grey surface of the 'town square', as his mother had always called it. The ruckled bed of the pool is filled with debris now – leaf dust, a fanned-out newspaper, a scattering of plastic clothes pegs. Aaron's sight is not what it was, but somehow he can still see rubbish clearly.

Looking up a little he notes that about a hundred yards away, after the demolished section, the rest of the walkway is still standing, arcing through the estate towards the foot of the tower by the river, meeting it at the second floor. A ripped and ragged tongue of tarmac and concrete pokes into the damp air towards him, tempting him into a ridiculous leap. He takes another step backwards.

He looks at the envelope again and recalls seeing the walkway as a single, bow-shaped piece of white card, curving its path through the model in his mother's studio. Clive picked it up once – one evening when they stalked, shoeless and giggling, into the room and stared at the blocks and towers, all a perfect Lilliputian white. The studio was forbidden territory. They were allowed entry only with express permission. Even gazing upon Zöe's creations required her personal supervision, it seemed. Clive had glanced at Aaron, and, without a word, reached his arm over into the middle of the board and tested the walkway with his finger. Then, realising it was not stuck down – Aaron knew exactly what his twin was thinking – Clive clasped the slim piece of card in his curled fingers and lifted it. Stepping back from the model, he brandished the long card sabre at Aaron, sweeping it across his face and aiming its point at his eye, until Aaron hissed, 'Stop it!' and, careful not to damage the piece, prised it from his brother's hand. He replaced it carefully on the thick cardboard cylinders his mother had crafted as supports, delicately pressing it down, tracing the length of its elegant curve through the scissoring blocks, over the town square with its pool, above the little parks, and finally to the tall tower on the riverside.

Aaron turns with closed eyes and makes his way back to the road and then, via the cramped alleys and awkward, dog-legged route created by the construction company, through the estate towards Marlowe Tower. As he approaches the town square again, he passes the windowless end wall of a block. The mural that was painted on it thirty years ago has been draped with a veil of green plastic net. It's come away from one corner and hangs down, revealing part of the faded scene: a dirty-grey Marlowe Tower is recognisable, but it is oddly bowed, bending over a group of children with skin in a variety of flesh tones, but with faces that are flat and unshaded, and look out at the viewer rather than at each other. Aaron remembers the group of artists coming to paint it. Residents watching from their balconies with folded arms. Asking the artists to come and paint their kitchens. Do something worthwhile for once. This is worthwhile, Aaron once heard an artist retort. It brings everyone together. What if we don't want to be brought together? came the reply.

The group of teenagers is still in the dry reflecting pool. Most of them are black kids. One white. Maybe two. One he thinks is Asian, but he's not even sure. They're clustered together now, looking at something in one boy's hands. He wonders whether they've ever looked at the mural. He's not even sure they live on the estate. He doesn't recognise any of them. He wonders if they recognise him. The skinny white man with long grey hair who still lives in Marlowe Tower.

Past the town square he notes that one of the longest blocks is completely gutted now. The workmen have removed nearly all the windows and Aaron can see blooms of wallpaper in the exposed living rooms. Further on, though, another block stands as it always has: all the windows curtained; plants and bikes on the balconies; music pulsing out of an open door; its raw concrete still a proud cliff face.

But when he turns the corner by the school, he stops. Ahead of him is a view he's never seen before. The workmen have demolished not only the long section of walkway that passes over the school, but also the spur leading from it, south towards the park.

But they haven't yet toppled the sculpture.

It once stood at the end of the spur, on a circular platform, high above the stage of the park's outdoor theatre. Now though, with the branch of walkway gone, it sits alone on an unscalable pillar. More than twenty feet of moulded concrete, its shape still eludes Aaron's eye, and the grey sky behind it now makes it seem obstinate. Its base is a hollow drum, perforated by a lattice work of slots and apertures. Inside there's enough room for a person.

Aaron wonders how they'll bring it down. He imagines it hitting the stage below. The loud crack of the impact. The thought makes him jerk, and he hurries on his way, little reminding yelps travelling up his leg from his bad right knee.

Finally, after a journey made at least ten minutes longer, Aaron is sure, by the destruction of the walkway, he reaches the tallest building on the estate: the riverside Marlowe Tower. The name can now only be read in the paleness left behind where the letters have been removed.

Aaron heaves aside another contractor's fence and pushes open the door to the service stairs.

On the second floor, he pauses in the main foyer, glancing out at the river through the wired glass of the vast window as he fruitlessly pushes the lift buttons. For a second – a tiny, hopeful second – he thinks he hears the homely clunk and hum of the lift mechanism waking up and sending the lift down to collect him. But no; it's been weeks now since the contractor turned off the power to the communal areas. So Aaron heaves another of the many sighs of which his days are made, and begins the long, slow ascent to his flat on the twenty-fourth floor.

As he opens the door to his corridor, he is met by the gush of grey wind that has become familiar since the window at the other end was broken by some careless workman. But this time, along with the unvoiced breeze, comes a chirr and a thud. He stops, his hand keeping the door to the stairs open. The wind picks up and finds its voice: a quiet clarinet. He lets the door swing shut and listens again. Nothing. It was a piece of scaffolding rattling. Or some blend of draughts and pressures opening and closing a door in one of the empty flats above him.

Aaron pulls out his key and limps towards his flat.

As always now, when he arrives home, he tours the rooms, flicking all the light switches on and off to check he still has electricity everywhere. Then he turns on the taps, letting them run.

Finally he takes off his coat and stands at the living-room window, glancing alternately at the thicket of towers across the river on the Isle of Dogs, and at the envelope, which he has dropped unopened on the dining table. He has had to collect all his mail from the post office for weeks now; the postman no longer delivers to Marlowe Tower. Another way his path has been narrowed. He never opens anything until he gets home, though; he reads his correspondence in his own living room, as if refusing to acknowledge the tiresome daily trip. His old neighbours told him many times to get himself an email account, sign up for the internet. Perhaps he should have taken their advice. But that would have been cut off by now too, wouldn't it? And no company would come to Marlowe Tower to install those wires and boxes. And he doesn't have a smartphone – he barely uses the small mobile he keeps in a drawer.

He realises now that he has laid the letter on his mother's place, and, for a moment – a moment when he thinks he should be opening it; a moment when anyone watching would wonder why he isn't – he thinks of her. He imagines her long fingers holding the corners of the envelope and examining his name on the label, then turning it over and squinting, as if trying to read the print through the paper, before handing it over to him and watching, eyes avid with expectation.

Aaron takes a single, long step to pick it up. The stretch is unwise; his knee screams with the strain. But Aaron ignores the pain. He stands back at the window and hooks a finger under the flap. The envelope opens with a little cloud of white dust.

Inside: a single sheet.

The Residents' and Tenants' Trust
3 April 2021

Dear Mr Goldsworthy,
Many thanks for your letter of 12 March regarding the offers to purchase your home you have received from Deptford Borough Council.

The trust is already aware of the redevelopment of Deptford Strand Estate and of the proposed sale of Marlowe Tower to Clive Goldsworthy & Co. We have been assisting former tenants and owners of properties on the estate with their negotiations with the council, so we feel well positioned to advise you about your case.

In regard to your question about Compulsory Purchase Orders, we'd like to reassure you. It is not possible for a local authority to force someone to sell their home without good reason. If the local authority does apply to a government department (in your case, the Ministry of Housing, Communities and Local Government (MHCLG)) to gain the power to purchase your home without your consent, that government department will then have to make a decision about giving those powers to the local authority. Its decision will be based on whether there is what is known as 'a compelling case in the public interest' for the local authority to force you to sell your home, and whether the local authority has made every effort to negotiate with you on the sale. The local authority cannot force you to sell purely out of commercial interest.

In terms of your specific case, it is our considered opinion that the various commercial interests involved in the proposed sale and redevelopment of Marlowe Tower will make it difficult for Deptford Council to argue that there is 'compelling' public need for you to sell your home to them, simply for them to sell the entire building on to another party. The proposed purchaser, Clive Goldsworthy & Co., clearly wants to profit from buying Marlowe Tower, redeveloping the property and reselling the renovated apartments. The commercial benefit to Clive Goldsworthy & Co. could therefore be deemed as greater than any public benefit from the sale.

This case is further complicated by the fact that Clive Goldsworthy & Co. has also been contracted to redevelop the rest of Deptford Strand Estate. Our work with former residents of the estate, and with other interested parties, suggests to us that there may be several ethical questions around the relationship between the two deals: the contract to redevelop the estate, and the proposed transfer of the ownership of Marlowe Tower from the Council to Clive Goldsworthy & Co.

Overall, we believe that you would have a strong case against any CPO should Deptford Borough Council attempt to serve you with one.

We do stress that if you decide to make any challenge, you should only do so with the appropriate legal representation. We would also advise that any dealings you have with Deptford Borough Council should be done in cooperation with other residents or former residents of Deptford Strand Estate, and again with legal representation. We are coordinating a collective challenge to many aspects of the project, so would be happy to add you to the group of residents and former residents we are working with. We also have a team of advisers who deal with cases like yours every day. You can speak with one of them should you wish to discuss your case further.

Please keep us updated on your situation, and do let us know should you wish to join our efforts to challenge the development.

Kind regards
Sally Perry
Advice Manager

Aaron looks out of the window again, this time directly at the white tower that stands slightly apart from the cabal of heavy buildings where bankers sit in rows. This tower lacks their height but is tall nonetheless. And it is nearer the river, with a good view of the estate. Of Marlowe Tower. Of Aaron himself, perhaps. Aaron stares at the top floor. Is Clive there today?

He looks down at the letter in his hand, its white similar to the white of Clive's tower. Not once does Sally Perry mention that Goldsworthy is both his name and the name of the 'proposed purchaser' of Marlowe Tower and developer of the estate. Did she wonder about this apparent coincidence as she composed this letter?

He lifts it a little closer to his face and reads a few phrases again. The tone is personal and impersonal at the same time. Studiously so. He puffs a little snort of air out of his nose. What does it matter how she says what she says? What's important is that the letter tells him what he wanted to know – what he thought, in general, lumpen terms, was the case.

He turns and floats the single page onto the table; at this distance the paragraphs are dark, uneven blocks.

He sighs. He should be victorious, but instead he is sad. Sad and thirsty. And after his extended walk and the climb up the stairs, his knee is complaining. He shuffles across the worn parquet to the kitchen, pours himself a glass of water, then shuffles back through the living room and steps out onto the balcony, where he sighs into a metal chair, propping his leg up on another.

He drinks. Closes his eyes. A friendly breeze plays a little with his long hair. He threads it back from his face and behind an ear, and turns his eyes across the river once more, staring with what feel like unblinking eyes. He sits very still for a very long time. It's as if, as his limbs relax, they set and harden, becoming immovable. As if he'll never get up from this chair again.

3

Clive is in the tower. And it could be that he's staring back at his brother. It could be that their eyes meet above the impermanent furrows of the river, where the tide is just at its turn.

But here, at Deptford Reach, the Thames is too wide for them to see into each other's eyes. And Clive isn't in his apartment on the top floor. He's in his office, three floors down. And while he is at his window, he's not focused on the pale smudge on a balcony on the twenty-fourth floor of Marlowe Tower.

They haven't seen each other for forty years.

Clive's look lingers on a spot at the very top of the tower. His fine fingers find the edge of the model that sits on a table beside the window. Unlike the maquette his mother made fifty years ago, only the tower on his model is in three dimensions. The rest of the estate is displayed as a plan. Shapes and zones in various shades. He stares at the grey of the real block, caught briefly in a flash of sun. His mother insisted that it stood at just that angle, at just that place on the riverbank, towering over Deptford Strand.

He glances at the model version of the tower – renamed for her. Reclad. The blunt top smoothed with a parabolic curve of roof, beneath which two, perhaps three new penthouses will offer views of the bristling city.

The curve is itself a tribute, mirroring that of the long walkway. On the model he can trace the path it once took from the road to the tower, threading through the narrow spaces between the old, long blocks, the open spaces and the town square, then flying over the intersecting curve of the estate's main road before passing over the primary school, widening outside the health centre and tapering to a point as it arrived at the main entrance to Marlowe Tower. Home.

Clive has been informed the walkway has now been partially dismantled. The school is already empty. The health centre and community centre both closed long ago. The plan shows no trace of them.

Clive recalls creeping into his mother's studio with Aaron, both trembling with mischief, the evening of the day her model was brought back to their house in Blackheath. The sun slid through the slats of the half-closed blind. The card and balsa-wood blocks cast neat shadows over the greens. The façades of the towers were lit gold. And the walkway's sinuating journey was proud and prominent. It was a perfect little world. And that was surely the problem, he thinks now. It could only exist for a moment, when the evening sun shone in horizontal stripes and the tiny stick figures in the town square and outside the school and shops made grey letters on the impossibility of the white concrete.

Try as she might, even Zöe Goldsworthy couldn't make full-sized, fleshy humans stand in the right places. And not even a Goldsworthy building could awe its inhabitants into living in a different way.

The glass door to Clive's office creaks. A hinge hidden in the edge is misaligned, he thinks. Details, he thinks.

—Clive? says his assistant.

He turns. Kulwant has a folder in his hands. Papers to sign. Permissions. Instructions, Proposals. Somehow today, the folder looks limp.

—Do we have any news? Clive asks as he moves over to his desk, gesturing to Kulwant to take a seat.

—Yes, we do. Deptford Council just called. Kemi.

Clive looks up as he's opening his pen.

—About Marlowe Tower?

—Mr... Kulwant coughs ...Mr Goldsworthy refused the council's latest offer.

—Of course he did.

He opens the folder and sifts through the pages, looking for yellow stickers, signing as he finds them.

—Did Kemi say anything else?

—Royal Mail hasn't delivered to the tower for several weeks now, says Kulwant. Unsafe access.

—I suppose he'll be collecting it from the post office, then.

Clive glances, just briefly, at the window. Even from his desk at the back of the room, he can see Marlowe Tower. And for a flash of a second he imagines what Aaron is doing. He imagines correctly, even though he doesn't know it. Having rested his knee, Aaron has fetched a loaf of bread from the kitchen, and is now sitting at the table, buttering a slice. Clive doesn't know that there are blue-grey streaks in Aaron's hair.

—And there really is nothing else she can do?

—He's still a resident, says Kulwant. The electricity and water firms can't deny him services. She says the council has done everything it can to make things, well...

Clive taps the nib of his pen on his jotter. His irritation concentrated into the tiny tattoo. For Clive dislikes – intensely dislikes – having his plans thwarted. 'Why must you always have your way, Clive?' Zöe used to say, as Aaron folded his lips to hide a smile. 'It's so unattractive.'

Just once he replied, 'For the same reason you do. Because I think my way is best.' He had expected some slicing reprimand, but Zöe focused her pale-green eyes on his and said, 'And you're most probably right. What you need to learn is the trick to getting your way.' She widened her eyes. 'I'll teach you one day.'

Now he nods, and tells himself that she knew him all too well. He must have his way, and usually does. But this time his brother is preventing it. He sits unmoving on the other side of a screen that they drew between themselves forty years ago. And if he doesn't move, the meagre money Clive will receive, and major effort it will take, to renovate the rest of estate is for nothing. 'Aaron's obdurate,' Zöe used to say. 'Aaron, you are infuriatingly obdurate. You can

never be persuaded of anything.' Clive tried to tease his brother
with the word, but Aaron seemed to quite like the label.

Clive taps his nib with such energy now, a drop of ink flies out
and lands on his cuff. He raises his hand slightly in order to gaze
at it as it soaks into the fabric.

—There's a lot of other, non-Marlowe stuff to discuss, says
Kulwant. There's the cladding issue, of course. They're not
convinced by the specs for the new stuff. They're saying that post-
Grenfell they need more assurances. They want a meeting.

Clive doesn't bother to stifle his sigh before saying:

—If there's a space tomorrow, let's meet them then. Make an
agenda. Five minutes each issue. And have them come here. I can't
be bothered with the fuss of getting down there.

Kulwant has already pulled out his phone. Makes quick notes
on the pad in his hand.

—Have we had any more questions from Knights about
funding tranches? asks Clive.

—Not yet.

—I'm surprised; they're usually over-punctual. They're bound
to call today. Don't mention... Clive waves his ink-stained cuff ...
I don't want them spooked.

Kulwant stands up, takes the file from the desk and makes the
door creak as he leaves the room.

Alone, Clive moves back to the window. As if the light and air will
help. He carefully places the fingertips of one hand on the model
table, twitches his wrist so they hop and fall in a quiet drum roll.

It pains him to see Marlowe Tower still shabby, still brutally
grey, still blunted. Still thinking it is the future, still believing it is
standing above the docks and a river busy with tugs and barges,
when all of that has gone, leaving it an unloved tombstone. He
swivels, as if to make for his desk, as if to write this thought down.
But instead he taps his fingers, more roughly this time. The model
quivers so that the curve of the new roof shifts, and the tower now
wears it like a jaunty cap.

4

This time Aaron cannot wait to get back to his flat to open the envelope. It's brown, and when he sees the Deptford Council logo it's all he can do not to tear it open in the post office. He refused the council's last offer, and they acknowledged this refusal. Have they found some new way to force him out? It's four days since Sally Perry asked about joining her 'collective challenge'; he's still unsure what his answer should be. Have the council now slipped in front of him? Clive always told him he was too slow.

But the queue in the post office fills every part of the tiny shopfloor. He doesn't want to open the letter here. Out on the street is no better; the growl of slow-moving truck traffic would prevent him from properly understanding what he's reading.

He nearly squeezes through the gap in the fence to take the footbridge over Evelyn Street, onto the walkway. But he remembers in time and crosses the road to take the disjointed path through the estate.

At last, at the foot of Marlowe Tower, it's quiet and lonely enough for reading. He could wait and climb the stairs, he thinks. But no, he doesn't want to be breathless and dizzy. He slips a finger under the flap.

Housing Development Team,
Deptford Borough Council
8 April 2021

Dear Mr Goldsworthy
We are writing to you to invite you to a meeting with our housing development team and with the proposed buyer of Marlowe Tower, Clive Goldsworthy & Company.

This meeting has been suggested by the company as a way to discuss the options around the sale of your property that would allow you to remain living in the area, and possibly on the estate or in Marlowe Tower itself.

Present at this meeting will be myself, Alexa Douglas, Kemi Olawale of the housing development team, representatives from Clive Goldsworthy & Co. and Holly Bridges of Hearst and Binfield Conveyancers. We are also inviting the other owner-occupiers still resident in Marlowe Tower.

The meeting will be held at our offices in Deptford Old Town Hall, New Cross Road, on 23 April at 3pm and will last approximately one hour. Please let us know as soon as possible whether you will be attending.

We look forward to your reply.

Kind regards
Alexa Douglas, Assistant Housing Development Manager, New Projects, Deptford Borough Council

The page flaps in one of Aaron's hands; the torn brown envelope flaps in the other. Two questions have formed in his head:

Will Clive be at the meeting?

Who's still living in the tower?

He drops his hands to his sides and looks upwards, scanning the windows of the tower. Here and there a scrap of left-behind curtain, a concertinaed blind.

He turns his head. He cannot see Clive's tower from here. The view is obscured by the two plane trees that shade the riverside path. He notices, fleetingly, their divergence: one leans towards the water; the other reaches upwards.

He's been so sure no one else is left. He has felt for weeks – for months – that he is the sole occupant. He has grown comfortable with it. It has become something he might wear.

Clive is behind this letter, he thinks. It may be from the council, but it bears all his marks. Aaron can almost catch the smell of his twin; a semitone away from his own; how he knew which was his shirt, his shoes, his golden tie.

He looks at the letter again. The writing suggests someone junior. He probably met Alexa when the team visited the estate. It was last year, after the first lockdown, he remembers. They set up tables and chairs under a marquee on the town square, he recalls. A small group of the remaining estate residents put on masks and sat in a safely scattered formation to listen to the council's reasonableness. This was Alexa's first job, he expects. One more than him, though. A hair licks his neck.

How many exchanges has he had with the council now? Double figures, it must be. And this is the first mention of anyone else in the tower.

He looks up again, fruitlessly. Then across the river once more. Has Clive installed someone in the tower? No – Aaron can't make sense of such a move. He stuffs the letter into the envelope and makes his way to the service stairs.

He doesn't bother pressing the lift buttons as he stalks through the foyer on the second floor, on his way to the main stairs. The intention hasn't formed in his mind quite yet, but once he has ascended the first three flights to the third floor and taken the necessary pause, he sees the door to the corridor ahead of him, steps forwards and pushes it open.

He stares down the length of the corridor. The doors to the flats stand open. Pale rectangles of light lie like mats in front of each entrance. At the end, the window is cracked. No one on this floor.

On the fourth floor he goes through the same procedure: standing in the doorway to the stairs and registering the open doors of the flats, the wedges of colour inside. Only now does he wonder why the doors have been left ajar like this. In the past, an empty flat would be secured. Steel anti-squatter barriers fastened over the frames. But not here, not with Marlowe Tower. Why was no one interested?

Zöe's declarations about housing trail after him up the stairs to the fifth, sixth and seventh floors. 'People need homes,' she would say, at dinner tables over wine, on the telephone. To him and Clive at breakfast. 'Good homes. Ones we'd be happy to live in ourselves. And that's why we're moving.'

He's struggling for breath now and has to pause on a landing between the eleventh and twelfth floors. He remembers Zöe's hands on their shoulders in the lift the first time they visited the estate – they were still so young he didn't differentiate between the hand on Clive's shoulder and the one on his own – and her saying, 'You're both going to love it here. It's a completely new way of living.'

It was a phrase they'd heard her use to anyone who frowned at the idea that she was taking her boys out of the elegant modern house she had designed, and down to the dirty banks of the Thames at Deptford, to live cheek by jowl with a woman who probably worked on the line at Peek Freans.

'When I built the house in Blackheath, I said I'd be prepared to live in it myself, and I did,' she would say. 'And Deptford Strand Estate is the same. I'll be proud to call a factory worker my neighbour. It's a completely new way of living.'

The twelfth floor offers the same emptiness as the others. The new way of living is over. Aaron frowns. Did he say that out loud? He says it out loud:

—The new way of living is over.

His voice bounces off the concrete floor, the cracked render of the walls.

But there – is that a closed door?

His footsteps echo his voice as he walks along to the third flat on the right. Yes, closed. His stomach tightens. Stupid, he thinks. He spots the glint of the keep, halfway down the door frame. So the door's not locked. What will he see if he pushes it open?

It takes some effort to raise his hand, brace two fingers and press them against the wood.

The door swings open, and Aaron is greeted by something very familiar. This flat has exactly the same layout as his own. He steps over the threshold, looks along the corridor and down the flight of steps to the bedrooms. Then enters the living room and stares around the dusty grey box. Yes, it is exactly the same as his flat twelve floors above. Only the angle from which he can see Clive's tower is different. Fractionally.

Aaron taps his fingers on the gritty window ledge, glances at the walls: grimy Anaglypta. The floor – stains bloom; someone spilled something and let it soak through the carpet. He walks out and leaves the front door ajar.

He and Clive hadn't been happy at first – to leave Blackheath, their garden. The view over the railway line from the back fence. The thick-trunked trees in the street. Their friends. But on that first visit, Zöe had promised them a glimpse of something secret. Something she had built especially for them. 'A home is somewhere to play too,' she'd said. And in one of the empty flats – pristine white and filled with the crunchy plaster smell – she'd opened a cupboard and pressed her fingers against one corner of wall at the back. A door had opened and Zöe had gasped dramatically, making them chuckle. Then she had passed through it, beckoning Clive and Aaron to follow. 'You see how the flats are split-level – the living area on the higher level, the bedrooms on the lower one? Well the stairs in between create room for hidden passages. There are lots of places like these. And only the three of us know about it.' Zöe had widened her eyes and her thick hair had fallen about her face, and in the dim light of the secret space she'd looked like the best kind of witch.

If she had really gone to the trouble of inserting all the 'hidden places', as she called them, just for Aaron and Clive's benefit, then her plan had worked. Deptford Strand Estate was a vast playground built especially for them. They came to know every inch of it. Felt they owned every step and every alley. They'd gloried in it. And Zöe had gloried in their glory.

Re-entering the staircase, Aaron's footsteps make a sharper echo. He takes the next flight with a little more energy. He got his breath back in the empty flat. But still he needs to pause on the next landing.

And as he rests, does he hear his footsteps continuing to sound up the stairwell above him?

Or does he hear some other feet?

Now stopped. Just after his.

He moves on, but freezes on the third step of the next flight. Again, he hears it: an echo? Or other feet?

He recalls a game he and Clive used to play on this staircase. One starting at the top, on the thirtieth floor, the other at the bottom, they each attempted, by slipping into the corridors, to pass the other unseen. It was exhilarating – the scramble up the stairs to escape. The last-ditch attempts to wrestle himself free as Clive clung to his ankles. The stairwell had peeled with their screams. But it was quietly terrifying: the crowded-chest feeling he had as he craned towards the sound of Clive's feet, trying to guess how far away he was.

Aaron blinks and twitches his mouth. How did he play it? By leaning heavily on the banister and treading as lightly as he could, he recalls. He tries it now. Reaches the next floor. And there, as he places a flat foot on the landing, he hears it. Hears them. Two steps. Two feet dropping one after the other. His heart breaks into a brief dance. He grips the banister, not to quieten his footsteps but to prevent himself sliding to the floor. He can't seem to hear anything over the thump of his heartbeat.

How stupid.

But wasn't this exactly how spooked he was by the game, back when he and Clive played it? He often gave up. Allowed his brother to catch him, so they could finish with the giddy grappling.

But how does this other person know how to play their game? Unless the other person is Clive.

No. That's impossible.

Aaron has finally reached his own floor. He stops, listens; stops, listens. Then makes his way to his door. His opponent will win, it seems. Clive always won. He only ever played games he'd win. Games Aaron might win – the exquisite corpse, hangman – Aaron had to seek out Zöe for. Then Clive would move restlessly from room to room until Zöe stopped the game and said, 'Go and play with your brother now, Aaron. Before he starts kicking the skirting boards.'

Aaron pauses at his door, fumbles in his pocket for his keys. As he pulls them out, he hears – distinct, clear, not playing a game, but moving with intent, footsteps passing quickly along a corridor somewhere above. Then the creak of a stairwell door swinging to. A pause. Then the slam of a flat door. The sounds form a little film.

He puts his key in the lock, and opens the door. Places the letter on the narrow shelf in his hall then goes back into the corridor, closing the door with the quietest of clicks.

Back at the stairwell he takes the flight with care but also with certainty. He's no longer listening for someone playing a game with him, but for a clue as to which floor they might be on; which flat they have closed the door to. He checks floor twenty-five only briefly. He's already presumed it won't be that one; he's lived in Marlowe Tower long enough to recognise footsteps directly above his head. The next floor he checks a little more carefully. All the doors are open. No one is here. The same for the twenty-seventh and twenty-eighth. And for the twenty-ninth. His breath is laboured now. A quiet dread somewhere deep in his belly has woken.

Floor thirty. A floor he has visited many times in the past. He pauses for a moment before opening the stairwell door. He looks through the wired glass and sees what he has been expecting – the regular rhythm of dark and light shapes on the corridor floor is interrupted here. One of the doors is closed.

He opens, passes through, and closes the stairwell door silently, then soft feet for all of the nine steps to the closed door of flat 304.

He stands in front of it. He thinks he can feel a kind of muffling warmth. The rounded scent of a body that's just come by. He holds his breath. Yes, there's a thunk, a pink, a shuffling drag from within the flat. Someone is inside. Doing indoor things. In the flat where Annette and Christine did their indoor things forty years ago.

5

The summer they met the twins, the sun had scorched almost to white the grey concrete of the blocks and towers, of the river terrace, of the town square, of the parade of shops. The grass of the verges and lawns had faded to yellow and then almost to ash.

Zöe had been jubilant. See how the estate has matured, she would say, almost every morning, calling in through the balcony door. Aaron and Clive would come across her with her camera, photographing the end of Evelyn House, where the stack of balconies gave the impression of a ziggurat cutting into the solid blue of the sky, or in the town square, where the reflecting pool was filled with water again. She had pressed and cajoled until the council had agreed to turn the taps on, and it had become a paddling pool, not just for the estate's children, but the adults too, cotton skirts and old suit trousers hitched to the knees.

Smashing, Zöe had said as she expounded upon the weather, telling the 'tourists', as she called the colleagues who would make the excursion into Deptford to visit her, how perfectly the estate had responded to the new climate. How perfectly the residents had adapted to the heat. Smashing, she had said, as if the weather and her design were one and the same, or least came from the same source. Something high above. Smashing, she had said, each morning that had dawned early and hot, bringing her out onto the balcony in her voluminous kimono, to look down on her creation.

By the middle of June, Aaron and Clive had finished their A levels, and the rules Zöe had about her sons' timekeeping had relaxed in the heat. University, for Clive at least, wouldn't start until late September. They took full advantage, staying out late into the tropical nights. Zöe would make a little show of disapproval in the morning, but they caught her on the phone to their grandmother one Sunday: 'They're out to all hours these days. But I'm happy to loose the shackles.' Clive raised an eyebrow at Aaron. Their freedom had been bestowed.

It was one such evening, as they came home from a party with old schoolmates in Greenwich, that they met Annette and Christine.

They had jumped off the back of the bus as it passed under the walkway on Evelyn Street, the conductor shouting back at them that the stop was just here, you daft ha'p'orths, then mounted the stairs and swung idly along into the estate, playing the game where they collided with each other every few steps, bouncing shoulders, doing it harder and harder to push the other off course.

As they reached the town square, the blocks on one side of the walkway still half lit and awake, music drifting from a couple of windows, and a dog splashing around in the pool below, his owner smoking shirtless on a bench, they noticed two figures approach them from the opposite direction. Two young women. They were dark with the walkway lights behind them, but then, as they came nearer, both with the same swinging gait, the lights from the town square below lit up their dark skin, their dark hair in coiled braids, their dark legs beneath their skirts.

It was rare to see black people on Deptford Strand Estate, Aaron remembers thinking. This part of Deptford, and Bermondsey next door, still hadn't started to mix. And wouldn't. Not for many years. He and Clive knew the estate inside out, and he didn't believe a single black family lived there. But there was something about the way these girls walked – the easy slowness, the way their slim bodies occupied space – that suggested they were at home.

The women both smiled and slowed as they approached Aaron and Clive, parted as if to allow the brothers to pass between them, but then stopped.

—Twins! they shouted, in gleeful stereo. Then they put their hands to their ears and let out a tuneful scream.

The dog paddling in the pool below stood still in the water and let out a single bark. Its owner frowned at the little group of silhouettes he could see on the walkway, then shook his head, as if to say that the heat was doing funny things to people.

The twins' scream spread across the estate, breaking in little waves over the sills of the open bedroom windows. Those that slept stirred without waking. Those still awake opened their eyes wider and held their breaths.

Zöe, who had dropped off just minutes before, woke with a start. She looked around, as if searching for the reason she was suddenly sitting up. Her mattress was on her bedroom floor. She had asked the twins to drag it out onto the balcony earlier that evening. She had seen people sleeping outside on hot nights when she'd visited Turkey and Lebanon, before they were born, she'd told them. But her balcony wasn't big enough for a double mattress, so she had settled for sleeping beside the open door.

She stood up and stepped off the mattress and out onto the balcony, gazing over the constellation of fluorescent lights, squinting a little, as if she needed her glasses. She certainly couldn't see Aaron and Clive, far off, over the town square, with Annette and Christine. She leaned against the concrete parapet for a moment, her face thoughtful, her eyes still half in sleep, then stepped backwards. As she did so, her polyester nightdress caught on the stipple of the raw concrete, pulling the fabric away from her body. She plucked it back with an irritated flick.

Turning back inside, she stood, slightly unstable, on the mattress and pulled the nightdress off over her head, before opening a drawer and pulling out a lighter, cotton one. But in the act of unfolding it to put it on, she froze, looking sideways at her reflection in the mirrored door of her wardrobe. She dropped the nightdress on the floor and turned her body at an angle, the blue darkness and blue light welling up the sides of the tower from the depths of the estate.

She stretched out an arm and put her leg forwards. Then stood straight, her arms hanging by her sides. The swell and sag of her belly showed that she had had babies. She placed her palm on her navel. Was she thinking she might have more?

She shook her head and lay down, naked, on the mattress.

On the walkway, as the scream still spread in a rolling ring, the four figures at its centre, Aaron and Clive glanced at each other, with the same wide-eyed expression on their similar faces. On Aaron's it was shy but amused; on Clive's, surprised and challenged.

Aaron took two steps past the women.

—You're twins too, said Clive, staying where he was.

—We are, said one.

—Annette, said the other, touching her chest. This is Christine. She touched her sister's shoulder.

—I'm Clive, and that's Aaron. Clive gestured almost dismissively towards his brother.

Annette and Christine had moved slightly along the walkway, towards the road, and Aaron had drifted in the other direction, towards home. Clive still smiled, still waited, intrigued. A little drunk. The line connecting him with Aaron had stretched, the gap had widened; between them stood this new pair of twins.

—You live in Marlowe Tower, don't you? said Christine, pointing past Aaron.

—We saw you. Annette looked over her shoulder at Aaron, then at Clive. But we didn't see you were twins until now. You dress yourselves different.

—So do you, said Clive, pointing at their gypsy skirts – Annette's cream; Christine's dark blue with lace trim.

There was a pause, everyone smiling in the warm darkness.

Both Aaron and Clive sensed they were outranked. These were women. No longer teenagers like them. Aaron moved another few paces towards the tower, and Clive was pulled an unwilling step in the same direction.

—Are you going home? Annette turned on the spot as he moved. Her eyebrows were raised.

Clive stopped again, as if she was challenging him.

—Where are you off to, then? he said.

—A party, said Christine. Then, directing her words down the walkway to Aaron: a late, late party.

—We're just coming back from one, said Clive to Annette. Finished too early.

He looked over at Aaron. We're ready for more, aren't we? his expression asked.

—Come with us, then, Annette said. We're only just starting. It's not like you got school tomorrow or something. And she delivered a laugh like she was ringing a bell, throwing out a hand as if she held a clapper.

—I'm going to university in September, said Clive, a little too loudly.

—Time to celebrate, then.

Annette threaded her slim arm through his. Her smooth, dry skin made him feel damp and sweaty. And try as he might, he couldn't stop the smile on his face giving him an innocent, eager look.

Aaron expected Clive to look back and check. They'd told their mother a vague time they'd be home. If they were going somewhere else, they should tell her a new time.

But Clive didn't turn. He'd never not turned before. Aaron stayed where he was, his shoulders angled away from the other three.

It was Christine who turned. Even in the darkness her small smile told him she knew what it was to be the cautious one. She sauntered back. He couldn't hear anything, but he felt she was quietly singing a song. She held out a hand towards him as she approached. And then, with a lighter touch than her sister, placed one hand on his forearm and moved it just a little, so she could put her arm through his.

—The best parties are in the middle of the night, you know. And anyway, you have to come now. We're twins, you're twins. I don't know why that's a reason for you to come with us, but it is.

A spritz of delight made Aaron grin. Christine grinned back even larger. She was impossible to refuse.

—Listen to my sister, Aaron. There's no way you can't come too.

Annette's voice bounced along the walkway like a colourful rubber ball.

Clive looked back too. Christine was talking. Aaron attending, relaxed, in her care, in the curl of her smile.

They crossed over Evelyn Street, then tripped down the steps and into the park, the darkness here a hunter green.

—Where's the party, asked Aaron, the empty vault between the trees oddly unfamiliar, seeming to hitch his excitement.

—New Cross, answered Christine, Annette saying the same a split second later, their voices juddering.

—At a friend of our landlord's, said Christine.

—It's his birthday. Annette produced an envelope from the fringed handbag that swung at her side.

—Fifty, said Christine.

—Fifty? repeated Clive, and stopped himself saying, we're going to a fiftieth birthday party?

—Fifty, said Annette and Christine, and laughed as if it was funny. A dog barked somewhere out of sight.

◆

The party was in a battered Victorian house in the centre of a short terrace, a remnant of the long rows that once spread among the confusion of railway lines between Bermondsey, New Cross and Deptford. The front door was open and the sash windows at the front were pushed up; silhouettes swayed across the nets inside, the music broadcasting from the bay and echoing off the long, low block of flats opposite.

People were draped over the front steps. And even now, Aaron and Clive can both remember the smell of grass – still rare then. Aaron can recall looking at the windows of the block across the road and wondering if the police might not turn up soon, if he and Clive shouldn't turn tail. He must've caught Clive's eye.

Clive saw Aaron's face, flat and still, his eyes blinking, roving over the tableau on the steps, the man with the impressive afro, leaning against the doorpost. The twins surged up the steps – Annette pulling Clive with her; Christine and Aaron close behind. The man in the doorway nodded his afro low, smiling, and they pushed into the narrow hall, people lining the walls on either side. And Clive realised, just as Aaron did, that they were the only white people. Clive looked back. Aaron gave him a smile. The noise was warm. The heat loud.

—Ronald, called Annette.

Ahead of them, a man turned around.

—My girls. His rasping tenor cut through the music, and he put his arms out – one for each twin.

In the net of low lights from the various rooms, Clive saw the man's fat dreadlocks, held back at the nape of his neck and falling over his shoulders as he bent to hug the twins.

—We've brought some new friends, said Annette, touching Clive's arm. Christine pushed Aaron forwards.

—They live in Marlowe Tower, said Annette.

—And they're twins too, said Christine. Look.

They lined themselves up either side of Clive and Aaron.

—A pretty picture, said Ronald, and held his hands up as if taking a photograph with an invisible camera.

—I'm Clive. Clive put his hand out to shake, trying to recover his confidence.

—Ronald.

—And this is Aaron. Clive put his arm on his brother's shoulder. The muscle was taut.

—Welcome, boys, said Ronald.

—Happy birthday, said Aaron.

Clive realised in a rush that their hands were empty.

—Sorry, we haven't brought anything. They ... And the names escaped him for a second.

Aaron noticed before Ronald did:

—Annette and Christine, they only just invited us.

Annette spun round from a conversation she'd been having with a tall woman behind them.

—We found them coming home just as we were leaving, and decided to bring them. Twins, you see.

—Neighbours, said Christine.

—Don't fret, boys, said Ronald. On my birthday, bring yourselves, and bring love, and that's good enough for me.

He laughed with a hissed kissing noise. What he said had tickled him, but Aaron and Clive didn't know why.

—Get yourselves some drinks, boys. Kitchen's down there, said Ronald, his warm hand pushing Aaron gently towards the stairs. And then he turned, someone's arm wrapping itself around his shoulders.

The twins were gone. Clive saw their slim arms raised in the middle of the dancing crowd in the front room. Aaron was pressed against his side.

◆

They stayed together the whole time they were at the party. Mostly touching, arms pressed against each other, squashed on the same seat, one hanging on the other's shoulder. At the time, they probably couldn't have given a reason for it, but now, as sixty-two-year-old men, they'd likely tell you it was because it gave them a sense of security. Because, at that party, they felt a little young, a little daunted, a little green – because they were white. People chatted to them, they were pulled into the front room to dance. They joined in 'Happy Birthday' when it was sung. There was no reason to feel insecure. But somehow they did. So they kept close. Felt each other's heat. In the darkness between the moving bodies, they held hands. Thinking back to that party as adults – prompted by the beat of a song on the radio, or by the wet-garden smell of grass drifting onto the street from a downstairs window – they have both thought they now understood why Annette and Christine took them to the party that night.

Clive has always known – has always told himself – that he didn't need this proximity as much as Aaron did, that as they grew older, he allowed it rather than wanted it. Aaron knows he needed it. Knows Clive needed it too, whatever he might profess.

Aaron and Clive didn't really speak to the twins again that night. They saw them – they heard them. And, although they'd arrived at the party with Annette and Christine, so couldn't really know, felt that the women's presence jolted the atmosphere of the house, accelerated it from the lounging, walking pace, first into a tight trot, and then a zipping canter. The music they persuaded – or rather cajoled – onto the record player had a more urgent beat. The talk was louder, the laughter came in squalls. Aaron remembers being slightly breathless. When Clive was particularly close, he felt sure he could feel his pulse galloping. Aaron smiled at Clive, and received the same smile back. They would have laughed had they had the puff to do so.

At last, the frenzy got the better of them both.

—Do you want to sit outside for a bit? Clive said, noticing the sweat on his chest and knowing Aaron's was the same.

Aaron nodded and they found themselves on the front steps. Ronald was there, leaning easily on the slope of the balustrade, smoking a cigarette.

—Hello, boys. Enjoying yourselves?

—Yes, it's great, replied Clive.

Aaron picked his T-shirt away from his body.

—From dancing, he said, grinning – at Ronald, but also at the cool air on his skin.

—Girls leave you swinging? Ronald drew on the cigarette, making its tip glow.

Aaron began with a 'sort of', but Clive spoke at the same time, so he closed his mouth.

—They're with friends.

—Everyone's their friend, said Ronald. You can't not be. You've realised that already, I suppose?

Aaron and Clive looked at each other – it was a reflex.

—But they're actually difficult to get close to.

Ronald paused. Looked back through the open door.

—But, you know, maybe you'll be special. And he laughed the hiss-kiss laugh.

A police car drove slowly past, almost coming to a stop outside the house, then moving on again.

—Third time they've been past here, said Ronald. Harassing a university professor.

And he laughed again.

Clive almost frowned and asked who the professor was. But Aaron stepped in front of him, quicker to understand, for once.

—Which university do you work at? he asked.

—Southbank Poly. Engineering. Some of the kids in there are my students. He gestured over his shoulder.

—I'm going to university in the autumn, said Clive.

—To study...?

—Architecture, said Clive.

—That's a long course. He looked at Aaron. And you...?

Aaron tucked himself into Clive's side a little more. He still wasn't comfortable with this question. With giving his answer to it.

—I haven't decided. I'm waiting to get my A level results, and then I'll have a think. Travel for a year, maybe.

—Without your brother? Ronald laughed gently. That'll be a big change, I bet.

—We need to start doing separate things, said Clive.

Ronald's eyebrows raised in reply. He looked at Aaron, expecting a comment.

—Maybe I'll come to more parties like this, said Aaron, surprised and pleased with his reply.

Ronald rolled another cigarette. Then placed it in his mouth, unlit, and put his head on one side.

—What are you two boys doing living on that estate, then?

The question they'd been asked often in the ten years they'd lived there. A council estate in Dirty Deptford – the most run down of all the run-down areas of London: not a place for well-mannered, well-spoken young men like them. But Zöe permitted no dropped h's, no poor grammar, and their manners were those she'd learned in her upper-middle-class home in Godalming.

—We've lived there ages, said Aaron, trying to slacken his speech.

—Our mother designed it, said Clive, clearly, standing a little straighter. Aaron felt him go rigid for a moment.

—She did? Ronald readjusted his posture on the balustrade, sitting a little straighter himself.

—Yes. The first woman architect for a whole scheme like that, Clive went on. It took her years.

Ronald nodded and shuffled around again. Lit his cigarette and took a few long drags, the smoke thick and languid around his head.

—I knew a female architect. I met her many years ago, when we'd both gone to work over in Jamaica. Very talented she was. Very talented.

He paused, looking towards the other end of the road, it seemed. Aaron followed his gaze, and then Clive did the same – their unison already beginning to fray, although they didn't yet know it.

Ronald looked back at them.

—I caught up with her here a few years later. She'd had a family by then, and she told me...

His voice was less conversational now, more as if he was reading from a book. They were standing on a lower step than him.

—She told me something strange. She said she only felt really creative when she was pregnant.

He let the words hang in the air for a moment.

—She said that of course she could do her work – her sketching, planning, all of that – at any time. But she felt her real inspiration only came when she was ... with child.

He sat back from these words a little. Then gave a clicking chuckle.

—She might have just been play-acting.

He looked at Clive from the corner of his eye. Then Aaron. Then back to Clive again.

—Just something to say, you know? A woman doing her kind of work, the guys around her were always going to say, 'What about when she has kids?' She can come back at them with, 'That's when I do my best work'. I don't know if that's what she really thought, though.

Aaron felt Clive move. He'd sensed the insinuation here. This man knew Zöe. Or had known her years ago. Ronald was still looking at them. He blew a cloud of smoke into the air between them. The expression that appeared as it cleared was slightly amused, slightly expectant. Clive was constructing a reply.

—Our mother designed the estate long before she was ever pregnant with us. It was her dream project. It took her years to get it built.

Ronald stared at Clive, the stretch of a smile now on his face. Aaron knew Clive didn't like this – felt that he was being ridiculed, even if, as Aaron suspected, the smile was one of appreciation.

—It won prizes, said Clive. And as soon as he spoke, he knew he sounded juvenile.

—Did it? Ronald nodded. Flicked his cigarette butt with a skilful thumb. Then said:

—I asked her, what do you do, though, after you've given birth?

He held his hands in front of himself, as if demonstrating a delivery.

—Hi, guys.

Annette and Christine were standing at the top of the steps, silhouetted against the yellow light of the hall. One of them – Aaron thought it was Annette; Clive thought he knew it was her – took a few steps down towards them.

—Enjoying the party?

—Hope Ronald is looking after you, said Christine, joining her sister. Sorry if we abandoned you. That wasn't nice. But there are just so many people we haven't seen for yonks.

—It's my party, said Ronald, and I'm sitting out here, while you girls get all the attention. He laughed.

Annette and Christine laughed. Aaron joined in. Clive did too. A little late.

—Come up to our flat this week. Top floor. 304. Evenings are best, said Annette.

—We'll get to know each other properly, said Christine.

Ronald looked at them all in turn, his quiet smile difficult to read in the thick night-time air.

6

Aaron is right. Clive is behind the letter that has led him up the stairs to the door to flat 304. Clive's little scheme was prompted by information let slip in the meeting he and Kulwant had with Kemi Olawale and Alexa Douglas from Deptford Council, three days ago, now.

Clive had allowed Kulwant to lead the meeting. There was some dull discussion about access roads to the estate. Updated schedules. News on decanting the remaining blocks. Clive pushed himself back from the table and folded his arms. He no longer cared these days if it made him looked disengaged.

At last Kulwant opened a new folder, turned a page in his notebook, wrote a new heading and underlined it.

—Marlowe Tower. Where are we?

Kemi, the more experienced of the two officers, began:

—There's been another little hiccup.

Clive sighed.

—We thought we'd agreed sales with all apart from...

Here Kemi smiled at Clive, clearly hesitating to say 'your brother'. Then continued:

—However, now there's a different issue. One of the other owners seems to have had a change of heart.

Alexa, who was less experienced, and, it seemed, more excitable, butted in:

—We've no idea why or how, but for some reason, they've actually moved back into the tower. I mean, who does that? Into a block that's basically derelict?

Clive's eye was attracted to a sharp flicking movement below the table. He was sure he saw Kemi's hand knock against Alexa's leg.

Alexa's colour rose.

—How much do they want? Clive asked.

—We're offering good market rates, Mr Goldsworthy, said Kemi.

—I can add the amount to our offer to the council, if it's proving too much.

Kemi held her pen at both ends, studied it for a moment and expelled a little puff of air from her nostrils.

—We're not clear yet whether money is the issue. We'll have to investigate further.

—Everyone has a price, said Kulwant.

—Sometimes that's not a cash price, though, Clive added.

—Sometimes that's not a cash price, Kemi repeated. Look, we've had incidents similar to this in developments in the borough before. It's a question of sensitivity. Negotiation.

She left a pause. No one filled it.

—Leave it with us. We'll see what we can find out, what these owners' needs are, and how we can get towards something that means we can move forwards together.

Clive stared at her. Having interested him momentarily, her words had become like the vast, baggy bubbles entertainers make with hoops.

◆

After the meeting Clive sat, as always these days, at his window, the model near to his hand, his eyes staring at Marlowe Tower. He let them skim its surface, starting from the ground floor and travelling upwards, counting. At every floor he moved his eyes sideways, examining each bay of windows. Counting them out separately. It was a tricky mental task.

At last he was at the thirtieth floor. He paused now before looking across. Blinked a few times, widened his eyes. Looked across at the bays.

There.

He squinted. Whereas almost all the other windows were an anthracite grey – the shadows of the rooms inside making them dark – this set were pale. It was as if he was staring at an old woman with cataracts.

These windows had curtains. Or nets. His mother hated that residents of the estate – and particularly Marlowe Tower – hung nets across their windows. They made a messy patchwork of her clean, monochrome façade.

Clive moved sideways a little, to adjust the angle he was looking from. Could he see nets or curtains from here? What was it – three hundred yards? He scanned down a few floors to Aaron's flat – formerly his own home. Yes, he could see the edges of some curtains. No nets there, of course. He raised his gaze once more.

So there was someone living in flat 304. He checked once more that he was looking at floor thirty, counted across to be sure the bays were those of 304. Then he stared long and hard, as if his gaze might eventually penetrate the fabric. As if he might see the occupants. Who was now living in the flat once occupied by Annette and Christine?

A little pit of panic put out a shoot, climbed a tendril up his throat. In a moment he was at the door to his office. He pressed the opener and called out to Kulwant as the door swung open.

He was back at his desk as Kulwant came in.

—I need you to perform a Land Registry search on a flat in Marlowe Tower.

—246?

—No. We know everything we need to about my brother's flat. I want information on flat 304.

Kulwant wrote the number on a new page of his pad. Clive saw it: the clean page, the figures upside down and underlined. For a moment they made him dizzy. He blinked, looked up. Kulwant's expression was expectant. But Clive's mind was full of other upside-down thoughts. He couldn't find his words.

—Is this something do with what Kemi and Alexa were saying? said Kulwant.

—Yes it is.

—How do you know it's that flat? They didn't mention the number.

—No. But I ... But I ... But I lived there for a long time. I looked at the windows.

Clive raised a hand, but he felt suddenly too weak to even point.

—Look at the windows. Flat 304's are the only ones with curtains.

7

The first time Aaron and Clive climbed the stairs to visit the twins was a day after the party. An evening. The sun was low in the sky but still hot, driving straight into the corridor of the thirtieth floor, making the tiles under their feet golden. Warm.

When Clive led the way from the stairwell to the twins' door, he saw that it was ajar. A thick hum of voices, music, patchouli and grass washed through the gap.

Clive paused in front of the door. Aaron drew up beside him. This was supposed to be the most casual of visits. But Aaron's face was taut, excited – anticipating the new. Clive couldn't pretend he felt different.

Clive rapped lightly on the door and waited. No one answered.

Were they supposed to simply push the door open and wander in with a casual greeting? Clive knocked again, harder this time.

A lock clicked; the light brush of another door opening nearby. From the next flat along a woman's head emerged. Iron-grey hair in batteries of blue and pink rollers so rigid they seemed to be at least partly responsible for the indignation on the woman's face.

—You're Mrs Goldsworthy's boys, aren't you? she said, in a voice too loud for the few yards between them.

From the corner of his eye, Clive saw Aaron nod.

—Yes, that's right, Mrs Ledbury. Clive smiled brightly, then knocked on the twins' door a third time. Loud and brash.

—I've told your mother about those girls, said Mrs Ledbury.

She had stepped out into the corridor now. She was wearing a full-length, pale-blue nightie. It was only eight o'clock. Aaron thought he saw a sheen of sweat on her forehead.

—They've been nothing but trouble since they moved in.

She took a couple more steps towards them, folding her arms across her waist.

—The noise. Having people round at all hours. The smell. I don't know what they're smoking, but it's something.

She was close now. Aaron found that his hand was on Clive's upper arm.

Despite himself, Clive edged backwards.

—We've never had coloureds here. Not on this estate. I've told your mother that. She knows people at the council. She should be able to tell them. There's only ever trouble when you start mixing...

Her voice fell away and she retreated a few paces as a waft of sound and warmth and scent engulfed Aaron and Clive. They turned and realised the door had opened. One of the twins leaned out.

—Evening, Mrs Ledbury, she said with the broadest of smiles.

Aaron remembers thinking this must be Annette – she was the one who'd take pleasure in this little impudence.

Mrs Ledbury's face twitched. Clive could see she was working out what to say.

—Doing your hair tonight? You should let me or Christine do it for you, said Annette. Feel free to knock anytime.

A wounded Mrs Ledbury now had a foot inside her door.

—I shall tell your mother you two were up here.

She released a hand from under her armpit and thrust a finger at Clive and then at Aaron.

—She'll stop you if she's got any sense.

—Let us know about doing your hair, Annette called, sing-song. Corn rows would look nice on you.

Almost out of sight, Mrs Ledbury shot her reply from behind the closing door.

—I wouldn't have you touching me. Not in a million years.

And her door slammed shut.

Annette widened her eyes and raised her brows high. Christine was behind her now.

—Hello, you two, she said, her head over Annette's shoulder. You've met Mrs Ledbury, then?

They were moving back along their hallway.

Both Clive and Aaron hesitated. It was for the briefest of moments, but both would remember it for years after. It's a pause of which they should be ashamed. They know it now, and they knew it then, very nearly in the moment it happened.

Annette and Christine looked back at them from inside the flat.

—Come on, then, Christine said. It was almost a question.

—I hope you're not going to let that old bag tell you what to do, said Annette.

Aaron strode forwards, almost knocking Clive aside as he passed. Clive was a beat behind him. Annette pushed the door to.

The layout was similar to their flat downstairs. A short flight of steps led to a lower level. But almost everything else seemed different.

—Shove up, said Annette to two men sprawled on the sofa. One in a wide-open shirt; in the heat his chest a polished teak. The other shirtless. He wore a necklace of large wooden beads. A white woman sat on an armchair. Clive stared at her. She was the oldest person in the room, he decided.

—Gorton, Albert, Jenny. Annette slapped each of them lightly on the head as she named them. They made pained faces. The shirtless man cowered away.

—These are Aaron and Clive, said Christine as they squashed together in a space for one. Or Clive and Aaron.

—Twins too? Jenny said. Then to Christine: Shouldn't you be able to tell them apart?

—We've only just met them... Christine began.

—But you all look the same anyway, said Annette. We don't know who's a twin and who's not.

And then she jerked herself back with a spray of laughter, grabbing at Christine's arm.

The shirtless man shot out a deafening laugh. Slapped his leg, then slapped the leg of the other man, who was laughing too, but almost silently.

—Don't know who's a twin, the shirtless man repeated.

Aaron wasn't sure if he should join in. Clive darted a look at the white woman. She was tucking her chin into her neck and giggling. He tried a chuckle.

Christine flopped onto a chair.

—We can make jokes like that in here, she said to Aaron and Clive.

Annette squeezed into the armchair next to Christine. She waved a slack hand at Aaron and Clive.

—Their mother designed this place, you know. She's an architect.

—What, this building?

—The whole estate, said Clive, sitting forwards a little and turning to Gorton.

Aaron felt like pulling him back.

—The whole thing, said Annette. The blocks, all the walkways, the square, the school ... everything.

—Even the door handles, the ways the windows open, said Aaron, pointing. She likes things done a certain way.

—Sounds like it, said Gorton.

Clive stopped himself saying that it was why Zöe had won so many awards. Instead he looked at Annette. She had a leg hooked over the arm of the chair, a finger resting on her upper lip, as if to hide at least a part of her smile. Her eyes were bright, staring at him. It was a challenge, or perhaps an invitation to dance.

—You know lots about her, he said, trying to send her an equally ambiguous smile.

—I hope so, she replied, taking her hand away from her face so he saw her full beam.

—We're at university, studying the built environment, Christine explained.

—Really? You're at university?

Aaron cringed and gave Clive an invisible nudge. Clive felt it. Had he put the emphasis on 'you're'? He had. Gorton was looking at him.

—Girl can't go to university?

Aaron felt hot. Clive wriggled around, first to face Gorton then Annette and Christine. Gorton maintained a questioning look on his face, one eyebrow raised, immobile. Annette and Christine looked like they were struggling to contain their laughter.

—You didn't say last night, was all I meant, Clive started. I didn't mean that...

Their laughter burst out now. Gorton let his face fall too.

—We know you didn't mean *that*. Christine widened her eyes and splayed her hands.

Annette did the same, saying *Thaaatt* with a rasp and her tongue out.

—And I was just going to say... Clive tried to speak over the laughter.

He could feel Aaron chuckling at his side. The vibration shook a laugh from his throat too.

—I'm going to study the built environment too, Clive finally managed. Architecture. What's your course?

—Town planning, said Christine.

—Which is why we know all about your mum, said Annette. She's a star.

—We love her work, said Christine.

—You should introduce them to her, said Albert. His voice was quiet. Aaron felt he'd said it just to him and not the whole room.

—Of course we'll introduce you, said Aaron, before Clive could hesitate.

—Now, that would be great, said Christine.

—We would have a lot of questions for her, said Annette.

—A lot of questions, said Christine.

Aaron smiled as he turned his head towards Clive, who drew in a breath.

Christine frowned.

—She wouldn't be keen on that?

—She'll put you through your paces first, said Clive.

—We've seen her with students. You have to earn her respect. But then she's fine, said Aaron. She can be great.

—When she wants to be, said Clive.

—We're great too, when we want to be, said Christine. We'll win her over.

—It's why we're here really. Annette sat herself up now, and gestured to the room around them.

—I didn't know that, said Gorton. I thought you just found a new place to live.

—It's a whole story, said Annette. In our first year, one of our tutors said he had a flat here. But we were settled in a house in New Cross, so we said no. He offered again a few months later, and we said no again. But then we started learning about the great, the incredible...

—The goddess of architecture herself – Christine almost sang it towards the ceiling, throwing her arms upwards – Zöe Goldsworthy...

—So when he asked a third time, we said yes.

—He did seem a bit over-keen, though, said Christine.

—Thought he was onto a good thing, did he? said Gorton.

—We worried about that, but fortunately no, said Annette. And by then we were both so into Goldsworthy buildings, we were regretting turning him down. We didn't think he'd ask again, and when he did we pretty much bit his hand off.

—And here we are. Christine spread out her arms.

—You're not no council tenant, then? said Gorton.

—Nope. He owns the flat and we rent from him.

—Don't know no one who'd buy a council flat, said Albert. Again Aaron thought he said it just to him. He even looked sideways at him as he did so.

—It's becoming a thing, said Christine.

—There are lots of people who want it to be a big thing, said Annette, standing up. Let's have some music. And who wants a drink? We have Coke, we have juice. And ice. Lots of ice.

She took their orders, pointing at each of them and repeating them in turn, as Christine got up too and went to a record player standing in the corner.

—Let's give Mrs Ledbury some sounds to enjoy, said Annette, and Christine turned the volume dial. The beat made the speaker buzz.

Annette danced to the kitchen door, stopped, cupped a hand around her ear and cocked her head towards the wall, rolling her eyes in anticipation.

A moment later there was a series of thuds. Someone banging hard on the wall of the adjoining flat.

—And there you go, said Annette.

It felt too loud to Aaron. But Annette's dance as she went into the kitchen and Christine's quiet, smiling glance at him as she sat back down made him unexpectedly comfortable.

Clive sat back, comfortable too. But the banging came again.

—Should we turn it down? he said. No point aggravating her for no reason.

—They've got reason, said Jenny. She's racialist.

—You heard her outside just now, said Christine. We've been nothing but polite to her. Loveliness itself. She complained to the neighbour on the other side that we were playing loud music before we'd got the record player. *Before* we'd got the record player.

—She's insane, said Annette from the kitchen.

Gorton let out another splitting laugh. Albert was giggling silently.

—She's racialist, repeated Jenny, taking a glass from Annette.

—Yeah, she's racialist, Christine agreed.

—Tabitha! Annette cried.

A small figure had appeared in the room.

—Thanks for leaving the door to, said Tabitha, then sniggered. Don't want Aunty Het nosing about, do we?

—This is the girl, said Gorton. Home delivery.

Aaron and Clive knew Tabitha vaguely. She lived in a block above the shops on the town square. She was a little younger than them. She claimed she was sixteen, but everything about her suggested a different age. Her speech and manner were those of a much older woman. She was quick with the kind of comebacks the old ladies shouted to each other from their balconies, and she touched her hair as if it had just been set. Yet her body seemed much younger. She was short, round-faced and had a plump, boyish figure.

She looked at all of them, examining Aaron and Clive carefully.

—You're up here too then? she said and creased her face up. Clive and ... Aaron, Air-ron? Aran, isn't it? I can't say your name. Can't say it. A-Ran. That's it, isn't it? I bet you can't say my name properly.

—Hello, Tabitha, said Aaron.

Tabitha chuckled. Then dropped unexpectedly to her knees in the middle of the carpet just as Annette was coming back from the kitchen with more glasses.

—Watch out, Tabs. You'll have me over. You got the shopping, then?

Tabitha was cross-legged now, as if she was in a primary-school assembly. Her face twitched and switched. She looked at everyone again, ending with Clive and Aaron.

—What about them? she asked as Annette handed her a glass. But she didn't wait for an answer.

—You won't say nothing to no one, will you, yous two?

—About what? asked Clive.

But Tabitha spoke over him:

—Are them two, you know...? She was asking Christine now.

—Them two are absolutely fine, Christine replied. They were at a party with us last night. And they're twins, so they have our special approval. And we love their mum.

—We love their mum, said Annette.

—What do you love their mum for? said Tabitha, rummaging in the pocket of her denim shorts now.

She sprang up and approached Gorton and Albert.

—Shopping, she said as she dropped a dark pellet wrapped in clingfilm in Gorton's open palm.

—Shopping, she said, as she dropped another in Albert's.

—Ain't got no shopping for you, she said, leaning over Aaron and Clive.

—I can tell the difference, she said. You're taller, she pointed at Aaron. I can tell the difference between you two and all, she said over her shoulder to Annette and Christine.

—I should hope so, said Annette, and caught Clive's eye.

Tabitha dropped to the floor again and took a big gulp of her drink, looking over the rim of the glass at Aaron and Clive as she did so. She finished with a gasp.

—Your mum don't know you're up here, does she? she said.

—Should she? Clive replied instantly.

Tabitha blinked and twitched her nose. Then turned to Annette.

—Their mum thinks she's the queen of the whole place, she said. And sniggered.

Then she turned towards Aaron and Clive, switching her eyes between their faces.

—Your mum thinks she's the queen of this whole estate, doesn't she?

Clive and Aaron presented her with smiles. They were genuine. Aaron remembered Tabitha always made him laugh, even when she wasn't trying to be funny.

—She kind of is, if you think about it, said Aaron.

—More a benign dictator, said Clive.

Tabitha's face screwed up like a snail on salt. Then relaxed in an instant, as she seemed to dismiss Clive's last comment.

—My aunt don't know I'm here, she said. That's why these left the door open for me. She'd go spare if she knew.

And Aaron and Clive realised almost simultaneously that Tabitha was related to Mrs Ledbury.

—I'm only doing shopping, she sniggered. You won't say nothing to nobody will you, yous two? she repeated.

—We won't say nothing to nobody, said Clive.

Aaron heard the ridicule in Clive's tone. He didn't like it.

—We won't tell anyone, he said. We promise.

8

The day of Clive's meeting with Kemi and Alexa, it took Kulwant a good hour to come back with the Land Registry search results.

Clive searched his face as he entered the room and placed the printout on his desk, his hand tensed over it so Clive couldn't see what it contained. Clive reached out to draw the page towards him, but Kulwant spoke.

—You're right. 304 is privately owned.

A slight warmth, that might, but shouldn't have been relief, spread across Clive's chest.

—The names?

Clive's tone seemed to make Kulwant's eyebrows gather for a moment.

—Annette and Christine Mayfield.

Clive nodded. He'd known it. For these last few minutes he'd been certain. Since he'd counted out the flats and floors from his window. But now, instead of warmth he felt cold. A chill that made him button his jacket and pull his shirt together at the neck.

Kulwant's fingers still stood over the printout. He had something more to say. Clive tried to read upside down again.

—There's something strange, though. Which is why it took me a while to do the search. I thought there'd been a glitch.

—What's strange? Clive buttoned a button.

—Well, these two women – the Mayfields – they didn't buy the flat under right-to-buy. They owned it a few years before that.

—Really?

Clive's chest twitched now. A nasty little spasm.

—I suppose it's not unheard of, he said. It was done here and there. My mother owned our flat since the sixties.

—Yes, I know. But look.

Kulwant held out the page. Clive reached out and again tried to grab hold of it, and just for a moment, Kulwant's fingers held fast. Then he released it.

Clive tried to read the print, but his eyes seemed unwilling to send the information to his brain.

And now they did.

But the black, fidgety marks wouldn't turn into comprehensible symbols.

And now they did.

But he couldn't understand them.

He heard a flutter and realised his hand was shaking. He put the page down.

—Transferred. They didn't buy it?

—No. It's written there. See? Purchase sum, zero. There's a note. Transfer of ownership. 1977.

Clive pushed himself back from the desk. He felt dizzy, as if he'd somehow stood up too quickly. Something seemed to press on each side of his head – a giant's pinch, making his vision narrow and dark.

—Can you give me a few minutes, Kulwant?

He didn't see Kulwant leave. Only heard the glass door click and clang shut.

1977. He pulled himself back to the desk. Picked up the page. June 1977. Of course it was June.

And of course, the figures of the two women, as they were more than four decades ago, were joined in his mind by Aaron.

Clive looked towards the window. But right now he hadn't the strength to cross the carpet to get there.

He had always channelled uncomfortable emotions into strategy formulations. One hot day when he and Aaron were eight – perhaps the first summer after they'd come to live on Deptford Strand Estate – they had badgered Zöe to take them to the seaside for the day. The trip on the train became, in just a few minutes, of

great importance to them both. Perhaps it was because they were
still not settled in their new home. Perhaps it was a new need –
to wrest a little control of their daily lives away from their mother.
Zöe, however, had refused. Aaron had sulked. But Clive had taken
out his summer homework books, sat at the dining table,
alongside his mother and her set of tissue-thin building plans, and
quietly started a comprehension exercise. Within twenty minutes,
Zöe had put down her pencil, folded the plans away and called
Aaron into the room. 'This hot weather won't last, I suppose,' she
had said. And they managed a long afternoon on the beach at
Broadstairs. Clive recalls catching his mother observing him
closely that day.

Clive's hands were still trembling from Kulwant's discovery, but
he'd already begun to organise his thoughts, and the brisk rushes
of emotion they brought with them.

Annette and Christine had owned their flat shortly before
they'd left it, in June 1977.

And now they were there again. Back in the same flat.

Clive snapped his head away from the hazy view. Did Christine
and Annette know that Aaron still lived in Marlowe Tower?
Without doubt they'd recognised Clive's name on the hoardings
around the estate. And on the letters Deptford Borough Council
must have sent, offering to buy the lease for flat 304 from them,
and detailing what was planned for Marlowe Tower and the estate.

Was that why they'd come back? Because they'd learned of his
plans?

He imagined their two heads close together over the letter, one
of them – Annette, he thought – saying his name aloud; Christine
repeating it: 'Clive? *Our* Clive?'

He felt a miniature flush of pleasure. Even now, even in his
imagination, they managed to have that effect on him. Sixty-two,
and he still wanted to be 'their' Clive.

They would be in their sixties now. They were older than him
and Aaron. They would be heading for retirement – if they had

ever worked. He allowed himself the spiteful thought that they'd probably danced and smiled through their lives, always charming, relying on that promise of specialness they seemed to be able to conjure out of the air. Would they be grey-haired now, though? Thick-voiced? Overweight and slow-moving? He couldn't picture it. It did not seem possible.

He glanced involuntarily at the glass wall that divided his office from the main one. His face was sagging in the reflection he saw there – the bags and furrows exaggerated by the strong lights above his head. Did Aaron look old now too? Did his lax life mean he'd aged better than Clive, or worse?

Clive blinked, and saw himself blink.

Did Aaron know that Annette and Christine were back in Marlowe Tower? He was almost embarrassed that this hadn't been his first thought. Was this why Aaron was still refusing to sell? Had the three of them met already? Had they moved aside for each other on the stairs, but, surprised there was anyone else still living in the tower, looked up to examine each other's faces, and after an open-mouthed moment, spoken each other's names.

Clive turned his head away from his reflection and back towards the window. If he began to imagine the conversations Aaron and the twins might have had, he would be frozen in this position all day ... all week. No. He had to drive his thoughts down a different road. Had to work out some way to discover what had brought Annette and Christine back to Marlowe Tower, and whether his brother knew they were there.

He drummed his fingers on the desk, then took himself over to the window to stare at the tower for a spell.

A meeting would work well. Or at least an invitation to one. Not from him, but from the council. He was sure he could persuade Kemi to send it. Or better, Alexa. To the owner-occupiers, he thought. He had no idea whether Annette and Christine would accept. But would Aaron? Would he wonder whether Clive would be there? Perhaps curiosity would get the

better of him. Or maybe he would send a message through his
absence, just as Clive was intending to.

Clive shook his head, as if he'd seen something unpleasant
passing down the river. If he and Aaron simply spoke, all this
would be so much easier. The efforts of the last few months would
have been unfrustrated if they'd just had a conversation. But that
conversation had always seemed impossible. Their split was an
amputation, the pathways any message might take permanently
broken.

But now Annette and Christine were back, and it was as if the
river had forgotten to turn at low tide, as if the muddy bed was
exposed, wet and treacherous and crowded with the past. Clive
felt almost as if he was stretching across the river, beckoning from
his tall building to Aaron's, wanting his brother to make the
crossing, wanting to meet his eyes and ask, 'Do you know? Do
you know that they've come back? Do you know why?'

9

Aaron isn't sure how long he has stood, staring at the shut door, hearing the small movements of someone at home inside flat 304. He realises that he is a little bent over. It feels too much to stand up straight, up here on the thirtieth floor.

He steps forwards and puts his ear close to the wood.

There. A voice. Three words, like three upward steps. A woman? Perhaps.

Then a reply. And a question.

The same climbing phrase. Another reply. None of it distinguishable.

Aaron realises he's holding his breath. He's still bent over, his knees slightly flexed. A quivering question mark.

He straightens up with a jerk that hurts his knee and steps back from the door. Footsteps are approaching, tapping down the hallway. And as their owner moves, she speaks. It's definitely a woman, and he's also sure of the words:

—Have you read the whole letter?

He turns and lurches to the stairwell, forgetting to hold the door, which slams behind him with a chiming bang. He stops, swaying on the top step, fully expecting to hear the click and squeak of a door opening behind him. But then he collects himself and starts down the stairs, his hand pressing hard against the banister to stop himself falling forwards into the faces that seem to foam up towards him from below, from forty years before.

Could it be Annette and Christine in flat 304? It feels so unlikely after all these years. Yet something about the voice he heard – its rhythm, its taste – placed the image of Christine's face in his mind – looking down at a letter. A copy of the one he has in his pocket.

Surely it can't be them. To find out, all he has to do is go to the meeting. But then they'll find out that he's here too. Perhaps they already know. Does Clive know who these other owners are? Does he know they're Annette and Christine?

10

Aaron and Clive slipped easily into the group of people surrounding Annette and Christine. And it seemed they were among several new friends from the estate the twins had gathered around themselves; or who had congregated about them – it was never clear whether Annette and Christine had chosen you, or whether you had circled towards their centre.

After that first evening, they told Aaron and Clive to come upstairs whenever they wanted – 'It's the holidays, so one of us will most likely be in.' The boys took to going up sometimes twice a day. In the mornings and afternoons, they'd arrive at the door to 304 panting from running up the stairs. Unashamedly eager. 304 seemed somehow brighter, the sky outside it bluer, the chairs and carpets softer than those six floors below. And at night, the flat seemed in a different building altogether from the Marlowe Tower of flat 246. Clive was sure the strands of lights below belonged to a different city.

It was all because of Annette and Christine, they would say, if you asked what made that difference. 'No one wears that kind of a face in here,' Annette once told Clive, when he'd turned up immediately after a prickly tussle with Zöe about how he was using his holiday time. But it wasn't an instruction to cheer up. It was a statement. Within minutes, Clive was crowing with laughter at nothing in particular. Then lay on the floor and watched Aaron tell Christine a long Zöe story, thinking his brother had never looked so beautifully unaware of himself.

—We should invite them to our place, Clive said to Aaron as they walked down from 304 to 246 one evening.

Aaron bounced his hand off the banister rail as he took each step.

—It'll be tricky, though, won't it? They'll really want to see

Mum. And you know what she can be like with students and what have you. Do we want to put them through that?

—You never know. First she'll call them upstarts, but by the time they leave she'll have started organising their future careers.

—We could ask, I suppose, said Aaron.

Zöe's answer was surprisingly emphatic. Her 'no' came out almost as a yelp.

But then she examined Clive and Aaron's faces, and immediately softened hers.

—I'm up to my eyes with work at the moment. And I'm up to – she placed a flat hand at waist height – about here with students. I don't need two more.

And then she flung her arms aside in mock exhaustion.

—Please don't make me. Please…

She was funny when she wanted to be.

◆

They didn't make her, of course. But they did invite Annette and Christine down to visit.

It was a Monday evening – the day Zöe always visited her mother for dinner. As children Aaron and Clive had had to go too, but their grandmother had since released them from the obligation, and now Zöe only insisted they pay a monthly visit.

There was an awkwardness in the first few minutes after Annette and Christine entered flat 246. Aaron was sure it somehow exuded from the furniture. The dining table and chairs, the long sofa and big paintings all seemed hushed and uneasy in the presence of the young women.

—We guessed that your mum wouldn't be here, said Annette.

—She's visiting our grandmother, said Clive.

—In Godalming, said Aaron. She drives down every Monday night. It'll be late before she's back.

—That's where she's from, isn't it? said Annette.

—Yes, grew up there, says Clive. It 'informs her vernacular' is what she says.

—Her language or her architecture? asked Christine.

—Both, said Aaron. That's the joke she likes to make.

Christine's laugh scurried round the room, and everything in it seemed to relax just a little.

—Does she bring everything back to her architecture, then? said Annette.

—It's more like she thinks her architecture can encompass everything, said Clive.

—Or more like she can encompass everything, said Aaron.

Christine laughed again, and Annette joined in, so their voices filled the room. Aaron didn't think he'd been so funny, but his body laughed along too. Clive stood up and opened the balcony door.

—Isn't it sometimes... Christine began, looking to Annette for assistance.

—Suffocating? said Annette.

Clive stopped between the balcony door and the dining table. He looked at Aaron.

—Being her sons, you mean? asked Aaron.

—You're always talking about how in charge she is of everything – you, the estate... said Christine.

—But when she writes, and when she's interviewed, she doesn't come across like that really.

Clive sat down again.

—Perhaps we overdo the 'Godsworthy' stuff, he said.

—The what?

—Gods-worthy – Goldsworthy, said Aaron. We tease her by calling her that sometimes.

—When she's getting carried away with the God-complex stuff, said Clive.

—And how does Zöe take that? said Christine.

—Oh, she laughs, said Clive. She knows it's true. But at the same time she won't change.

—She's a complicated person, said Aaron, and laughed at himself first this time.

—Do you want to see her office? said Clive.

Annette and Christine looked at each other.

—Of course, but...?

—Won't she mind? Christine directed the question at Aaron. He was pleased to see how clearly she saw his and Clive's roles.

—Probably, said Aaron.

—But she won't know, said Clive. He was already up and walking into the corridor and down the stairs.

When he reached the closed door, Clive knocked.

—You never know, he said, waited a second then opened it.

Satisfyingly for Clive, there were two small maquettes on a side table, an anglepoise lamp beside them.

—Sit there.

He pointed to the wicker chair. It was too small for both to squeeze into, so Annette sat on Christine's lap.

—This is our job, said Clive.

—Was our job, said Aaron. We generally refuse to do it now.

—She brings the models home, then sits there and we have to move the lamp around, lighting them from different angles.

Annette and Christine leaned forwards.

—Go on then, said Christine.

Clive popped the switch and the gold-white light flooded the two card buildings.

—That's gorgeous, said Christine.

—What are they? said Annette. Something municipal, I'd say.

—A library and a concert hall, I think, said Aaron. Somewhere in South America.

—Any housing? asked Annette, scanning the room.

—She's not done any housing since this estate, said Clive. She says it took so much out of her, she's not sure she has the capacity to do it again. She prefers these kinds of commissions.

He changed the angle of the lamp.

Annette stood up and examined the photographs grouped on the wall above the desk.

—I'm not surprised, she said. It must have been exhausting. Estates like this are always designed by a team. You never see one architect taking on the whole thing.

—Only someone incredibly single-minded could manage it, said Christine.

She'd sat back in the chair, still staring at the models with her chin on her hand. It was exactly the pose that Zöe would take as she examined her work.

—Move the lamp, she said to Aaron.

He grinned and gave her a low angle.

—At sunset, he said.

—Only someone as single-minded as her could have made it in the profession as a woman, said Clive.

He tapped one of the photographs, low down on the wall.

—Her class at college.

He put a finger on Zöe's shoes. She was front and centre. Her suit pale and sharp against the rows of dark clothes behind and either side of her.

—They all know she's the star, said Annette, bending at the waist.

—She has it there so it's directly in her eye-line while she's working, said Clive. To remind her of all the men she had to fight, she says.

Annette stood upright.

—I repeat: exhausting.

—She doesn't really have to fight them now, said Aaron.

—She commands, said Clive. Or cajoles.

—Or you find you've just done what she wants and have no idea how she's made you do it, said Aaron.

—Now that I like, said Christine, standing up and stretching.

—Trust us – you wouldn't, said Clive. You asked if it's suffocating; well, it certainly can be. We just wish she'd realise she can't control everything all of the time.

—I don't think she's ever accepted that things have a habit of going on without her, said Aaron.

This time, Annette and Christine's laughter seemed far too big for the room.

11

As the string of hot days became a stretch, Annette and Christine took to spending their evenings on the deck beside the river. A vast slab of concrete describing a shallow curve, the deck was cantilevered over the river on one side, and on the other, long, shallow steps led down from it onto the open space between Marlowe Tower and the next block.

Annette and Christine weren't alone, of course. As soon as they decided it was their evening spot, a group collected around them. At first it was no more than ten – the two sets of twins; Jenny and Gorton, the couple Aaron and Clive had met the first time they had visited Annette and Christine's flat; Albert, and another friend or two who stopped by.

Aaron and Clive were the youngest, but Annette and Christine kept them close, so they found themselves at the centre of the group, and the heart of the laughter. They began to look forward all day to these evenings. They'd sit as close to the water's edge as possible, hearing the tide making clucking waves against the concrete below them. It almost joined the flow of the conversation, and when someone brought beer, or a joint was passed between fingers and fingers, the waves seemed to become part of the hilarity that spread like catspaws around the group.

Aaron and Clive would have been happy to spend the rest of the summer lying across the benches and the warm, dusty concrete like a small, happy pride – sometimes gently tumbling around, other times almost sleepy with pleasure. But after a week or two, the group grew larger. There were Annette and Christine's university friends, who always came with bottles. There was the 'Goldsmith's crowd', many of whom remembered Aaron and Clive from Ronald's party – black men and women who seemed slightly older, and remarked on how the estate was so white. 'It's like crossing a state line, coming over that bridge on Evelyn Street,' said a woman in leather sandals to Christine as she gave her a book. Don't nobody on this estate mix?' 'We mix,' Christine had replied, pulling Aaron towards her.

Then there were the white hippies who'd been to Goldsmith's and had stayed on in the near-derelict flats the council had given them for virtually nothing, or in the squats that dotted the streets between the estate and New Cross. There was the Rastafarian who pulled off his striped woollen hat one particularly sultry night and laughed his locks free. 'Never thought it'd be that hot,' Annette had teased him.

There was the group of teenaged black girls whose numbers grew each night, and who all seemed to be friends of the daughter of Annette and Christine's former landlady. They acted shy, standing close together. It needed Annette or Christine to beckon them up the steps, to demand that others make space.

And there were the pale teenagers Aaron and Clive knew from the estate. They'd lived here nearly ten years, yet they couldn't say they were really friends with them. Not in the way they were instantly friends with Annette and Christine. At first the teenagers sat close by, not completely part of the group. Then the boys pulled off their T-shirts, displaying their scorched backs. 'Ow,' said Annette, and the next night she gave one of them a small medicine bottle. 'Coconut oil,' she said. 'It'll soothe the burn. And you'll go home smelling like us.' The boy gave her an uncertain smile, and after that the girls he was with drew closer. They wore shorts and bikini tops and admired Annette and Christine's skirts. They started careful conversations with the black girls. One took the joint that Gorton was passing round, took a drag, suppressed a cough, and passed it on to her pink brother.

One evening Tabitha arrived. She appeared at the head of a little troop of other girls from the estate, swinging a tape recorder at her thigh. She left her friends standing in an unsure line, and with hands pressed together, as if she were miming a fish, she inserted herself into the row of bodies on the step below Annette and Christine, sat down sideways and pressed a button on the tape recorder. Reggae tapped out of the little speaker. She turned her head up towards Annette, sniggering and squinting a little in the sideways sun. Annette dropped a hand on Tabitha's head, let a strand of hair run through her fingers.

—Turn it up, then, said Gorton.

The sound warped and crackled, and the voices seemed to strain.

—Shame it's such a little thing, said Christine.

The next evening, Gorton arrived at the deck a little late. It was an even hotter night – perhaps the closest evening of the summer so far. The air was thick, but the river seemed to give off the slightest of breaths, so the group on the deck was the biggest it had been.

—Looks like a party, said Gorton.

—Looks like you knew it would be, said Annette, pointing at the hefty silver box Gorton was carrying on his shoulder.

He swung it down by its handle onto the bottom step and the chatter around the benches hushed. Aaron felt Clive lean forwards; Clive felt Aaron follow him. It was like looking at the head of a robot with vast, flat eyes.

Gorton pressed a button and a drum stroke seemed to bounce from the box and trip up the steps towards them. Then a thud and the song began. Gorton spun a knob and the sound was as loud as at Ronald's party.

The hot air spread throughout the estate and carried the bass and drums through the maze of concrete buildings, turned golden in the evening sun. Behind the group, the notes fell into the shallow troughs between the sauntering waves, the river flashing lazily with the music.

Annette and Christine were up. Standing on the bench. Now

dancing. They held their arms high, gleaming in the softened sun. Their fingers seemed about to snap, but didn't. They looked downwards over one shoulder as they aimed a hip lower and swung.

Aaron blinked at the ease of it all. At the movement rippling from the twins into the rest of the group. And he knew that he wanted this moment to set, to remain like this, but also knew that it couldn't – its heat, its fluidity, its perpetual motion, prevented it.

He turned his head away from the twins for a moment and saw, above them on a balcony on a lower-down floor of Marlowe Tower, a topless man. He was standing at the balustrade, and even from this distance Aaron could see his hands were gripping the concrete. His belly was round and pale in the shade – it bulged like an angry eye.

And then a movement above him. And another to his side. And there, in the other direction, in one of the neighbouring blocks. People were out on their balconies, looking for the fuss and noise.

Aaron shared a glance with Clive. He'd spotted the white torsos and pink arms of the onlookers too. What were they thinking? He couldn't be sure, but he could guess. One of them confirmed his assumption, shaking her head and retreating inside. Clive, at the same time, saw the topless, big-bellied man turning his head to someone and throwing out a hand towards the scene below.

Of course, Aaron and Clive couldn't know for sure what all these people thought or felt, drawn onto their balconies that night by the heavy thump of music and the shoal of switching bodies.

But it was not long before they were told.

12

Just a few mornings later, after another evening on the deck, Gorton's cassette player staying loud into the darkness, Zöe frowned at Aaron as he joined Clive at the breakfast table.

—There's a residents' meeting tonight, she said.

Aaron watched Clive take the cereal box from the centre of the table and Zöe gather her hair from around her neck and clip it loosely at the back of her head. She let a long breath out through her nose. It was already warm. The door to the balcony was open but none of them could feel the slightest breeze.

—Can you think why it's been called? asked Zöe.

Clive put the cereal box back and reached for the milk jug. Aaron said nothing.

—No? Well I'll tell you. A whole group of residents are very unhappy about what's been going on down on the river deck these past few weeks.

She paused – as if expecting some reply. Clive's spoon chimed against the side of his bowl. Zöe looked from him to Aaron.

—Eat some breakfast, Aaron, she said. This isn't a telling-off.

Clive stopped eating and raised his head.

—Isn't it?

—No. No, it isn't. Right now, I'm just mentioning it to you.

Another pause.

—And telling you that I know you've been spending time with people down there.

Aaron put out a hand for the cereal box and nudged the milk jug as he did so. It wobbled and slopped. A drop of milk jumped out and spotted the tablecloth.

—Aaron, I wish you'd be more careful, said Zöe, picking up the jug and placing it further away from him with a thud that made another spot of milk slop out.

—We need something more stable, said Clive. He's always knocking it over. Something with a wider base—

—I wasn't watching you, if that's what you think, said Zöe. But other people have been. And I've had several come and talk to me. Telling tales on you, I'm afraid.

—Tales about what? asked Clive.

—We haven't done anything, said Aaron.

—Well you don't need to sound so defensive, then, do you?

Zöe hunched over a little and gazed into her cup for a moment.

—It's not like you're children.

Clive flared his nostrils.

—You're not a group of kids, playing out of an evening, she said.

—'Of an evening,' Clive repeated.

Zöe had developed a habit over the years of mimicking their neighbours' slang, but without adopting their accent. The mix sounded curdled.

She stared hard at Clive, a slight twitch in her lips.

—Our neighbours wouldn't mind a bit of high spirits and messing about, then all home to bed. But this – you're mainly adults, and there are more of you each night, apparently.

Neither Aaron nor Clive responded, so Zöe continued.

—It's the loud music until way into the night. I can even hear it up here. And smoking weed...

—You do that. Aaron spoke before he thought.

Clive glared at him, and Aaron knew he'd fired a big gun prematurely.

But Zöe was rattled.

—Not outside, with everyone to see ... and, and smell.

She slapped the table suddenly.

—You need to consider other people's feelings, she said. We *live* – her palm met the tabletop – in this community. We've been here years. I don't appreciate complaints about my own children.

Zöe often shouted, but she was rarely shrill. Now, though, it was as if the reed of her voice had cracked. She sat up straight, switched her gaze from Aaron to Clive and back again – her nose pointing at each of them.

—People – our neighbours – don't believe half the crowd down there are even from this estate.

—Some of us are, said Aaron, flatly, keeping his face expressionless, his hand on the table in front of him.

—Mrs Ledbury says that she didn't recognise any of the faces yesterday.

—She wasn't there, said Clive.

—And she'd have recognised us, wouldn't she?

—She said she passed a crowd on the walkway, heading for the deck. She didn't know any of them.

—Is that because they were black people, do you think? Clive turned his spoon over in his empty bowl.

Zöe sighed.

—Everyone is just a bit concerned that those twins ... those—

Her voice seemed to snag on her words. She coughed – an odd, dry cuss almost – then drank a long draught of tea to settle it. There was a sheen on her forehead and a flush on her cheeks.

—Those black women, Clive finished for her, sounding the words as if striking a bell.

—Annette and Christine, said Aaron slowly.

They didn't need to look at each other. They knew they had their mother cornered. They thought they both knew why.

—Yes ... Annette and Christine, said Zöe at last, but her voice was still strained. Everyone is just a bit concerned that ... well, that they're bringing an unsavoury element onto the estate. People who aren't from here – who aren't part of this community.

—It's racialism— Clive began.

—It is not racialism. Zöe held her palm flat and straight, like a knife.

—It is, Mum. You know it is, said Aaron. You've essentially said it yourself: 'People who aren't from here – who aren't part of this community.'

—I mean the estate. You know I mean that.

Zöe employed the other hand as a blade now.

—You know I'm not racialist. Not in the slightest.

Her voice seemed to have regained its strength, and she sat more upright, her hands flat on the table. Neither twin dared challenge her.

—Right from the beginning I wanted this estate to be a place everyone could live in. A proper community. You know that. Why would we even be here if that wasn't the case? I'm not Sir Basil Bloody Spence, living in Georgian splendour in Edinburgh while third-rate towers he'd never live in himself crumble away in the Gorbals. I built something I was prepared to live in. That I was prepared to bring my family to. And that something isn't just bricks and mortar.

—Or prefabricated concrete panels, said Clive.

But Zöe went on, undeterred:

—It's community. Trust. Ties. It means airing grievances. Talking about what worries us. That's why people are upset. They care about where they live. And that's a good thing. You'll see – that community-centre hall will be full tonight.

—We won't see if we're not there, said Aaron.

—I doubt we'll be welcome, said Clive.

—Honestly, I'm fed up to here – Zöe chopped at the air above her head – with your sarcasm. You should come tonight. If you were still children, I'd insist upon it.

She stood up and pulled their bowls towards her. Aaron's was still empty.

They were no longer children and she could not insist.

And neither of them had any intention of going to the community meeting that evening.

◆

But Christine and Annette did. It was, of course, Clive's idea to tell the twins about the meeting.

—Really? was Aaron's response.

—Yes. Airing grievances, talking about what worries people – why shouldn't Annette and Christine be there? It's them who'll be discussed. Why shouldn't they be part of that?

—Exactly because it's them who'll be discussed.

—And you think that's fair? said Clive.

—No.

—Or right?

—No.

—Well, let's tell them, then.

—It's making trouble, said Aaron.

—Good. Clive stood up. Let's make trouble.

Aaron washed the dishes. Zöe had been complaining they weren't doing their chores. If they were going to make trouble, he'd smooth a wrinkle elsewhere.

When he was done and was wiping his wet hands on the towel, Clive appeared and leaned against the door frame.

—Coming?

—Where?

—Upstairs. You don't have to. I'm going anyway.

Clive said it over his shoulder, into the living room, as if to someone else sitting there.

He always offered Aaron a get-out. But he never expected Aaron to take it. Aaron would always join him.

But this time he was surprised.

—I'm not going, said Aaron. I'm not saying any of this is right, and I won't stop going to the deck or seeing the twins or anything, but going up there and telling them about the meeting is just stirring the pot.

—They could find out anyway. It's bound to be on the noticeboard downstairs.

—Well, let them find out. And do what they want once they know. Telling them is as good as encouraging them to go.

—And they should go. I would.

Clive pushed himself off the door frame and went to stand beside the balcony window.

—Why don't you, then?

It was late morning and the sun was at its brightest – a heavy sheet of light behind Clive, making him a silhouette.

To Clive, Aaron, standing motionless in the kitchen, was all softness and diffused tints. But Clive knew he wouldn't be able to persuade him. He said nothing more and went upstairs without his twin.

It was the first thing Christine said when she opened the door:

—Where's Aaron?

—Downstairs—

—They don't have to be together all the time, said Annette, appearing in the doorway.

—No, they don't, said Christine, and as she turned her head to Annette and widened her eyes, it seemed to Clive that she said 'but we do'.

In the living room, Clive went to the window. It was the same view as downstairs: the river – clay grey, but flashing silver and tin at the bends at Rotherhithe and Greenwich; the expanse of derelict land opposite, on the Isle of Dogs, flattened heaps of gutted buildings lined up by the three oblong docks, the island fringed with little housing estates, low rises and the old point block. Nothing to rival Deptford Strand and Marlowe Tower.

But from this window, six floors higher than he was used to, the angle was subtly different. Everything was less real. Less immediate. And more malleable. As if he could pick up the pieces and move them around. And for the very first time he thought he understood how Zöe felt about her work.

He turned to Annette and Christine.

—There's a residents' association meeting tonight.

—Oh yeah? What about?

—Us.

—Who, you and Aaron?

—Drink? Christine turned towards the kitchen.

—No. Us. The crowd of us who've been hanging around down on the deck.

Christine stopped in the doorway and turned around. Annette sat down, but didn't lean back. Clive looked from one to the other – their expectant expressions were identical. Of course. Did they see him and Aaron that way when they were telling them something?

—Our mum told us about it...

He stopped. How to continue?

—And? Christine said.

—Apparently, people think ... people think 'outside elements' are coming onto the estate. People not in the community. The residents don't like it, apparently.

Clive realised he was hot. His armpits pricked.

Two pairs of eyebrows were raised. Annette and Christine were staring at each other, as if each was waiting for the other to speak. Annette went first.

—'Not in the community.' Well, we know what that means, don't we? She said it to her sister.

—'Outside elements,' said Christine. It seemed to amuse her.

—'The residents,' said Annette. Doesn't seem to include all of us that live here...

—Mum wants me and Aaron to go, but we won't.

Clive paused.

—We think it's just racialism.

Christine turned back towards the kitchen.

—Tea OK for you? she said.

And just like that, it seemed Annette and Christine were on

one side of the living room, and he was on the other, his back against the high windowsill. It was as if a glass wall had appeared between them. Clive thought he could see everything through it, but he knew there were things it masked. Things the twins knew that he didn't. Things he could never fully understand.

—Thank you, yes, he said.

—And what does Zöe Goldsworthy think about all this? Annette asked.

Clive frowned at the full name.

—Whenever she writes, Christine said, raising her voice a little to be heard over the kettle, she's talking about integrated communities – places where a college professor and a dustman live next door to each other.

—And want to live next door to each other, added Annette. Wouldn't move away to some suburb where all the neighbours have the same jobs.

—And are the same colour, offered Clive.

—But she's never said that, has she?

Annette's reply came like an arrow from a bow she'd whipped from its hiding place over her shoulder. Clive put his hand on the windowsill.

—We love her work, said Christine, reappearing from the kitchen. It's just she doesn't cover race. It's all about class.

—It's been interesting living here, you know. In a place she built, said Annette. The architecture is stunning, obviously.

—Obviously, said Christine.

—But it's the community that's confusing us.

—Confusing you?

The heat of the sun on the back of Clive's hand was almost like that of a person.

—All the shared stuff – the community centre, the health centre, the school... Annette began.

—The parks and the town square, the shops. Even the walkways and staircases... said Christine.

—Everyone uses them all exactly how she planned it. We've read what she says about her intentions. And it all seems to work.

—It's just that we didn't expect it to be such a... Christine stopped.

—Fortress, said Annette.

Clive laughed at the word.

—No, it's true, Christine said. That's how it seems. It's as if she's been so successful in creating a community, that community doesn't want anyone else to get a look-in.

—God, she'd hate to hear you say that, said Clive, glancing down at the sheer wall falling away below him.

—It's the way we see it, said Annette.

—You know, if she did find out you'd said it, she'd either spend all night and all day arguing with you, proving that it wasn't true, or she'd do something to change it.

—Like what? Annette threw back.

Clive raised his hands.

—Build something, I suppose. I don't know.

Annette and Christine giggled. Clive wasn't exactly sure how much of a joke he'd made.

—I'll need to tell Aaron you've said it's like a castle – a fortress. I don't think either of us have ever realised it might seem like that to ... to an outsider.

—Well I suppose you've never known any different, said Annette.

She turned and hummed over to the record player. She picked up a single, slipped it from its plain-white sleeve.

—But we do, she said, flashing her large eyes up towards Clive. The angle was odd. He couldn't quite read her expression.

—Mum says the hall will be full tonight. Everyone's complaining apparently.

—Did she say about what exactly? Christine placed a tray carrying full mugs and a bottle of milk on the table.

—Loud music. Smoking weed. That we're out until late.

—That'll fill about two minutes of the meeting, and then—

—The subject will turn to us, said Annette, pointing at her chest with her index fingers.

Christine did the same. And the last little wisps of confidence and defiance with which Clive had climbed the stairs from flat 246 were whisked away in the wind that curled around the top of the tower. 'You should go' was what he'd intended to say. But he feared the 'should we?' that would leap across at him.

Annette bent over the record player again, the needle touched the disc and a loud click came from the speaker.

—Is this...? asked Christine using the West Indian accent she and Annette sometimes swam in and out of.

—Mhm, replied Annette, and a drum ratt-tatted the introduction to the song.

—We love this, Christine said, beginning to dance. Gorton got copies from Jamaica. His cousin works in a studio. It's not out anywhere yet. You're one of the first to hear it.

—You're privileged, said Annette.

Two girlish voices began to sing, in the kind of patois Gorton would often use. Christine and Annette raised their arms and, swinging towards each other, joined the voices with their own.

Clive couldn't make out the meaning. The sounds of the words were familiar but he struggled to order them. He felt his discomfort return, the heat in the room making him flush.

But Annette and Christine were dancing towards him, each catching a hand, winding him now this way, now that, encouraging him to join in.

And he did. And with his movement, he felt for a moment he understood something. The voices from the record were everyday – sung in a kitchen or outside a back door. He could taste the blend of the sweet tune and the thickly textured accompaniment, yet he still couldn't grasp the meaning of the song. But it didn't matter. And it didn't matter. He was raising his arms too, dancing in the middle of the room in the middle of the day.

A thump-thump-thump came from Mrs Ledbury's flat.

◆

That evening, there were more people than ever on the deck beside the river. They all knew about the meeting. Those from the estate told those arriving from outside.

But Annette and Christine weren't with them. Aaron and Clive had been there for nearly two hours, and still the twins hadn't arrived, and without them the group was lacking something. It felt as if the heat was draining, whereas on other hot nights they'd revelled in it. Now they spread out across the deck, everyone seated or lying, the conversations few, murmured, fizzling out.

At last Tabitha stood up and wandered up and down the area at the bottom of the steps, for a moment her flip-flops the only sounds.

Clive watched her to-ing and fro-ing and realised from her frequent glances towards the walkway that she was watching for Annette and Christine. Between these checks, she looked at her feet, her face mobile, hopeful one moment and anxious the next. He wondered what exactly the little knot of conflict was she seemed to be struggling to untangle.

She saw the twins first.

—There they are.

She turned back to the group, her face now full of a child's satisfaction.

But Clive wasn't looking at her. He was standing up, ready to receive Annette and Christine. And as they reached the bottom of the steps outside Marlowe Tower, he realised: they were wearing identical outfits. Short khaki suits. They never did that.

—They never do that, said Aaron, at his side.

It was something the four of them had discussed – checking to avoid the same outfit and how difficult it was because they so often chose the same things.

Tabitha was already with Annette and Christine.

—I love your suits. She plucked at a sleeve.

—I can't tell who's who, said one of the estate teenagers. He was shirtless and his hands wouldn't leave his chest.

Christine looked up, meeting Aaron's gaze, just as Annette looked up at Clive, eyebrows raised, a little knowing. Or possibly she was looking at the older black woman who always brought books for Annette and Christine to read.

Clive met Annette at the top of the steps.

—How was the meeting?

—Oh yeah, how was the meeting? said Tabitha. She was awkwardly holding on to Annette's arm.

—Boring, said Annette.

—Just a lot of talk, said Christine.

—They clearly weren't happy we were there.

—Do you think it stopped them saying what they wanted to? asked Aaron.

—Well, of course. Annette took a step up onto the bench seat of the pub-style table, then sat down on the tabletop.

The group made room for Christine to join her.

—What they did was start everything with—

—'No offence but...'

—'I'm not prejudiced but...'

—'There's good and bad in everyone but...'

—And then there was a lot of 'ten years this estate's been here, and we've welcomed everyone...' said Annette.

—And 'they have to realise we have our ways of doing things here...'

—Then lots of blabber about community.

—Was our mum there? Aaron said quietly.

Christine looked upwards and Annette leaned sideways slightly.

—Yes, she was, said Christine.

—But she didn't say a word, said Annette. Now, why's it so quiet? Play some music, Gorton.

Gorton was sitting slightly apart, Aaron realised. As if he didn't need to pay as close attention. As if he already knew the gist of what they were saying. He was older, Aaron supposed.

Gorton clicked a cassette into the player, pressed a button and spun the dial with an open-handed flourish.

Clive heard the rat-tat of the introduction and realised it was the song the twins had played that morning.

—Louder, Gorton, Annette demanded, throwing her hands and her smile into the sky.

The song unfolded like a map, so big it spread halfway across the river, and covered the estate, all the way to Deptford Park, on the other side of the chugging traffic on Evelyn Street.

Christine had a baby in her arms now and was dancing with it propped on her hip. It clutched at the epaulette of her shirt, examining the brown button. Its mother, Sandie, was standing on the seat below, holding up her pink arms to wave to the child. Tabitha climbed onto the seat too, swaying and reaching out to grab Annette's hands.

The whole group was dancing now, but no one seemed to want to join Annette and Christine on the tabletop. Everyone seemed happy with their lower tiers – the seats, the steps, the deck.

Aaron and Clive moved through the group, dancing too. Aaron, unthinking, caught Clive's hands, and Clive, despite a minute pull away, let him. And they danced together. As they had as boys.

And because they danced, they didn't see Zöe.

She strode across the patio – as she called it – the undefined paved space at the foot of Marlowe Tower. Her gaze was trained on the undulating pyramid of bodies ahead of her, Annette and Christine twin queens at its apex. A chatter of laughter rose above the music for a moment.

And then Annette spotted Zöe. And straight after, Christine did too. Still dancing, Christine bent down.

—Aaron, she said.

—Clive, said Annette.

Zöe stopped in the middle of the patio, staring at the group for so long, many of them started noticing her, and their dancing drooped away. Aaron and Clive were both still now, looking back at their mother, both wondering if they should approach her, whether that's what her stillness meant. But she was staring not at them, they realised, but at Annette and Christine. It was too direct, and too long a moment.

A warm wind slipped up the river from the sea and was deflected into a spinning eddy that picked up a pile of leaves, crisped prematurely by the summer's heat, and threw it up in a playful little vortex, then took Zöe's hair from her neck and flung it across her pink face.

She turned, jerking her head so her hair fell away, and strode off again, her white linen trousers a sail crossing a grey, concrete sea.

13

On the day of the meeting between Deptford Borough Council's housing development officers and the owner-occupiers of Marlowe Tower, Clive and Aaron wait.

Clive waits in his apartment, fifteen floors above his office, at the top of the tower in Canary Wharf.

Aaron waits at the dining table of his flat on the twenty-fourth floor of Marlowe Tower. He sits in Zöe's place, his palms spread on the table in front of him. The varnish has worn away in places. Drop-shaped matt spots. He looks at the chairs, one either side – where he and Clive would sit. The place at the opposite end of the table was almost always empty.

Clive regularly glances at his watch. He is estimating the time it will take Kulwant to return from the meeting. When he thinks Kulwant is back, he'll go down to the office. He could text or call. He picks up his phone by its sides. He doesn't like to touch the screen, even though he knows it's made for touching. He turns it over in his hands. Puts it down gently. Looks at his watch.

Aaron looks through the kitchen door at the clock on the wall. The plastic casing is a chamomile yellow now. The red second hand moves with regular jerks. It advances one second, then immediately retreats a tiny fraction. As if time moves forwards only tentatively. The letter said the meeting would take an hour. Add to that the time it would take to get back here from Deptford Town Hall. Half an hour, with waiting for the bus then walking either end. Unless they have a car. He doubts they have a car. Why does he doubt they have a car? Because he doesn't have one? And then there's the time to scale the staircase. He has his bad knee, of course.

He moves one hand from the table and places it on his weak knee. The warmth of his palm cupping the cap is comforting. And he thinks about the fact that no one has touched him in such a way in a very long time. It's a flutter of a thought, as if a bird has flapped past the window. He doesn't have such thoughts. Hasn't had for years. So it's strange that this one sped past like that.

He places his hand back on the table. Should he assume they're fitter than him, and might get back more quickly, these people who now live in Annette's and Christine's flat? The twins stride into his mind. Loose-limbed, they hold each other lightly. Look at him quizzically, almost grinning, almost laughing. At him. At what they know. But they are as he knew them, he realises. Twenty-one, twenty-two. They will be in their sixties now. He can't imagine that. But they will still lean against each other. Still offer a knowing grin, then turn and make some surprising suggestion that he would never have considered but seems so easy when they say it – as if they have reached up with their slim arms and pushed aside a cloud.

He glances at the clock again, then turns and settles his gaze on Clive's tower across the river.

And as he does so, Clive consults his watch once again.

They both decide it is time.

Aaron stands up, collects his keys from the shelf in the hall, puts on his outdoor shoes and goes out into the corridor.

Clive calls the lift and prepares his case – his pen and notebook, his laptop and phone, painkillers, and moves over to the lift to wait.

Aaron doesn't go to the stairs. He walks to the end of the corridor, where the room with the refuse chute is located, and there's a low sink with a grate for placing mop buckets. At the far end is a cupboard. He opens the door and runs his fingers along the panel at the back, feeling for the catch. He presses down and, with a click, the back of the cupboard opens onto a slim, low-ceilinged stair, like you might find in a cathedral tower.

He treads cautiously down the ladder-like steps, counting the flights carefully. By the light of a small slotted window he spots another door, which releases like the first. He passes through and is in one of the between-floor passages.

He pauses for a moment, his eyes adjusting to the dim light. It is years since he has been here. Since anyone has, he suspects. He has no idea who now knows of the existence of these corridors, or how to access them. Zöe always told Clive and him that they were the only ones who knew of them. Of any of the spaces she'd hidden throughout the estate. Surely someone must have discovered them by now. Surely Clive has told someone – a contractor, an assistant.

The floor of the passage is slim, oblong white and umber tiles – the pattern forming a long, narrow maze, the white just large enough to place a human foot. A game that has sat unplayed for decades, hidden in the space created by the split levels of the floors above and below.

Ignoring the labyrinth, he walks in a regular way, albeit with his slightly stuttering gait, to a small, head-height window a little further along. It gives not onto the outside of the tower, but onto the stairwell. On the stairs side, it is high up one wall, so no one can look through, and most don't even notice it. From the passage, though, it offers a good view of the stairwell. It is an observation post in a medieval castle – perfect for Aaron's current purpose.

He takes up position and thinks about his mother. He's sure he heard her mention crenelations at some point. Arrow slits. He still doesn't see her justification for building this odd feature into a tower block on a council estate. It's as if Zöe couldn't help herself.

Aaron looks at his watch. He's left a wide margin of time. If he stands here for an hour, he must see the residents of flat 304. He's good at waiting. At standing still.

Clive looks at his watch. He's arrived in his office with plenty of time. As he approaches the window, his phone chimes. A text from Kulwant:

On my way back. Interesting meeting.

'Interesting' is a bland word for 'revealing', Clive thinks. He is tempted to call, but he needs all the details Kulwant can offer, in his looks, his movements. He'll wait.

Aaron's knee pain fades, as it does if he stands immobile for a few minutes.

Kulwant arrives sooner than Clive has expected. Clive is still sitting near the window, Marlowe Tower in view if he moves his head a few degrees to the right, the maquette of the reconstructed estate within reach should he need to touch it, the activities of the outer office a dumb show on the other side of the glass wall.

Kulwant shrugs off his jacket and leaves it on his chair. Now he's opening the door and crossing the grey carpet.

—Interesting? says Clive. What's interesting?

Aaron has never realised that from the window onto the stairwell there is a view of the town square. A section of it at least. He can see the faded pattern of flagstones, the labyrinth they once made making more sense there than the one in this passage. He remembers speed-solving the town-square one – Clive starting from the centre, Aaron at the edge. Zöe had told them that this particular maze had four possible solutions. Aaron wonders if anyone else knew that. Or ever even tried to solve it.

A distant thunk wakes him from his reverie. A quiet pause, then footsteps on the stairs. It's just a patter, but Aaron is sure there is more than one pair of feet. He stretches his neck a little and shifts his weight in an attempt to see further down into the stairwell.

And then he sees heads – two. One a little behind the other, moving steadily upwards.

—As we know, says Kulwant, the owners of flat 304 are Annette and Christine Mayfield. Twins, almost definitely. Black women. In their sixties, I guess.

—Yes, that'd be right, says Clive.

He still can't see them as women in their sixties, though. He sees them in their khaki suits, making him dance.

—And... he starts to say, but it's as if he stalls, chokes.

—He wasn't there, says Kulwant.

—Yes, that'd be right, Clive mumbles again, but it's as if his whole system is stalling now. He manages to move an arm, and slaps his thigh repeatedly.

Kulwant takes a step towards him. Bends. His face gets bigger.

—Clive? Are you OK?

Clive stops slapping. He feels cold – a prickly shiver. Then warm. And then in control again.

The heads are dark. Black hair. Black people's hair – the sit and shape, parted centrally. Locks on both heads, tied back and hanging, some grey showing there.

Then Aaron gets one clean glimpse of each face. He found it easy to tell them apart forty years ago. Neither he nor Clive mistook one for the other. They had to make no particular effort. Perhaps they simply had an extra sensitivity to difference. Now, though, as the first face turns the corner of the stair, he can't be sure if it's Annette's or Christine's. And it is this thought that clutches at him first. Not that his suspicion they've moved back into the tower has been confirmed.

By the time his brain has caught up, the first face has passed out of his sight line and the next is turning the corner of the stair. Again, he can't tell if it is Annette or Christine, but he does now register the years. This face – both faces seem extended, the jaws and cheekbones clearer cut; the mouths and eye sockets drawn with sharper lines. But their skin remains smooth, retains a warm lustre.

He leans his back against the wall. His shoulder blades seem prominent and awkward.

So he was right, he thinks. They are here, he thinks. They're back, he thinks.

Why? he thinks. And he wants to get back to his flat. Draw the bolts on the door. Lower the blinds, even. Keep the TV and radio low, walk about on soft feet.

How long have they been back? Have they been listening at his door as he has at theirs?

Do they even know he still lives here?

Has Clive told them he does?

And from there the next step: was Clive at the meeting with them?

Aaron lurches away from the window, and his knee screams at him for making such a sudden move. He should know by now. Should know after forty years. He doesn't stop, though; he limps over to the little staircase. And then pauses, turns as if to go back. If Clive was at the meeting, could he have accompanied them back here? Should Aaron go back to the stairwell to see?

No. He shakes his head. Almost laughs. That's impossible.

He goes through the door and starts to make his way back up to his own floor. But when he gets there he looks up. The grey light slips in through the slots between the concrete slabs of the tower's outer shell. He shifts about, trying to get an angle that will allow him to see to the top. He can't. It's too dim. But he doesn't need to. He knows that the last flight of stairs stops at a ceiling, set into which is a hatch, lockable from both sides. Open, it leads to what seems to be the reason for this staircase: access to the roof of Marlowe Tower.

Many times he and Clive climbed that final flight, concertinaing their bodies against the locked hatch as their feet continued to climb. Many times they had pushed and pulled at the hatch. They had even taken various bunches of keys from Zöe's desk drawer. One seemed to fit the lock, but the hatch still wouldn't open.

Finally they had questioned Zöe. Over the years she had only gradually revealed what she had concealed within her design for the estate. She rarely gave exact instructions about where and how to find these places. Instead she hinted at what they might find if they took a particular path, opened a particular door or got off at this or that floor of the lift in another block.

But when they asked about the hatch, what was beyond it, how they could open it, she turned the page in her book with a flick. It was just access to the roof. Only the caretaker and the council had keys. No one else could go up there.

—We want to, Clive had said.

Zöe had riffled through the pages of her book.

—Well, you can't.

She'd stood and turned, head a little bowed so the curtain of her hair obscured her face.

It was several years later that they finally passed through the hatch. And it was Annette and Christine who opened it for them.

14

It was the first time Aaron had considered Christine as a person separate from her sister. He felt a tweak of shame at the realisation.

Without Annette, Christine seemed a little chattier, more forthcoming. Aaron knew why. More often than not Clive would say what Aaron was about to. Clive simply got there first. It made Aaron seem quieter.

He'd knocked at the door to 304 alone. And when Christine opened it, he'd discovered she was alone too.

—Anyone would think we weren't twins, said Christine as she turned and walked into the living room, not inviting him in, but clearly expecting him to enter.

—We're not, Aaron laughed.

Christine laughed in turn.

—Where's yours, then?

Christine sat down at the table. Her feet were bare. She tucked one under her behind, and Aaron could see the pale sole.

Aaron sat opposite her and saw a small stack of note paper on the table between them. A clean sheet lay in front of her.

—You're studying. I've interrupted you, he said.

—You have. But don't worry. I was kind of hoping I'd been interrupted by someone, you know. And I'm happy it's you. Annette went out so I could get on with it, but that was hours ago. And I'm allowed a break.

—Clive's out with Mum. She's taken him to some event at the RIBA. She's introducing him to 'useful' people.

Christine widened her eyes.

—One of the benefits, I guess.

Aaron wasn't sure how to reply.

—He didn't want to go, he said instead. But...

—...after that meeting...?

—After a massive row, actually. She's basically tried to ban us from, well, you know...

—From seeing us?

—Yeah.

This was what Aaron had come up to say. He'd thought Clive might try to stop him, but he'd wanted to say it. And Clive wasn't here today to put out an arm.

—Sorry, Aaron added.

—Don't be.

Christine pulled her foot out from under her. Now Aaron could see the line between the brown skin on the top and the paler skin of the sole. She sat straighter, picked up her glass and drained it. The water cast a halo across her face as she tipped the glass. Then it disappeared.

—She tried to ban us from getting together on the deck too. We said no – to both, of course. But that's why we didn't come down last night. We thought it was better to keep the peace for a day or two.

—Well, if you had, you'd've had a surprise. Christine stood up. Drink? We have some ice.

—Please. What surprise?

Christine didn't answer, didn't call from the kitchen. Aaron waited patiently. He knew Clive would have raised his voice, asked again, eager to hear. And Aaron suspected Annette would have too. In fact he was sure he'd witnessed this very thing – Annette and Clive having a shouted conversation from room to room, over his and Christine's heads. He relaxed into the feeling of not being Clive.

Christine returned with glasses that clicked and popped as the ice cubes cracked in the lemonade she'd poured. He wondered if she was relaxing into the feeling of not being Annette.

—When we got down to the deck last night, she said, there was this big group already sitting there. Old people. Well, older. You're mum's age and older. They were spread out, deck chairs, blankets to sit on.

—Who were they?

—Just people from the estate. Her next door was there. Her face when she saw us ... Tabitha made a run for it as soon as she clocked her.

—So they were doing it to make a point, said Aaron.

Christine spread her arms and raised her eyebrows high.

—Did they say anything? asked Aaron.

—To us? No. But about us – yes. And they made sure we could hear them.

—Racialist stuff?

There was a silent beat. As if a glass ornament had toppled and soundlessly smashed.

Christine extended her neck a little.

—You might not think so. But it was.

Aaron took a sip of his lemonade so he didn't have to reply. Christine continued:

—Stuff like 'I don't care what anyone says, we've got it great here', and 'the people are smashing too' and 'let's hope it stays that way'. People won't call us names to our faces, so they do it like that.

Aaron cast his eyes around the room. Without so many people it seemed tidy, and much larger. Without Annette and Clive, he realised.

—The real dig was the chairs and blankets. There were only – what, ten of them? They all fit round a table and a couple of chairs. But they'd spread loungers and blankets out across the whole deck and down the steps too. Obviously to stop our lot using it. We hung around for a bit on the bottom step, but everyone drifted off in the end.

For just a moment, Aaron wanted Clive here with him – to serve a ready-made comment. He followed Christine's gaze out of the window. Yet another hot morning – the air bright and rigid, London a baked crust on the ground below them.

—You didn't suspect they might do that? he asked. When you went to the meeting, I mean.

Christine didn't look at him; her face was turned towards the glass brightness outside. The light laid a pale slip over her mid-brown skin, drawing out some yellows, some fawns. Her eyes flashed a little green, then turned back to hazel as she tipped her chin upwards and spoke.

—Annette and I both said something was coming up. This wasn't the end of things. There was a lot of 'if the council don't do something, we will' at the meeting. They even... she turned her face to Aaron ...They were even saying that kind of thing to your mum.

—That's not a surprise, he said. They hold her responsible for anything they don't like on the estate. If a rubbish chute gets blocked, they come knocking at our door.

—Doesn't she just tell them where to go? Just because she designed the whole place, doesn't make her in charge of everything. Shouldn't either.

—She doesn't help herself. She does kind of act like it's her little kingdom.

Christine turned in her chair now, leaning towards him a little.

—She'd hate that I've said that, said Aaron. 'It's a community', she'd say. But she sees herself as the leader, whether she admits it or not.

—In some ways it's admirable, you know? said Christine.

She stood up. Plucked at her blouse, looking thoughtful.

—Most architects don't stay involved like that. It's kind of why Annette and I are so interested in her work here.

Aaron drank again, observing Christine over the rim of his glass. Annette and Christine hadn't complained that they didn't meet Zöe when they visited flat 246, but when they spoke about her, they always had a slightly avid look in their eyes. He wondered whether they still wanted him and Clive to introduce them to her.

—Perhaps it's *because* we live here that she can't give up any control. She built something to be lived in in a certain way, and it's impossible for her not to ... not to... he turned his hand in the air ...police it. She'd probably be the same if she worked in one of her office buildings, or stayed in one of her hotels.

—All the windows and balcony doors are open, but I still feel like I want to open another one, said Christine.

—She's always saying it's not up to her what the council decides, said Aaron, but she's always doing something for the residents' association – always writing letters to the council, calling them.

Christine twisted her upper body, letting her arms swing loose.

—The people at the meeting certainly seemed to think she has some kind of power, she said. More than them, anyway. But really they should feel she has the same power as them. It should be a collective effort, running an estate like this.

Aaron nodded to the pile of paper.

—Yes, said Christine. Exactly. I write about this stuff all the time.

—We've never really fitted in properly here, though, said Aaron.

Christine stopped her twisting.

—No?

—We used to live in a big house in Blackheath. She designed that too. Gardens, big garage, ponds. Loads more room than our flat downstairs. Then she moved us here.

—Because?

—She believes anything she builds should be good enough for her to live in. And her family.

—Like I said – admirable.

—Kind of. But Clive and I didn't go to the same schools as all the kids on the estate. Our friends are all still in Greenwich and Blackheath. And none of her real friends live here. When they come here it's like they're visiting a gallery or something.

—Old habits die hard, said Christine. It's about the status quo

I suppose. She moved you all here, but kept her old life. But then, when other new people move onto the estate, they're expected to change their behaviour to fit in.

She stopped and stared at Aaron for too long a moment. He glanced at the carpet. It had been hoovered recently. He could see it in the brushed pile.

—I mean us. Me and Annette, she said.

Aaron nodded.

—I know.

—Oof. I've made myself even hotter moving around, said Christine.

Her laugh was loud and easy. She swung her long body to the balcony door, held on to the door frame and leaned out for a second.

—There's a garden here we can go and sit in if you like.

—Which garden? On the estate? The park?

—I'll get my sandals and we'll go.

She crossed the room in a few quick strides and disappeared into the hall.

—Is it someone's garden on the ground floor?

—No.

Christine reappeared and raised an index finger to the ceiling.

—Upstairs.

15

Sitting at his office window, or on the terrace of his apartment, Clive often counts the floors of Marlowe Tower. But he always loses his place. At this distance it's difficult to focus his gaze on one floor at a time, to be sure he hasn't already counted it.

He knows how many floors there are. Thirty-one. Aaron knows the tower has thirty-one floors too; but he didn't, and neither did Clive, not until Christine showed him.

◆

Aaron realised as Christine opened the door in the hallway that it was different from the one in their flat; 246 had a similar layout, but the door in the equivalent spot down there was for a coat cupboard, shorter than his own height – above it another cupboard from which things often fell on your head. This door opened onto a short flight of stairs. Christine led the way up.

—I thought you were the top floor, said Aaron as he followed her.

—Aha, Christine replied.

And then Aaron was at the top of the stairs and Christine was in front of him, her arms spread, presenting a huge room. It stretched ahead of him and behind him. He turned on the spot and realised it was the width of the tower. Windows on one side looked across the river. In one corner he could see the dirty dome of St Paul's, the City's stumpy outgrowth of towers nearby. In another corner was the tawny slope of Greenwich Park, and beyond that the wine-blue hump of Shooter's Hill.

And he recognised with a fragment of his mind that, from the outside, it must be easy to assume this floor was like any other in the tower – the strip of windows must look the same.

—How did I never know this was here?

—I don't know. How didn't you know it was here?

Christine's tone was toothed. It made Aaron twist back to face her. But she had already taken a step away.

Aaron wandered a little. The room was white-walled for the most part, with wooden partitions inserted in two corners. Through an open door in one he saw a kitchen. He descended two steps. This part of the room was lower than the rest, and lined with sofas. He tried to orientate himself in the building. This would be where the other flats split over the hidden corridors. He looked at the floor. He and Clive thought Zöe had revealed all her architectural secrets to them long ago. He looked ahead, out of a window, at a plaque of insistent blue. A bird shape tumbled across it, then soared through the air and away.

He was in a corner now, so he turned to take in the whole room from a different angle. Facing him on the opposite wall was a vast painting. The canvas took up most of the height of the wall and extended for several yards. On one side, a vertical stripe of messy reds crossed a white background, and in the centre, another pale, almost faded stripe – reddish but now pinkish – hesitantly traversed the white. None of the colours was uniform; each area was flecked with numerous shades, all loosely organising themselves into groups of white and reds. But even at this distance – some thirty feet – he seemed to know that some of this variation was the result of the thickness of the paint. He knew that up close, he'd find the surface pocked, churned and scored.

He set off across the room. He'd seen this painting before, he was sure of it. His mind insisted on Blackheath. But it wasn't. He remembered that house too well. They'd only left it ten years ago. He'd know if that painting had hung there.

—We need to go, said Christine. Our landlord went out a while ago, but he might be back soon. He won't like that we've been up here.

Aaron was close to the painting now. He put out his hand and touched the surface. Its peaks and craters tickled his fingers. Now he was sure. He'd felt this before.

And then he understood what Christine had just said.

—Your landlord?

—Yes. He lives here.

—So this isn't part of your flat?

Aaron stepped back, but his eyes remained on the painting. Hadn't he once also wondered about the central stripe? Was it an error the artist had tried to cover up? Why hadn't they ensured it was invisible? Or did they want this faded repeat?

—No, not really. Christine was over by the kitchen door, now. It was once, apparently. But it was split into two. We still have to share a hallway with him though.

Aaron pulled his attention from the painting. He wanted Clive with him – to share his bewilderment. To share the unease he felt at the discovery of their ignorance. At the odd familiarity of the painting.

—Come on. Christine beckoned with a jerking hand. We don't want to get caught. She was managing to grin and frown at the same time.

Aaron hurried over.

—Where are we going?

—I told you. A garden.

Aaron pressed his lips together, ready with a 'but'.

But Christine was already on the other side of the kitchen, opening another door. Aaron glanced back at the vast space behind him. This was another new angle. And it made him pause.

—Aaron... Christine urged.

He hesitated further. From here the whole room was familiar. Not in shape or size, but as if it were dressed in clothes he'd seen before, even worn. He could almost remember sitting in that chair, lying on that rug, pushing his hands into the woollen worms of the pile. Yes. It was like Blackheath. And that had to be why he thought he'd seen the painting before. The rest of the room was telling him he knew it. Wasn't that it? Wasn't it?

—For God's sake, Aaron!

And he was across the kitchen.

—Who is your landlord, anyway? Surely our mum must know him.

Christine didn't reply. She was opening the door, and stood back to let Aaron through. It was dark on the other side, but Aaron could see a single upward flight of stairs. He organised their position in the building.

—Is this part of the back stairs?

But he had no idea whether Christine knew of the back stairs. He and Clive still hadn't shown Annette and Christine any of those things.

—Yes, look.

Christine tapped her foot. The floor rattled, and Aaron saw that this was the hatch that had always blocked Clive's and his way.

—It's locked but you can open it from this side, said Christine. And now, the garden.

Aaron followed her up the steps, knowing now where the garden must be. The flight ended at a metal door. Christine leaned against it and they were outside, in the heavy sunlight. It seemed so much stronger here. As if Marlowe Tower was so tall it brought them closer to the sun.

Aaron's dazzled eyes struggled to adjust. He made a shade with his hand and stared across the space.

There were plants everywhere. Of all sizes. In all types of containers. Small trees. Shrubs grouped in clusters, stacks of pots between. Trailing white and blue flowers rose and sighed in the hot wind.

—I think I've got sunstroke or something, said Aaron. I can't believe any of this is here. A flat I knew nothing about. And now this?

—It's great, isn't it?

—Well, kind of. I don't know. I'm sort of disturbed by it all.

To look at Christine, Aaron had to drag his eyes away from the garden. He saw it was a garden now. The plants weren't arranged randomly. The gardener had organised them. There was a kind of avenue from the staircase to the centre of the roof, where a square container held water. Christine sauntered down the path and took a seat on a bench surrounded by thick-leaved palms. They draped her in tongues of shade.

—Tell me, she said as he approached the pool. It was large – probably ten feet across.

—Tell you what? Aaron put his hand into the water. It was only just cool. Tepid even.

—Why you're disturbed.

—It seems like we've been kept in the dark. Intentionally.

—We? You and Clive, you mean?

—Yes. Mum has to know about this. It might even be her that's done it all.

He pulled his hand out of the pool and threw it out to indicate the garden. The water slipped off his hand, almost viscous in the heat. A bloom of dizziness made him rock back. Then forwards. As if he was about to tip into the pool.

—Hey, hey, Aaron. Come and sit in the shade. Otherwise you will get sunstroke.

He took a few lumpy steps to the bench and flopped down next to Christine.

—But how on earth would she have got all the plants up here?

—He says it's his garden.

—Who?

—The bloke who lives in the big flat. Our landlord. He says it's his garden. We can use it, but it's his.

—But it's the roof of the whole tower, not just his flat. So isn't it everyone's?

Aaron knew he was parroting his mother's attitudes.

—How would everyone get up here? The hatch to the back stairs is locked. The only way up is through his flat.

Aaron looked out across the garden. In the foreground the greens were dusty and flat in the hard sunshine. Beyond was a tall trellis that looked to be almost at the edge of the roof, ready to fall, given the slightest push. From it hung a cascade of flowers, about ready to shrink and dry. The background was a dirty blue, organising itself occasionally into various planes of grey – distant buildings that had to be on higher ground for him to see them at this angle.

—How long has he been here? he asked.

—Not sure, exactly. He told us he had a flat going for rent last year. We've been here since – what, April? He said something about the garden really starting to look how he wants it. So he must have been here for at least a year or so, I guess.

She switched her head away, and her hand dropped onto the bench with a quiet thud. As if she'd forgotten about it.

—I'll ask Mum. She must know him, mustn't she?

—Are you asking me?

Christine sounded suddenly and strangely defensive. Aaron didn't think he'd yet heard her clip her words in such a way.

—No, no. It's just confusing.

—Perhaps I shouldn't have brought you up here.

Christine shaded her eyes in order to look at him, but the sun was behind her, not him. He wondered why she did it.

—No, I'm glad you did. It's just that...

—You want to talk to Clive, don't you?

When Aaron looked at her, she was smiling.

—Yeah, he said.

—I'd want to talk to Annette about something like this.

She stood up in one long movement. And it was as if the Christine he'd become used to had reappeared. The other woman – a little cautious, a little closed – had left. For a breath he wondered whether this was in fact Annette. But Annette was even more open, even more lithe. And he knew who was who. Just as he knew he was Aaron and not Clive.

As if to reassure him she was Christine, she spun round – a complete rotation.

—So, what do you think of us using this place for our get-togethers – instead of the river deck.

—But you said that it's your landlord's. Not everybody's.

—We make it everybody's. Me and Annette reckon he's put that hatch and lock in himself. We just have to find the key and unlock it. Let all our lot up the backstairs.

—You know once people like Tabitha come up, everyone will know. She won't be able to keep her mouth shut.

Christine stretched and shook herself a little.

—No, she won't. It's why we like her. But let her tell people. If we're saying this is everybody's, it's everybody's, isn't it?

It was a little like listening to Zöe, thought Aaron. He pushed one cheek out of shape.

—I don't know, he said.

—You know that Clive would jump at it.

—Perhaps I shouldn't tell him.

—You know that will never happen.

Aaron didn't reply.

—Come on, it's too hot here now, said Christine, making her way down the avenue of plants towards the door. And we want to get through the big flat before he comes back.

Aaron was loath to leave the shade of the bench, but pulled himself up and followed her.

—What's his name, your landlord? he asked as he reached the doorway.

—Leonard, said Christine from halfway down the steps.

The name made Aaron stop at the top.

16

Christine was right, of course. Aaron did tell Clive. It was almost the first thing he said when they were alone together that evening.

If you were to ask Clive if he remembers the conversation, without hesitation he'd answer 'Yes'.

He was on the living-room balcony. Yes, he's sure he was there. He even recalls leaning out towards the breeze like a plant towards light. It was after dinner, and Zöe was back in her study. He remembers the necklace of orange lights lying across the distance. He recalls looking downwards, his chin against the sharp stipple of the concrete balustrade, scanning the walkway, the area at the base of the tower, the deck, the purple section of the park on the far side of the estate, the luminous paving of the town square. He was searching for Annette and Christine and their band. It was late, and they still hadn't arrived at the deck yet. If they did, would he and Aaron go down? They hadn't been since the night of the meeting. Would they go tonight?

Aaron appeared by his side.

—Looking for Annette and Christine?

Clive didn't reply.

—I went up to see Christine today. She showed me something.

Clive, sitting now on the terrace of his apartment, looks at Marlowe Tower, its dirty grey even more discoloured by the sea-green glass of the balustrade. He remembers the prickle of irritation at the news that Aaron then related: that he'd discovered something new without him.

Clive recalls straightening up, the heels of his palms pressed painfully into the concrete in front of him. Why had Christine chosen Aaron to show this grand apartment, the roof garden above? He wanted to go straight upstairs, knock on Annette and Christine's door and demand they show it all to him too. More than anything he wanted to close this gap that had opened up between him and Aaron, with Aaron ahead of him, seeing things first. Clive remembers the exquisite pain of this desire. For a moment it obliterated any other train of thought. For a moment it made him deaf.

It took Aaron three attempts to make Clive acknowledge what he was saying.

—Listen – Aaron hissed it. The man's name is Leonard.

Clive came round with a sway.

—Leonard, he repeated. It could be another Leonard?

—I don't think so, said Aaron. You haven't seen that ... that apartment. Mum must've designed it. There's no way she doesn't know about it.

—Unless it was altered after.

—It doesn't look like it to me.

—I'll have to see it for myself, Clive said.

—You do. But, well, you can't just walk in. Christine seemed very cagey about it all. I think they're very careful around him.

—And he teaches on a built environment course.

Aaron was right beside Clive now. They were both leaning, bellies against the concrete. Clive could feel the front of Aaron's arm against the back of his own.

—I feel as if somehow I should've known, said Aaron.

—You're really sure?

—You will be too when you see the apartment.

—Or we could just ask Mum.

Clive was already halfway through the door, foot in the living room. But Aaron's hand was on his shoulder. He held him strongly. He rarely used this kind of force.

—No, not yet. Aaron's voice was low. Telling Clive his had been too loud. You need to see it all first.

◆

—I definitely haven't seen this painting before, Clive said, as if Aaron had asked him.

Clive turned. Aaron was one step behind him; Annette and Christine stood in the centre of the room. They looked uncharacteristically anxious, Annette more, even, than Christine. Her chin pulsed and Clive saw she was chewing her lip.

—But I think I must have seen something similar. Probably something by the same artist.

—And what about all this? Aaron took in the whole space with an outspread arm.

Clive properly understood now the reason for Aaron's heavy grip on his shoulder the previous evening. Aaron wanted him to see how familiar everything in the room was, and to have this sour sensation in his stomach. It was like the house in Blackheath.

He didn't respond to Aaron for a long while. He stared around them. If he examined this chair, this pot or the rug under his feet for long enough, surely he would finally be able to place them. But they were obstinate. They wouldn't settle in any corner, in any room in that house. He strained. It was only ten years. He should be able to recall these quiet objects, which seemed almost to be refusing to speak to him. His irritation chirruped inside him. He frowned and shook his head when Aaron nodded to a floor lamp: no, I don't remember it. But I feel like I should.

Now, looking through the sea-green glass of his roof terrace, it is as if Clive sees Marlowe Tower in the past, and the same cheeps of frustration sound inside him. He should be able to arrange all the pieces of information into a logical pattern. But he can't. He cannot find a good reason, a safe reason, why Annette and Christine have come back to their flat. And because he doesn't have all the pieces, he is scared. His stomach feels empty but food is far from his mind. His fear is a sealed vacuum, lying in his belly.

And it seems like this feeling hasn't just arrived. It has being sitting inside him for forty years. He thinks he knows – no, he knows he knows – that it has been sitting in Aaron's belly too.

Clive needs more information. To gain that information, he needs to ask for it. But something stops him.

Something stops Aaron too – from hobbling along the corridor of the thirtieth floor and rapping on the door of flat 304.

And something stops Clive from picking up his phone and asking his driver to collect him from the foyer in half an hour and take him to Deptford.

Something stops them from asking their questions. Something still stops them from speaking to each other.

◆

Aaron is back in his flat now. It feels like he has been away on a long trip. He hasn't travelled for years. But he remembers this feeling – of coming home. The curdled mix of comfort and disappointment. The childish thought that the furniture, the ornaments, every object, stopped gesturing and speaking a moment before he opened the door.

He stands in the centre of the living room and listens. He has lived in silence for so long, the tiniest of noises is loud to him. The ever-present hum of the wind round the tower, the tinks and thuds of cranes and lorries, the regular chime of a pile driver – all find their way through the walls and windows to his ears. But there is no sound that tells him what's happening upstairs, no matter how hard he listens. No matter how long he stands, a little stooped, his arms slightly in front of him, his hands hanging, useless. He feels like he's been stood this way for forty years.

A clump he can't identify makes him move out of his dead-puppet stance. Was the noise from outside, or from within the building? From upstairs perhaps? He looks up at the ceiling. Stupid. He crosses to the balcony door and pulls it open. It shrieks.

It always shrieks. But this time he wonders about other people hearing it. He walks to the balustrade and turns, propping his back against the concrete and attempting to look upwards.

The sky is grey, but a too-bright shade, as though the sun is insisting its way through the cloud. And his head feels too heavy now. As if it might fall off his neck and tumble to the ground, bumping off the tower a couple of times, his face turning through the air. He's giddy now, a little sick, but he clutches at the rough wall behind him and stretches himself out even further. Now he can see the gap-toothed profile of the tower above him, the protruding balconies gun-metal against the silk grey of the clouds.

Nothing though. No one. No pair of grizzled heads, locks falling around their faces. If there had been, what would that tell him? Wouldn't the bubble of fear in his belly – for he's brave enough now to name it as fear – have simply expanded further?

He has to shuffle and turn to ease himself upright. His back-bend has made him dizzy and sick. He staggers back into the living room and falls, slack, onto the sofa. He's forgotten to close the balcony door. The draught is cold, but he doesn't think he can manage to get up again. Not for the moment. Everything has become too much.

Through the open door he can see Clive's building. Its clean lines are cleaner and the almost turquoise glass is more marine without the unwashed balcony door to mask his view.

He's sitting at a yaw. It's uncomfortable; all the horizontal lines around him – the table, the lintels of the doors, the floor and the balcony wall – are askew. But he understands now that he and Clive must speak.

Zöe had set up the folding table on the living-room balcony. It was too big and only just fit. If someone wanted to sit down or get up, everyone else had to do the same.

—I thought we'd eat outside. We should make better use of the balconies. They're not just for drying washing.

Neither Aaron nor Clive protested. They brought out the breadbasket, the knives and forks and the water jug. The wind plucked at the napkins.

Clive hadn't warned Aaron about what he planned to say. He just plunged in.

Aaron broke into a sweat at Clive's first words. They were eating ice cream.

—We were on the thirty-first floor today, said Clive.

Aaron locked eyes with Clive, so they both missed Zöe's reaction. Clive squirmed. He wanted to start again.

Zöe didn't speak until she'd finished her ice cream. She ate slowly. Her spoon against the bowl made it seem like she was ringing a bell.

—You went up through the door in the flat those girls live in, I suppose.

She was holding up her spoon. She'd licked it almost clean.

—I went up yesterday too, said Aaron. Christine showed me.

Aaron felt as if his tongue was tap-dancing.

—Then Clive came up today, and—

Clive's hand was on his leg, staying him. Aaron was glad. And he saw what Clive had seen. That Zöe was constructing a reply. She stacked the empty bowls, the three spoons in her other hand.

—Did you meet him?

Clive let go of Aaron's leg.

—Leonard? Clive said. He wanted to sound airy but felt like he'd spat out a bullet. No, he wasn't there. But he lives up there now, you know.

—I know.

Zöe braced herself, the bowls in her hand, as if she were going to stand up. But then she set the bowls down again.

—We were going to live up there, she said.

—In that big apartment? said Clive. That was supposed to be ours?

—The whole thing. Flat 304 and the whole floor above. I designed it as one big apartment originally. For us. The top floor was one of the hidden things, you know?

Zöe's smile was badly drawn. She bit her lower lip with her teeth. She never smiled like that.

—I suppose I liked the idea of something special for us. After Blackheath I didn't want you thinking you'd lose out by moving.

—We didn't, said Aaron. And wondered why the conversation had taken this direction. Why Clive had allowed Zöe to steer it here.

—We do now, said Clive. I do, anyway. We could've been living up there all this time? Why haven't we?

—Because it would have defeated the whole point of the estate. The whole point of us moving here.

It might have been the fading pink of the evening light, but Zöe's face had changed again; she tipped her chin up when she argued politics.

—So you crammed us in here? said Clive.

—We're not crammed in, Aaron said. This wasn't how Aaron wanted this discussion to go. And he was sure Clive hadn't intended this either. He slung his knee against Clive's thigh.

—No, we're not, said Zöe. There's space everywhere on this estate. Shared space. That's the point. You have more room here than you ever did in Blackheath, and you meet people while you're using it. Look at you two out on that deck with those twins and their ... their gang.

—But you hate us going down there. Clive's voice was metallic.

—The point is you can use the space. It's your living room. The whole estate is. It's the people you're with I – Zöe took an unexpected breath – object to.

And she stood up, barging against the table as she did so. Water slopped out of the jug and she caught her foot in the leg of her chair. But she pushed on, escaped the furniture and made it into the living room.

—I think we can fold the table away, she said over her shoulder. It's too cramped really to eat out there.

Aaron stood and started clearing away, but Clive was already following Zöe into the kitchen, and Aaron found himself inside too.

—Who's been living up there all this time? demanded Clive. He blocked the kitchen doorway, so Aaron could only see Zöe's head. She was standing at the sink.

—I really don't know.

—Christine says Leonard's only been living there for a year or so, said Aaron.

—When did you find out he'd moved in? said Clive.

Water clattered into the sink, as if Zöe was squeezing the tap to make the flow stronger.

Clive was undeterred.

—Have you been up to see him?

Aaron had to nudge Clive aside to stand in the doorway with him.

—Has he been down here? Aaron found himself asking, and looked over his shoulder into the living room.

—Down here? No. Zöe seemed to sing above the chimes and thumps of cutlery and crockery as she dropped it into the washing-up bowl.

Aaron felt Clive inhale and stiffen. He placed two fingers on

Clive's forearm. Clive breathed out, not speaking. They waited. Zöe stopped banging the plates and bowls. She leaned forwards over the sink. Her hair made a tent. They couldn't see her face. Aaron thought he noticed a strand of grey he'd not seen before.

She turned her head towards them, their two bodies filling the door frame. She raised a finger to push her hair from her face, and left a clot of bubbles behind. She assumed a smile.

—As you're obviously so interested, I'll tell you how it was, shall I?

She advanced towards them, standing straighter now. Her nose pointed at each one of them in turn. They slid out of the doorway so she could pass. She sat at the dining table and waited until they'd sat down in their usual places.

—As I said, I designed that apartment for us. I meant for us to go in through the door to the corridor, like with the rest of the flats, but the layout to be totally different, and of course there was the extra floor. It was going to be huge, the whole thing. Two or three times the space we had in Blackheath.

—Sounds fantastic, said Clive.

Aaron felt the vibration of Clive's voice.

—But towards the end of construction, when I was visiting the site, well, it just came home to me how ... elitist the whole idea was: us living in this vast apartment at the top of the tower, but the front door looking like it led to a flat the same as all the others. It was hypocritical. I couldn't have lived there and faced everyone – all our neighbours. The whole reason I'd brought my family here, to live on the estate, was to prove that this new way of living worked: the professional classes could – and should – live alongside the working class.

—Would they have known? Clive asked.

Zöe raised her eyebrows in reply.

—So I decided to have them fit out the interiors differently from the plan. It was too late to extend the main stairs upwards and make the thirty-first floor separate flats. So we just laid 304 out the same as all the others, and the top floor was left as one apartment. I tried to have the entrances sorted out. A hallway, a flight of stairs. And then two or three big flats on the top floor for large families – it wouldn't have been difficult. But by then – Zöe coughed and adjusted her position in her chair – the developer and construction company were involved and, well, it was out of my hands. And they ended up with the fudge that's up there now.

Aaron saw Clive shift in his seat. Again Zöe had guided the conversation somewhere else.

—So who's been living up there all this time? Clive repeated. It can't have been Leonard. You can't have hidden him from us for that long.

—I don't know. Zöe directed her words towards the open balcony door. There was some deal made with the council so the big apartment and 304 weren't part of the general housing stock. It had a separate lease and was sold off.

—Like this flat. You bought the leasehold to this one. Did Leonard buy the lease to the big one? And to 304.

—Yes. Yes he did. So ... so those flats have been empty, or occupied by his tenants, whoever they are.

—How does nobody know about all this? said Aaron.

Clive and Zöe both looked at him. As so often happened, the conversation had become a two-hander. His interventions were always a mild surprise.

—Well, I wouldn't say nobody knows about it, replied Zöe.

—We've lived here for a decade and we didn't, said Aaron.

—Because you didn't tell us, said Clive.

—But now the twins are here, it's not so much of a secret, is it? said Aaron.

Zöe looked at him again, almost shocked now. The point of her nose seemed blunted as she folded her lips together.

—And now, because of them, we've found out about Leonard, said Clive. If they hadn't moved in and we hadn't made friends

with them, it might have been months, years, before we found out
he's up there. You weren't going to tell us, were you? ...Was *he*?

Zöe gathered herself, put her hands on her knees and stood up,
making for the kitchen again.

—So, there you are. That's all there is to know about flat 304.

She was at the sink, banging the pots in the water again.

Clive was up and in the kitchen doorway again.

—Have you seen the apartment, though? Since he's been here?

Zöe moved her head, but it was neither a nod nor a shake.

—What about it?

—There's a painting. Aaron nudged Clive aside. Was there a
big wall painting in Blackheath once? Is it upstairs now?

—Well. Yes. I suppose—

—Mum. Clive took a long step across the kitchen. Almost
lunging at her. The furniture, the art up there. It ... it could be
from Blackheath.

—Blackheath? Zöe pronounced the name as if she'd never
heard of the place.

—Yes, Blackheath. Clive almost shouted – intended to shout.
Held back, despite himself. He was too close to Zöe, Aaron
thought. But she wasn't moving. They were too close to each other.

And then Zöe whipped a hand out of the sink, a blade of water
slashing across Clive's T-shirt, making him jerk backwards.

—Well why the hell wouldn't it? Her face was pink, her nose a
dart, pitched at Clive's face.

He didn't have a reply. He glanced at Aaron. A few steps away,
Aaron found the words they wanted.

—Because we thought that house was yours – ours. We didn't
know he'd had any hand in it – we didn't think that it was his, his,
his ... home too. You've always said that when it was over it was
over. When you split, he never looked back. Wanted nothing to
do with us.

Zöe put a hand to her head, as if she'd just knocked it on an
open cupboard door.

—It's too hot to stand over a bowl of hot water, she said.

She grabbed a tea towel and buried her face in it. There was silence for a moment. Then the wind hummed a note outside.

—Get out of my way, I need some air.

Zöe flung the towel aside and made for the living room. But Clive was a beat too slow to step out of the way.

—Move! she yelled, barging him aside.

Aaron and Clive stared at each other, at the empty space where she had been. The tea towel had landed on the floor. Aaron bent to pick it up.

—I told you to fold this table up, Zöe shouted.

There was a slam and a scrape from the balcony. Zöe was out there and had kicked the table, hard.

They walked out onto the balcony too. The table was now askew, three of the corners touching the balcony walls, leaving only a tight triangle for the three of them to stand in. Their faces seemed close and big.

—We'll do it. You go inside for a minute. Clive tried to make his tone level, placatory.

—*You* go inside for a minute.

Zöe's words trod on the heels of Clive's. He tasted salt, his appetite for this argument waning. Aaron felt a little sick.

—Go on. Zöe tried a smile now. So close it looked like anguish. You know any mention of him turns me into a horrible ratbag.

Aaron and Clive stayed where they were. Both expected Zöe to put out her arms for the double-hug she always gave them after arguments and tellings-off. But instead her raised arms shooed them.

—Go on, go on. Leave me to it.

Aaron drifted inside and turned on a table lamp, and they sat down at opposite ends of the sofa. They watched Zöe's back. She propped herself up on the balustrade. Her shoulders were high around her dropped head. They watched her in silence for several minutes, exchanging just one look. It seemed to them both that if they waited, she would come inside and speak. And she would speak about Leonard.

He and Zöe had separated before she'd given birth to Aaron and Clive. The reason Zöe always gave when they asked was 'incredible unhappiness'. She'd say it with a big grin. It was the same answer they'd seen her offer at countless dinner parties, when wine had given a guest the courage to question her about her marriage.

'We delighted in each other's company once,' she would say. 'We lived together, worked together, built things together. And then we didn't. I set up Goldsworthy Limited, and he wasn't really part of it. He hated that. But he's not an architect, so how could he be involved? He was the numbers guy – the business man. He wanted to contribute to the design decisions, the aesthetics, the creative elements. And he couldn't. I wouldn't allow it. Having good taste in art and furniture isn't enough.' Here Zöe would snort. 'He said I used him, because in those days it was virtually impossible for a woman to get business loans or incorporate a company without a man involved somehow. And he was right. I couldn't have set up Goldsworthy without him. But I was clear. His position was nominal. He was a director, but it was my practice, my company. And anyway, he had his own business.'

Zöe's success had soured everything, she said. They'd struggled on 'manfully' – she'd always say this with another grin – but when they won the contract for Deptford Strand Estate, it was the last straw. The years it took to get the project off the ground broke them. 'Architects and developers never get on,' she said. Then she'd turned to Aaron and Clive: 'Be thankful you were preserved the worst.' The guests would look at them and laugh kindly. Sometimes someone put a hand on one of their shoulders.

Zöe and Leonard had divorced in 1969, when the law finally allowed them to, and just after the estate was complete. 'I count lawyers among my very best friends,' was Zöe's final quip, at the dinner parties and when questioned by her sons. And then she'd change the subject.

But now, Leonard was seven floors above them. A dinner-party story wouldn't give them the answers. They needed something more. And they understood their mother well enough to know she would supply it.

And she did.

When she turned and stepped through the doorway, she gave them the slightest of smiles, then sat sideways on a dining chair, put an elbow on the table and observed them for a moment with her chin cupped in her palm. It seemed that she'd spent at least some of her time outside deciding on this pose.

—I suppose you're old enough now to hear this.

She paused. Perhaps for effect. Perhaps wondering exactly how to begin.

—Leonard was...

She stopped. And didn't speak for a long time. Warm air stole into the room from the balcony, but stopped, seeming to sense the unsaid words waiting in Zöe's throat.

—This is going to sound awfully egocentric, but Leonard was obsessed with me. It wasn't just love, it was ... a sort of ... God, I hate saying it about myself, but it was a sort of worship.

Zöe seemed uncharacteristically fuddled. She looked up and spoke to the ceiling.

—I know your grandmother and aunt have told you this before.

—Grandma always says, 'He worshipped the ground your mother walked on,' said Clive.

—Exactly, but it wasn't just an expression. He did.

—She says he'd have done anything for you, said Aaron. And Aunt Elspeth said he did, but she wouldn't say what.

Zöe darted a glance at him.

—Elspeth shouldn't tell tales, she said. But they're right. It was part of why I had to finish with him for good. It was impossible for us to go on like that.

She looked out of the open balcony door now, her voice becoming quieter.

—You know the other reasons why our marriage broke down: the business, the estate ... what we went through together ... But what you don't know is how suffocating he was. I just couldn't live with it a moment longer.

She turned back towards them and covered her mouth with her hand. Behind it her face seemed to fold, and she made a couple of muffled squeaks. As if she were about to spit up a draggled mouse. After a moment she took her hand away and, with effort, spoke more clearly.

—I thought making him leave was the solution. But it didn't stop him. He just wouldn't stay out of my life.

—What do you mean? said Clive. We never saw him. He had no interest in us.

—It sounds dreadful to say it, but in you two, no, he didn't. But in me, he did ... He's been a constant presence. Constant.

Zöe let the word settle for a second or two.

—At first, the fact we couldn't divorce without him battering me or something was the biggest problem. But once the law changed and we managed to get the divorce, he was still forever bothering me with phone calls and letters ... and telegrams to my office. All ostensibly about legal arrangements – about property, our affairs, the businesses. And then he'd be at professional events, or some architects' do at a mutual friend's. Even when I travelled, I'd find him at this or that conference – in the States, in Japan. He turned up at an obscure exhibition in Naples once. It's gone on to this day. I'm always coming across him. But he always seems to have a 'professional' reason to be wherever I am, so there's little I can do other than ignore him. Thankfully he seems satisfied with making me feel uncomfortable. He doesn't approach me anymore, wanting to have a conversation or anything. I've become used to it over the years, knowing he could be round any corner. If I don't see him for a while, I start wondering where he is.

She gave a stuttered laugh.

Aaron and Clive didn't have to look at one another. They each knew the other's thoughts. They'd been told many times – by Zöe, their grandmother, their aunt Elspeth – that Leonard had made no effort to see them, paid not a penny for their upkeep, made not one enquiry into their wellbeing. It wasn't something that surprised them. It was as simple a fact as that they were twins. What was news to them, however – what gave them both the urge to rearrange themselves on the sofa so their legs, their arms or their shoulders were touching – was the fact that he had been so much a part of Zöe's life all this time. The betrayal was winding. It took some time before either could speak.

—And now he's living upstairs, said Aaron at last.

—Now he's living upstairs, said Zöe.

—And the furniture, the art upstairs. That's all his obsession with you? said Clive.

Zöe opened her hands, then brought them back together with a hushed clap and a nod.

—There's no danger. There'll be no problems. I've lived with this for eighteen years – your entire lives. More. I know how to manage him now. I'd prefer him not to be here, but he has a right to be, and well, we haven't seen him, have we? And he's been here quite some time, it seems. I don't think there's anything for you to worry about. But, well, now you've made friends with those... she stood up; almost a leap... girls, I suppose you might see him, and you need to know...

She stopped. Turned on the spot, apparently choosing between going back out onto the balcony or into the corridor.

—You need to know, well, what was what, and what's what now.

She heaved a sigh, then observed them for a moment – passively, not attempting to hook an answer.

—I know how to deal with Leonard, she said, her tone almost cross. I have everything under control.

Then she strode through the room and down the corridor.

They heard her clogs on the short flight of steps, then the door to her study clicked shut.

18

It was when Clive was standing in the middle of an arbour – created by a crowd of pots, plants of various heights curling over his head and brushing his bare ankles – that he heard Annette, somewhere across the roof, say:

—We should hold a get-together up here. Show everyone this is our new place.

Clive snapped the tip of a frond between his thumb and finger. He'd had that idea. This was what he'd been mulling over in the shade of this bower, out of sight of the other three. A messy party. A provocation. In Leonard's garden. But now Annette had made it her idea. Something easy-going. People sitting around, coming and going as they pleased.

—What? Annette's voice leaped over the shrubs at his back.

But it wasn't meant for him, and he realised without seeing that Aaron and Christine had exchanged looks.

—Aaron and I were talking about that, said Christine.

Clive emerged from the arbour and strode across to the other three.

—Were you? he said. I was just this second thinking about it.

Annette's eyebrows were raised high.

—These two have been having secret discussions. Her pointing finger was taut and scolding. It's a good idea, though.

Clive ducked into the shadow and perched beside Aaron on the arm of the bench.

—We should make it a big thing, Clive said. Drinks. Food. Proper music. Make sure people can hear it from the ground.

Annette was now the only one still in the midday sunshine. She looked perfectly comfortable, her face a quiet matt.

—You want to go big? she asked Clive. We can go big.

Clive heard a challenge in her tone.

—We could unlock the hatch and let everyone up through there, he said. We know all the places in the tower where you can get into the back stairs, so nobody would need to come through your flat.

—Or Leonard's, said Aaron.

Clive looked down at him. Saw the blinks that meant Aaron was in doubt.

—He's away at the moment, said Christine. But he's often back for the weekends, so—

—Let's do it Saturday. Clive trod on Christine's sentence.

—Midweek is better, though, if he's not here, said Aaron.

He looked up at Clive, and saw him blink slowly. He disagreed. He wanted the party at the weekend. He wanted to do it while Leonard was at home. He was pulling them towards something sharp.

—No, said Clive. You can't have a big do midweek. Saturday. People will dress up. Everyone will come.

—We can keep it relaxed, though, said Annette, spreading her arms out wide. We just have to let people know, ask them to bring booze, food. I'm sure Gorton can organise some sounds.

—Are we sure? Christine said.

She turned towards Aaron slightly. Annette dropped her arms to her sides and looked at him too now. He could feel Clive's eyes on him, his glare.

Aaron scrabbled, looking out across the rooftop.

—Is it safe, though? He raised his hand, gesturing towards the edge. There aren't even any rails. And at night. In the dark.

Clive laughed and dropped his hand onto Aaron's shoulder.

—Are you saying that someone's more likely to fall on a Saturday than midweek?

—No, of course not.

—Well, there you go, then. Saturday it is.

Clive stood up, walked over to Annette and began a discussion about where to put things. A folding table. Speakers. Candles. Aaron didn't like his excitement. The way his hands pointed and gestured in the sun. He looked at Christine. She widened her eyes at him.

—Our little get-together is turning into something else, she said.

Aaron sat back and folded his arms across his chest, as if the hot day were still too cool for him.

—You know Leonard… he began, not looking at her.

—A little, but yes. Why?

Aaron examined her face now. She put a finger to her top lip.

—How do you think he'll react if he hears a party going on up here?

Christine left her finger on her lip for a long moment. Then dropped her hand into her lap.

—I think we'll find out, she said.

◆

—We'll ring the Goldsmith's guys, and the rest of our lot, Annette had said. You invite the estate people.

Aaron frowned at Clive. Had Annette just drawn a chalk line – you and your people on that side, us with ours on this? Did she think like that? Or was it him thinking like that, and seeing chalk lines where there weren't any?

—We'll tell Tabitha, said Clive, after they'd left Annette and Christine. Get her to invite everyone. It'll be as good as an advert in the paper.

Aaron stopped. They were on the main stairs, halfway between the thirtieth floor and the twenty-fourth. Clive took just one more step before halting and looking back up at his brother.

—Why are we doing this? said Aaron.

Clive started walking again.

—Telling Tabitha? You think she'll ask too many people – the wrong people? That's exactly what we want. All comers welcome.

Aaron hadn't moved.

—We know where he lives now. You could just knock on his door and talk to him if you really want to. Why throw some stupid party to get to him?

Clive paused at a turn. There was a whole flight between them now. He stood on one foot and let the other dangle over the tread. He held on to the banister and glanced up at Aaron.

—Would you come with me if I did try to see him?

Aaron slowly descended until he stood next to Clive. There was no question that if Clive went to see Leonard, Aaron would be beside him – or a little behind him, the front of his arm touching the back of Clive's.

—Zöe can't stop us if we want to do it, Aaron murmured. For a second he feared the stairwell's metallic echo.

Clive stared at him, then he blinked and let his eyes travel away from Aaron's face.

—Your hair wants cutting, he said. Then began to skip down the stairs. Let's go and tell Tabitha now.

◆

Tabitha's flat was in a block flanking one side of the town square, the parade of shops on its ground floor.

It was mid-afternoon and the reflecting pool was choppy with small bodies. Adult shins made a messy fringe around the edges. The sun was still strong, and the concrete of the paving, the blocks and the walkway radiated the heat it had been absorbing for several weeks now. The spritz of drops on Clive and Aaron's arms and legs, and the breath of cooler air from the pool were welcome.

—There she is. Aaron pointed upwards.

Tabitha was leaning over the rail of the gallery walkway three floors up. Clive could see the dark space of her flat doorway behind her.

And now she saw them.

—Oo-oo. Her voice reached them over the chatter around the pool. It was the kind of call an old lady might use.

—Come up. She beckoned with her skinny arm. Her hair swung about her face in straight strips.

—Is that my Tabby?

A woman standing at the pool's edge turned around, one hand extending a cigarette, as if she had to smoke it but wanted to keep it as far away as possible.

She looked up to Tabitha, shading her eyes.

—Who you inviting up, Tabs? Her voice was big. Several faces turned towards it.

—Those two, Tabitha shouted, pointing. The twins.

Tabitha's mother looked at them. The ash on her cigarette seemed incredibly long. But she took a drag without tapping it off.

—You're what's-her-name's two, aren't you?

—Zöe. Zöe Goldsworthy, said Clive. Yes. And he made himself smile and lean forwards. A minute bow.

The movement was almost invisible, but Tabitha's mother definitely leaned away. Aaron saw it. They were on the lip of a little conflict.

—Oh yeah, she said. Zöe. I know her.

She stretched out her arm and tapped one finger against the brilliant-white shaft of the cigarette. The ash fell to the floor. Specks blew onto the surface of the pool.

—Go up, then. Get Tabitha to make you a drink. It's too hot, isn't it? It's like blinking Africa.

She stopped just long enough for Aaron and Clive to take one step each towards the block.

—Specially with all these blacks we've got on the estate now.

Aaron froze. Would Clive reply? Was he about to? Aaron saw his weight shift.

But before Clive could speak – he was going to; he was going to say something about family; it was half formed in his mind – a large woman, her hands spread each side of her on a bench, said:

—We'll all be the same colour if this weather keeps up.

Both women laughed. A man sitting on the next bench hacked out a laugh too.

Aaron touched Clive's elbow. Clive felt the tap of two fingers. They went on their way.

◆

Tabitha was delighted.

—I'll tell everyone, she said, before Aaron and Clive had even asked her to. I love a secret.

She put her hands on either side of her neck and gave it a gleeful squeeze. Her smile threatened to burst her face, and Aaron realised she didn't see the contradiction between the two things she'd said.

—We'll need to remember never to tell Tabitha about any of the other hidden places, said Clive as they left.

Clive stopped at the top of the stairs back down to the town square.

—Shall we use the bridge to get back?

—Isn't it a bother? Aaron was already halfway down the first flight. We have to go right to the top of this block, then back down. What's the point? We'll be quicker going the normal way.

Clive didn't reply. He held on to the banister and swung his body upwards, making the sulk face that meant he wanted something. But Aaron couldn't work out what. And this made him take a step back up. Clive responded by taking the next flight in leaps. Aaron followed, his mind suddenly dimmed, as if a shade had been pulled.

Clive moved quickly, and soon they were on the top floor, pushing at the railings to find the section that opened and would allow them onto the narrow hidden balcony running just below the roof line on the other side of the block from the town square.

—What's made you want to come this way all of a sudden? asked Aaron.

—Old time's sake, maybe?

Clive found the catch and set off down the balcony, one foot in front of the other, as if on a tightrope. He didn't really know why he wanted them to take this secret route. If he looked down over the parapet, he could see the long strips of scorched lawn that ran down the centre of 'the avenue' – Zöe's name for the stretch of parallel blocks that ran from Evelyn Street all the way to Marlowe Tower. It seemed deserted right now. Then he saw a movement. A man alone sheltering under a tree.

—We won't be doing any more of this, I suppose, Clive said.

That was it, he thought. That was why he'd made them come this way. They wouldn't be here again. Something was about to change.

The thought made him stop, and Aaron walked into the back of him.

—Watch it, Clive said.

—Why haven't you asked me what I'm going to do? replied Aaron. You know, once you're at university.

Clive started moving again, without turning his head, Aaron's hand on his shoulder.

—I have. You said something would come along, and you'd know if you'd want it or not.

Aaron realised he had said that. He'd forgotten. He immediately thought of Annette and Christine.

And then he thought that what he'd maybe meant was something would be sent along. That Clive doing something would lead to him doing something too. That was how it had always worked. What Clive did was a function of what the two of them had thought or discussed. Aaron's legs and arms were always in there somewhere.

But not now, Aaron saw. He let his arm drop from Clive's shoulder. He realised that he'd mentally turned, thinking a door was open, as it always was, and found it closed, for the first time almost.

—Why are we having this party? he said.

—This weather can't go on forever, said Clive.

—You know what I mean. You're doing it to provoke him.

Clive stopped and turned in one movement. Aaron raised his hand as Clive raised his, and for a moment their fingers touched. Their faces were so close it was difficult to focus. But neither stepped back.

—Let's go now. Knock on his door, said Aaron. If you want to confront him, let's confront him.

—And say what?

—Everything. There's a list. I know you've written letters to him that you haven't sent.

—So have you.

The heat seemed to chill for a second as the same – almost the same – image appeared in both their minds: the other holding a lined page, reading the words he'd hidden from his brother.

Aaron recovered quickest.

—Why not tell him what we wrote, then? Why throw a big, messy party? Why make trouble? Why not act like adults?

—I don't want to be an adult...

Aaron pulled back his head, eyes wide.

—Not about this, said Clive, and turned around. Not about him. You heard what Mum said. He's been crossing her path for years. But not once has he made any attempt to contact us.

They walked on in silence, and entered the next block through a plant cupboard in the fifth-floor stairwell.

19

The day after the meeting Clive is in his office early, waiting for Kulwant. The deeds Kulwant has retrieved are laid out in front of him.

When Kulwant arrives, Clive watches as he approaches his desk. He is in his cycling outfit. Folds of belly as he bends over to unpack his bag. He glances across the room towards Clive's office. Clive raises his hand, beckoning.

Kulwant has removed his helmet and is carrying a large metal water bottle. He sits down. Clive can smell his sweat. He spreads the deeds out and plants his fingertips on them, as if he's playing a chord.

—I know about the thirty-first floor, he says. It was sort of a secret of our mother's.

Clive stops. He said 'our'. He hurries on.

—But then we all found out about it and, well...

Kulwant blinks at him, in the way a cat does.

—But who owned the lease and when: I'm unclear on all of that. As far as I knew, it was originally held by the developer, along with the lease to 246—

—Your brother's flat, says Kulwant.

Clive is tripped.

—Yes, that's right, he says, patiently. 246 was held by the developer, and then passed to my mother's firm, and on to...

He stops. But Kulwant obstinately refuses to complete his sentence.

—What I need to know, Clive continues, is how the lease to 304 arrived with...

—The Mayfields, say Kulwant. He pushes his hair around. The

ends are a little damp, and the mark on his forehead from the helmet is clear.

—I think I've pieced it together, he says. Let me get my shower then I'll bring it all to you, OK?

Clive nods, though he'd prefer Kulwant to piece it together for him right now.

Kulwant stands up. Before he opens the door, he pauses.

—You think knowing this will help us find a way to get them to sell the lease back to the council?

Clive looks at Kulwant's body; it is drawn in wide lines, the Lycra exaggerating the shapes. He seems very thick in the middle, his arms and legs too slim compared to the expanses of stretching fabric.

And then Clive realises he needs to answer Kulwant's question. In truth the answer is 'no'. But he needs to know anyway.

—It'll tell us what we're dealing with.

Then he looks down at the papers on his desk, picks up his pen as Kulwant opens the door.

◆

It seems a long wait. Clive wonders what Kulwant is doing in the shower all this time.

He wonders a little about Kulwant's body. Wouldn't cycling make him fitter? Burn off that belly fat?

Clive considers his own body for the briefest of moments then jerks himself away from the thought. But before he manages it, a glimpse of Aaron's appears. As if he's dashed naked across Clive's sightline. Clive doubts Aaron can dash these days.

—OK...

Kulwant is carrying his laptop. He sits down next to Clive and opens the lid. Clive can smell the sharp, blueish scent of whatever product he has showered with.

—From what I can tell, 304 and floor thirty-one were all part of the same lease when Marlowe Tower was completed in 1969.

—Yes. This I know.

—And the first holder of the lease was Derring Limited, which we know was one of the original builders for the whole estate.

Clive looks at Kulwant's finger pointing at the screen. There are tables with dates and names. He looks up, but he can't see out of the window and across the river. Kulwant's head is in the way.

—I'd have to dig further to find out how they squared it with the local authority to hold on to this lease – and the one to 246.

Clive waves a hand.

—My mother.

—OK. But whereas your mother bought 246 for peppercorn – a pound and a penny – the lease to 304 and floor thirty-one was sold for the same amount to L. Harrington Limited. Owner, Leonard Harrington.

Clive thinks he should say something, but finds himself unable for the moment. He knows that Kulwant is staring at him. He daren't meet his eyes. He sits back and pushes himself away from the desk a little. Now he has a view out of the window.

—Yes. Leonard Harrington, Clive says. He was involved in the development side.

Kulwant is looking over his shoulder at him now. Still Clive won't look at him.

Kulwant turns back to the laptop.

—Where it gets really interesting is here.

Kulwant scrolls down and points at another place on the table.

—1976.

Clive tries to focus on the area of the screen beside Kulwant's finger. But he's too far away. And something is stopping him moving closer.

—In September, the lease to 304, etc. passes from L. Harrington Limited to Goldsworthy Limited – us, or the original company.

Kulwant pauses. He's expecting answers. Clive is clotted with them.

—And then, in 1977 – Kulwant floats his finger down the screen – June, the lease is split in two. Floor thirty-one goes to Deptford Borough Council, which makes sense. But the lease to 304 passes to...

He pauses. A ridiculous piece of drama that makes Clive shake his head.

—...Annette and Christine Mayfield.

Kulwant removes his finger from the screen, sits back and drops his hand in his lap.

Clive moves back still further and turns himself a little towards the window.

—There's evidence of my mother's involvement in this, he says eventually. Or did—?

Kulwant interrupts.

—Her signature is on the grant of permission for the transfer of the lease to the Mayfields.

20

The next time Aaron and Clive went up the stairs into Leonard's flat was on the afternoon of the Saturday-night party.

There was no pausing in the living room this time. Aaron glanced at the painting and checked to see if Clive was doing the same. But Annette and Christine were already in the kitchen, with Clive close behind. Aaron caught up as they opened the door to the back stairs, and then all four were standing over the hatch.

It was a tight space. They were pressed together in the close heat.

—We've swiped a load of keys from our mum's desk, said Clive. Hopefully one of them will fit.

Aaron tapped the padlock with his foot and held up the fat bunch of keys. Annette took them from him and started to sort through them.

The space was lit from above by a skylight at the top of the flight leading to the roof. Right now sunlight fell heavily through the glass and hit the hatch, almost with a thud. Aaron squinted.

Clive took the keys out of Annette's hand. Aaron noticed that her mouth opened a little. But Clive was already squatting down, trying each key in turn, efficiently separating them with his finger. Aaron caught Annette looking at Christine with a raised eyebrow and a slow blink.

—This one, said Clive, and pulled at the lock. It's stiff – done it.

Annette bent down and heaved at the handle. The hatch shrieked.

Aaron and Christine laughed, and then they were looking into the grey glow of the staircase below them.

—We've told people to go to the seventeenth floor and into the chute room, from around seven, said Clive. We'll leave the cupboard door open for them. And we've put arrows on the wall to show the way.

—It seems there's only one way, said Annette, and let the hatch fall against the wall with a clatter.

Clive stood up and handed the keys back to Aaron, looking from face to face. He had the sense for a quick moment that he'd done something wrong. He brushed the dust from his palms.

—We'd better go up and decide where we're putting stuff, he said, placing his hands on his hips in a way Aaron hadn't seen him do before.

—No, said Annette. We don't want to do things differently because it's a different place.

Aaron saw Clive fighting a frown.

—But I thought we were making it a party. Clive instantly heard how childish this sounded.

—Yes, but not organised and fussy. Annette shook her hands in front of her.

Aaron felt sweaty. Clive plucked the T-shirt from his chest. The space was really too small for this discussion.

—We thought we're just telling people to bring drinks and food and music, said Christine, looking up at the skylight. And let it be a party by itself.

—We've bought booze. It's downstairs ready to bring up. And candles.

Clive looked at Aaron. But he knew no support would come from there.

Aaron stared back at him. He'd helped with the drink and arrows. But he wasn't going to argue Clive's case for him.

—OK, said Christine. But we don't need a big do.

Clive moved away from the hatch and put his foot on the first step up to the roof.

—I wanted to make a point. I thought we were making a point.

Telling them all to fuck off. Showing them we're still here. There's loads more people coming than usual. I thought that's what we were doing.

Annette shook her head now and tilted it to one side.

—We never said that, Clive. We just want to get people together. That's all.

She didn't look at him as she spoke. She seemed to direct her words down through the hatch.

—If you want to make a point, fine. But who are you making it to?

She looked at Clive now. But on the way Aaron was sure her eyes flicked to the door to Leonard's flat. Clive had seen it too. They'd still not mentioned to Annette and Christine that they knew who Leonard was. But now, in this hot little space, Aaron wondered if they didn't need telling. Clive was suddenly sure they didn't. He looked from twin to twin to twin.

Annette broke the lattice of looks by raising her arm, leaning towards Clive and dropping it across his shoulders.

—We didn't really want to make a statement, she said. Sometimes just being around people gets more done.

Her touch was light. But Clive felt it as an admonishment.

—Perhaps you're more like Zöe than you'd like to admit, she said.

—Probably, he replied. He knew he was. Was even proud to be. A few months ago he would have said so.

—Let's go up, then, said Annette. Just to see.

Christine put her hand on Aaron's back, and ushered him up the stairs with a smile that she intended would say at least a sentence or two, he was sure.

◆

That evening Aaron couldn't find Clive. They'd hefted the drinks up earlier and agreed to go upstairs again at a quarter to seven.

Annette and Christine would be late, of course. They always were, and everyone accepted it; in fact they relished the anticipation of their arrival.

Aaron guessed immediately that Clive had gone up ahead of him. It was happening more and more these days. The time when Clive wanted to be at the front, but only if Aaron was directly behind him, was over.

Aaron didn't rush up. Instead he stood on the balcony and looked down at the estate. The stretches of grass were almost the colour of cream. The trees surprising spots against the scorched expanses. For a moment he couldn't imagine the estate being anything other than this. The concrete seemed cleaner and lighter against the combination of green and straw, as if that was Zöe's design all along. He looked behind him into the flat to see if she was there. To perhaps ask her: did you have a summer like this in mind back then, when you were creating all of this?

But she wasn't there. She was in her study, he presumed. And Clive was upstairs, waiting.

He remained a little longer on the balcony, looking down.

And now, if he finds himself on the balcony in the early evening in summer, he looks down at the estate and remembers that moment. Remembers tasting how it might be to be alone like this. High up, looking down, the whole city below, each item visible, yet everything important out of his view.

◆

Clive stood over the open hatch, staring down and listening. He could hear pinks and thunks, a long, continuous hiss. Occasionally a voice would travel through the concrete and the air and reach his ears.

He'd decided to be the first, the one everyone saw as they reached the thirtieth floor. Annette would gently mock him for it, he thought. Christine would suggest that he did something else.

Aaron would look on. But he'd know that Clive wasn't yearning for attention. It was anxiety that made him stand there alone. A habit inherited from Zöe. A need to be prepared. To see the whole event from the very beginning, so that anything unexpected was made expected. Clive glanced at the door to the thirty-first-floor kitchen. He expected Leonard to turn up to the party. And he was increasingly certain that Annette and Christine expected him too.

He heard footsteps below. He adjusted his head, trying to peer down the stairwell to see who it was. They were already just a few flights down. And he realised it was Aaron. He turned the final corner and paused for a moment, looking up.

—Why didn't you wait for me?

—I called you. Said I was coming up.

—No you didn't.

Clive didn't bother to contradict him.

—You're the first one, he said as Aaron emerged through the hatch.

—Are you going to stay here the whole time?

—No. I just wanted to check stuff out, you know.

Aaron sat on the flight leading up to the roof. The sun was low now, so the light from the open door made a gentle layer on his head and shoulders.

—You haven't seen him, then? He nodded at the door to the kitchen.

—Leonard? No. They said he was away.

Clive looked down into the stairwell.

—And that he comes back at the weekends, said Aaron.

—Yes, I hope he's come back, OK? Clive widened his eyes and shook his head as he spoke.

Aaron allowed a suitable silence before speaking again, his voice a little lower.

—Do you think he'd be able to hear us if he's in there?

—I reckon he would. He might be listening now. Clive kept his voice at the same volume.

—He won't know our voices though.

—No.

Each looked away from the other now.

Aaron sighed and stood up.

—Let's go up.

—I'll stay here for a bit. I want them to know they're going the right way.

◆

Tabitha arrived first, at the head of a group of teenaged girls. Each had a bottle of beer in her hands. Before he saw them, Clive heard their laughter. He squirmed. He and Aaron were always cautious and quiet in the hidden places. But they knew there was no keeping this a secret. And Annette and Christine were clear – the roof should be for everyone. Nevertheless he glanced once again at the door to Leonard's kitchen.

—Clive? Aaron? I still can't tell the difference. Well, I can, but... Tabitha's voice sang up and down the stairs. Are Annette and Christine here yet?

—It's Clive. No, not yet. You know them.

—Where do we go? Whoops...

Tabitha tottered backwards as she came through the hatch. Acting a fall.

—Up there. Clive pointed. Prepare yourself.

—Don't scare us, Clive.

But she was already climbing. The others – four of them – looked to have dressed themselves for a party. Clive smelled perfume. He noticed they all wore the same high-heeled sandals.

Aaron heard their exclamations before he saw them. He was sitting on a bench, concealed by vegetation. He thought to get up and greet them. But he remained seated, listening to Tabitha's voice.

She was able to keep up a continuous flow of talk, managing to

listen and speak at the same time. Asking questions, answering
them and commenting on everything around her in the pauses.

—Are we the first? If Clive's down there, where's Aaron? Just
look for Clive and you'll find him. I can tell Annette and Christine
apart easier than I can them two. Oh my God. But there's no, like,
rail or anything. Don't go near the edge. I'm going be scared of
falling the whole time I'm up here, aren't you? We'll just stay in
the middle. Here. I'm not moving from this spot. Here he is!

Aaron twitched. Tabitha's head was poking around a shrub.
He'd followed her curling flow, but not heard her footsteps or her
voice coming closer.

—Where's everyone else? This is amazing. How did you find
it?

—Annette and Christine.

Aaron stood up. Tabitha had to look up at him now. She
squinted, her thick make-up sharpening the creases. Aaron
thought he saw what she would look like in forty years.

—I needn't have asked. Course those two found it. Can't go
down there by the river anymore, can we? My mum and her mates
go down there now. I'm not drinking and puffing in front of them.

Tabitha's speaking voice was loud, but when she laughed it was
always a snigger. It gave her just enough time to swing round
towards the door to the stairs. There were more bodies. Loud
voices. People emerging onto the roof, stopping and looking about
with open mouths.

The stream of people soon became strong. Within half an hour
all those who had usually gathered on the riverside were present.
But they all remained standing, as if they weren't sure where to
put themselves. It wasn't like the deck by the river, where people
heaped themselves on any surface. It was as if the air was stiff up
here, in the evening brightness, the wind far more confident –
there were no soft folds. Even when Gorton arrived, and the music
started and people began to dance, they didn't look relaxed. Their
limbs were gripped by a tension. And the wind seemed to snatch

away the beat before they could grasp it. Perhaps it was because Annette and Christine still weren't here, Aaron thought. And then he saw Clive appear from the stairwell. His arms were a little crooked. He looked ready to pick something up. Anxiety? Or excitement? As Clive approached, Aaron wondered whether he did the same thing when he was stressed.

—What's happened? Aaron asked. But knew.

Clive placed his hand on Aaron's back and guided him towards the edge of the roof.

—Annette just came up to tell me. He's come home.

They were standing side by side. But Aaron needed to face Clive. He turned around. Clive blinked then frowned at him.

—What's he said? asked Aaron.

—She didn't say.

Clive looked over Aaron's shoulder, across the river to the Isle of Dogs. The flat, empty acres looked like mud in the lilac light.

—Why are you worried? Aaron asked. This is exactly what you wanted, isn't it?

Clive turned a little and cast his eyes across the thickets of shrubs, the configurations of containers and pots, the people moving among them, their pale clothes and dark shoulders an elegant animation against the stillness of the vegetation.

—I'm not worried. This is exactly what this garden is for, don't you think? It looks like he designed it for this. For all these people.

Aaron followed Clive's gaze. He wasn't convinced. He thought it was too crowded. He thought people looked pressed together, huddled at the top of a precipice, their walks nervous, their hands jerked and snatched. He thought that Clive had a sudden regret.

—So he doesn't want everyone to leave?

—I told you, Annette didn't tell me what he'd said. But she said don't worry, go ahead with the party – she said 'get-together'. Just that her and Christine would be late, and that he was in their flat, chatting, and it might take a while.

Aaron felt an odd pass of air at his back. A warmth that moved upwards, brushing his bare legs then stirring the hair at his neck. He was far too close to the edge of the roof. His heart hopped, and he stumbled forwards against Clive, pushing at his chest.

Clive staggered back with a gasp, alarmed at being attacked.

—What was that for?

—Sorry. Sorry, I felt too near to the edge.

—Calm down. You're too worked up, Clive scolded.

—So Annette came up specially to tell you that? Aaron said, attempting to shake off his sudden fear. They're always late. And if he's not bothered about the party…

—I know. And she seemed, I don't know, agitated, but pleased when she said it. Sort of smiling but couldn't keep still. Wasn't like her at all.

—Sure it wasn't Christine?

—That's what I thought, but she's never like that either.

Tabitha was walking towards them now. She was holding a plastic cup in the air and stepping in time to the reggae track that had just started to play.

—So where are the twins? The other twins. Not you two.

She chuckled, jerking slightly out of time with the music.

—I just saw Annette. They'll be up in a minute.

—What are they doing? Always late, them two. This is great up here, though, isn't it? Who did all this gardening? Not them, surely. I've asked loads of people up. They can't believe those stairs. Wait till they see this.

She waved her cup in a wide arc. A little beer slopped onto the floor.

—Who have you asked? said Aaron.

Tabitha's face creased, and Aaron realised it had come out a little scratchy.

—Just, you know, friends. You said everyone was invited, so I invited everyone. Don't say everyone's invited if you only want some people to come and not other people to come. That's not fair, is it? And why shouldn't they come? It's their roof as much as anyone else's if they live here, isn't it?

She'd run ahead of herself, excusing the arrival before it occurred, because a moment later, Clive saw grey heads appearing at the door and moving through the greenery.

—You invited your mum and her mates?

—No, replied Tabitha, scowling in defence. I didn't invite her. I just said. About us coming up here, like. I didn't invite her, though.

—You said earlier you didn't want to drink and smoke weed in front of her, said Aaron.

—I don't. I don't.

She was a distance from them now, her face a smile and a grimace all at once. Her snigger seemed to come from the hunching of her shoulders.

Clive felt his anger flare. He turned to Aaron and swore, to stop himself swearing loudly at Tabitha. He'd wanted a big party. He'd wanted anyone and everyone, but somehow he didn't want this. Things were slipping through his fingers. And up here it was as if you couldn't save anything you dropped. Before you could grab it, it had rolled to the edge and disappeared.

The group of older people was large. Too large, thought Aaron. They stopped as soon as they stepped onto the roof, so those behind had to bob their heads to see and began pushing at those ahead of them. There were barks and shouts, frustration fizzing on the stairs.

Aaron caught sight of a head of tight grey curls. Its owner's hands were batting at people's backs, making them move out of her way. He tapped Clive's hip.

—Mrs Ledbury.

—Oh, fuck. How did she find out? Surely Tabitha didn't bring her. She can't keep her mouth shut, can she?

Mrs Ledbury stood at the head of the group now. She seemed to lean forwards slightly, as if she had stopped on a hill. Her arms were loose, hanging in front of her, and her mouth chewed as she took in everything she saw.

She turned back to her friends. Neither Aaron nor Clive could hear what she said to them, but her head was shaking and now a finger pointed – downwards, towards her flat; then at the tape player – at the beat as it flew to meet her. Then she moved back to her friends, and in that instant became part of a ripple of turned heads that spread from the door all the way to where Aaron and Clive were standing. Faces that had been in the shade brightened as the ochre sunlight caught them. In the middle of the gang of older white people were two brown girls, dressed again in their khaki suits.

Annette and Christine slid through the bodies. Everyone moved in response. The older people seemed to jerk back. The younger group swayed forwards. Tabitha was silent and fast, and had her hands on the twins in an instant.

Clive found himself halfway across the roof before he realised that he'd left Aaron behind. His eyes were scanning the group by the door. Seeing who else might have come up with Annette and Christine.

Leonard, he thought. I'm looking for Leonard. His pulse ticked up. He scanned the faces in front of him quickly, efficiently.

His eyes fell on Mrs Ledbury again. She seemed to be straightening up, ready to grapple. Christine had slipped out of Tabitha's grasp and was advancing, arms extended towards her neighbour. Mrs Ledbury took a small step back. But suddenly Annette was at her side, and Christine had slipped to the other and taken her by the arm.

—Mrs Ledbury. So glad you came up. It's amazing, isn't it? said Christine.

Annette looked up briefly and caught Clive's eye, her face impassive. And then breaking into a smile to match Christine's.

From Aaron's position on the edge of the roof, it looked like a stand-off. The older, greyer, paler people on one side, occupying the space by the door, the younger and the darker on the other. For a second, every face in each group looked across a glass line at the other.

And at the centre, the limpingly regal figure of Mrs Ledbury, trying to stand straight, but surrounded, almost overcome by the warm beams of her foes.

And then it was as if something gave way. A knee flexed. Mrs Ledbury split into a smile and swatted at the twins' hands.

—Get off me, you two. Honestly. Where's the drink, then? A woman could die of thirst up here.

Clive heard her close up and thought she sounded conciliatory; but to Aaron, at his distance, it was hectoring. He stepped back from its rasp.

The gust – that warm updraught – prickled the back of his legs again, his arms, his neck. He looked over his shoulder. Again he was one step away from the edge.

By the time he'd sprung forwards – off balance and giddy as the wave of vertigo reached his head – the scene had broken up. People were looking in every direction. The lines between the groups had become ragged. The music had become louder and voices were raised over it, becoming a clatter. Merriment, perhaps. But close his eyes and it could be a ruck.

Aaron tried to see who was talking to whom; who stood together in what groups. But things had become blurred. The more people arrived – another group was just coming through the door; young white men in T-shirts and jeans, jerking their heads in search of a threat – the darker the crowd became, bodies obscuring the light, hips merging into backs merging into breasts, so that the party was now a long, flickering strip in various shades of tan.

Clive, dropping out between two conversations, searched round for Aaron, and found him alone, over towards the roof's edge, his fingers worrying the loose frond of a climber.

—We'll need to light the candles and tilley lamps, Clive said. It'll be dark soon.

—August, said Aaron. It'll be autumn in a minute.

Clive let the wind whisk the comment away.

—I was worried when that other lot turned up, he said.

—Were you? Aaron asked. I thought you were looking forward to some kind of bust-up.

—No, said Clive. I wanted to prove a point, yes. Show all those old white people complaining about Annette and Christine that this is as much their estate as anyone's. And I think my point's been proved. Without a bust-up.

—There's still time, said Aaron. The gardener hasn't arrived yet.

He found another whip of vegetation – a pliable length that bent between his fingers but didn't snap. Clive grabbed it out of his hand, anger pluming in his cheeks.

—He won't thank you for ruining his plants, he said.

—That's the least of our worries if he comes up and sees all these people.

—So you think you know what he'll say, do you?

—You think you do? Aaron clapped back without a breath.

Clive thought he had a reply, but it was gone, dropped over the edge.

—Why aren't you chatting to anyone? he demanded instead. You've not even got a drink. If you're not going to join in, you could at least light some candles.

Clive felt like he'd shoved Aaron in the chest. And was glad he had.

Aaron knew what to do. He knew what would annoy Clive the most.

—I'll fetch some matches, he said, smiling, but couldn't quite leave it at that. And call me if Leonard arrives, won't you?

21

From above, where the evening light still offers some clarity, the roof of Marlowe Tower is spotted and speckled in a way it has never been before. There are swifts up here, playing with the thermals, picking off insects as they ascend from the pale expanses of grass below, finding a final meal before their long journey south. They hover over the tower for a few moments, attracted by the hum, the movement. One bird allows itself to drop a few yards, then rises again, banks and veers off to a more profitable column of air.

We stay though. Perfectly still. Our gaze fixed, as the clots and patches grow and merge, fed by a fidgeting drip from one side of the roof – the door to the stairs. As the bodies increase, they spread, and the dark, stationary figures of the plants are soon surrounded by swaying, darting, sliding shapes, so many that they reach to the edges of the roof.

The noise is loud, even from up here; the music is reggae, some rock, some disco. Different parts of the roof move in different ways as the song changes. And behind the music, but often in front of it too, the ceramic rattle of voices.

Up here it's impossible to distinguish a word.

But there is a shout. It seems to make a splash in the middle of a group of people, and they move away from it in a wave, leaving three figures at the centre.

Now, between the bodies we see Annette – talking urgently, but smiling. Christine is beside her. She speaks too, adding harmonies to the ends of Annette's phrases. Smiling too, nodding too.

Annette stops, and the short, dark-haired man standing opposite her starts to shout again.

—I TOLD you, he says.

—I TOLD you you can have this bloody party in my garden. On my bloody roof. Of the bloody tower that I fucking built.

His hands are flat and in front of him, seeming to hold each emphasised word in a box.

—I've even come up here, like you asked, to see all these shits kicking over my pots.

He throws a hand into the air. Some people shy away, some advance.

—But I TOLD you I'm not going to play happy families and talk to them.

Annette takes the thrown hand in hers and lowers it between them.

—It doesn't have to be anything, she says. Have a drink. Sit on a bench. Have a chat.

Christine touches him too. They're confident, assured. They've already tamed one tiger tonight.

—They know you're here now, so what's the point in avoiding them? she says.

—What's the point? His voice flattens, widens, sharpens. Her. She's the point. Your blessed Zöe.

He shrugs off their hands with rolling shoulders; his whole body roils as if he's bound in a sticky net. Then he freezes. Looks from Annette to Christine.

—Is this her idea? All this?

He flings his gaze around, at the crowd, the roof, the sky.

—You finally met her, did you? And she got you to do all this? God, she's good. Don't believe a word of what she says.

His hands are flat again. More words in more boxes.

—You'll regret trusting her, believe me.

He laughs. Just a snort. Then a forced, clapping clamour.

—She's here, isn't she? You'll take me over to them, and she'll be there. All smiles.

Annette and Christine are shaking their heads now. No, no, no-ing. Raising their hands.

—Zöe! he barks.

It's an explosion.

◆

Aaron heard the shout before Clive. He was closer. Clive further off – dancing near the tape player, buzzing as it strained to handle its full volume.

Aaron heard the acceleration, the voice taking off. He twisted himself in its direction.

There was another shout. And then another. Someone was screaming his mother's name.

He left the hippy guy he'd been speaking to and barged his way through the bodies – some turning towards the ever-louder yells, some still oblivious.

Aaron collided with someone, another man pressing in the same direction. Clive.

Clive felt, smelled, Aaron beside him. Saw the same knot on Aaron's forehead that he felt on his own.

—Did you hear? he said.

Above his question were other shouts now – men telling someone to pack it in, reel his neck in. Leave it.

—It's him, isn't it? said Aaron.

Someone pushed past in a steam of beer, making Clive stagger against Aaron. They each put a hand on the other's shoulder.

—Leave 'em to it, I say.

They looked sideways at the man who'd elbowed them. It was their neighbour from floor twenty-four. He was gone before either of them could reply.

They looked in the direction from which he'd come, towards the scattering shouts. But neither seemed to want to approach. They were stuck. Not brave enough now to find out what was happening.

The music and chatter were growing louder, now, as if the

shouting had quickened them. And with the noise, there seemed to be a switching of the current. People were turning in new directions, moving faster, singing louder.

So it wasn't Aaron and Clive's choice. They didn't push their way through. They didn't force a path, breathless and desperate. A group simply parted – like curtains on a small stage – and presented to them a trio of figures in intense, rapid-gestured discussion.

Annette and Christine, and Leonard. Aaron and Clive's father.

22

Leonard is Aaron's first thought when he wakes up each day. When he opens his eyes: Leonard. His father, Leonard. He has no term of intimacy for him. He doesn't see his face and think Dad, Daddy, Pop; he thinks Leonard, my father. And when he thinks these words, the image of the man arrives in his mind with an ache.

He wakes up aching today. It's as if he's spent the night fighting. His frame is sore. He feels like he needs a rest after such an exhausting sleep. He swings his legs over the side of the bed and sits for a moment, recovering.

Annette and Christine had never mentioned that they knew Leonard was Aaron and Clive's father. And Aaron and Clive hadn't told them who he was either. Later though – quite a lot later – Aaron perhaps was beginning to understand what Annette and Christine had been doing by showing them the big apartment on the thirty-first floor, the roof garden. Steering them towards a party, a gathering, a get-together. Bringing an unwilling Leonard along. But still, Aaron has never been entirely clear about the twins' intentions. And he and Clive have never had the opportunity to ask them.

Aaron stands up, visits the bathroom, and, like every day, examines the cream scar on his knee, the bald, bony clearing. Then he takes his blue dressing gown from the back of the door – it's decades old, the towelling thin at the elbows and seat – and wanders into the kitchen.

Neither did he and Clive ever have the opportunity to ask Leonard why he'd brought the twins to the tower. But then they had more than enough questions for him – a list that had grown in fits and starts over the years; left in the back of a drawer sometimes, occasionally brought out again and added to. As children they'd interrogated Zöe, and she had done a thorough job of answering.

'He was furious. Permanently furious, when I wouldn't allow him to be part of the design team for the estate. And then when things completely fell apart while I was pregnant with the two of you, and I demanded a separation, he used you as a weapon. "If you make me go, I'll not come back and see them. I won't be a father to them," he said. "You won't see me in this house, cooing over babies." I didn't think he'd keep his word, but he did. He has.'

Aaron tries to rerun this scene in his head, but Zöe said it so many times and in various ways, so he can't recall any specifics. He stands in the kitchen doorway, now, gazing at the living room – still as it was when Zöe lived here. The kettle pops and hisses behind him. She'd most definitely have said it sitting at the dining table, him and Clive on the sofa. Or sitting in her armchair – wingbacked and not in keeping with the rest of the room. But Zöe liked that about it. 'Your father was appalled by it,' she would say. 'I had to hide it away in my study when he still lived in Blackheath.'

It must have taken some effort, Aaron has always thought, for Leonard to keep his word like he did. Never to see his sons. Never to enquire after them. Was his determination to punish Zöe that strong?

'He saw us as a unit. Not just as a married couple, but a creative and social entity: "Goldsworthy and Harrington"; "Harrington and Goldsworthy". Actually, "The Harringtons" was what he really wanted people to call us. But it didn't work out that way. People wanted my ideas, my work, my talents. And his only by default. His bitterness about that poisoned everything. When you were born, he sent me a telegram. No congratulations. No questions about your health. Just an instruction: "DO NOT NAME TWINS HARRINGTON STOP". Which is why your surname is Goldsworthy.'

Aaron's sitting at the table now with his cereal. He's sure Zöe gave this speech sitting right there – he points at her chair with his spoon. A drop of milk falls on the table top. He dabs at it with his napkin.

The reasons Zöe gave felt weak then. And still feel weak. Could a relationship become so toxic, it cauterised every paternal feeling. Could Leonard's inability to accept his subordinate position in the professional partnership really destroy not just his marriage, but his instincts towards his children? Weren't these arguments to have within a relationship, not to end it?

But what does he know? he thinks. He puts the spoon back in the bowl, his cereal suddenly unappetising. None of his little list of encounters – with men or women – could ever be described as a relationship.

Leonard's picture appeared occasionally in magazines about architecture, building and planning. As Zöe claimed, his businesses were all successful. She made no effort to hide these articles from Clive and Aaron. But equally she didn't encourage them to contact him. 'If he wanted to see you, he could have years ago. And he has never tried. So why waste your time on him? You have others in your lives.'

They were small when she had said this, he remembers. Eight or nine. So still at Blackheath. It had silenced but not satisfied Clive. But Aaron had accepted it. It was the first rift between them – the first time Aaron had felt his individuality. The first time he had felt he didn't know every facet of his brother's feelings.

◆

Looking at the printouts Kulwant left him, Clive tries to focus his mind on the dates, the prices, the names, the mechanics of the transactions. But the flat facts seem swollen, distended. He feels dyspeptic. Why did his mother hand a large flat over to those two young women?

He's in his apartment, his breakfast things drying on the table. He can smell the sweetness of the melon. A fly can too. He moves away and repositions himself by the window. It's too windy and cool to go out on the balcony, and he can see Marlowe Tower clearly enough. He stares for a time, as if examining those top two floors long enough will give him some indication of Zöe's reasoning.

He looks away. And searches his mind – as he has all night – for some mundane detail that, turned over, will clarify the picture. But there's nothing. Nothing that he knows.

Annette and Christine would always open the door to 304 and then turn and walk away. They didn't ask you in. It was as if the invitation had already been made, and they assumed you'd accepted it. They never said 'not today', that it was inconvenient, that they wanted to be by themselves. That they were doing things or thinking things they didn't want you to know. Instead they accepted whatever you offered with ease and smiles. And they seemed to offer you everything. All they had was themselves, but they spread it out like a feast.

Yet in reality they offered very little, he thinks now, and gives the page he's holding a little shake, so it whips around the curve made by his thumb. They were fascinated by Zöe, of course. They wanted to hear all his and Aaron's stories about growing up in the house she designed in Blackheath, about visiting her office, about the move to Marlowe Tower, the architects who'd dined in flat 246. About his and Aaron's lives on the estate, speaking as they did, going to a different school from the rest of the estate's kids, going on different holidays, having a different mother. Having money. But he can't recall a conversation in which Annette and Christine talked about their childhood. Where they came from. What doors had closed and opened. Did he ever ask? Did Aaron? He puts down the page, straightens the little pile of documents. He doesn't think they ever did; it was almost as if such questions were proscribed. Yet Annette and Christine had never proscribed them.

He thought he knew them, that they were an intimate foursome. He might have even used that phrase to Aaron, to describe them all. But they'd been friends for three or four months only. Less perhaps. Weeks. A number of encounters he might be able to recall individually if he tried hard enough. Between him and Aaron they would be able to supply the full account.

He casts his eye across the river. What he didn't see, what he didn't ask, Aaron might have seen and asked. And the thoughts Aaron is having now might help Clive. He always relied on his brother's observations: 'Aaron's analysis' he sometimes called it. But he's gone without Aaron's analysis for forty years. Why can't he go without it now?

Because this is different.

There's a screen through which he cannot see. And until he can, he won't be able to move forwards with anything else.

23

The sight of Annette, Christine and their father was brief. The crowd had parted, but the space was filled again. A new, poppy disco song had begun on the cassette player and everyone seemed to rush nearer to the sound.

Clive grasped Aaron's forearm and began to edge forwards through the bunched bodies.

But Aaron hung back and Clive's grip dragged at his skin.

—Wait, Clive. What are we going to say?

Clive looked back. Two women were bouncing, one behind the other, between him and Aaron, not realising the twins' outstretched arms were barring their way. Clive had to let go.

—I don't know, he said over the women's perms.

—None of us do, love, said one of the women.

She put her hands on her friend's shoulders, and they laughed as if she'd made some scandalous joke, jigging a two-step further into the crowd.

Aaron closed the gap between him and Clive.

—I don't know either. But this is what you wanted, isn't it? What were you planning if it wasn't to say something to him?

—I didn't think of what we'd actually say, though. But we've talked about it – what we'd do if we ever met him.

—*You* talked about it, replied Aaron.

They'd drifted now to where they'd seen Leonard standing, remonstrating with the twins.

—They've gone, said Clive, raising and dropping his hands.

They stood side by side, arms touching, and scanned the layers of people. It was dark now. The black above was thick. The weak orange from the candles and the greyish-blue glow of the tilley lamps lit the thickets of legs, but the bodies above were partial, hinted. It was difficult to see any single person, and the moving mass was almost sinister. The music was loud, but the voices were louder. And there was a tiny bite on the breeze now.

Aaron looked sideways at Clive. What was he going to do? Clive's chin slid from side to side and he rolled his lips between his teeth. Aaron wondered how much he'd had to drink. This summer was the first time either of them had been properly drunk, properly stoned. Aaron had noticed that they responded differently. He sank backwards and inwards, sagged into a bust armchair. Clive stood up, excited and defiant, ready for fun or fights.

—There.

Clive was walking away, not bothering to grab Aaron this time. But Aaron still followed as if pulled.

—Have you decided what to say?

A tower of questions grew in Aaron's mind as he caught up with Clive. It was tottering, and at the top was something heavy and simple. The first thing he thought Clive would ask; exactly what he'd ask himself.

Clive stopped. Leonard, their father, was a few yards away, near the roof's edge. Leonard glanced for the briefest second at his sons, then turned to look out across the river, at the dark, flat expanse of the Isle of Dogs, pulled out a pack of cigarettes and lit one, the flame flashing big, making him jerk his face back.

Clive strode the last little distance, Aaron in step, but a step behind.

—Hello.

Leonard turned towards Clive's hacked greeting. He was short – shorter than them – and hunched over, so he looked up at them slightly, smoke drifting from the dark leaf of his mouth. His eyes moved back and forth between his sons' faces. But he didn't speak. No hello in response.

Aaron wanted to ask why – why his father didn't greet them.

Wanted to declare sarcastically to Clive that the man couldn't even say a polite hello after eighteen years. That they shouldn't bother with him. He wanted Clive to say it. He expected Clive to say it.

But Clive said something else.

—Why did you really bring Annette and Christine to live here?

Clive had not planned to say it. It was never the topmost in his own tower of questions. But then he'd seen how Annette and Christine had touched Leonard, leaned towards him.

Aaron moved, his arm nudging Clive's. Leonard dropped his cigarette.

—Your mother deserves everything she gets.

He jabbed a finger at Clive, as if intentionally poking a bruise. He looked at Aaron. Then back at Clive.

—What does that mean? said Clive. He hadn't known how Leonard would reply, but this still wrongfooted him.

Leonard took a step towards him. He was taller than his father, Clive realised again.

—I have every right to live here, said Leonard, and to invite whoever I want to live in my property.

Aaron now heard his father's accent. He'd never considered what he might sound like, but now the capped, rounded sounds and click-clack rhythm seemed to be wrong.

Clive had moved forwards to meet the smaller man. To confront him, Aaron thought. He was squaring purposefully. Neither he nor Clive had ever been in a fight. Except with each other. Violence they'd reserved for themselves. But perhaps Clive was ready to extend it to other family members. Aaron wouldn't have it.

—When did you move in? he asked. Why didn't you come to see us?

The questions he'd wanted Clive to ask.

It worked. Leonard looked down, the tension in his body released, and Clive's weight shifted as Leonard turned to Aaron.

—I'm sure your mother has plenty to say about me. But you've never heard my side.

—Because you've never bothered to contact us – and we've had no idea how to contact you.

As Aaron spoke, he saw Clive brace again.

—How long have you been here? said Clive. The twins came in April, and said you'd been here a while. Enough time to plant all this... Clive gestured around them, more violently than he'd meant to.

Leonard twitched and blinked.

—We haven't seen you, said Aaron, keeping his voice flat – neither pleading nor challenging.

—And you've been just upstairs, said Clive, intending it as an accusation.

Leonard pulled out his pack of cigarettes again.

—These architects talked about 'villages in the sky'. Your mother droned on about it all the time. But it doesn't work, does it? It's not like a street, where you see people walking past your door. Who knows who's above or below you in a place like this? You could live here for years, decades, and not exchange a single word with one of your neighbours.

Clive caught Aaron's glance – they were both wondering at their father. He was disconnected somehow – everything he said seemed intended for someone other than the two of them.

Aaron decided to ask something else.

—What did you mean when you were shouting at Annette and Christine – when you said you *told* them?

The triangle flexed. Leonard and Clive were looking at Aaron with the same expression on their faces. Puzzled and angry. Did he look the same? he asked himself. The question was like being kicked.

—When? said Clive. I didn't hear that.

Leonard drew on his cigarette.

—It was made quite clear to me what my role was.

As he spoke the smoke shot from his mouth in chugging puffs.

—I was to serve a purpose, and once that purpose was served, my services and purposes were no longer required.

He looked upwards, arms out and palms up, and laughed a nasty, coughed 'Ha!'

Aaron and Clive studied him for a second.

—I heard him shouting, said Aaron. Before we saw the three of them together. I could just hear 'I *told* you', loads of times. Like they hadn't listened.

Clive was silent for a moment. Aaron tried to keep up with his thoughts. He was just getting there as Clive swung towards Leonard again.

—They were trying to make you talk to us, weren't they?

Leonard put his cigarette in his mouth and flapped his hand, moving out of their small triangle as he did so, ready, it seemed, to walk away. The trellis near the roof-edge stopped him. He walked around it, and Clive followed him, while Aaron found himself rounding Clive and blocking another direction by which Leonard could escape them. Aaron had his back to the river now, to the edge of the roof – which was uncomfortably near.

The trellis now screened them from the rest of the party, and it was almost pitch-black here – the light from the candles and lamps unable to reach this far. The city below was draped in a net of stars – orange and pink and white – but nothing strong enough to illuminate this narrow stretch of roof. Aaron knew where Clive was – he always knew that; but Leonard was more a shape, his silhouette appearing and disappearing against the bars of the trellis, his expression invisible.

—And did you tell them not to? said Aaron, speaking quickly, as if Leonard might disappear completely. You told them you didn't want to meet us?

Clive saw Leonard's hands: twitching bats crossing the space between them.

—If you didn't want to meet us, why the hell move into the fucking tower? he said. You could have lived anywhere.

—Yes, I can live anywhere. Anywhere I want. And right now, I choose to live here. And she can't stop me. She likes to act like this whole place is her creation. Like she's some kind of Earth mother who, who, who – Leonard's shadow fluttered for a moment – who can dispense and withdraw her love, and never have to face the consequences.

Leonard's voice came from further away now – closer to the roof's edge. Clive realised that he had stepped away. And now he saw his shape against the muddy glow that lay above the city. How had he not seen him move? It was a jump cut.

—But she's not, said Leonard. She can't. She's human like the rest of us. She never would have got her practice off the ground without me. She couldn't have got a loan – a woman architect, without a man looking after the finances. And no investor would've even looked at her. But they did, because of me. I showed them the books, made them see it would be in good hands. It's all well and good having a vision, but to build the bloody thing you need a man like me. This whole estate is as much mine as hers.

Leonard laughed again. Another bark. A click and a scarf of yellow light – his face orange, creviced. He was lighting another cigarette.

—If she can live in a place she designed, I can live in a place where, without me, the foundations would never have been laid.

The orange of his cigarette soared like a comet, as his dark, short shape moved between them, as if to get away, as if to fall back into the crowd. But now there was a row of planters in the way, containing some of the bigger shrubs Leonard himself had placed there. Aaron saw his father's arms spread, as if to tackle figures blocking his way.

—But what's that got to do with us? said Clive.

—What have we done? said Aaron.

They'd followed Leonard, spreading out instinctively,

Leonard seemed to turn, the pleats of blacks shifting around the bright ball of the burning cigarette.

—She should never have had children, he said. The cigarette end danced a jerked jig. Never have had them. Other people are just a means to an end for her. She works out what she can get out of you, and when she's done ... well, you're done. And that includes her children.

—What are you talking about? said Clive, lunging forwards into the darkness, thinking as he did so that he might collide with his father.

Aaron reached for Clive's shoulder but couldn't find it. He stepped towards him. Towards Leonard.

—You two. You were just a means to an end. You've never heard her party piece? About having to be pregnant to do her best work?

Clive and Aaron were close enough to distinguish the expression on Leonard's face, but it was unreadable, a theatrical mask, poorly painted.

Aaron stuttered the beginnings of a protest, but Clive laughed, mimicking his father's bark.

—She's just play-acting. Your friend Ronald told us the same thing.

—So you've met Ronald, have you?

—Annette and Christine took us to his party.

Leonard's shape became still – the cigarette end hovered a few feet from the ground.

—And what did Ronald tell you?

Leonard's voice was quieter now. Clive felt like he'd stepped on something.

—That she used to say it to shut people up – men who asked what would happen to her job when she had babies.

—And you're sure he's right? asked Leonard.

—Yes, said Aaron. I'm sure. We're sure.

—Well, I'm not. Not at all. Not. At. All.

Leonard's voice was loud again, his hands pale blades, chopping the air.

—It was her choice. Her choice! – The 'her' was almost a shriek – After everything she'd done to me, I had to make a stand. I told her, if you want me to be a father to those brats, after everything you've done, then you have to accept me as your husband too. If you throw me out, after everything you've done – after everything I've done for you – that's the end of it. They won't have a father. And that will be your doing. But your mother, your blessed mother, she went ahead and showed me the door.

Aaron felt Clive edge backwards, felt himself step backwards too.

—But that's not our fault.

Today, neither twin can recall which of them said it.

—And it wasn't mine either, said Leonard.

—And what about Annette and Christine? said Clive. Do you love them? Are they your daughters?

It was a leap. A conclusion he'd only just reached. Aaron saw it spring across the darkness. Clive had seen it just a blink before.

Leonard swung around.

—No, of course I don't. Of course they're fucking not. How could I be the father of ... of ... of those two?

—Then why the fuck are they here? Why the fuck are *you* here? The words burned Aaron's throat as he yelled them.

Leonard paused for a third of a second.

—Let's go and talk to your mother. She's up here somewhere, isn't she?

He swung around again, away from them.

—Zöe? His voice was hot and loud. Zöe, where are you?

He advanced into the darkness, his head switching from side to side. He stretched out his arms.

—Where is she? ... Zöe?

It was a screech now. He was moving towards the trellis, hands ahead of him, trying to find a way around it, confused by a tangle of foliage. He stepped back, sideways. Then turned and barged forwards, colliding with his sons, trying to walk through them, as if it was darker up here for him than it was for them.

Aaron was shoved back and sideways, and the back of his heel found the air at the edge of the roof. He drew himself in, sharp, reached out to grab something, and found his father's shoulder, warm and round.

At the sight of Aaron's stagger. Clive grabbed at Leonard's other arm, felt his biceps, warm and round.

—Get off me, the both of you.

And Leonard was suddenly too strong for them – loud power springing from his body as he shook off their hands. The cigarette dropped like a meteorite, in a gasp of little sparks.

—Zö–e, he called – a nasty sing-song. Where are you?

He strode forwards.

And stepped off the edge of the roof.

24

That night in 1976, many of the residents of Marlowe Tower are on its roof. But not everyone, of course. If we float past, at a short distance from the bright slots of windows and the dim balconies – feeling the concrete slabs radiating the heat they've accumulated during the day – we might see people going about their Saturday-evening business. Those at home are mostly parents of young children. The younger people and the older people are the ones who've been able to dress up and go upstairs. But the children are now in bed. Some are still not asleep – it's another humid night. But their mothers and fathers are generally sitting on sofas now, watching TV, limbs spread wide in the warmth.

Zöe is alone in flat 246. She's in her battered wingback. She's draped it with a shawl of Indian cotton – most likely to stop her arms and legs sticking to the leather. She has a glass of water and another of wine beside her. The TV and radio are off, and she has no book or paper on her lap. She blinks regularly, presses her lips together and scratches at the strands of hair that have escaped her ponytail and are sticking ticklingly to her neck.

There's a possibility that someone has told her about the party taking place on the roof above her head. Mrs Ledbury, perhaps, or someone she met on the avenue, in the lift or on the walkway, keen to hear her opinion. But in fact she has been out all day, and arriving home encountered no one between her parking space and her flat door. So maybe she knows nothing of what is happening eight floors above.

The balcony door is open, and sounds wash in, then out again. A few bars of music and a staggering beat. Then a swell of voices. A shout. Another. But the eddies of updraughts and down-draughts in the column of air beyond her balcony mean the sounds could be coming from any direction – from a party in another flat, a group in a garden somewhere below. The summer has been full of noisy nights.

She stands, walks to the balcony door, leans her head out, listening, maybe, then turns and drops back into her chair, her cheeks puffed out a little. Dissatisfied.

A crooked shape passes the balcony. It drops through the dark-blue air just beyond the balustrade. It makes a noise – like a sip. The black is legs. The white a shirt. The fabric flutters. It's what makes the sound.

Zöe stands, her wine glass tips, but somehow its contents splash into the tumbler of water.

Others in the tower see the shape too. A flicker, like a wing flapped in the corner of the window, a bird late to settle for the night. Below Zöe, a young woman is smoking, her arms propped on the balcony wall. She picks at her elbows, brushing bits of grit from her skin. Then the body huffs past. She jerks back with a grunt of surprise. Her husband, stretched topless on the sofa, swivels his body and puts his feet on the floor.

—What was that?

She turns to face him, the light from the room bleaching her sunburned face.

—Someone fell ... I think.

—From the party?

They were invited by Tabitha, but they couldn't find a babysitter. All the teenaged girls were going upstairs.

The last person to see the body is the tower's caretaker, Albert Bishop. Albert will also be the one who eventually scours and scrubs the paving stones where the body lands.

Now he is in his pyjamas. They look like thick winter ones; perhaps his summer ones are in the wash. He's removed the top; it lies on the sofa cushion beside him. In his reflection in the balcony door, his distended belly and sagging breasts seem to glow.

He huffs and pulls himself straighter, squares his shoulders, and, levelling his head, takes a drink from his mug. Over the rim he sees the body. A glimpse, but enough that he might be able to replay the last few yards of the body's descent over and over in his head. The U-shape the body makes, as if the man is attempting to touch his toes, while falling back first through the air. The white shirt with the sleeves rolled up. The legs of the trousers, wind-stitched to the back of the thighs and calves, but the bottoms billowing.

The face – turned towards Albert in that moment, as it happens – the mouth flopped loose, already given up on words. The eyes are closed. This might be a mercy for Albert – not to see the expression of a man about to die. But Albert has seen this some thirty years before. Three times in just a few weeks in 1943.

A moment later, the sound of the impact darts through Albert's open window. A sack of vegetables dropped off the back of a delivery van.

●

25

Aaron takes his tea out onto the balcony and places his mug on the flat top of the balustrade.

He comes out here almost every morning, after his breakfast, and almost every morning he thinks the same thing.

And then, almost every morning, he leans against the wall, bends a little and looks down at the ground below, at the spot where Leonard landed.

At first, he did it to remind himself that what happened that night happened. The kink of discomfort it gave him ignited the full memory, and it would then burn all day: the sight of his father striding into the darkness in search of his mother, running out of roof to walk on. But over the years the habit has struck fewer and fewer sparks, so most days he's just staring at a piece of ground, no different from the rest surrounding Marlowe Tower.

But now, with Annette and Christine four floors above him, the sight of the patch of tarmac strikes a match. The night comes back to him, burning loud.

The tarmac is relatively new, poured over the concrete that was there before, and that replaced the large paving stones on which Leonard landed. Aaron stares. Did they pull up the paving stones – the pattern of pale and dark flags in Zöe's own design – a piece of functionless decoration, rare on the estate? He can't remember. Maybe they poured the concrete directly on top; then, years later, the tarmac directly on top of that. So he's now attempting to stare through the layers at the rusty stain left by his father.

A figure appears from between the green-netting fences surrounding the gutted block adjacent to Marlowe Tower and, on the other side, the remains of the avenue. The path is redundant now. It was created to give Marlowe Tower residents access to the main road, now that the walkway is partly demolished. All the Marlowe Tower residents have left though. Almost all. This person is using the path. He stares harder. Leans further. Not a workman. A woman. No high-vis jacket. But not Annette or Christine, he is sure. The glimpses of their heads were different. This hair is dark. But the fidgety walk seems familiar.

She is directly below him now, so her figure shrinks to an ellipse. She's stopped. Then she walks backwards. She's looking up. At him? It's too far to tell. Too far for their eyes to lock. And perhaps that's why he doesn't pull back, trying not to be seen. It seems that she's moving her head now, from side to side, scanning. And in a rush he knows who it is. His chest and belly snap tight. He has to grip onto the wall. It's Tabitha.

Now he does jerk back. Is it really too far for her to see? He saw her face. Recognised who she was. Did she recognise him? He wrestles for a stupid second. He guesses at what she saw – the pale oval of his face. Perhaps two flecks of flesh – his hands. The grey of his jumper too similar to the concrete for her to distinguish. But none of that matters. She knows he stayed in the building – the only person to do so when everyone was decanted. So if she saw anything like a head – a human – she would automatically think it was him, wouldn't she?

Tabitha moved out of her mother's flat when she married. Aaron is not sure exactly how long ago this was; thirty years, perhaps? She has grown-up children now, he thinks. She and her husband were given a flat in Marlowe Tower. He recalls the discomfort of meeting her in the lift and discovering that she was now even closer. 'We're neighbours now,' she said, squinting. 'Me and Mark have moved in. Floor twelve.' And her snigger had come in two waves.

Yet, despite being just a few floors apart, he and Tabitha have spoken very little. They'd occasionally pass on the stairs, in the hallway, on the walkway or in the town square. Stood behind or in front of each other in queues at the shops, at the doctor's surgery, and once, he now recalls, at the cinema at the Elephant. But they've exchanged no more than a hello or a nod.

From her side, however, there has always been a scent of mirth. 'Hiya, Aaron, you all right?' Then the snigger, as if greeting him is amusing; and the creasing smile, which screws up her face, making her true expression disappear, but not before Aaron thinks he has seen something knowing and pointed there. Something he has also heard in her greeting. The something that has made her laugh: how funny that she should be saying hello to him, of all people.

For thirty years, he knew she was below him somewhere. Sometimes he would stand and feel the floor under his feet, then try to visualise the storeys beneath. He would count down from twenty-four to twelve. Try to think of her in her flat. He wasn't sure which it was – whether it was directly below his, or further along the corridor. But somehow, when he did this, he thought he could feel the heat of threat through the soles of his feet.

And this despite the fact that she had said that she would say nothing.

26

The moments after their father strode off the top of Marlowe Tower passed like the river below – unseen in the darkness, carrying an assortment of objects; but what they were, neither Aaron nor Clive could know.

The music was still loud, and the chatter pulsed like a squeeze-box. They found themselves looking at each other. Had they turned their heads – away from the empty space a foot away from the edge of the roof? Neither knew. There was a gap.

They needed to speak. Clive – of course, Clive – opened his mouth. But the voice they heard was not his. It was Tabitha's.

—What have you two done?

And then she sniggered.

She was on the other side of the trellis, looking at them between the slats. Her body was hidden, but light from somewhere caught her face, her eyes and mouth mobile, as if she were considering a new flavour.

Then it froze, mouth and eyes pulled into Os.

—Don't worry. I won't say nothing.

Clive was working hard on their denial, so Aaron spoke first, unguarded.

—But we didn't do anything.

Tabitha's eyes moved between them, her face now pressed against the struts of the trellis.

—Didn't do nothing? You pushed that bloke off.

She sniggered. Paused. Sniggered again.

—We didn't.

Clive advanced on her. Aaron followed him round the trellis.

They found her in the corner, whips of foliage reaching out to her. Lit by the rash of lights from the party.

—We didn't push him off, Clive said.

He wanted to reach out and grab her, use the pressure of a hand to make her understand.

She was all movement now, her eyes switching between their faces, looking over their shoulders. She was palpating her feet, tiptoeing up on one, then the other, her hands now holding her arms, now plucking at her shorts.

—We didn't, Aaron repeated, as if she'd said something.

Tabitha twisted sideways and placed her hand in the gap in the trellis where her face had been.

—I saw what I saw.

She allowed a long pause this time before releasing the snigger. Then she became more still.

—But, like I said, I won't say nothing. I promise. I didn't see nothing.

—Because there was nothing to see!

Clive's voice rang out too loud. Aaron placed a hand on his arm and told him to keep it down.

—Yeah, Clive. You don't want everyone to hear, said Tabitha.

—But he just walked off the edge, said Clive to Aaron.

And then, in a kind of stage whisper, as if he couldn't modulate his voice effectively, he said to Tabitha:

—He just walked off the edge.

—He must have thought he was facing the other way, said Aaron. He couldn't see the edge in the dark.

—He just walked off the edge.

Clive felt jammed – a bolus blocking his mind.

Tabitha took a step out of her corner, and Clive and Aaron made way for her a little.

—Well, I know what I saw. You was arguing with him. He barged into you, and you both grabbed him.

She stopped. And at the same moment the music stopped too. There were cries of disappointment. Then a reggae beat started up.

—And then off he went – over the edge.

Aaron rushed to replay the scene.

The ember darted through the dark. Leonard was too strong. Writhing too much to hold. He stepped forwards, calling for Zöe.

—We weren't touching him when he fell, he said. We were still arguing—

—Yeah, and grabbing onto him. And he didn't *fall*...

—He did, said Clive. He walked off the edge.

He turned to Aaron, pleading eyes.

—He must have been disorientated.

—I don't know what he was, said Tabitha. I just saw your hand on his arm, and yours on his shoulder, and he was trying to get you off of him, and then you both gave him a good shove.

She pushed at the air with flat hands.

Clive couldn't speak now. Aaron held his breath. The moment had been rewritten. And there was no reorganising the words.

—But don't worry, I won't say nothing, said Tabitha. A snigger. What do they say? Mum's the word. We don't grass round here, do we? More than your life's worth.

She'd edged between them now, her head turning.

—Come back to the party. Act likes nothing's happened, she said. She was twitching a little in time to the beat. Whoever he was, just don't say nothing. And I won't either.

She was sauntering away, her hand stretched behind her, beckoning, telling them to join her.

They were still for a second.

And then, far off, the two-step keen of a police siren.

Tabitha froze for a second, then spun on one foot, stamping the other down to stop herself falling. She looked at them, widening her eyes theatrically.

—You gonna come and dance, or what?

27

Clive decides to stay in his apartment. He emails Kulwant. He calls the office downstairs to tell them he's not feeling fit enough to come down today. He turns off his phone.

He takes up his position outside, on the terrace. It's windy today. It's almost too windy to think. But it's what Clive needs. Inside is too quiet and empty; he designed the space himself, for 'contemplation and focus' he always tells his visitors. But contemplation and focus haven't helped him with this problem. Outside his thoughts are tugged and battered, and scurried away; when he reels them back in they are shredded, but somehow more useful to him.

Annette and Christine are back in Marlowe Tower, living in the property that Zöe gave them one year after Leonard's fall. Zöe's gift explains something about Leonard's fall; or his fall explains something about her gift. Clive can't decide which end of this to grab hold of. For now he moves forwards and grips the steel rail at the edge of the terrace, then bends a little and rests his chin on the cold metal. He feels his teeth press together – the weight of his head on his jaw.

His scheme for Marlowe Tower must have been the trigger. Being asked to sell their flat – Zöe's gift – to the council has to be what has brought them back here now. According to Kulwant's research, they've owned flat 304 for forty-four years, but as far as he knows they haven't lived in it for more than a few months until now. If they'd been back living there at any point in between, Aaron would have seen them, surely. He hasn't left the tower in all that time. But then he and Aaron haven't spoken in all that time either.

Clive's eyes drift down from the top of the tower to floor twenty-four.

He left; Aaron stayed. There was an explosion – a mine on their road. It propelled him forwards, at a blinding speed, but it had stopped Aaron dead in his tracks. Clive has never dared allow himself to look back for his brother; never glanced over his shoulder. Because, he thinks now – he knows now – the thought of finding Aaron stationary, far back in the distance, was too much to bear. A dark, badly drawn figure, arms hanging useless at his sides, his face too far away to read, but Clive knowing – always – that it holds a soft frown, a set mouth and a blink of accusation.

According to Alexa and Kemi, Annette and Christine's move was recent. Has Aaron spoken to them yet? What has he said? No. He's sure that conversation hasn't taken place. The news of that confrontation – because that is what it has to be – would have travelled across the water at speed, and the strongest wind wouldn't have altered its course.

And he does now what he has always managed to prevent himself doing. He looks at the top of Marlowe Tower, then flicks his gaze to the open area at the bottom. From here it is just a grey trapezoid – like the fragment of a tile. Then he raises his eyes back to the edge of the roof – and describes the fall, holding them fast on the point of impact, as if to make some kind of mark. As if to reassure himself that his father really did accidentally walk off the edge of the thirty-one storey building.

He performs the same action again. His body otherwise immobile. Just his eyes moving. His chest, a little. His nostrils, minutely with each breath. And then he holds it as he pauses at the bottom of the tower.

Every day that he is here, in his apartment, or downstairs in his office, he is tempted to think of the fall. And every day he resists. Every day for years and years. Until now. Until Annette and Christine came back.

They never demanded anything of anyone, that he can

remember. Yet somehow they insisted upon your engagement with them. And they did this, he thinks now, by suggesting that you were completely free to walk away – or even never to approach. No one walked away, of course.

A particularly violent gust boxes his ears. There's a numbing ache that's almost welcome. People did walk away from Annette and Christine in the end. He knows they did.

And now they are back, and engaging with them once again is almost irresistible. But again, they have done nothing. They've made no attempt at contact with him. They have simply turned up to a meeting arranged by Deptford Borough Council. And he is now sleepless and bedsore and cramped and strung. He's in a corner that he'd almost forgotten was there, and turning, finds them right behind him, arms out, ready to wrestle him down. Because they haven't forgotten. Of course, they haven't forgotten.

Clive pushes himself upright, and the pressure is released from his jaw. He realises his teeth are aching from the strain.

No one but Tabitha saw his and Aaron's argument with Leonard. It was Leonard's row with Annette and Christine that everyone remembered. Would remember to this day, if asked. What happened on the far edge of the roof, behind the trellis, in the blue dark, has been blown away by the eddies of air, by the up- and down-draughts, and by the winds from all points that have swirled around Marlowe Tower for four decades.

A spit of rain lands in Clive's eye.

28

That night in 1976, it is Albert who calls the police first.

A moment after the sound of the body hitting the ground enters his flat, Albert puts down his tea, slopping it over his hand. Then he is out on his balcony, leaning over. The stale orange of the lamplight illuminates the body. The legs are twisted to one side, making it look like the man has landed at a run. The dark gloss emerging behind his head seems like a deep pool.

Albert lumbers back into the flat to make the call. He has no phone, but there's one in the corridor just outside his front door. He reaches the door and is about to open it when he seems to check himself. He hustles into the living room and returns, pulling on his pyjama top.

Outside he dials, then buttons himself up with one hand as he waits for the operator to answer.

'Someone's had a fall' are the words he uses. It's like he's telling the operator about an old lady who's missed a step on the stairs. But Albert doesn't know anything about the party on the roof. The three or four people who have encountered him over the previous couple of days and who were going to the party were careful not to mention it. Albert is the kind of caretaker who would trouble himself to put a stop to anything like that.

This means he is of little use to the police when they arrive. He offers to conduct them on a floor-by-floor tour of the tower, but they say they can do that themselves, and keep him to his own floor, two or three staying with him, asking him carefully and quietly what he has seen. Then they ask him again. And they go out onto the balcony, look up and down. They go out into the corridor and talk to each other, and, alone, he says to the empty

room, 'Three lads in three weeks, I saw die. So him out there' –
Albert jabs a thick finger – he's the fourth.'

It's when the police officers reach floor nineteen that they begin
to understand a little of what has happened. The young couple are
waiting on the landing. Like Albert, they have no phone
themselves and have been trying to find someone who is in and
does have one. The husband was putting on his shoes to go down
to use the payphone outside Albert's flat, when his wife called out
from the balcony that the police had arrived below. They thought
then that it was best to wait. Catch the police as they came
upstairs.

—We wouldn't have all this if we lived in a street, she said. We'd
be straight outside on the pavement, telling them what we'd seen,
not waiting around for them to make it up a hundred flights of
stairs.

—If we lived in a street, there'd be nobody getting shoved off
the top of our building, said the husband.

—How do you know whoever it is was shoved?

—Had to have been, didn't they? Must've been a dust-up at
that party. Things got out of hand.

And this is what he says to the police as they climb the last
flight to his floor. He calls it down:

—You know there's a party on the roof, don't you?

Radios click and chirrup. Groups of officers take the lift and
stairs to the upper floors. The group with Albert are told to ask
him about access to the roof.

—The roof, he replies to their question. He was on the roof?

—There's a party up there, we've been told.

—A party? But I'm the only one with a key. Well, apart from
Mrs Goldsworthy.

29

The police didn't arrive on the roof in force. Aaron noticed them first – a cough of black and white, a glint of metal. He touched Clive's arm. Almost felt the sweep of fright pass through his fingers and into Clive's body.

Clive saw them too. They were in shirtsleeves, no jackets. Talking and standing straight. Pink hands doing the explaining. It was Mrs Ledbury they were talking to now. The music was too loud to hear what was said.

Clive felt Aaron's hand tight around his forearm. There were more of them coming. White shirts emerged, one by one, from the door to the stairs, faces obscured by bent, helmeted heads, then appearing as the men straightened up.

The music ended mid-phrase.

—Ladies and gents, ladies and gents, ladies and gents ... An officer in a peaked cap repeated the words until the rumble of chatter faded.

There was more light now. Several policemen were carrying fat torches, casting them around the roof. The beams caught on scowls of uncertainty, paused on a brown face, slid over a burnt-pink one, a grey coif, paused again on dark skin and thick locks. The officer in the peaked cap seemed to examine the faces as they were illuminated. He turned and pointed at another area of the crowd. Again, the torches found the faces. Performed the same pattern of slides and pauses, like a code – a kind of Morse. The officer watched on, then, apparently satisfied, drew himself up.

—All right, ladies and gents. We're going to have to close this little shindig down. Sorry to spoil your night, but there's no safety up here. What my officers will do is come round, ask a couple of questions, and when you're done you'll be free to make your way downstairs. So stay where you are for now, and you'll be told when you can go down and get yourselves home. All right…? He left a short pause. All right.

Aaron caught a glimpse of Albert standing by the door to the stairs, his thick pyjama top buttoned wrong, so he looked lopsided, his mouth gaping. Aaron thought he knew what Albert must be thinking: How have all these people got up here? Where had all these plants and trees come from? How did Albert, the caretaker, not know about all this? But it wasn't Albert's block, thought Aaron. It was Zöe's. Zöe's and Leonard's.

—Can I speak with you gentlemen, please?

Aaron felt Clive at his shoulder. They didn't need to look at each other, but they did. And quickly looked away, convinced they'd just winked guilt.

—Yes, of course, said Clive.

Aaron nodded. The peak of the policeman's helmet came low over his face, so he couldn't read his expression. But he wanted to tell the truth.

Clive didn't. Clive wanted to lie. And, as always, Clive spoke first.

—What's happened? We're allowed up here, aren't we?

—I don't know about that. But we're not actually here because of the party. You live in the block?

—Yes, we do.

The officer's eyes were almost invisible under his helmet. He took a loud breath.

—We've found the body of a man downstairs. At the bottom of the tower. We think he may have fallen from up here.

—Fallen? From here?

Aaron thought Clive's disbelief was particularly forced, particularly suspect.

—He's wearing a white shirt and black trousers. Shortish bloke.

In his late forties, early fifties, we think. Is that someone you know? Someone you've seen at the party?

He's our dad, Aaron wanted to say. He walked off the edge. We didn't do anything. It was an accident. We don't know him. None of this was what Clive wanted to say, he thought. Yet he couldn't sense what Clive did want to say. It was somewhere among the choppy pool of bodies around them.

—I think... said Clive.

He allowed a long pause. Then he turned to Aaron, gripped his upper arm and formed his face into a look of concern Aaron had never seen before.

—Wasn't he wearing those clothes? Clive asked. Did you notice?

Aaron couldn't answer. He couldn't understand what Clive was doing. The policeman, impatient for a reply, said:

—Who are you talking about? Who's 'he'?

Clive kept his hand on Aaron, hoping it would keep him quiet. He knew what Aaron wanted to say, and he knew it was different from the lie he'd been building in the moments since Leonard fell.

—He's our father, Clive said.

He felt the pressure of his blood in his neck. He was ready, clear-sighted.

Aaron had the same sensation, but was fearful, confused.

The policeman stared at them both for a second. Aaron saw the glint of his eyes now. Then he turned, raising an arm, beckoning another policeman over.

—We'll need to ask you some more questions, boys, all right?

—Yes, fine, said Clive. Do you think...?

Clive's performance was atrocious, Aaron thought. This was going wrong. He should speak. Step in front of Clive and explain. Tell the truth of what had happened.

But over the policeman's shoulder he saw Tabitha. She was talking. Talking and talking – to another policeman. Her arms were folded, but one continually escaped, to gesture, to point.

And, then, turning to demonstrate something – a where, a who. She caught sight of Aaron and Clive. Her gaze skipped from Clive's to Aaron's. 'I won't say nothing,' she had said. But would she? Her version of what had happened was different from theirs.

Their policeman was turned away, and Clive and Aaron exchanged a glance; but Aaron couldn't see what Clive was telling him, and there was no time for Clive to say, 'We'll tell part of the truth, but nothing that makes Tabitha right, OK?' He just had to trust that Aaron would keep quiet or agree.

And Clive could trust Aaron. Because at that moment, with Tabitha still talking, still pointing, Aaron could see no other option than to allow Clive to dominate. A right hand picking up a pen.

Their policeman was joined by two others now, one of them the officer in the peaked cap. They were ushered away from the main group of people, corralled, separated from the herd.

—All right, lads. The senior officer stepped in towards them, displaying his palms. You told my colleague that your father was up here, correct?

—That's right, said Clive.

Aaron nodded, his chest at Clive's triceps.

—And he's in his late forties, early fifties? Wearing a white shirt and black trousers, yes?

—Yes.

Aaron nodded.

—And you live in the tower, do you?

—Yes, with our mum.

—Flat 246, said Aaron.

—And what's your dad's name? The officer put his head a little to one side.

—Leonard, said Clive.

—Leonard Harrington, said Aaron.

—We're Clive and Aaron Goldsworthy. We took our mother's surname, said Clive.

The officer's face twitched minutely.

—And I can see you're twins. What age are you?

—Eighteen, said Clive. Eighteen this spring.

—All right, boys, I'm afraid you'll have to stay up for a bit longer while we go over a couple of things with you.

—It's OK, said Clive. We understand what's happened. It might not be him though, eh?

Aaron thought the officer looked unconvinced by Clive's acting.

—Let's just ask you a few more questions, first, all right?

Aaron nodded. Clive didn't reply.

—So, when did you last see your dad?

—He was over there, by that trellis thing.

Clive pointed towards the edge of the roof, and for a moment he thought he had it wrong. Which edge was which? Where was the river? But then he was sure.

—That was the last time I saw him.

The officer turned the peak of his cap towards Aaron. Aaron realised he had to speak.

—Same for me. I saw him over by the trellis thing.

—Did either of you talk to him. Who was he with?

—I didn't see if he was with anyone, said Clive. He was standing there, smoking. But... Clive had to twist round to exchange another look with Aaron. We don't talk to him. Our mum and him split up years ago, and we didn't stay in contact. He only moved in here a few months ago, but we've not been in touch.

There was a small, listening frown on the officer's face now. Aaron wanted to tell Clive to shut up. Or at least look more upset, anxious, fearful. But Clive felt confident. He waited for the question he expected.

—Not been in touch when he's living in the same block of flats? The officer's frown was punctuation now.

Clive shrugged, raised his hands a little, but tried not to seem blithe.

—It's our mum and dad. It was years ago, but they still don't talk. And, well, they separated before we were born, so...

—OK. Understood. Is your mum here, at the party? Or did she keep away?

—No, she wouldn't come to something like this. She's downstairs. In our flat.

—We'll need to speak to her too.

—Yes, of course.

The officer left a silence, during which he turned to Aaron. And Aaron was unsure whether he was meant to say something. What did Clive want him to say? The truth – but only a bit of it. Something convincing. Something that wouldn't make what Tabitha said she saw true – or even possible.

—Mum's not spoken to him either, since he came back. It's a big tower. You can go months without seeing your upstairs neighbours.

It was too many words. The officer looked too interested. His head extended an inch forwards.

But then he dropped his eyes to his feet.

—And neither of you saw who your dad was with? Whether he was talking to anyone earlier in the evening? Arguing?

—We saw him and kept our distance, to be honest, said Clive. We didn't think he'd be here.

—Otherwise we might not have come. You know, because of Mum and that, Aaron added.

Too many words again.

—So I didn't notice him with anybody, said Clive. Did you?

Clive glanced at Aaron, but Aaron couldn't help flicking his eyes across the groups of people, searching for Annette and Christine. He saw Mrs Ledbury in animated conversation with two, no three policeman. He couldn't see Annette and Christine.

—Aaron? Clive prompted.

—No, I didn't see him with anyone. I hardly saw him the whole night. We avoided him, like Clive said.

Aaron hated to lie. He hated when Clive made him.

But the officer seemed comfortable. He put his hands together and used them to point at Aaron and Clive.

—Thank you, boys. You've been very helpful. Now, I'd like to meet your mum, but first I'd like you to do something for us.

He softened his face, his mouth a little open and his eyebrows raised. It was as if he'd decided that a fatherly look, a gentle tone to his voice, would help them agree to what he wanted.

—We'd like you to come downstairs with us and identify the body.

He stopped, froze his hands in mid-air, then started again.

—You can say no, of course. But you know, you're men now, and the quicker we know for definite that it's him, the quicker we can find out what happened and why. That all right with you, boys?

—Yes. I can do it, said Clive.

He wasn't acting now.

—I'll come too, Aaron said, a little too quietly, he thought.

—Thanks, lads. It'll be brief. You just have to say whether it's him or not.

The officer made a small turn, some gestures with his head, his hands, and Clive and Aaron were being escorted across the roof, towards the stairs.

They never did it normally – they'd learned not to in public years before, and this discipline had extended to their moments alone too – but now, as they walked close beside each other, each reached for the other's hand. Found it. Laced together their fingers.

As they reached the stairs, their escorts stopped. There was a stutter, shadows, the shouts of white shirts among the dark bodies. Another group was going downstairs too, escorted by police. And there, illuminated for a beat, Aaron saw linked hands, fingers interlaced. Brown arms, then brown faces.

The senior officer put himself between the two groups, so

Aaron could no longer see the impassive faces, dark in the darkness. But he realised, now that they were screened from him by a policeman standing with feet wide apart and arms spread, that in that moment he'd not been able to tell Annette from Christine, Christine from Annette. They'd disappeared behind twins.

Clive saw the group tighten round two black women and knew instantly it was them, but couldn't understand why the policemen were so intent on coming between them, why their frowns and glances at each other were so wary, so baffled. Was it the coincidence of two sets of twins at the same party – one set, black girls; the other, white boys? No. There was something else.

—Take those two down first, Sergeant, said the senior officer. We'll follow after.

But then the officer drew his sergeant a few steps away, a hand on his back, lowering his voice a little. Clive didn't look, but concentrated hard, angling his head so his ear would catch what was said. He took a casual step backwards. Two.

—I'd say nick them right now, only it looks like there's a few of their mates up here, and I don't want a riot on a roof, if you know what I mean. So get them downstairs, nick them there. Then in a car and straight to the station and let them stew. You know how it is with them lot. It'll take hours to get anything honest out of them.

Now Clive wanted to look at Annette and Christine. He could see their khaki suits, pale against the policemen's black trousers, but dark against their white shirts. But he couldn't see their faces. Their heads were bowed, or they were simply watching their feet as they were led through the doorway, each held by a policeman, their big hands tight around the slim brown arms.

Aaron felt Clive brush against him. He saw him checking around them briefly. Then he murmured,

—I just heard him say they're going to arrest them.

30

When Aaron dares to step forwards and stretch his neck over the parapet, Tabitha has gone. He draws his body closer to the wall, leans out, looks further. He'd be able to see her if she'd headed back the way she came. But there's no one. He scans the open areas at the foot of Marlowe Tower and under the fractured walkway, the paths alongside the nearby block and community centre, both half-deconstructed now, concrete frames, their front walls missing.

No one.

Tabitha must have entered Marlowe Tower.

He turns, three quick steps to the balcony door – catches the toe of his shoe on the lip, tips forwards and places the next foot inside with an unintentional stamp, which stabs upwards into his knee. He gasps, but keeps going, to his front door, then out into the corridor.

He stops and holds his breath through his whole body, his arms crooked, as if for balance.

There are always sounds in Marlowe Tower. Its relationship with the wind is more than five decades long. The wind has taught the building to breathe – not regularly, but in fits and starts. Sighs and hisses, clicks and grunts. They're all familiar to Aaron, and he tries to brush a wash over them, so a door creaks and footsteps can appear.

He has to breathe out eventually. He places a hand on the cool, smooth wall, and he hears the footsteps he's been expecting. They're below him, he's sure. Tabitha is coming up. The steps come in chattering little groups. She's moving briskly, but stopping on the landings. He imagines her snigger. Strains to hear it. He seems to wait a long, long time. But then the footsteps seem suddenly close. He thinks he sees a shuffle of shadows further up the corridor, near the door to the stairs.

He steps back inside his flat and pushes the door to. Waits. Holds the latch open, then settles the door into its frame and eases the latch closed with an almost inaudible click.

He immediately wants to go back outside. He can't hear anything in here.

By now, if she'd come to see him, she'd be in the corridor. And by now she'd be knocking. He'd have to wait a moment before opening. She can't know he's behind the door, his ear almost touching the wood, his little finger hooked over the door knob.

He remembers the peephole, and puts his eye to it. The wall opposite, a patch of the floor. The light is soft, coming from the broken window at the end of the corridor. No one is outside his door.

He turns the latch tentatively, opens the door – enough to put his head out – and looks up and down the corridor. No one. Which means Tabitha has gone somewhere else in the tower. Not to her old flat. That's floors below.

A door slams. The ring of it fires through building.

It came from above, he's certain. He's a few steps along the corridor now. He's at the stairs, opening the door. The draught slips around him and hurries behind him towards his flat door. He'll not get back before it slams too. His key is inside.

But the door only sways. He puts his foot out to stop it but stays in the corridor, listening.

Nothing, now. But he knows the only place Tabitha can be is with Annette and Christine.

He slips inside and closes his door again.

He walks into the living room and looks up. The ceiling is greying. He looks at the back of the kitchen door. It needs paint. He looks out onto the balcony. A wall of undecided cloud, the top of three towers across the river. Clive's is invisible from this angle.

Now Aaron glances at the phone. It was disconnected weeks ago; the company said the council were denying access to the tower, so they could no longer provide a service. His cheap mobile is in a drawer. He could take it out. He could call Clive. Because, with Tabitha upstairs, talking to Annette and Christine, he feels as if he's on the outside of something. He's been the sole occupant of this tower for months, now, yet has the tight stomach of an intruder, despite standing in the living room of the flat that has been his home for fifty years.

He wants to feel at home – he's homesick. He wants to speak to Clive. Yes, he wants to speak to Clive. Tabitha, he wants to say. Annette and Christine, he wants to tell him. And he wants not to speak in normal sentences. Not to have to explain. But just to say a few words, pause, wait and understand that he's been understood. That his fears are recognised, are shared. And then he'll feel like he can sit down.

He opens the drawer and takes out the phone. The buttons crackle under his thumb. The charger sits beside it. The battery will be flat.

He goes out onto the balcony again, turns his head to take in the entire view, as if he needs it if he's to begin to think what Tabitha's visit means. The stand of towers across the water, grown from nothing since the night of the party. The banks of new flats wedged into plots that once held warehouses and timber yards. The cartoon crown of the dome downstream. The wreck of the estate below.

Over the years, Aaron has often wondered about Annette and Christine. What they did after. Where they went. What they did for a living. Did they become successful, like Clive? Or did they waste and shrivel, like him?

He leans his weight against the balcony wall. Why does he imagine that they both followed the same course? Perhaps they didn't speak for years either. Perhaps they are only now mending their relationship. Perhaps Tabitha is helping them.

And he thinks he hears her snigger – snatched from her mouth six floors above, whipped out of their open balcony door, dropped, then danced in front of him, before blowing away, downstream to the estuary. And he cannot bear it. He needs to know what they are saying.

He pictures himself rushing – or lurching – up the flights to the thirtieth floor, knocking at the door to 304, breathless and smelling his own sweat. Calling out his name, saying that he needs to speak to them. All of them. Now.

But no. The person he imagines doing this is someone else. Someone who looks like him, but who does things he would never do.

Eavesdropping, though. He can convince himself that he would do that. And he knows where he could do it. Zöe's keys still lie in the drawer of the desk in her study – everything in there as she left it.

He goes back inside and stops just inside the door. He was about to walk down to the study, a question on his lips: shall we do it now? he intended to ask as he opened the door. He's never got used to doing things alone. So he does very few things.

31

When they passed floor twenty-four in the lift, the senior officer and two others with them, Clive gripped Aaron's hand.

—We should tell Mum.

His grip and the floor number lighting up would have been enough. But Clive spoke the words aloud. And Aaron knew why. They were to lie to Zöe too.

—Let's get this out of the way, the senior officer said. Then we'll go and have a chat with your mum. You'll be next of kin, as they're divorced. And you're eighteen, you say? Keeps it nice and tidy.

—Clive gripped at Aaron's fingers again, but didn't say anything this time.

The lift rocked a little and quietly clanged, and Aaron thought of one of their games. They'd stand in the lift and one would close his eyes while the other chose a floor to go to. The one with closed eyes would say whether they were moving up or down. They both mostly got it right. The delight was the few times when, for dizzying moments, they couldn't tell. That was the winning of it. But they were going down now, and Aaron couldn't trick his brain into believing any different.

And they were shuffling out of the lift now, through the big hallway to the main entrance, then down the steps to a ring of officers, torches all trained on the heap on the floor. Aaron and Clive's hands curled into a tight clutch. Their arms pressed together and they were ten years old again.

—Boys.

The senior officer ushered them forwards with an outstretched arm, bunched lips and kind eyes.

—Yes, that's him, Clive said almost immediately.

Aaron thought it was too quick. As if Clive had said it without looking, without being sure. As if some other person had stumbled into the hot night.

But it was him. His body was covered with a red blanket, and an officer was holding back a corner, just enough to reveal the face, little enough that the wounds, the smashing, the pulping impact remained concealed. Aaron could still see blood.

—Yes, that's him, said Aaron. He could do no more than simply repeat Clive's words. His tongue felt like a pebble in his mouth. His limbs seemed difficult to move.

Clive flexed his arm.

Aaron felt it.

And the officer drew the blanket back over their father's face. Clive thought how unpleasant it must be to have your face covered with such thick wool. And in this heat. It would be impossible to breathe.

And then they were being moved again, feet, now yards away from their father's body. Until they couldn't see it anymore. Nor would they ever again.

Which somehow reminded Aaron that Zöe and Clive and he weren't the only ones affected here.

—What's happened to Annette and Christine?

Clive made an attempt to pull his hand out of Aaron's. Aaron held on tight.

The senior officer stopped.

—Annette and Christine? he said.

The group were on the front steps now, each person on a different step from the others.

—Who are they, then?

—The two black women. The ones you brought down before us, said Clive.

He managed to pull his hand out of Aaron's now. It came away with a kick. He wouldn't have mentioned them. But now Aaron had, he would find a way to work with it.

—You know them, do you?

—Yes, Clive replied straight away. It was their party.

Aaron didn't like this. Wouldn't someone say it was his and Clive's party too? Wouldn't this unnecessary lie drop a trail to the other one?

The senior officer seemed to consider something.

—We're chatting to them about what happened. Now let's go upstairs.

◆

—I have a key, said Clive as the junior officer knocked at the door to 246.

—Use it then, lad, said the senior officer.

Clive turned the key in the lock, and as he opened the door he saw Zöe staggering back, her hand still raised to unlock it from the inside.

—Clive? She moved her head. Aaron?

She stepped aside as the policemen entered the hall.

—Mrs Goldsworthy?

—Miss. Zöe. I called 999 – about seeing someone fall. I saw your cars more than an hour ago. I've been waiting.

Aaron noticed she had brushed her hair and had neat, fresh eyeliner beneath her eyes. She turned and led them into the living room. The policemen's uniforms seemed too big for the space.

—Chief Inspector Markham, said the senior officer. Sorry we've been so long getting to you.

—No problem at all, officer, said Zöe. Her expression was clear and interested. Her chin a little raised. I imagine there's a lot to do.

She examined first Aaron, then Clive, but remained silent. The policemen seemed to be waiting. If it was for hysterics, thought Aaron, they'd come to the wrong place.

She took a step towards the kitchen.

—A drink of something, gentlemen? It's a hot night.

There was a pause before anyone answered. Long enough for Aaron to glance around and understand that they all knew something Zöe didn't. That Leonard had died. He had an urge to say it: 'It's Leonard. He's the one who fell.' Did the officers expect him to? Expect Clive to? They didn't even have a name for him: should they say 'Father's had an accident'? 'Dad died'?

—A glass of water each would be very welcome. Then we'll sit down and let you know what's happened tonight.

Zöe was already moving towards the kitchen, but paused minutely, her top lip contracting. Clive was closest to her and expected her to ask Markham just to come out with it. But she caught Clive's arm as she passed him, tugging him with her.

In the kitchen she put a tray in his hands and on it placed glass after glass of water poured from a jug that had been in the fridge. As she put them down she caught his eye, looking up at him from under her brows. It was the look that told them off, that asked them what they were hiding, that insisted they do this or that thing, at this or that time. But then she turned to pick up another glass and the same expression seemed to be asking for reassurance, for some glib 'Clive' answer to the question she still hadn't asked.

He carried the tray to the dining table, where the policemen were all now sitting. The glasses chimed against each other. The tray was heavy. Clive thought he might drop it. Aaron's face told him that he thought he might drop it too.

Zöe pulled out her chair – at the head of the table – sat down and folded her hands in front of her.

—Please, officers, take a glass. It's chilled. Now tell me. Who was it that fell?

—I'm afraid it's someone you know well, Miss Goldsworthy.

Zöe looked at both Aaron and Clive, as if to double-check that they were both present – within reach.

—It's your ex-husband, Leonard Harrington.

Zöe picked up her glass and took a sip, then bobbed her head as if the water wouldn't go down.

—I ... He was wearing a white shirt and black trousers?

—Yes, said Markham.

—That's what I saw. That's what I told the operator when I dialled 999. A body. A white shirt, black trousers. I didn't see enough to know who it was. To recognise ... Leonard.

Her voice was level. She seemed very still, her hand around her glass.

—We're very sorry, Miss Goldsworthy. It's definitely him. Your boys have identified him.

Now Zöe became animated.

—How? They barely know what he looks like.

She darted out a hand and clutched at Clive's, looked straight at Aaron as she did so.

—You should have come to me first. I should have been with you.

Aaron wanted her to stop. This was her at-home voice. The one she used for the two of them. For her mother and Elspeth. A few close friends. It was as if she'd erased the thick, stiff uniforms crowding the room.

—We checked their ages, Miss Goldsworthy. They're grown men now. And I can tell you that they've acted like it. You'd have been proud of them.

Clive saw Zöe's face sharpen, her mouth tighten. Her nose almost extended into a point as she refocused on Markham. Markham responded by placing the edges of his hands on the table, opening his palms once more.

—We'd have fetched you, but we had a bit of a situation. There were a lot of people up there and we needed to get an identification as soon as, so we could start bringing them all down.

Zöe frowned. Blinked.

—A lot of people? In his flat? He was having a party?

Her fingers were mobile now, turning the glass. It was a warning sign. Clive decided to speak. Before it began to seem like they were holding too much back.

—The party was on the roof. Annette and Christine organised it.

Aaron thought he should object. This fabrication could be so easily pulled apart. There were paper cups and boxes of candles in their rooms.

—On the roof?

—Yes, Aaron said. Annette and Christine thought the garden would be a good place for a get-together.

He saw Clive looking at him, telling him to shut up, that he had a plan and Aaron was complicating it.

—Because, you know, people don't want us down on the deck any more.

Markham broke in.

—It seems that Mr Harrington was at the party himself. If it was his garden up there, then perhaps he objected to a party taking place, I don't know. But at some point he fell. An unsurvivable height, I'm afraid.

—Thirty-one floors, said Zöe.

—And you weren't at this party yourself, Miss Goldsworthy?

—I didn't even know it was happening. And I wouldn't have gone – or let my sons go – if I had known about it. There are no balustrades or rails up there. It's not designed for anything like that. I had no idea Leonard had started using it as a roof garden – not until recently.

—The boys say you have no contact with him.

—Yes, that's correct. We fell out many years ago. Over the design and build of this estate, as a matter of fact.

Markham pulled back from the table a little and frowned.

—I designed this estate, Chief Inspector. Leonard took care of the business side of things. The project was very large, and the strain was too much for our marriage. We separated, at first. Then divorced – seven years ago. Since then, all our communication has been through third parties – lawyers and business associates.

Clive stared at her. Would she mention what she had revealed just a few days ago? Would she say Leonard had been harassing her for eighteen years? No, he decided. That would be suggesting weakness, giving up power.

—But you were aware that he'd moved into the block? said Markham.

Zöe cast her gaze around the table, and when it settled on Aaron he saw wet glints.

—Yes, I knew he'd come back.

There was a scratch in her voice now too. She gave her head a small shake.

—This block is owned by the local authority, but the leases on a couple of properties are privately owned. This one, and Leonard's, which occupies part of floor thirty and the whole of floor thirty-one. Leonard's owned it since we separated, but he's not lived there, and as far as I know, it's been empty. But he recently moved back in. I found out from a neighbour. He didn't tell me – in person, or by any other means. And why would he? He doesn't have any reason to.

Aaron thought he heard the shuffle of feet under the table.

—Perhaps so he could speak to his sons?

Markham sounded like he was making the observation reluctantly.

—Perhaps, replied Zöe. But he's made no attempt to see them before. He... She seemed to lengthen her neck, level her gaze ... He made it clear that if I insisted he left, he would relinquish his role as their father. I insisted he left.

She paused; expecting a reply, perhaps. Then continued.

—It could be that now they're grown men, as you've described them, he feels he should be in touch. I wouldn't have got in the way, of course.

Zöe looked down suddenly, and put a thumb and finger to the bridge of her nose. The light from the overhead lamp made a pool on the table below her face. A single tear hit the wood with a minute click. Had everyone seen it? Aaron wondered. He was sure they had.

Markham placed his palms flat on the table, then drew them towards himself, almost in a caress.

—And what about these two young coloured girls – Annette and Christine Mayfield?

Zöe looked down the table at Markham. Her eyes were still teary, but her expression was hard. She didn't blink, her eyebrows were still. No, Aaron thought. They were slightly raised.

—My sons would be able to tell you more about them than I can, said Zöe. She approached a slight smile. They've been quite friendly with them this summer.

—I wonder how happy you've been about that? said Markham, his face as impassive as Zöe's.

Zöe looked like she was going to answer, she definitely took a breath. But she let Markham continue.

—It's just that we've been hearing from the older residents that these coloured lasses aren't so popular on the estate. They're putting noses out of joint, bringing in outside elements and troublemakers, that kind of thing…

Zöe's face was suddenly mobile, as if she were fighting a sneeze.

—There have been a few problems with them and their little crowd, yes. The residents' committee has met about it, and one or two members have been to speak to the young ladies. Tried to encourage them to be more, well, neighbourly.

—They live on the thirtieth floor, we're told.

—Yes, they…

Zöe adjusted her position in her seat and addressed her comments to the table in front of her now.

—They live in 304, which is part of Leonard's apartment – officially at least. Alterations were made so the two parts are more like separate flats.

—So they're his tenants?

—Yes. He's their landlord. As far as I know, anyway.

Clive thought Zöe had been trying to make herself difficult to read over the past few moments. And he wondered which parts of what she was saying were approximations of the truth and which were downright lies. Because she wasn't being completely honest. Maintaining this impression of calm control was clearly causing her some distress. It was as if she were experiencing some kind of guilt. Or was it that she could feel his?

But why should he feel guilty? He had to glance at Aaron now. There was nothing to feel guilty about. Leonard had walked off the roof by accident. So was he feeling guilty because of the story Tabitha had invented? Was he guilty over something that hadn't occurred?

But he had lied – they had lied. Was this what Zöe was sensing. Was the scent of their guilt mobilising her defences?

—Have you any idea how they got on, the three of them? said Markham.

—Zöe now pulled a handkerchief from somewhere below the table. The pocket of her smock, Clive thought. It was a small baby-blue square. *ZG* was embroidered in the corner, he knew.

—I really don't know. It was news to me that he'd moved in. And then I heard about these young women who'd move in upstairs and were disturbing their neighbours, but I didn't make the connection. Not until Mrs Ledbury, who's in flat 305, told me they were right next door to her, and she could hear their music. Then I knew they had to be in 304 and couldn't be council tenants – they had to be Leonard's.

—Yes, I spoke to Mrs Ledbury personally, said Markham. Or she spoke to me, I should say. A lady with very strong views. Justified most likely. And she's actually provided us with some very useful information.

Zöe unfolded the handkerchief and placed it flat on the side of her neck.

—That's been much of the problem, you see. If they were

council tenants, we could appeal to them, possibly have the girls moved on. But the council's powers are limited when it comes to private renters. They have so few, you see.

Markham took a loud breath in, caressed the table again, but with just one hand this time.

—So Mr Harrington wasn't in any kind of ... relationship – Markham stretched the word out, almost lewdly – with either of these girls?

Zöe's chin twitched to one side, as if a falling leaf had hit her cheek.

—No one has suggested anything like that to me.

—You might be wondering why we're asking these questions.

—I assume you have to ask about everything, and everyone, Zöe replied, almost snapping back, Clive thought.

—We do, said Markham. And we've been asking everyone up at that party what they saw regarding Mr Harrington. Several people have told us they saw him arguing with the Misses Mayfield – the two coloured girls.

Clive felt something hit his shin. Zöe had kicked a leg out. It wasn't intentional, he was sure. She had slipped down a little in her chair, too, her eyes studying her glass.

—So you see why we're interested. Markham's hand sat in mid-air for a moment. But you've given us some information we can follow up. Thank you for that.

Zöe moved her glass and raised her eyes.

—They were arguing with Leonard? What about?

—We're not sure, Miss Goldsworthy. That's what we'll be asking them.

Aaron wanted some truth in the air. It had become too thick with hints and lures. Everything seemed to be true, but Markham's hands were too active, Zöe's tells too obvious.

—You've arrested them, Aaron said.

He'd intended it to be a leading comment, but it flew across the table to Zöe as a statement.

Markham started nodding and opened his hands, but Zöe spoke before he managed to.

—Arrested them for what?

Clive felt another kick as she drew her legs back and sat up. Markham shifted too, and once again his hands started his reply for him.

—I realise things haven't been good between you and Mr Harrington, but he's still these lads' dad, so I'm telling you this because I think you have a right to know. This isn't official, but in half an hour on that roof we've heard enough to put those two girls in the frame for this.

Aaron couldn't look at Clive. Clive couldn't looked at Aaron. They both turned to Zöe instead. Her head seemed to move with her pulse. She was drawing her chin back, as if she couldn't get away from something putrid.

—You think they pushed him off the roof?

—I'm sorry, Miss Goldsworthy, but that's what it's looking like to us. Now, we're unsure what exactly their reason could be. But this tenant thing might give us some idea. And the fact, as you say, that they've brought trouble and outside elements onto the estate, that could be part of it too. And of course there might be a racial element, as there is so often around here these days.

Clive studied Markham. He seemed to be talking too much now, justifying something, and for a moment this dizzied Clive's head. Did Markham think he knew the truth – or the truth as Tabitha had seen it and had described it to the police? And was Markham now trying to shift the blame away from Aaron and Clive? He almost expected Markham to wink at him: 'Don't worry, boys, we'll pin it on them.'

The table shifted with a loud clack. Zöe had stood up sharply, knocking the edge as she did so.

—I'll get some more water. This jug's almost empty. It's still so hot, and it must be well past midnight.

—Don't trouble yourself, Miss Goldsworthy, said Markham, rising too.

The other officers all stood up, and the room changed, the shadows thrown differently. Zöe stopped in the kitchen doorway and turned around. Clive had to turn to look at her. Aaron saw her face on. The kitchen was bright and against it her long hair fell black and heavy across her shoulders, like a headdress. She held the doorposts with both hands and a nearby table lamp lit her face from below.

—Leonard ... Leonard was a difficult man.

She was immobile apart from her moving lips. It was impossible to tell whether she was gripping the door frame or her raised arms were about to bestow something. For a moment, Aaron expected – was certain – that she was about to tell Markham what she had told him and Clive: that Leonard was obsessed with her to the point of hatred. Worshipped her and detested her in equal measure. And he was sure Markham and his officers, having been in her presence for these few minutes, would understand.

He was wrong though.

—He could be impossible to live with, she said at last. But I can't see a situation in which those young women would do something like that.

Markham stood his fingertips on the tabletop.

—But you said you don't know them, Miss Goldsworthy.

—I don't. I think I've only met them once, briefly.

Her head sank a little, and the shift in shadow made her face look like a theatrical mask.

—They're pleasant young women, by all accounts. Just a little troublesome. Not capable of...

She took one hand from the door post and gestured towards the balcony.

Markham tapped the table sharply.

—We'll take that into consideration. Now, we'll thank you for your hospitality and we'll be off. You've all been very helpful. I don't see this taking too long or being too painful for the three of you. As you're estranged from Mr Harrington, I doubt you'll be needed for much else. I assume there's some other next of kin?

He raised an eyebrow in Zöe's direction.

—Yes. A sister. I have her address.

Clive moved just his eyes to catch Aaron's gaze. An aunt they didn't know of?

—Please give it to the constable here, said Markham.

There was a lot of slow shifting – it seemed to take them several minutes to funnel out of the door. But finally Clive closed it behind the last officer and returned to the living room. Aaron was alone, sitting on the sofa, his gaze focused ahead of him. Clive studied his brother, unsure what he was looking at. Then stepped forwards and caught the reflection of the room. Aaron was studying himself. But then there was movement outside – Zöe on the balcony, leaning against the parapet, gazing out at the night.

Aaron looked up at Clive, and Clive expected his silent question to be 'How are we meant to feel?' But it wasn't.

No such question was in Aaron's mind. He knew how he felt. He blamed Clive. He couldn't quite form the argument, but he glared at him with the shape of it.

I shouldn't have, Aaron thought. I shouldn't have followed him this time.

32

Following Zöe's gaze takes us to the lights of the police cars as they drift through the estate towards Evelyn Street. They move in a small herd, turning off the main road and disappearing under the railway, in the direction of Deptford Police Station.

It's the early hours of the morning now, but it's still warm. The summer of 1976 hasn't relented quite yet. Most of the doors and windows in Marlowe Tower are open. There are plenty of lights on too. Those who were on the roof are awake and enervated. Mrs Ledbury has put on her cotton summer nightie. She presses her ear to the wall adjoining Annette and Christine's flat. On the other side, the police are combing through the twins' things. Above them, two detectives are standing in the middle of Leonard's flat – the single vast room like a pool of grey water. One detective has his arms spread out wide, as if he's enjoying the coolness. The other is staring at the painting. A short upward flight and we see that the roof is deserted now. The police have finished here for the night, leaving only a few chalked dashes. Several pots have been overturned, some earth has been scattered. Something floats in the pool. A bottle. Someone's cardigan is draped over the back of a bench. It will stay there for months, to be picked up by a council worker, finally clearing the dead plants from the roof. He'll notice the greyish marks from the bench's slats, then throw the cardigan in the bin with the tangles of dead tendrils he's pulled off the trellis by the roof's edge.

At the police station it is now 3am. Markham has separated Annette and Christine, of course. And now they are being questioned. One, then the other; then the first again. The officers are confused as to who is who. They suspect each is giving the other's name. But they're not. They're answering honestly. The police don't believe them.

—You can't tell them apart, a detective tells Markham.

—I find it difficult enough as it is, but when you've got them as twins... Markham laughs.

His sergeant laughs. The detective waits for Christine to be taken to a cell, then Annette is brought up to the interrogation room, and the detective walks in and says:

—Which one are you, then?'

—I'm Annette Mayfield, says Annette Mayfield.

Later, the detectives let Annette and Christine see each other in the corridor. Markham and the senior detective watch from the doorway of an office. The WPC taking Christine to her cell has been told to 'have a gossip' with another female officer.

Christine and Annette hold hands for a moment. But they don't speak. They stare at each other. They don't hug, or cry. They blink once in unison. The officers don't notice. The senior detective gives a nod, and the WPC jerks Christine away from her sister.

—Well, I couldn't tell a thing from that, says Markham.

—Cold, say the senior detective. That's what that is. Cold and hard.

In their interviews Annette and Christine answer all the questions put to them. They're clear and polite.

—He's our landlord.

—We've known him, what, a year or two?

—He's a lecturer at our college. He was looking for some reliable tenants. We needed somewhere to live.

—We like the architecture.

—We keep to ourselves, and he keeps to himself, mainly.

—He's invited us up for a drink a couple of times.

—No, nothing like that.

—No, not with my sister either.

—She'd tell me. And I'd know.

—Neither of us was put out. He could be our dad.

—I mean he's our dad's age.

—If he was annoyed about us having friends over, he never said. But he's not home much.

—We did tell him that people had been complaining. We told him about the lady next door – Mrs Ledbury.

—Yes, we know about that. Some people from the committee came to see us. But I don't think we've really disturbed anyone. It's just music. A crowd of people enjoying the weather.

—Maybe because we're new on the estate.

—Maybe people here just don't like seeing black people having a nice time.

—I didn't use that word.

—The roof was Christine's idea at first. Then everyone got involved.

—We all thought it was great. Out of everyone's hair, you know.

—We didn't expect that many people.

—It's fine if everyone wanted to come.

—Yes, we had an argument with him.

—That was the first time. There's been nothing to argue about before.

—About his sons.

—About Aaron and Clive.

—He wouldn't talk to them, and we thought he should.

—No, it's none of our business. But they're our friends. What have they done wrong?

—He's living in the same building.

—It's just a shame. That's what we thought.

—We weren't telling him to speak to her, no.

—I didn't think it was something for him to shout about. But maybe Annette went a bit too far.

—I probably shouldn't have kept on at him. Christine told me to leave it, that he obviously didn't want to hear what I was telling him.

—I said to her to leave it, but it wasn't so bad. Nothing like a big row.

—And then he just exploded.

—He started ranting at the top of his voice, saying he'd already told us no.

—Nothing. We just stood there and took it.

—Yes, it was embarrassing.

—No, we weren't angry. Upset, a little. Not angry, though.

—No, not angry.

—He just dried up in the end. And walked off.

—I don't know where.

—I don't know where.

—No. That was the last time I spoke to him.

—I don't think she saw him again either.

—Neither of us saw him again after that.

—We just tried to forget about it.

—We just went and danced with our friends.

◆

—That's blacks all over though, isn't it? They don't stop talking, but they're not telling you anything, the senior detective says to Markham at 6am.

—And twins too, with that secret language thing. It's a double dose.

—They did it, though.

—No question. We'll get this Mrs Ledbury in to take a proper statement.

33

When, after much rummaging in Zöe's desk, Aaron finds the key attached to a cardboard fob with *LEONARD – 31* written on it in her bold and jagged hand, he first thinks it must open the door into Leonard's flat from flat 304. He almost drops it back in among the mess of keys in the drawer, but hears a voice full of mights and why-nots and give-it-a-trys, pushes the drawer shut, the key still in his hand, and makes his way to the service stairs.

Aaron unlocks the hatch from below, and gives it a hopeful push. It opens and a shower of gritty dust sprinkles onto his face. No one has ever reattached the padlock from above, he thinks. And he realises with a nip of irritation that Leonard must have fixed the padlock there to stop anyone else using his garden.

He climbs through the hatch and looks at the door to flat 31's kitchen, and in the milky, indirect light, spies a lock. He tries the key. And it fits. He ignores the told-you-so that drifts from across the river.

Somehow he expects to see the kitchen – he thinks it was yellow and white, small and unused – then to walk through to the large room that was so like the house in Blackheath. So his brain struggles to reconcile these images with the view that unfolds when the door swings open.

There is no kitchen. And the room is even bigger; there is no wall and door to a bedroom at the far end. Flat 31 is now one large space. There are no dividing walls. No furniture, no carpets. The walls are white, a little grey in the corners. The wooden floor remains, but is covered in a thick sheet of dust. The windows ring the room with Morse code – translucent dots and dashes. A panorama of the city, the distance making everything dishwater blue. Zöe used to say that of her eyes, he thinks. A dishwater blue.

He realises he's still in the doorway, so takes a step inside and is surprised at the flapping echo his shoe makes. The key is still in his hand. Why did Zöe have it? he now wonders. And wanders further into the room.

Leonard must have left this place to her, then. He loathed her, but wanted her to inherit his estate. Even now, Aaron admires her ability to endure such a love. So at some point, she owned flat 304 too, he thinks. Yet Annette and Christine are back, living there. He can't make this stack up without instant collapse.

The stairs, he thinks. The stairs down to 304. This is where he intended to eavesdrop. But there is nothing, no banister, and the floor of the big room is uninterrupted – a calm of dust. He tries to work out where the stairs must have been. He judges a line down the centre of the room, above the corridor below; the position of 304. Here must be 305, Mrs Ledbury, dead thirty years nearly. So here is 304. The front door. Two steps. The stairs.

He looks at his feet, and realises he has left a trail of footprints in the dust, from the door to where he now stands.

A ripple of guilt travels through his chest. It's a familiar feeling. But on whose property is he trespassing. Could it be his own? Clive's? Who does flat 31 belong to now? Very few people even knew of its existence. Yet the trail of footprints is so very clear, the marks he's left so distinct, he considers somehow scuffing them away. But that's impossible, he'll only leave new marks. Unless he brings a broom up here and sweeps and sweeps. For half a year, he thinks.

—Stupid fool, he murmurs.

And with his foot he starts to brush away the dust. He glances at the walls again to judge he's roughly in the right place. And there. A clear line in the wood – cutting through the boards. It extends feet – yards. On one side the elegant parquet Leonard must have had laid, on the other a piece of cheap chipboard, set in the floor where the stairs once descended to flat 304.

He hesitates for a moment. Looks over his shoulder at the stuttered view from the line of windows on the river side of the room. Can he see Clive's tower? Not without walking over.

He braces himself, chooses to bend his good leg and crouches down. It's painful, his knee on the hard floor, but he lowers himself further, hands planted in the dust. And at last he manages to place his ear to the floor.

Voices instantly hit his eardrum. He expected to wait, doubled over. Expected to struggle to hear anything at all. But it's as if he's tuned in to a song mid-verse. Three voices harmonising. Two humming, low, above them a staccato descant. A pause. Then that snigger. A full-throated laugh. Then words he can distinguish.

—We said that.

—Yes, we said that.

He gropes back in time. He's sure the voices are familiar. It has to be Annette and Christine talking. But how did they really sound? The memory feels perished, and he can't tell which is which, who is who.

Footsteps now, a rush of water.

—As we told you, we own this place, you see.

He has suspected this since finding their flat door closed, since seeing them return from the meeting.

—Well, Aaron owns his too, doesn't he?

His name has taken form in the room. A drop condensing as it falls.

Tabitha. Without a doubt.

There's movement and he can't make out anything else for a long stretch.

But then they're directly below him. They're saying their goodbyes.

—It was nice seeing you again and catching up properly.

Tabitha. Just feet away from his ear.

—You too. And thank you again. For your honesty, I mean.

—Yes, thanks from both of us.

Tabitha sniggers at that.

—Well, you let me know what you girls are going to do.

—We will.

—We will.

—I'll love you and leave you.

—Take care on the way down.

The flat door opens. A tap of shoes on the floor of the corridor. Aaron pushes himself up. He's on his hands and knees. Dust clings to his jumper and jeans; wisps irritate his ear, trickle down his cheek. He needs to speak to Tabitha. He needs to know what she's told Annette and Christine, what honesty they were thanking her for. What they are going to do.

He hears a clang. The sound of the door to the stairwell swinging shut. She's walking down already. By the time he staggers up, gets to the back stairs then down a couple of floors, through the next chute room and to the main stairwell, she'll be way ahead of him. And his knee will never allow him to run down the stairs, taking two steps at a time.

But there is another option. One Clive sometimes employed to win the stair game. It involved a clever bit of strategy that Aaron never quite mastered. You had to get to the twenty-eighth floor without the other person catching you. And then you could pass your opponent with ease. He'll be downstairs waiting for Tabitha when she emerges from the ground floor.

He lurches across the room, leaving scudding marks in the dust, and stumbles down the back stairs, breathless now in his rush. He has to stop for a moment. His arms and legs are weak. The excitement has sapped his strength and he's not kept track of the flights. He has to look upwards, count the turns of the stairs. He's on floor twenty-nine. So two more flights. He takes them more carefully, and is out through the chute room and into another empty corridor of open doors, a lattice of light thrown across the floor. He walks straight through it towards the lift, the cross beams catching his ankles, and pulls at the long grille set into the wall

beside the lift doors. Somewhere here a catch, a tiny lever – there.
He flicks it up, and the grille swings open with a whine. Behind it
there's three feet of space, and then a panel. Another door, like in
the chute rooms, with a press-release catch. Aaron has to jiggle it
and dig his nails into the edge to get it open. And when he does,
he reveals a barrel-shaped space, the floor and ceiling descending
in a curve away from him.

The slide.

It was one of a few secrets that Zöe intended to share. The other
hidden passages and backways were easy to slip into the estate's
design without attracting too much attention from the construction team. But quietly inserting a spiral of metal tubing
around the lift shaft for twenty-eight floors required cooperation
from plenty of people. 'I want it to be a surprise,' Zöe had said.
'This tower is as much a playground as it is a building full of
homes.' Her plan was to reveal it once all the first tenants had
moved in and had been using the lift, unaware of its existence.
'Architecture should be full of moments of delight,' she said.
They'd used a separate firm to install the tube, bringing them in
after the main build and obfuscating over questions from various
contractors about the extra space around the lift shaft.

But Deptford Council got wind. And before a single tenant
had moved in, had instructed that the slide should be sealed up.
So of all the tower's residents, only Zöe, Aaron and Clive knew
of its existence; where it was, and how to open the hidden access
points Zöe had quietly had inserted.

Aaron has removed his shoes and has one leg inside the tube
now. He can feel the polished metal through his jeans, still slick
after all these years. He remembers to sit sideways so he can pull
his other leg in and hold on to the lip of the tube while he prepares
himself for the descent. The tube is dark. There are lights in the
ceiling, but they were never connected to the tower's electricity
circuits, so all the rides he and Clive took were through the pitch-
black, a grey glow appearing as they shot through the final yards.

He feels a faint upward draught, the open grille and door pulling the stale air out of the tube. He smells dinners. No one but him has dined in the tower for months. He corrects himself: Annette and Christine must have. He glances at his watch. It's three minutes since Tabitha left 304. He clutches his shoes to his chest, aims his socked feet downwards and pushes off.

His button cheeps against the metal and the zip of his jacket clatters at his side. He's accelerating, trying to keep his body slim and straight – a soft missile. The air passing over his face is almost warm, oddly humid. The memory of a laugh stretches in his belly. He recalls Clive's giggles ringing out as he slipped away.

This ride seems long. Longer than he remembers. It seemed too short back then. Just when the constant turning, the clockwise curl that was forced upon you, became familiar, you were out, your body a jumble.

He and Clive had taken the ride together a few times – always Clive in front, between Aaron's legs, gripping his knees while Aaron gripped his shoulders. The double weight had felt dangerous. They'd shot up the side and bounced down again, their two bodies not connected enough, not one. Individual slides were better, they agreed.

But Clive will never do this again. Can never do this.

Aaron's throat tightens – an effect of the speed, the turning, the sliding?

And then he's out of the pitch-black, the grey grows and he's crumpled, shoulders pinched, against the curve of thick foam that serves as a crash pad. He can't see the grand puff of dust his impact makes, but he can feel it raining down him, and he begins to cough. He's dazed and something hurts. The crimped position isn't good. He shuffles himself around until he's in a sitting position, and waits for a moment, listening. And he realises he's listening for the whisper and clang of Clive coming down behind him.

But there is no Clive. Not on this side of the river.

Tabitha.

The thought has been knocked out of his head. He grasps at it and staggers to his feet, then scrabbles along the wall until he finds the wood of the panel and opens it, emerging on the entrance floor beside the lift.

He pulls his shoes on, listening again, for Tabitha's footsteps this time. He hears them, still a little way above. Confident but a little stuttered. Where to meet her? Right here? She'll see him from a few stairs up. She'll stop and he'll have to crane his neck. Outside seems better. In the grey air. If he waits by the main steps, he'll catch her whether she takes the main entrance or comes out through the service door.

But once he's pushed through the door and limped down the big steps onto the forecourt of Marlowe Tower, he decides to scurry round behind them. An ambush? Or is he scared? He's shaking and his knee pulses with pain. He has to steady himself against the back of the open treads of the steps.

The door above opens. Bangs shut. Tabitha's shoes appear above him. He watches them taking each step. Her ankles in grey tights. At the bottom she turns, about to take the path between the hoardings.

And he steps out, hands outstretched, stopping her.

—Oh my godfathers...

She steps back, turns with a hand to her chest, bends a little, looking at the ground.

Aaron drops his hands. He can't tell if she's acting or if she's really in difficulty. Her face is lined, he sees. Like his.

But then she straightens up. Her expression is still young. The reddish hair is dyed and styled, and looks like a hat she's put on to provoke a laugh.

—Fucking hell, Aaron, you could've killed me, jumping out like that.

The giggle she adds is a tic, not amusement.

—What are you doing, hiding behind there? she says.

—I wanted to speak to you.

There's no pump behind his voice. The words seem puffed out of an empty paper bag. He's not spoken to anyone other than himself for days.

—Well, you could've just said 'Oi, Tabby', rather than jump out on me like that.

Aaron coughs. Dust from the thirty-first floor, from the slide, from the crash mat, has caught in his throat. But the coughing doesn't help, and it doubles and trebles. It's in his chest now, spasms.

—You all right? Tabitha is saying. Sit down on the step. There.

She's beside him, her hand on him. The little thrust of a human's touch, guiding him by the elbow, pushing him down so his knees bend and he's seated. The step is gritty and cold. He's below Tabitha now. She's standing in front of him, looking down. What he didn't want.

—Better? I'd give you something to drink, only I ain't got nothing.

He looks up at her. From below the plump of her cheeks is jowly, her neck in folds.

—You've just come from seeing them, he says.

—Who's that, then?

She looks to the side and back. Her mouth describes a swift circle – making her nose switch back and forth. Is it a new tic she's developed?

—Annette and Christine. Who else?

—Who else lives here? she says.

—Only me. And them, now.

Tabitha's face is still for a moment, but her eyes move, from his face to the tower, the sky; then her mouth and eyebrows join in. She's made a decision:

—So you know they've moved back in, then? she asks.

—I've seen them yes, and...

He has another, smaller, coughing fit, and when he looks up he

sees that Tabitha has stepped away from him, almost as if she's
telling him she's leaving, that she shouldn't talk to him, shouldn't
reveal what she knows. But he can see her hesitation. Her feet are
too heavy. Temptation is too strong for her. It always was. They all
knew that about her.

—How did you know they'd come back? he asks, standing up.

Her body turns back towards him, her mouth describes another
circle so he can see the snigger coming. It propels her words.

—Well, I met them, didn't I? Because of all this.

She nods at the broken buildings around them.

—Everyone that used to live on here, all of us as got chucked
out, we've been meeting. Trying to getting compensation and all
that. I hadn't seen the twins in years. Not since all that...

Her mouth and eyes perform a new trick, a squeezed blink –
her lips lids.

—It's forty years, you know, Aaron.

She leaves a long pause, as if he's been stupidly unaware of the
passing of time.

—They're still the same, though. Don't look their age at all. But
they say that about blacks, don't they? Don't age like us. Must be
nice.

Aaron could interrupt, could prick her on. But she's talking like
she always did. Singing all the parts so you can't quite make out
the melody.

—But you know what surprised me...?

She pauses. Expecting him to say no, he didn't know what
surprised her. He doesn't.

—They've owned that flat all this time. And the council has
offered to buy it off them. And I said I never knew you owned
that place. And they said, well they didn't, not when they lived
there when we knew them. But after ... well, all that, your mum
gave it to them.

She stops. Looks at him, her head crooked purposefully,
properly smiling now, but not showing her teeth. Did you know

that? she seems to say. Cos I did. Aaron strains to keep his face straight, strains not to reveal his confusion.

—They've been renting it out ever since, she says. Money coming in for them. But they've still lived together all this time, you know. Not like you and Clive, eh? Bet you can't imagine living with him your whole life, can you?

She takes a step forwards. Another. It's an advance, an attack impending.

—They were furious they said, when they found out it was him.

Aaron twitches, knows his mouth has dropped open.

—His company buying the tower, you know...

She looks pleased that she's made him jump, then calmed him down.

—It's like a slap in the face, after everything, she says. Why does he want to do that? He's not lived here in forty years.

She folds her arms so the straps of the bag she's carrying are entwined between them. It swings heavily at her waist.

—Was it you? she asks.

Aaron sags into the step, as if she's jabbed a finger into his chest. But she's standing back a little, studying him, and he's not sure whether her last question is part of what she and Annette and Christine said to each other, or is directed at him.

—I've not spoken to Clive in forty years, myself, he says. The only contact we've had is through letters to lawyers and what-not.

—That's what I said. As far as I know, Aaron's just stayed there in his mother's flat all this time, while Clive's been off everywhere. We've not seen hide nor hair of him round here. And Aaron's left by himself in the tower now, I said. I reckon he's refusing to sell. Because it's his brother.

She raises her folded arms and shoulders a little, then settles them back in place again.

—That's what I said, she says.

He nods. He's hardly spoken to her in all these years, but she seems to have been inside his life.

—Clive's doing it because of Mum, Aaron says. He doesn't believe what she believed anymore. He thinks it's naïve, short-sighted. He thinks private enterprise has to be involved in social housing. He's written magazine articles about it.

Tabitha frowns slightly.

—I don't know about all that. But Annette and Christine, they said they're not selling to the council, not if it's his company that'll benefit. Not after everything. And they know all about all this stuff. So Clive better watch out. They're not taking no prisoners on this one. Not again.

They hold each other's gaze for a second. Aaron knows the blow will come soon. A real attack. He could simply ask her: 'Did you tell them what you think you saw? Did you say you saw us push our father off the roof? Did you keep up the lie?' But he can't manage it. He thinks she'll offer it herself. He thinks he can trust her need to tell him.

—But why move back in? he says.

—Why have you stayed? Tabitha snaps back. Why don't you take the money and leave?

Because Clive didn't come and ask me. Because he had it so wrong and won't admit it. Because he made us lie back then when I wanted to tell the truth. Because I should have done what I thought was right, no matter what he did. Because he betrayed me.

—I don't know, he says. Spite?

—Cos he's made it big and you've done nothing with your life? Aaron isn't surprised at this swipe.

—That too.

He looks away, and she seems to take the chance to get the real jab in.

—I told them what happened that night, she says.

Aaron wants to sit down, but he's already sitting. He needs more support. Needs to lie down. But even that won't be enough.

—What you *thought* happened, he says. As if it's something he's told her many times.

—I've kept it to myself for years, Aaron. And I expected to be treated right in return. So this whole thing... she twists round, unfolds her arms and gestures to the tower, making her bag swing wildly ...and knocking down the rest of the estate. Putting us out of our homes, where we've lived our whole lives, some of us, that's not right. I didn't keep no secrets so yous could do that to me.

—I haven't done anything to you. This is all Clive.

—You, Clive, whatever. I've told Annette and Christine what I saw, and whatever they decide to do about it, that's up to them.

—What you thought you saw.

Aaron places his hands either side of his body on the gritty step. He needs to steady himself. He leans against the step behind. The edge seems to bite through his jacket and shirt.

—I know what I saw, Aaron.

Tabitha has raised her voice suddenly. He's never heard her speak like this. It's always been a noisy flow. Never this staccato shout.

—I saw you and that twin of yours shove him off that roof.

And she pierces the marbled sky with an outstretched finger.

—Your own dad, for fuck's sake.

—It was an accident. He just walked off it. You were standing there, behind the trellis. You said you saw us push him, but you can't have. He just walked off by himself.

—I didn't see nothing like that.

She's quick and sharp, her voice more tempered now.

—He walked off the roof. By himself. He must have been confused – it was so dark up there and we were arguing with him. He was looking for our mum and went in the wrong direction. He just stepped off. By himself. We didn't touch him. Well, we touched him, but we didn't push him. And then we turned around, and you were there saying we had pushed him, that you'd seen us do it.

Tabitha doesn't snigger – she laughs, her tiny mouth almost square.

—What are you talking about, Aaron? You're not making any
sense. You're in denial, you are. I remember what I saw. Clear as if
it was yesterday. I saw you two push him. And then you saw me
looking through that trellis thing. And I said I wouldn't say
nothing. Well now I have.

—But it was an accident. He just walked off!

Aaron's shout hurts his throat. He slaps his palms on the steps.
Once, twice, three times. So he can feel the pain.

Tabitha is undisturbed by his noise. She shakes her head.

—I've told Annette and Christine the truth. I told them what
you two did that night. And they know you let them take the fall
for it.

Aaron's limbs feel weak, his legs not strong enough to hold
themselves upright. His knees splay, his heels slip off the step. He
lets his head fall forwards, his chin resting on his chest.

When he raises it again, Tabitha has stepped a few feet away,
her arms at her sides, feet slightly apart, as if braced.

—You didn't say anything for years either, though, says Aaron.
Why?

—Cos I'm not a grass. We were never big mates, me and you
and Clive, but I wasn't about to go to the law about you.

Tabitha looks less confident now. He sees his chance.

—But what about Annette and Christine? What about your
aunt? As I recall it was a lot of what she said that made the police
arrest them. Why didn't you speak up then, if you knew it was
us?

—Everyone saw that argument. It wasn't just Aunt Het. And
she never said she saw them actually do anything.

—You know she told the police a lot more than that. She stood
up in court and said it, for God's sake.

Tabitha is uncomfortable now. She lets her bag swing down to
her side, arms loose.

—She was their neighbour. She only said what she'd seen going
on next door, and all that.

—There was a lot more than that. She wanted to make as much trouble as she could for those two. You know she did.

—No I don't. Your memory's going, Aaron. Why would she do that, anyway?

—You know why.

—If you're going to say she was racist...

—I am, Tabitha. And she was. Her and everyone else around here back then. They hated Annette and Christine even being here.

Tabitha looks sulky now. Aaron can see the teenager he knew.

—Well, they didn't help themselves, did they?

—How can you say that? You loved being with them. We all did. And they didn't do anything we didn't do. But they were black. And people wanted to keep this estate white.

Tabitha doesn't reply. Aaron leaves a long gap – enough for her to fill. But it seems she has nothing to fill it with.

—Even Deptford Council were in on it.

Tabitha looks as if she's about to object, but Aaron won't let her.

—They were, and you know they were. That bloody residents' association used to go on about it all the time. Not just about Annette and Christine, but after them, when any black family moved to the estate: 'The council told us they'd keep our estate for local people. We've been given assurances.' The council said they wanted to avoid 'social friction'. They did the same up in Bermondsey and Rotherhithe. Why do you think the National Front was so big around here? And then the British National Party, and now—

—Now everyone's moved. All my relatives live down Sidcup.

Aaron's eyes find the gable end of the long, eight-storey block nearby. Its front faces the river with gaping, toothless windows. Behind him, more blocks. The ones that are still occupied are on the other side of the estate, so here it's just the two of them. And Annette and Christine, high above. He wonders if they're looking down at them. He leans back, gazes up. The bright grey is too bright.

He looks back at Tabitha. It feels like they've stopped fighting.

—You can't say that your aunt wasn't racist, Tabitha. Why else would she purposely finger Annette and Christine?

Tabitha's head jerks to one side and her shoulder rises.

—And all that time you said nothing, says Aaron. Whether you saw us push him, or you saw what really happened – that he fell off by accident – why didn't you say something? Why didn't you save Annette and Christine? Is it because me and Clive are white and they're black? Are you racist too, Tabitha?

—No. Course not. How can I be racist? I've got black neighbours. Black mates. Mixed cousins, and nieces and nephews.

Her pout makes her look older rather than younger.

—And what did Annette and Christine say about you keeping what you call the truth to yourself all these years? Why did you let them take the fall, when you knew full well they didn't push him off.

He gets up, his strength returning, but his limbs stiff from sitting on the concrete steps. He take the three steps down so he's beside her. She raises her shoulders and takes a step away, but only so she can swing round with renewed energy.

—Why did *you*? You and Clive let them take the fall just as much as me. And now Annette and Christine know it.

She takes two more strides away. Swings back again.

—So watch out, cos they're angry, those two. And they aren't going anywhere.

She's heading for the path between the hoardings along the avenue now.

—Go and speak to them yourself, if you like.

When she reaches the path, she stops.

—But you won't, will you? You're too scared.

Her face forms its customary smirk.

—S'pose you'll just have to ask Clive to do it.

She lets out a brief snigger and walks away.

34

From above, Deptford Strand Estate is tawny squares of burned-up grass sitting between concrete bleached to ash by weeks of sun. Here and there is a sad grey-green tree top, almost ready to give up its fight against the drought.

No one sits on the deck by the river anymore. Annette and Christine's group don't dare return without them. The older people who spent a few evenings there before the party have found other things to do. Not many people use the town square, either. The day after the party the council drained the pool, telling the residents it was part of their drought measures.

If we dip down and pass between the blocks lining the avenue, we see most people inside, waiting for the sun to finish. 'We need a drop of rain now,' they say to each other across the divides between their balconies, or on the stairs and in the lifts. 'We've all had enough of this,' they agree.

If we linger while they lean towards each other, though, we might hear them take the subject away from the weather. 'You've heard about those two coloured girls, I suppose.' That's how the discussion begins. 'Pushed some fella off the roof of Marlowe, they did.' No one says 'some bloke fell'. It's always that two black girls pushed him.

—Well, that's the end of them, then. They won't be coming back here.

The woman standing next to Tabitha's mother outside the launderette says this. They're waiting for their washes to finish. The machines make it too hot inside, so there is a row of women outside, leaning against the window, smoking. Tabitha's mother pulls on her cigarette and watches a man from the council standing in the now-dry pool, fiddling with a drain cover. She doesn't reply, nod in agreement or even look at the woman beside her. Perhaps she's heard too much from her aunt and from Tabitha about this.

Someone else eventually nods and agrees.

—You see what happens when you start mixing. It always ends up with trouble. I've nothing against them myself. I'm sure some of them are very nice people. But in my book, we're better off living apart.

—I've got something against them, says an older woman. She's dragged a plastic chair into the doorway, which means no one can get in or out.

The women chuckle gently.

If we now flap away – irritated, uncomfortable and reminded – we might find ourselves sweeping across the river. And in minutes, seconds, words, we are in north London, on Camden Road. Holloway Prison is brand new still – red bricks and big windows.

Annette and Christine share a cell. They have been quiet, calm and compliant. Except for during their first few nights, when they were apart – given beds in separate cells, on separate corridors. A simple decision based on empty spaces on a blackboard.

They both banged on their doors that first night. Annette fought her cell mate over it. Christine fought hers. 'I want my sister,' they both said, shouted, screamed. The second night they banged again. Annette barked the knuckles of her right hand, Christine those of her left.

The wing governor heard the noise as she was locking her office door. She put her head into the duty office and raised her eyebrow.

—New inmates, ma'am. The mad black twins. Screaming to see each other. Two nights they've kept this up for.

—And in the day?

—Well, they see each other then, so they calm down.

—No trouble otherwise?

—Good as gold when they're together, ma'am.

—Then put them in a cell together. We've one free now, I see.

The wing governor placed her finger on the board – two spaces next to each other in a square. The two guards don't reply.

—Yes, it's giving in. But weigh it against this for weeks and months on end.

The guards don't know it, but the wing governor is a twin herself.

From that moment on, Annette and Christine's behaviour is impeccable. They appear for roll call in the mornings, do the work assigned them. Eat their meals. Smile sometimes, if it oils the moment. It's been a few weeks now, and they've become popular with the other inmates. They've been forgiven the first two nights. Been forgiven the concession. 'They're twins,' everyone says. 'You can't split up twins.' The guards notice a little group of women sitting in the twins' cell with them during association. A cluster round the door.

But what do they say to each other, in their cell, alone? If we come back here later, when they lie on the same bunk together for a few minutes before sleep, what will we hear? The window is open – it's the last hot night of summer. And, anyway, we can slip through the bars and hover up by the ceiling light, watch and wait in the blue prison dim. They're talking, they're murmuring. It's a long conversation. Annette makes her point, Christine hers. There are questions, it seems, opinions, explorations. But none of it seems to reach our ears. Perhaps, after all, we can't hear everything. And if we could, perhaps we wouldn't understand. Perhaps these words are not for us.

◆

The rain comes, of course, and washes Clive away. It pours for the entire week before he leaves for university.

Aaron is standing on the balcony. Clive comes out to say

goodbye. They hug. Clive says he'll miss Aaron. Aaron says he'll miss Clive. Zöe is in the living room, watching through the glass. The door is closed, and she seems to be trying to read their lips.

Aaron stays on the balcony and is watching when the Citroën leaves down the access road. He's still there a few moments later when it turns onto Evelyn Street. And he's still there two hours later, when the Citroën returns. It's as if no time has passed at all – or an endless blank moment has elapsed. He's hardly moved, he's hardly blinked. But when the car pulls into the parking space, he leans over the parapet and looks down.

Zöe doesn't get out. She's sitting behind the wheel, still, staring straight ahead, her eyes unfocused. She turns her head and looks at the deck. Her eyes flick around, taking in a corner of a building, the angle of the walkway as it meets Marlowe Tower, then she sits forwards a little, gripping the steering wheel, staring at the tower in front of her. She sits back and looks down into her lap, biting her lips and tapping the wheel with a flutter of fingers. Finally she sighs, and drags herself and her bag out of the car.

Inside the lift, she presses the button for floor twenty-four. But, pausing for a second with her hand still raised, she presses the button for floor thirty.

Floor thirty has so much more light than twenty-four. It seems blown in in bigger, billowing sheets. Zöe is wearing clogs. Their clack on the floor tiles is incredibly loud. She stops, perhaps considering whether to slip them off. She walks on to the door of flat 304. From flat 305 comes the rhythm of a voice. It continues in an uninterrupted flow. Mrs Ledbury is listening to the radio. But then the sound stops abruptly. Zöe stands looking at the door to 304. Her hand is in her handbag. She is about to pull something out, when the door to 305 opens.

Mrs Ledbury has a head full of rollers again. As if she can only appear at her door with them in. They are arranged haphazardly this time, not her usual rows of pink and blue.

—Hello, love.

Mrs Ledbury usually calls Zöe 'Mrs Goldsworthy' – always forgetting it's 'Miss'. Zöe hesitates with her mouth open, as if shocked to be addressed in such a familiar way. Or perhaps it's a look of guilt. Her hand is still in her bag.

—What are you doing up here, then?

Mrs Ledbury settles against the doorpost, and the door swings gently against her shoulder.

Zöe musters an 'I'. Then pulls her hand out of her handbag. Mrs Ledbury nods at the door to 304 and says:

—Sorry about all that ... you know.

Zöe nods and wrestles her face into a smile.

—Why don't you come in for a bit? says Mrs Ledbury. I'll put the kettle on.

Zöe seems reluctant. She looks back at the door to 304, as Mrs Ledbury steps back inside, clearly expecting her to follow. Zöe looks at her feet. The clogs are decorated with pineapples – one on each big toe.

—I really need to go in here. I have to, you know, check through his flat.

Mrs Ledbury crooks her head.

—I know what it's like, losing your husband.

—We'd not spoken in eighteen years. Not since the boys were born.

Mrs Ledbury leaves a pause, in respect for the falling-out it seems.

—Still, he was your husband, wasn't he? At one time. The father of your boys. That still counts for something, even after all these years.

—It's made things very complicated, says Zöe.

—Complicated sounds like the least of it. I mean, he was living up there. She points to the ceiling. But sort of with them – she twitches her head towards 304. It doesn't seem right. He...

She stops herself. Watches Zöe, then starts again.

—I didn't even know there was anything upstairs. No one did. We just thought it was storage or what-not, and then the roof.

Who knew there was a whole other flat up there, and someone living in it all this time?

—Well, I'd better get on with this, Mrs Ledbury.

Zöe's smile is slight, but Mrs Ledbury accepts it.

—You take care of those boys of yours. And yourself, of course, she says, and she backs into her flat, her rollered head last to disappear as the door closes.

When Zöe is inside 304, she takes a moment to work out which is the door to the upper storey. She has not been here in a very long time. She climbs the stairs and stops at the top, her hand resting on the banister rail, slowly turning her head to take in the whole room, all its objects, all its air. She pauses on the large painting. Her face, impassive until now, droops a little, a slumped sadness. She takes a few steps around the room. Her lips are moving. The words she mutters are addressed, perhaps, to the painting, perhaps to the floor, perhaps to the furniture she glances at as she passes, but all are meant, it's clear, for Leonard.

She has a simple question:

—What happened? she says. And again: What happened?

She flicks her eyes towards the painting, as if it's from where Leonard's reply might come.

—I'm sure the police have it all wrong. But I can't show them how it's wrong if I don't know what really happened. So I need to know what really happened. Because whatever really happened, I'm sure it's our fault. Our fault to correct.

She stops walking and lurches towards the painting.

—But you're not fucking here, are you? So it's down to me to … correct this. But how can I if I don't know?

She glares at the thick, ruckled paint, as if affronted by its silence. She turns her back on it and heads for a window. Stares at something for a moment. The plump grey dome of St Paul's is within her vision; the red dash of a distant bus sliding along towards Surrey Docks. She drops her head, directing her words behind her.

—I didn't just build a place, I built a world. So if something goes wrong in it, isn't it up to me to fix it? Especially when...

She puts her hands on the windowsill.

—You'd give me that 'God-complex' stuff, I know. But ... but...

She turns once again and surveys the whole room.

—I don't believe it was the girls. And I can't believe it was our boys – can I?

She's halfway across the room again, her eyes beseeching.

—And if I can, then I have to do something, don't I? I have to.

It seems she waits for a long time – as if truly expecting the layers of paint to shift and the answers to her questions to be daubed across the dusty floors.

And then she turns and heads back down the stairs.

At their foot, she doesn't really straighten up – she maintains the slight crouch and careful steps we all take when descending a staircase. With this stance she enters each room in flat 304, one of her hands always raised to her cheek, her lips, her hair, as if she fears discovering some little beast under a bed or behind a chair.

She scans every inch of the flat. She takes her time, observing every detail. And every object she comes across is touched – lightly, respectfully, even; the tips of her fingers brush everything. She caresses the spines of the books on the shelves in the bedrooms and living room, crooking her head to read their titles. She riffles through the records beside the record player. She opens the kitchen cupboards, and examines the tins and jars, turning the labels to face the front so she can read them. And finally, at the end of her exploration, she stands in the hallway and breathes in deeply through her nose, her eyes closed.

And then she leaves – carefully, cautiously.

Like a thief.

35

Clive came back to Deptford for Christmas. He got off the bus, with his heavy bag, at the stop in Evelyn Street and wished he'd not brought so many books back with him.

But at the bottom of the steps of the footbridge leading to the walkway, he met Aaron. They both stopped. He dropped his bag. They smiled, weakly. Aaron raised his hand and placed it on Clive's shoulder. It felt heavier to Clive than before. Aaron's hair was longer. He was wearing a winter coat, but his shirt was unbuttoned so Clive could see the speckle of hair across his sternum.

—What, are you a hippy now? Clive said.

—Maybe. Not sure yet.

They each took a handle of the bag and climbed the stairs in an odd, mis-articulated stagger.

—It's punk now, you know, said Clive. You're already out of fashion.

Aaron didn't reply. Clive was ahead of him, two steps up, and as they reached the flat of the walkway, the bag stretched out between them, making Aaron stumble up the last few steps, he pulled forwards, arm outstretched.

Clive looked back and stopped.

—Sorry.

Aaron shook his head, but when Clive began to move off again, he didn't follow. Clive felt the tug of the bag and turned, his face a thick frown.

—They're still in prison, you know, said Aaron.

Clive started walking again. Aaron had to follow or drop the bag.

They didn't speak all the way to Marlowe Tower. Clive had known Aaron would do this. He'd managed to ignore the conversation all the time he'd been away. But now he was back, and Aaron wouldn't let him ignore it. Because Aaron couldn't. Because Aaron was paralysed by it, and wanted Clive to start him moving again.

But Clive didn't think he could. He didn't even think he wanted to. Because if he did, he'd have to consider the things he hadn't had to consider for three months.

He broke the silence in the lift.

—What have you been doing, then?

Aaron let three floors pass.

—Not much. There's not much to do.

And this was how Christmas passed. Clive and Zöe had their inevitable argument. But it wasn't over some challenge Clive made to Zöe's architectural ethos, as they had both expected it would be – it was over Aaron.

—Why are you letting him do nothing with himself? Clive asked one day when Aaron was out.

—Because he needs time.

—To do what?

—To decide what he wants to do.

—You've changed your tune. You've been on at him to find something to focus on for years.

—Don't cheek me, Clive. And anyway, everything's changed, hasn't it?

—I'm still getting on with it, though. He should too.

—He's not you, though, is he?

Clive felt as if the balcony door had blown open. Cold December air, ready to raise gooseflesh on his arms. But it was closed. And Aaron was out. And Clive didn't know where. Because Aaron left without telling him. And Clive wanted to cry. Someone was clutching at his throat.

Zöe's face melted, and Clive was in her arms.

◆

Aaron tried to talk to Clive, but what he wanted to say and what Clive wanted to hear were now too different – two different – things.

—They're in Holloway, he said.

Clive didn't know this, but he tried to make his expression look like he did.

To Aaron, Clive looked like he was drinking milk that was on the turn.

—I keep seeing Tabitha, he said.

—Well, she lives here, doesn't she? replied Clive.

Aaron could feel him shaking.

But Aaron couldn't ever take a second step, ask a second question. He knew why. He'd never had to take second steps alone before. He'd always had the first confirmed before he'd taken another. Either that, or he'd been led. And Clive was refusing either to lead or encourage him further. So Aaron stayed standing where he was. Sitting. Lying. Leaning on the balcony wall, watching the buses pass along Evelyn Street.

On Boxing Day, however, Aaron managed to provoke something more from Clive.

—I want to write to them, he said.

Clive snapped his head up from the building plans he was looking at. The tape sticking their seams together was yellow and brittle.

—What the hell do you want to do that for? Are you an idiot or what?

He glanced at Zöe and managed to dam the flow before it was too late. Managed to bite back 'Everyone thinks it was them. Why do you want to spoil that?'

But Zöe twisted round. She looked from Clive to Aaron and back again, her nose pointing at them.

Aaron tasted salt on his tongue. Clive had finally engaged. But Zöe was here. It was bad planning. He had no idea how to proceed now.

—Who do you want to write to?

Zöe looked at Clive as she said it, as if she was confused between her twins. She had never been confused between her twins.

—Annette and Christine, said Aaron.

Zöe sighed through her nose, and turned back to her book.

—I don't think that's a good idea, she said.

◆

Clive didn't come home for the Easter break.

Aaron hadn't offered to visit him at all since he'd been away, and Clive hadn't invited him. They didn't write to each other. They didn't even speak on the phone. When Clive called – which was about once a week – Zöe would chat for a few minutes, then take the handset from her ear and hold it towards Aaron, the coiled lead bouncing leisurely.

—It's Clive. Do you want to say something?

Aaron would twist out a movement halfway between a shrug and a head-shake.

In Clive's first term away, Zöe had insisted that Aaron spoke to him.

—Talk to your brother, she'd say, and shake the handset at him.

But after |the Christmas break she gave up. In the spring term, she would simply put the phone back to her ear and start quizzing Clive about his professors.

Aaron did want to speak to Clive, though. And Clive knew, by his refusal to come to the phone, that he was burning to have the discussion Clive was avoiding. So Clive stayed away at Easter. Aaron was disappointed, but it was a blunt pain – a dull blade pushing against thickened skin.

◆

In May, Aaron sent Clive a letter. He kept it short. He didn't say what he thought Clive should do. He didn't try to persuade him of anything. He wrote just a greeting, and signed it 'love Aaron x'. And between was a single line:

Their trial starts tomorrow.

He used a first-class stamp and posted it from the post office on Evelyn Street, to ensure it arrived the following day, to ensure 'tomorrow' was accurate. To ensure Clive felt the right amount of apprehension.

There was a time when a touch of the elbow would have sufficed.

◆

Clive opened the letter from Aaron in his room the next morning. He generally ripped through envelopes while standing beside his pigeon hole, reading the letters while he climbed the stairs. But he recognised Aaron's handwriting – careful and neat; he never joined up – and slipped the letter between two books, as if he needed to hide it from someone.

Once he'd read the letter's one line, he made a decision within thirty seconds. Tutorials and lectures were coming to an end. He could revise at home. Zöe had many of the key texts on her shelves. There was a family emergency. His twin needed him. It was an easy sell.

His tutor seemed unable to inhabit his suit – his neck and wrists wandered around inside it. He nodded at Clive, signed a chit and handed it to him, saying that he hoped everything would sort itself out in a favourable way.

Clive could have called from the payphones in the hall, opposite the pigeon holes. He could have called from the station.

From King's Cross. Instead he let himself into flat 246 expecting to have to explain his surprise return. But the flat was empty.

Clive put his bag in his room, then checked the whole flat to be sure no one was there. He stood in Zöe's study. It was uncommonly messy. She wasn't obsessively tidy, but she was organised. She wouldn't normally leave her desk like this – covered in papers and files, as if they'd fallen from an autumn tree. On a side table he found a card model, crushed by two heavy books. The wicker chair she read in was piled high with unbound documents in pale-pink and pale-blue covers. What was she working on?

Zöe generally left her study door open when she wasn't at home. Clive closed it. And then walked down the corridor to Aaron's room.

Only one curtain was pulled back, so the light was uncertain. He could smell smoke, and a body. He tried to recall Aaron's smell. Did he smell like this? Did *he* smell like this?

There were paperbacks in a pile on the nightstand – all with bookmarks. Aaron read novels, Clive knew. But several at once? He picked up the first. Iris Murdoch. And then he noticed that the bookmark was in fact a photograph – the white strip along the top was glossy and he could see the tops of people's heads. He edged it out from the pages a little. Aaron's face appeared, his hair now long. Clive shifted the book so the spine sat in his cupped hand and let the pages fall open at the photo.

Aaron was flanked by a man and a woman. He wore wooden beads; his shirt was unbuttoned and they rested against his bare chest. And they matched beads worn by both the man and the woman. Aaron's arms curved behind their backs. Their bodies were pressed against him too intimately, Clive thought. Aaron was smiling, but he didn't look happy.

Clive snapped the book shut.

He stood out on the balcony for a long time. From here nothing seemed to have changed, which at first calmed the disquiet he felt – in his stomach, his limbs, his mind. But then he leaned against the wall and felt annoyed at the roughness of the concrete. And when he stared down at the estate below, the arrangement of the buildings irritated him. This shouldn't be here and that should be there, he wanted to say to someone – to Zöe. People don't live like this. You can't make them.

And then he noticed, directly below, a black rhomboid of concrete. Zöe's paving design had been covered over. Leonard's blood had been stubborn. At Christmas there had still been a yellow cloud on the slabs between the walkway steps and the big cupboards where the bins were kept.

A bang made him jerk upright. Someone had entered the flat and the draught had caught the living-room door and flung it into its frame. Clive turned and looked through the window. For a moment he saw both his own reflection and Aaron's figure, one laid over the other, his eyes unable to decide which was on top, but finally they refused the double image and made him see Aaron clearly.

They stared at each other. It was not uncomfortable. They met in the balcony doorway. A small hug. Their cheeks brushed together. Clive was clean-shaven, Aaron noticed. Aaron was stubbly, Clive thought.

But he was wearing a shirt and a suit jacket and trousers. There was a rolled-up tie in his hand.

—Where have you been? Clive asked.

Aaron didn't answer straight away. As if he hadn't spoken since they were last together and he had to make an effort to do so now.

—Court, he said.

He saw Clive tighten.

—I was just in the public gallery. Not a witness or anything.

—What the fuck are you playing at? This is exactly why I knew I had to come back.

Clive swung round, back out onto the balcony, pulling Aaron with him – so he thought. But Aaron remained inside the flat.

—I had to go and see them.

—And what if someone saw you?

—What if they did?

Aaron turned away, pulling his jacket off. Clive tried to stay where he was, but Aaron sat on the sofa and watched his brother until he came inside. He knew Clive didn't like this, but he was of a mind not to give in to what Clive wanted this time. Clive dropped onto the other end of the sofa, making Aaron bounce a little.

—They might not have thought anything. Or they might have wondered what you were doing there.

—He was our dad. Families always go to murder trials.

—Yes, but we didn't know him, did we?

Clive looked through the balcony window and dropped his voice a few notes, speaking in a straight line.

—We are supposed to have never spoken to him. And especially not that night.

Aaron stood up and pulled the balcony door closed.

—How would anyone suspect anything just from me sitting in the public gallery?

—Look, we should be baffled, uncomfortable, sad, but we should be at a distance from the whole thing. Showing as little interest as possible. Getting on with our lives. You still hanging around here is bad enough. You should have gone on some hippy pilgrimage – Morocco or India or whatever. And now you go to their trial. What are you even getting out of it?

—I feel guilty, all right?

Aaron threw his hands in the air then let them drop.

—For what?

—They're innocent. They're on trial for something we did.

Clive found himself leaping up.

—We didn't do anything!

It was a shout, and it masked the sound of the flat door opening again. Aaron was about to reply, but he saw Zöe in the living-room doorway. Her eyes searched the scene.

—Clive? she said.

Clive started to approach her. She looked between him and Aaron.

—Are you fighting?

Clive found a tone, a posture, and took Zöe into a hug.

—Just bickering, he said into her hair.

Aaron saw Zöe look him up and down over Clive's shoulder.

—And why are you wearing a suit?

Clive felt Zöe's hands push at him. He wanted to hold on to her, to stop this conversation pulling away from him. But she pushed. She took a breath. He released her and stepped back.

—Aaron? she asked.

—He went to court today. To their trial, said Clive.

Zöe sighed. Walked to the kitchen, staring into Aaron's eyes as she went. They heard her putting her bags down, opening cupboards, the fridge.

—Is that why you're back then, Clive? Did you go too? she called.

It seemed that she banged the tins and jars and slammed the cupboard doors.

—No. I just thought I'd come down. Tutorials and lectures have finished. I wanted to see you both.

Zöe appeared in the doorway. She appraised them, a tin of tomatoes in each hand. Then turned away again.

—And what happened at the trial?

Her voice scratched. Aaron saw her reach up to a top shelf.

—It was just opening statements and lots of stuff about the way they were arrested.

Aaron could see that Clive wanted him to stop talking – even to lie, however innocuous his descriptions.

Clive wanted to tell Aaron what to say.

—And how were they? Zöe asked.

Aaron and Clive moved closer to each other, as if their elastic bond could no longer bear the stretch.

—Who? said Aaron weakly.

They could see Zöe at the sink. She held on to the edge with both hands for a moment. Looked upwards.

—Those girls – Annette and Christine, she said, as if talking about someone she'd met at a party.

—Just quiet. They said their names and then their plea.

—Which was...?

Aaron feared he might answer this question incorrectly, as if there were several versions of what happened in the courtroom. Clive bumped into him. A nudge? A nudge.

—Not guilty.

Zöe remained at the sink, hardly moving. It seemed she was staring out of the window. It took her a long while to speak.

—How long are you here for, Clive? I wish you'd called. I've just done all this shopping, but only for two.

—We'll go out now and get what we need, said Clive.

He took Aaron by the arm.

Zöe had come into the living room now; she was drying her hands on a cloth. She stared at Clive's hand where it clasped Aaron's forearm. She looked up, raised her brows.

—Another pint of milk. You might as well get a loaf. You're just going to the town square supermarket? Eggs – and a few more potatoes.

Her head made a couple of small, stuttered movements, as if she were swallowing something down.

—Don't rush, though.

She turned away, but then gave them another look – underarm, sly.

Clive still had hold of Aaron, and now they were in the hall.

—Keys, said Aaron.

—And this...

Zöe was directly behind them – she was soft-footed when she wanted to be. She held up a pound note. Clive reached out to take it. He felt her thumb and finger maintain their pressure; she didn't immediately let it go. But there was no mischievous smile on her face. She wore a sharp, searching expression.

Clive gave Aaron's arm a small tug, and they were out of the front door before Zöe's face could interrogate them further.

As Clive pulled the door closed behind them, they heard the bang of the living-room door. The wind, they thought to each other.

36

But it isn't the wind. It is Zöe.

Zöe is slamming: the living-room door. Then her hands on the dining table – flat, spread. She's surely about to scream. She pulls open the balcony door and goes outside. Stands against the wall and closes her eyes. She remains there for a few minutes, quite still, but for a flicker under her eyelids, a fidget in the fingers that lie on the gravelly concrete of the balustrade. And then, as if she's counted out two minutes, she looks downwards. Almost on cue, two figures appear on the walkway from the direction of the tower's entrance. Zöe's eyes focus on them, her head lowered, as they make their way along the walkway. It's not the shortest route to the town square. They could have taken one of Zöe's quick cuts, or even descended the steps to ground level and wound between the neighbouring blocks. But the walkway is as good as any.

Yet Clive and Aaron don't continue on to the town square. They turn off onto the little spur that extends over the park opposite the primary school. They're still visible from the balcony of flat 246. Zöe's eyes are still on them. They've never glanced away. Not until the twins stop on the circular platform at the end of the spur, where the sculpture sits, floating high over the little amphitheatre.

Zöe turns away and darts back inside. She clutches her keys from the hall table but she doesn't leave by the front door. She strides into her study, closes the door, moves the wicker chair, and opens the cupboard behind it. Pushing the books and folders and dusty boxes aside, she locates a corner with her finger, presses, and the back of the cupboard opens onto a dim passage between the floors. But this one doesn't lead to the service stairs. Two-thirds of the way along – where the lift shaft passes through, she opens a door. A staircase curving down and up, following the curling pipe of the slide to the main entrance floor, then continuing down into the foundations of the tower.

She passes swiftly, knowledgeably, through the short corridors and concealed doors she added when lying in her bed more than two decades before, her belly swollen with bodies. The builders shook their heads at the plans. But there were much bigger questions about the estate. A strange access corridor or an inexplicably invisible door-opening mechanism caused little trouble for them in comparison.

From the basement of Marlowe Tower she enters the underground car park that lies beneath the paved area and stretches under the health centre. She passes the serried cars at a half-run. At the other end, she checks no one can see her, and lets herself into a dim corridor, which leads, after a minute's brisk walk, to the basement of the school. She's close to the town square now. Music can be heard from somewhere – faint and tinkling.

She passes through two or three large rooms below the school. Discarded, childish art is piled on a table. A life-sized cardboard king and queen are propped against one wall. Their crowns are huge. Their limbs painted in different thicknesses – by different children, perhaps. She opens the last door – onto the passage that leads to the open-air theatre.

The builders did ask questions when it came to the platform floating over the stage. The stepped semi-circular outdoor theatre made sense to them, but the complexity of making the pillar supporting the platform at the end of the walkway spur hollow and inserting into it the narrowest of spiral staircases didn't. 'It's like a trapdoor in a conventional theatre,' Zöe explained. 'The staircase leads to a passage that takes us to the basement of the primary school. Actors will be able to appear on the platform above the stage, completely unseen. You'll understand it when the sculpture arrives. It's hollow too, with a door. The actor will be able to stand inside, waiting for their cue.'

She reaches the staircase, and the light dripping down from the lattice of concrete above illuminates her face for a moment. She stops. She's listening. The light is like a layer of powder on her face. She is momentarily the age when she argued over these stairs with the construction company.

She takes the flight with great care, each foot placed gently, toe then heel, her body gliding. At the top is a small, circular room: the inside of the base of the sculpture. It is a grotto, the ceiling is stacks of geometric shapes; the walls are a fretwork – open slots and grilles letting in a net of light. Zöe peers through one of the apertures. She moves her head forwards, narrowing her eyes, then jerks back and to the side, as if hiding herself.

On the outside, the sculpture is a confusing image. From some angles, looking up from the park or the tiers of brick seating, it suggests a human figure, perhaps two, in an embrace. From other angles – the first floor of the school, the windows of the blocks overlooking the park – it is a truncated tower. From the wide platform encircling it, and from nearby, on the walkway spur approaching it, the sculpture is a building grown out of control: the round, hollow base, with its latticework walls, seeming to shoot up of its own accord into a strange excretion – something the sculptor never intended but could not prevent.

At the sculpture's foot, directly over the stage below, leaning against the rail surrounding the circular platform, are Aaron and Clive. They are just yards away from Zöe. If they looked closely they'd be able to see her eyes staring at them through one of the holes in the concrete.

There's a metallic clunk. Aaron twitches and stands up straight, looking down. Zöe frowns. The noise is from the gate in the rail, inserted to allow ladders or steps up from the stage below. Flexibility for the plays Zöe had intended to be performed here. There were a few in the early days, when the estate was brand new, when newspapers came to make picture stories about modern community living. But there has never been the summer festival Zöe built the outdoor theatre for. And no one has ever used the sculpture as part of a play. No character has ever needed to appear from within it, making their entrance onto the platform fifteen feet above the stage.

Zöe edges closer to the aperture. The conversation between her sons is becoming heated.

—We agreed what we'd do, said Clive. We'd say nothing. Do nothing. Annette and Christine were arrested, so why offer ourselves up as suspects?

—Because it's wrong, Clive.

Aaron leaned against the rail again and it moved with another worrying creak. He stood away from it.

—They didn't do it, he said. They could be found guilty of murder, and that could be our fault.

—Look, we know they didn't do it, said Clive. We know no one can have seen them do it. So there can't be any real evidence.

Clive chopped the air with blade-like hands. He wanted to break his argument into small pieces. Make it easier for Aaron to swallow.

—They'll get off, Aaron.

Aaron turned away from Clive's face. It seemed leaner than before. A line, almost invisible, but present nonetheless, lingered between his eyebrows. Once more Aaron leaned against the loose section of rail, and this time it gave a little with his weight, sending a surge of fear into his thighs and belly. He jumped away and moved to Clive's other side.

—And what if someone lies, Aaron said. What if someone who hates them, some racialist – takes the stand and says they saw Annette and Christine pushing him off?

—No one would go that far. Even the worst racialists wouldn't lie about that. Look, it's not like we're not sure. We know they didn't do it. We know what really happened.

Inside the sculpture, Zöe inhales. Steps back. Splays her fingers over her mouth and nose. Puts the other hand against the wall to steady herself.

—And that's exactly why we should come forward, said Aaron. Go to the police station. Or the court. Tell them what really happened.

Aaron lunged towards Clive.

—Tell someone, he said, and grabbed his brother's arm.

It felt thin. Thinner than before. Thinner than his own.

Clive felt the strength in Aaron's grip. He shrugged and shook it off.

—But tell them what? he said.

—What really happened!

Aaron couldn't understand Clive's urge towards complication, when it was so simple in his mind.

—We can't do that. For fuck's sake, Aaron, what do you think would happen to us? We'd never get out of the police station. Markham's not going to say, 'Thank you, boys, for the information. Very helpful.' We'd be arrested on the spot.

Inside the sculpture, Zöe grips the concrete with both hands. It seems she would fall if she let go, tumble down the stairs. Or the sculpture would collapse around her. Her eyes are pink. Sore-seeming.

—And what about Tabitha? Clive continued.

Aaron didn't reply. He was defeated at the first skirmish.

Clive knew it. He leaned forwards a little, stabbing his words like a finger.

—She says she saw everything. And she said she wouldn't say anything. If we do, though, how do we know she won't break her promise? She'll tell the police everything she says she saw: us arguing with him. Us grabbing hold of him. Us pushing him off the roof. Our father, who abandoned us as babies, who came back to live on our fucking estate and didn't even bother to make contact with us. We'd be handing ourselves over in a neat package, all tied up: victim, perpetrator, motive, witness.

—But if we say—

—They'll say we're lying, Aaron. For God's sake, when did you get so stupid? Who are you now?

Aaron rushed forwards. Someone – something pushed him. Some animal impetus. His hands were on Clive now, simultaneously pushing him away and pulling him towards himself.

—Who are *you*, now, Clive? Who the fuck are you? When did you get so fucking cruel?

Clive didn't like Aaron's strength. Didn't like that it bound him, that he couldn't meet it, exceed it. He twisted his torso and snaked his arms.

But Aaron snaked his tighter. Clenched his grip. As if he could physically force Clive to reorder his thoughts, to share Aaron's mind. To return to him.

Clive made a last effort, bending his knees and twisting his whole body away from Aaron's embrace.

Inside the sculpture, Zöe's body tenses. She fumbles along the wall, searching for the catch that will open the door onto the platform.

Aaron was about to lose hold. Clive was taut, sprung, urgently resisting. Aaron slammed a foot forwards to brace himself against another pull. But as he did, Clive wrenched himself backwards and felt his back hit the rail. Aaron was coming towards him. Bigger and heavier than just a few months earlier. Bigger and heavier than Clive. Their chests were pressed together. Aaron felt Clive's heat. His bones.

And the rail gave way.

Aaron heard a shout. He turned his head.

Zöe was somehow inside the sculpture. But now she was outside it. Leaping towards them.

Clive, mid-air, heard a scream.

Zöe.

Then something black – a blanket. The sky.

They hit the stage.

Clive's back took the full impact.

Aaron heard a strangely loud crack as Clive's head hit the concrete, and then a sword of crystal pain thrust through his knee. He was on all fours over Clive's body. He couldn't stop his limbs collapsing. Their chests pressed together again. Clive was bony. Too slight. Aaron pushed with his arms and managed to roll himself off his brother.

And saw Zöe, looking down at them.

Her hair hung too straight. Her face looked old. Sagging. She was speaking. Singing? Shouting perhaps. The pain danced through Aaron's leg and up through his body.

What pain did Clive feel?

Aaron rolled his head to the side. To Clive.

Clive was still. Asleep.

37

Aaron and Clive didn't see each other in the hospital. The week during which Aaron was an in-patient – his leg immobilised, metal braces around his knee – Clive was still unconscious, ten floors above him in the big, new, grey tower of Guy's Hospital. He was still in a coma on the day Aaron was discharged. Zöe, Aaron's doctor and the sister on Clive's ward, all advised against Aaron visiting. Aaron was pliable, as always.

When they arrived home, he asked Zöe for the newspaper, then hopped out onto the balcony and dropped into a chair, spreading the paper across the table. He scanned each page, but there was no report from the trial. He looked through the window, into the living room. Zöe was briefly a shape in the hall doorway, then disappeared. Could he ask her whether she'd heard anything? All their recent conversations had been about Clive.

When she assisted him into his seat at dinner, he took the opportunity – him half on the chair, her slightly pink from the effort.

—Have you heard anything about the trial? he asked. Have they given evidence yet?

Zöe let go of him, stood back a little.

—Tomorrow, she said. Then went back into the kitchen.

When she returned, her hands inside oven gloves, holding the orange casserole dish, she used the same tactic he had. Serving him a portion she asked:

—What was the argument about?

Aaron picked up his knife and fork. He wished he already had a mouthful of food to chew. Zöe rested the spoon in the dish, waiting.

—Clive was angry because I'd gone to the trial. You heard us. You came in in the middle of it.

Aaron ate a forkful of potato and meat. It was far too hot. Zöe served herself.

—Not then. When you were at the theatre.

Zöe was the only person who called it 'the theatre'. Everyone else knew it as 'the scoop'. Aaron swallowed.

—It was the same argument. He seemed to think we should keep away, not appear interested. Because of, well, Leonard. Our dad.

Zöe looked uncomfortable. Stared at her plate. Aaron took the opportunity to drink some water. He held it in his mouth to calm the scald on his tongue. Should he leave it at that, or go further? She was on the hunt for something, he could tell. And she was dangerous when in this kind of mood. Her senses seemed heightened, always ready to pounce, to ambush. He wasn't sure whether he should put her off the scent, or if it was too late and he should provide her with a trail. He decided on something that could be either.

—I think they're innocent, he said.

Zöe stopped reorganising the food on her plate and looked up, her fork in mid-air.

—I think so too.

And she dropped her eyes before Aaron had a chance to read them.

38

The nurses adjusted the height of Clive's bed and kneaded the pillows behind him so that he could see out of the window. If he tipped his head too much, his neck ached, but he could just see the roof of Marlowe Tower.

He'd repeated the word 'paraplegic' to himself four times since the doctor had said it to him. The nurses had already stopped tickling his feet.

Zöe came every day, twice a day. She told him what she and Aaron had eaten for lunch and dinner. He knew breakfast was always the same. Her words came out in a clatter. Nothing seemed considered. She talked a lot about Guy's tower. He couldn't picture the outside, although he was sure he'd seen it many times. She brought him a leaflet from the foyer downstairs with a photograph of the tower on the front. As he took it, he anticipated the kind of argument they would have engaged in before. But his fires were burning low; Zöe's were apparently extinguished.

One evening, she said:

—I'm sure Aaron will come and visit soon.

Clive didn't speak. He'd recently discovered that he didn't need to respond to everything anyone said to him.

—He has a wheelchair, and it's OK in the lift, and then to the walkway. But getting him to ground level and into the car is really tricky. There's the ramp on the other side of the school, of course, but then I'd have to wheel him all the way back. I should've designed more ramps and fewer steps, shouldn't I?

Zöe's laughter never seemed genuine in the hospital. Perhaps the clean surfaces made it more shrill. It ended, and the weary look returned.

—He'll come and see you when he has his next check-up, I'm
sure. They said they'll give him crutches.

She placed her hand, palm upturned, on the bed. Clive didn't
take it. She withdrew it, and then seemed to study it, where it lay
in her lap.

—Why were the two of you arguing about what happened that
night?

She said it without raising her eyes.

Clive wanted to cross and uncross his ankles, curl and uncurl
his toes. He stayed silent. His brain worked, but it was still slow.
His wit was no longer quick.

—Aaron thinks they're innocent – Annette and Christine, Zöe
said at last.

She lowered her head to one side and raised her shoulder at the
same time, as if to grip a telephone receiver.

—Do you? she asked.

Clive realised with a slow flash – all his brain was capable of
currently – that Zöe had a strategy here. That it was quite possible
she already had him surrounded. He made sure he kept both his
gaze and his voice steady.

—We liked them. A lot. They were good friends.

Zöe blinked at him several times. As if something was irritating
her eyes.

—There was nothing going on between the four of you, was
there?

Clive tried to pedal his thoughts faster. His brain felt so slow.
But then he saw that she'd unwittingly given him an opportunity
to feint.

—What are you talking about, Mum? There was never anything
like that. We were just friends. They'd probably think we were too
young for them anyway.

—I didn't mean anything ... romantic. I mean...

Her face collapsed into jowly desperation. She gripped the
corner of the bed cover.

—I mean something the police might want to know about.

For a moment Clive wanted Aaron beside him, ready to fill in with the answer he would give – back-up power he could rely on in his weakened state. But then he thought, no. Aaron would be no good right now. Clive couldn't be sure he'd say the right thing. Tell the right lie. Stick to the best version of events.

—Why would the police want to know about our argument? he said.

Zöe seemed confused by this. She dropped the bed cover and examined his face. He'd made a connection for her. His sluggard of a brain was leading him into mistakes.

—We just think differently about going to the trial, that's all, he mumbled.

The long silence made Zöe's face unbearable to look at. Clive turned his head and made his neck ache staring out of the window at the roof of Marlowe Tower. But perhaps even that hinted at guilt, he thought. Then told himself that he – that they – were guilty of nothing.

39

Aaron became fixated on the news. He watched the television bulletins at one, five-thirty and nine, and the rest of the day he marked the hours by turning on the radio. He became adept at placing the aerial at the best angle to pick up Radio 4 and Radio London. The former he realised was less likely to carry the report he was waiting for. But the latter occasionally reported from the Old Bailey and the High Court. When he discovered they were not one and the same, he felt deficient. He was still not completely an adult. And with a clarity he still remembers – the day was gusty; the wind sang a few feet out from the balcony – he wondered if he ever would be now.

On the first Friday in June, the midday radio news told Aaron that two Deptford women had been acquitted at the Old Bailey of the murder of Leonard Harrington.

Annette and Christine were found not guilty. Clive had been right.

Flat 246 was suddenly a prison.

—Acquitted, said Zöe.

She was in the doorway to the hall. Aaron had to twist round to see her.

—Yes, he said. Not guilty.

Zöe stayed silent. Aaron's neck was starting to ache, and his eyes, looking out of their corners, couldn't focus on her face. Was she relaxed, sad, angry? Blank? He could only see blank from where he sat.

—They didn't do it, he said, as if he needed to explain 'not guilty'.

—Who did, then? said Zöe.

Now Aaron adjusted his position in an attempt to see her better. He pressed his hand down on his injured leg and his knee gave a little cry. And now Zöe moved. But he saw, or thought he saw, something accusatory. A glare.

She was out in the hall now. He could hear her bare footsteps.

—Will you tell Clive? he called.

But then he wasn't sure whether he'd meant it as a request or a query – was he begging her to make sure Clive knew, or to keep the news from him?

◆

Zöe did tell Clive, during that evening's visiting hours.

Clive was bothered more and more by her demeanour when she came to see him. She looked increasingly lost when she walked through the doors, even though she'd been here countless times now. She'd stare at him, her face suggesting she was trying to place him, searching for the context in which they had met.

He told himself it was the shock – renewed each time, twice a day – of seeing him paralysed. For him it was a continuous drone. It had started when he awoke from the coma, and was already becoming familiar. For her it was gunshots.

Today it seemed she'd been hit. Her gait as she crossed the ward was almost a limp. She clutched her bag against her body, as if the handles had broken.

She sat down without a hello or a kiss.

—The girls have been found not guilty, she said.

—They didn't do it?

Clive just managed to inflect the last word upwards, to prevent his words coming out as a statement. But he saw Zöe's brow twitch and eyes widen a fraction nevertheless. She was suspicious. He wanted to move his leg.

—That's what the jury thinks, she said.

Clive saw his opportunity to steer her suspicion away.

—Does that mean you think the jury are wrong?

—Not at all, she said. From what I've heard there's simply no evidence to suggest they were responsible for ... for Leonard's...

The urge to cross and uncross his legs became stronger. He almost thought he was about to do it.

—You've always been mistrustful of them, though, he said. You took against them from the start.

Zöe looked down the ward.

—Those people at the end are so noisy, she said.

The man in the bed laughed the same short laugh in response to everything anyone said.

—You still think they did it, don't you? said Clive, placing his hands on his thighs, feeling only one side of the contact.

—No, I don't. But I do wonder who did, Zöe replied, her tone flat, her voice oddly soft, her eyes watching his hands.

Clive turned his palms upwards.

—I suppose the police will have to start from square one again.

—That's exactly what they're doing, she said.

Clive kept perfectly still, but he felt a fraction shrunk – as if his body had retracted from her words. Zöe was examining him. He thought she must have sensed it.

—Markham called just before I came out, she said. They officially reopened the case this afternoon, he said. But he also said not to expect any results, as they have nothing to go on – no new information.

The lure lay between them like a dull coin. Clive knew Zöe well enough not to pick it up. But his brain was too fogged to divert her onto anything else. So they sat in silence until she decided it was her time to leave.

40

There is a party in the town square, to celebrate the Silver Jubilee. Zöe decides to show her face during the afternoon part, when the kids are lined up at tables and fed from red, white and blue paper plates.

—How was it? Aaron asks when she comes back.

—The town square looked dreadful, with all that bunting, she says. I didn't design it for that.

—Not for a party for an unelected head of state, do you mean? Aaron doesn't look at her as he says it.

If he did, he would see her sway slightly as she stares at the back of his head, his hair long and a rich chestnut now. She grabs the door frame as if to stop herself toppling. A strand of hair has caught in an eyelash. It must blur her sight. Must irritate.

Aaron turns, to see why she's not replied, perhaps. She puts her hand in her hair and hauls some back.

—Tabitha was there, she says. And her aunt and mother.

—What did they say? asks Aaron.

—That Annette and Christine are back.

Aaron picks up the ruler from the cushion beside him and pushes it down his cast. His face seems intent on the scratching. When he pulls the ruler out, he turns back.

—How do they know? he says.

—Mrs Ledbury complained that she could hear knocking from their flat the whole weekend. She says they're trespassing. But Tabitha said she saw them on the walkway with empty bags and flattened cardboard boxes. So I said they must be moving their stuff out.

—They must be, says Aaron.

He picks up his book. It's clear he's trying to look like he doesn't care. Zöe studies him carefully. She's sure to see the small movements of his jaw, the tightness of his lips.

—We have been a happy family, the three of us, haven't we? says Zöe.

Aaron doesn't speak, but he nods, his mouth a little open.

—Yes? Zöe asks.

—Aaron nods more vigorously.

—Yes, Zöe confirms. Blackheath was lovely, wasn't it?

She turns into the kitchen.

—But here has been lovely too. We've made it our home.

She stands still in the middle of the kitchen. She doesn't pick up a pot or open a drawer. She speaks into the air.

—And it will always be our home, won't it? This community. There are good people here.

Her voice is becoming quieter. Her mouth movements small. She's fading to a whisper.

—It was right to come here. I know you weren't happy to move, but you did well. You loved it so much. And you made friends. And now Clive is at university – he'll be going back, I'm sure. You'll do something like it yourself soon. When you find your purpose. Your metier. You'll come across one without knowing it, probably.

Aaron has turned back to the book he's been reading. It looks as if he can't hear Zöe's words. He couldn't from that distance, she's speaking so quietly now.

—Your father made his choice. I didn't keep him away. He stayed away. If he'd made any kind of attempt to see you, I'd have allowed it. Of course I would. I don't think you've been damaged by it, though – by his absence. I know that's what people will say. But I don't think it's true. Is it? Is it? Is it?

Her words are less than a whisper now. No vocal-cord tremors, no hiss of air aspirates. Her tongue, lips and jaw work the words from her mouth, but Aaron doesn't hear them. Only we do. They emerge as droplets.

—That's not why you did it, is it? Is it? Because he stayed away. Because even when he was here he wouldn't see you? I told him to. I went up there and said. I sat in that room and looked at my damned painting until he came home, and I said, 'You have to see them. You can't be here and not acknowledge your sons. Your own fucking children.' And he called me a hypocrite. And threw me out. I lost my temper with him then. I would've hit him if he hadn't closed the door. I would've hit him, he's that maddening. Was that what happened with you two? Did he make the two of you furious? Did you lose your tempers? Did Clive? Was it Clive? I think I know it was Clive. You're too gentle. You would have tried to stop him. But he's too much for you sometimes. I know that. But you'd never betray him, not even to me. I know that too. But if it was him, I'd understand. And if it was you, I'd understand. Because maybe it was you, after all. You might have got that angry. Over something like this. Like your father. He might have driven you to it, he's so infuriating. So selfish. Is that why you did it, the two of you? Is that it? Is it? Is it? Is it?

She continues to repeat those two words, making them two silent syllables, a meaningless sound, a simple drumbeat. Aaron is oblivious. Not a word reaches his ears.

Her mouth is still moving as she walks back through the living room, along the hall and down the steps, her hands skimming the walls on either side, as if she mistrusts her balance.

She reaches her study and drops heavily into her chair. Her mouth is still moving, but imperceptibly now. It finally stops when she picks up a pencil and pulls towards her a sketching pad. Her body seems to settle, her eyelids drop, pencil poised over the page, about to draw something – a curve? But no, something is stopping her. Some broken connection prevents the information flowing from her brain to her hand, to her fingers and into the blue top of the pencil.

She lets the pencil drop. It falls tip first and skitters a chain of tiny dots across the page. She places both hands on her face and holds them there for a long moment.

When she removes them and opens her eyes, they have a

different cast, her mouth a different set, her chin raised, her nose a sharp point. A decision made. A strategy before her.

She walks back to the living room, upright now. She goes out onto the balcony for a moment. The music from the party in the town square is faint and tinny. She turns and stands on the threshold, looking into the room at Aaron.

—When I was with Clive last night, I was asking him about your argument.

The book Aaron is holding closes. Aaron seems not to notice that he hasn't marked his place.

—I told you, we were just arguing about the trial, he says.

Zöe steps into the room now. If we're beside Aaron, we see her figure dark against the light outside.

—Clive said it was you.

Aaron seems to retract a little. The heel of his cast rasps against the rug.

—What was?

Zöe adopts an indulgent expression. Her eyes aren't committed to it though. It comes out as fearful.

—The two of you did see your father at the party. After everyone saw him arguing with Annette and Christine. Clive says you argued with him...

Zöe's pause is forced, hammy.

—And that there was some kind of fight. You were on the edge in the dark, and...

Here she should swallow, sob, touch her face before she can speak the words. But she seems unable to perform the dumb play; instead she stalls, is still, then starts up again.

—You pushed him – Leonard.

And then she adds:

—Your father.

It is almost comic. Aaron might be forgiven if he laughed.

Aaron does laugh. But without humour. It is in disbelief – coughed up like a pellet. He picks up the ruler and grips it tight.

Zöe stares at the brittle slice of wood. She's told him several times that he'll snap it.

—Is he wrong?

—Clive said that? Aaron replies.

—He's right, then?

—No. No he isn't. But he said it? Like that? I pushed Leonard?

Aaron lurches sideways and reaches for the crutches that are propped against the sofa's arm. They make a metal clatter as he pulls them over and slides his arms into them. His movements are all jerks and snatches. His hands shake. His face flushes, then blanches. Zöe observes, but makes no effort to help. He heaves himself up, his injured leg slightly bent, his foot hanging in the air, the toes naked.

He straightens himself up.

—We did speak to Leonard, he says at last. But we didn't really argue. We talked and then ... He fell. He just...

Aaron winds his hand in the air, teetering on one crutch and one leg.

—...fell.

Zöe leans on the back of her armchair. But it's the wrong height; she looks awkward and uncomfortable, her limbs like a doll's – messily arranged.

—That's different from what you've told everyone, she says. Me. The police.

Aaron hops in an arc so he faces her.

—We.

He stops. Allows his foot to touch the floor. He doesn't appear to place his weight on it.

—We, he says again.

The two of them stare at each other. They must both be making decisions.

—We decided, when Annette and Christine were arrested, that we'd better just say nothing.

—Why?

Zöe is rigid, still in her unnatural pose.

—Because we'd look so guilty.

—And now – now they're free? she asks.

Aaron tries several times to start speaking. He hops on the spot a little, fiddles with the placement of his crutches.

—While they had Annette and Christine, they had suspects. Now they don't, we'd look even more guilty. And the police have reopened the case. This is the information they're looking for.

—And are you, Aaron? Are you guilty?

—No! It was an accident.

—He just fell?

—He just fell.

Zöe pushes herself upright. Her face is a blank – an expression she has perfected. But she doesn't seem to be doing it purposefully now. It's more that she's out of strength.

—You don't believe me, says Aaron.

He spins a half-turn away. Half turns back to her.

—You really don't, do you? he says.

Zöe presses the back of her hand against her lips.

—You believe Clive? Aaron says, the crutches splayed now.

—You believe Clive, he says quietly. Then: Clive said that?

A pause. He adjusts the crutches, takes a swing to the window. A bird hovers outside. Another joins it. Dives away.

—Clive said that, Aaron says.

It's almost a whisper.

◆

At the hospital Zöe sits with Clive while he eats his meal. He tells her she doesn't need to stay.

—I know, she says. Then tells him all the details of the children's party.

When he's finished the last spoonful of his dessert, Zöe glances from side to side. The next bed is empty. On the other side is the window. Zöe leans forwards. Much further and her chin would rest on the bedcover. It seems she does it to make her voice low.

—I was chatting with Aaron earlier. About the argument you were having before you fell.

Clive's hands find the fold of the sheets.

—Oh yes?

He's busy now, adjusting the lie of the covers.

—He says you saw Leonard that night on the roof. You spoke with him. Argued.

She pauses. She's bent over in her chair still, holding her belly as if she has stomach cramps.

Clive fidgets. He looks out of the window, down the ward, at each bed and its occupant. Then back at his mother. His words emerge, but his lips barely move.

—Yes, that's right. We did. We just thought it was best not to mention it. He was a bit odd with us. We said a few things. I wouldn't call it an argument, though. Maybe he rowed with Annette and Christine again after—

—Aaron says it was you.

Clive pulls his head back, jerks his chin, as if he's caught a punch. But he quickly gathers himself.

—What was? He twists his mouth into a hint of a smile.

—He says you pushed him.

—I pushed Aaron? Clive does something with his eyebrows now – a pretended confusion.

—He says you pushed Leonard.

Zöe finally sits up, but slowly. She drops her hands to her sides. Flat, exhausted.

Clive's face twitches and pulses. His mouth looks like it wants to speak, but he seems to have lost control. He lifts a hand and appears to point at the window – at the grey air outside. Then drops it. It bounces on the bed.

—Can you get a nurse, please, he finally manages to say.

◆

The nurse gives Clive more pain relief and he falls asleep before he and Zöe have spoken another word. She watches him for a few minutes, standing beside his bed. It is past visiting hours now. The men are reading books or magazines. Several are sleeping.

Zöe turns away from her son and steps up to the window. It's light – a June early evening, but the sky is busy with clouds. She must see the profile of Deptford Strand Estate. Her eyes have certainly come to rest in that direction. She sighs. Blinks. Then holds her breath – for a long, long stretch, it seems. Finally she gasps air in, as if remembering she should breathe.

Sighing the air out again, she turns back to the room, picks up her bag and leans over Clive. She kisses him gently on the forehead, on the cheekbone, drifts her fingers over his hand. Then she leaves in a kind of rush – her strides light and long. An old man with white, slightly yellowed hair looks up from his newspaper and follows her flight over the top of his spectacles.

In the foyer of the hospital, Zöe finds a free phone in the line of booths by the seating area. Taking her phone book from her bag, she drops her coins and has to chase them across the floor. A woman with a stick places a foot on a two-pence piece to stop it rolling on.

When Zöe makes the call, it's only a few words. A greeting and then:

—Are the papers all ready? And everything else? I'd like to come down right now, if that's convenient? ... Sorry to disturb your bank holiday, but I just can't see a time to collect it all, otherwise ... Excellent. Thank you, Thomas. For everything. Above and beyond, I think it's called ... Yes, I'll be half an hour at most.

Then she's outside, half walking, half running to her car.

It's almost a straight line from the hospital to her destination in Blackheath. Her expression as she drives suggests she's staring down the length of it. She doesn't seem aware of the traffic around her – doesn't check at the junctions or look in her rear-view mirror. It's luck, perhaps, that today is a public holiday. The Old Kent Road is deserted – boarded-up shops between the long stretches of corrugated-iron fencing. She drives fast. She doesn't even slow down for Canal Bridge. It seems the 2CV's wheels leave the ground for a moment. Her body absorbs the rattle as she lands, but her eyes are still fixed ahead, focused on something far off.

Even when she turns off the A2 on Blackheath and weaves between the elegant villas before pulling into the pavement outside a particularly hefty cream one, her eyes seem to be staring at something more important.

She emerges from the house twenty minutes later with a cardboard file in one hand and a thick envelope in the other. Sitting in the car, she opens the file and briefly examines the documents inside. Then she parts the mouth of the envelope with one hand and uses the fingers of the other to riffle through the contents. She closes it and looks out of the window at the peaceful street – the little arcadia on the fringes of the heath that wealth buys. The tiniest of sighs escapes her lips, accompanied by a long blink. It looks like resignation, but something like determination has settled in her eyes. She places the file and envelope on the passenger seat and starts up the engine.

It is only when she is coming to the end of the road, about to emerge onto the green expanse of the heath, that her gaze changes. She stops at the junction, casts her eyes down into her lap, then back over her shoulder. She blinks a few times as if her eyes are suddenly smarting. Then raises her hand and makes a large, rough U-turn, mounting the kerb as she does so.

Her detour takes her back down the road she stopped on, through a few similarly curving avenues of expensive properties and effusive trees, until at last she enters a close. She comes to a halt outside a long-fronted house. Concrete, modern, with large windows and a terrace on the first floor. In the garden is an oblong pool with a short bridge you have to cross to reach the front door. Neat rushes emerge from the dark water at one end.

Zöe gets out of the car slowly, gazing at the rest of the close now – a mixture of early twentieth-century houses: detached, large gardens, wide drives. She leans her back against the car and examines the modern house – her head tips a little, her finger to her mouth as she seems to trace the line of the roof, the fall to the terrace.

The front door of the house opens, and a woman clutching a large tablecloth appears. She's halfway between the porch and the pool before she sees Zöe.

—Oh, she says. Then: Can I help you?

Zöe is staring at the bunched-up tablecloth. Several large yellow-and-white blooms burst from the creases. She seems to wake up.

—Sorry, I'm fine, thank you. I'm just ... I used to live here. In fact.

The woman waits for a moment, an expectant precursor to a smile fixed on her face. Her hair is an unfashionably stiff yellow bob. Then she takes a little step forwards and shakes out the tablecloth with a practised flick. Zöe watches the crumbs land on the glossy surface of the pool. Specks.

A bone-shaped, bone-coloured face rises out of the darkness, mouth gaped, and swallows a flake of bread.

—Carp, says the woman. They wait for the crumbs every evening.

She offers a social smile, and slowly folds the tablecloth, looking up at Zöe between each movement. Zöe's finger goes to her mouth again. Then she walks back round to the driver's seat. The woman, politely perplexed, remains where she is, the tablecloth now a perfect square in her hands.

Just as she's about to get in the car, Zöe seems to remember something. One leg inside, she calls:

—There's a staircase hidden in the back of the pantry, behind the shelving. It takes you down to a little room under the terrace at the back, where the land falls away.

She ducks into the car, shuts the door and turns the ignition, and doesn't hear or see the woman say 'we know' at the car as it makes a circle of the close and exits it at speed.

◆

The air around the bottom of Marlowe Tower is cool and thick when Zöe gets out of her car. A few notes of music blow over from the town square. The adults' party has begun.

When she reaches the lift on the entrance floor, she finds Mrs Ledbury there, waiting with two children. The boy is still wearing his Union Jack hat.

—I'm taking these up to mine for the night, so their mum and dad can enjoy theirselfs.

—That's nice, says Zöe.

—You love the queen now, don't you? says Mrs Ledbury to the little girl. Then looks back at Zöe: It's great isn't it, all this? I thought it's all gone out of fashion, you know, queen and country, up the Brits and all that. But no. We still love our country, don't we? They can put us down as much as they like, but we've still got our queen and our royals, haven't we? And our armed forces and all that – best in the world, still. No matter how many blacks or Asians or whatever come over here, we're still Britain and nobody can say we're not. And today we're saying it, aren't we, kids? Hurray!

Mrs Ledbury takes the girl's hand – she is holding a plastic flag – and shakes it in the air, so energetically the girl's whole body judders and her face creases, almost as if she's about to cry.

In flat 246, Aaron is on the sofa, watching TV. Zöe looks at the screen from the doorway. Aaron doesn't turn. He says:

—I've eaten. I didn't know how long you were going to be.

It seems to take a while for the words to form in Zöe's mind.

—I'll go down to the evening party shortly. There'll be food there. It's started already. I heard the music.

She stops, her face immobile.

—Your brother had a little dizzy spell or something.

Aaron twitches. A tiny gasp. But doesn't say anything.

—But they gave him some pain relief and he was asleep when I left, so...

Aaron's head moves a little to the right. His shoulders rise very slightly.

Zöe approaches him from behind. Her clogs clip the parquet, so he must hear her, yet he flinches when she puts a hand on his shoulder and leans over him.

—You need to be kinder to each other, you boys. Especially now. You're going to need each other.

Aaron puts his head back and looks up at her. Their faces are opposed – they see each other upside down. She leans down further and kisses his cheek.

Then walks away in a kind of rush – her strides light and long.

When Zöe reaches her study, she closes the door and pauses a moment in the middle of the room. Her hands find her face, they cover her eyes and mouth. The noise of her gasps is magnified by the cups of her palms. It takes some time, but at last she drops her hands. Her face is flushed, but it seems she has stifled the sobs.

She opens a drawer, roots round in it for a moment then pulls out a canvas shopping bag. She picks up her handbag, removes the file and envelope she collected in Blackheath and places them in the other bag. Then she pulls the wicker chair away from the big built-in cupboard, opens the door and begins to move the box files and books from inside. Her movements are quick and efficient. Once cleared, she opens the panel at the back. Then steps back to the study doorway and looks at the scene: the two open doors. The one at the back of the cupboard, onto the corridor, swings gently, then glides to. Zöe takes a pile of papers and places them so they prop the door open.

Now she opens a desk drawer and selects three keys, turning the card labels and checking them before putting the keys in her pocket. Then she sits down. A whole-body sigh. Her palms flat on the desk top. A long pause with her eyes closed. Then, opening them, she takes a notepad and pen, and writes. Quickly. Large letters. Kisses. She folds the page and places it in another pocket, then picks up the bag containing the folder and envelope, and, seemingly in a hurry now, is out of the chair and ducking into the cupboard.

Her clogs echo in the dim corridor. This time she takes the stairs around the lift upwards. A few steps down from the top, she stops, panting – the long climb has made her breathless – and searches the wall with her fingers. It's dark in this staircase – the slithers of half-light that reach her from the grilles and apertures dotted up and down the shaft aren't enough to light her task.

—Oh, for God's sake.

Her voice is low, but you'd hear it if you were somewhere below. No one is. No one ever has been.

At last she stops. Her hands have found something. The wall opens and she steps through, folding the narrow door back – leaving this route open too. She's on a landing on the service stairs, just a single flight from the hatch. The key is already in her hand and she opens the trapdoor with ease, lowering it to the floor, once again, leaving a door open. As if she expects someone to follow her.

She opens the door to flat 31 – but this she carefully closes behind her. She passes through the kitchen almost at a trot. She has a destination.

She's more than halfway across the big room, when she steals a single glance at the large painting. It stops her in her tracks.

She can't look at the painting again, it seems. Yet is desperate to turn towards it. Its gravity is irresistible.

—It was them, she whispers as her head turns. Aaron and Clive. I know it was them now.

She's looking at the painting through her hair. She makes no attempt to pull it from her eyes.

—Which of them it was, I don't know. It might have been both at once. I've tried to find out. I needed to know which one will need my help most. Who I have to ... to make room for. But they wouldn't say. They won't say. And ... and ... and...

She grips her hair now, but doesn't brush it back from her face; she clenches it in her fists, almost ready to pull the whole forest out by its roots.

—And now I think I've broken them.

She lets her hair loose. Looks through it at the paint.

—They were in pieces already, and it's like I took a hammer to them. But I had to know. I had to ... Didn't I?

The tension in her body vanishes. She steps towards an armchair and slumps down into it.

—So now I have to save both of them. And I have to make sure those girls down there stay safe too. Because if there's anyone in all of this without blame, it's them. Isn't it, Leonard?

It's the ceiling she's talking to now.

—Why did you have to bring them here? Look what it's done.

It's almost a whine. A sound unsuited to Zöe's lips.

She's silent for a long stretch. Her gaze lingers on the painting, then travels from object to object in the room, her head making the small fidgets of a bird on a high perch, scanning for threats and prey.

At last she draws her fingers through her hair, easing the worst tangles, smoothing it behind her ears.

—If I don't make sure this all this turns out the way it should, then who will? she asks.

There is no reply.

—And if I can't do it, then what's the point of me?

The room remains still. Tacit.

—What is the point of me? she asks again.

Then stands up slowly, checks her bag, runs a final hand

through her hair. She is at the stairs to flat 304. She steps quietly now. She must be curling her toes to keep her clogs from clapping. She stops by the door at the bottom. There are voices beyond it. Movement. A splash of water in a sink. A question – called from one room to another. A response. She has another key in her hand now. She slips it into the lock. Stops. Her chin flexes. Her nostrils flick.

She turns the key, the door opens and she's down the last step and into flat 304.

From where we are – behind her, still a few steps up, we hear an 'Oh'.

And then another.

41

From above, the roof of Marlowe Tower is stained, unscrubbed. The plants Leonard covered the space with some two years ago now have succumbed to the elements. The wind is always blowing up here, so evaporation rates are high. Leonard must have come up every day, watering. Now the climbers are taupe, tangled clouds. The majority of the shrubs are crisp-leaved or thickets of twigs. The trees he somehow pulled up the stairs – surely with several people helping him – are saddened. And every attempt made by the smaller plants has been scorched and blasted. It's hostile at the top of a tall building. The pool still has some water in it, but mainly courtesy of the rain. The scum on the surface is almost the only green up here now. Everywhere pots have tumbled and rolled, scattering dead stalks and biscuits of desiccated soil.

The door to the stairs has been propped open with one of these empty pots. Zöe has used a largish one, with some heft. It keeps the door from shutting, but the door wants to shut, so a mezzo-forte chime – metal against ceramic – spreads over the scene, and is harried away by the wind.

This wind finds its way down the service stairs. Flat 31's kitchen door is closed, but the trapdoor is open and a tentacle of quick air extends down the flight and finds the open door to the stairs that curl around the lift. Halfway down it meets another tongue of wind, singing a quiet note, now that it has found the way from the balcony in 246, through the flat, along the hallway and down the little flight of steps, into the low cupboard in Zöe's study and the hidden corridor, to the spiral stairs. The two currents serpent round each other, twisting past and flowing on to their escape. Their tug and tumble rattles all the doors that Zöe has so carefully opened. Her study door seems closed, but the catch hasn't quite caught. It shuffles against the strike plate and the door yawns. A rush of wind, and it slams.

In the living room, Aaron leaps from the sofa, then drops back down, cupping his knee, his face pulled tight.

The same gust that slammed the door has been at work up on the roof. It has pulled free from under a pot at the roof's edge the piece of notepaper Zöe wrote on and placed in her pocket before heading for flat 304. But the wind is not solely responsible. A bird, a peregrine – the rarest of rarities in London in 1977 – is using the upturned pot as a perch. It's usefully close to the edge, and its bottom makes a comfortable grip for the bird's talons. But when the wind huffs, it's caught off-guard, raises its wings and flaps. The pot shifts beneath it, the wind coughs stronger and manages to slip a finger under the page, then flutters it out from under the pot, where Zöe placed it a couple of hours before, after her visit to Annette and Christine. The peregrine is startled and takes off, yawing sideways as it spots the pale page flipping and twisting in the air below. The falcon hovers, observing: is it the white underside of a pigeon's wing? The page turns over, revealing Zöe's words.

It has taken me a year to admit what I'm writing in this letter. A year that has harmed people I never wanted to harm.

I was at the party the night Leonard died. It was my fault he fell. We argued, and I pushed him.

I'm not asking for forgiveness, because what I have done is unforgivable. I expect that many people will think I should face justice, and that I am taking the coward's way out.

They are probably right. I am a coward. I cannot face my children and admit to them what I have done. But I hope they will one day find some peace in knowing who was really responsible for Leonard's fall, and in knowing that whatever I have done I have loved them completely.

—Zöe Goldsworthy

42

Aaron only noticed Zöe's disappearance the following morning.

He had the thought as soon as he entered the living room. He leaned on his crutches, foot dangling, frowning. Everything was as he'd left it the previous night. The newspaper he'd been reading was still sprawled on the sofa. Two hops into the kitchen. His plate, bowl and mug were still sitting in the sink. Since the accident, Zöe had stopped telling him off about his laziness, had been clearing up after him. Had she now had enough?

But the balcony door was open. She would at least have shut that. There were drops of rain on the window. It was a cool, blowy summer's day. He swung over and pulled the door closed. It was quieter now. He listened. He could only hear himself, the squeak of the rubber feet of his crutches. He went into the corridor. Her bedroom door was open; the bed was made, the room empty. Down the steps, her study door was closed. The rules since their childhood were: if the door was closed, they should knock. If there was a knock, she should reply.

He knocked and called out.

—Mum?

A thin draught slid over his bare calves. The door clunked in its frame. His body unstiffened a little, she was about to open the door. But the knob didn't turn. The door shifted again. Sucked back, then settled. He grabbed the knob and turned it.

The room was empty – as he'd known it would be. And across from the door he saw straight away the open cupboard. The draught of air spread over his legs now, as it found the open door and corridor behind him. He moved forwards and bent down a little. The cupboard door had been propped open with the wicker

chair, and at the back of the cupboard, another door, held open
by a stack of papers. He crouched lower, his arms heavy on the
sticks. There was a corridor. Much like the one a few floors below,
from which you could look into the main stairwell. Zöe had never
told them about this one, though.

He pushed himself upright. Had she told Clive, but not him?

He flinched, as if from a bang. A collision. Clive had lied and
told Zöe that Aaron was responsible for Leonard's fall. Were there
other discussions they'd had together? Other secrets they'd shared.
Like this passage out of the flat.

His organs seemed to shudder. He felt a little nauseous. He let
himself fall into the wicker chair.

Clive had betrayed him. Had lied. But why? And now this odd
little scene.

She's gone.

He may have mouthed it, he may have spoken it, he wasn't sure.
Clive had lied, and Zöe had gone. He glanced around the room,
searching for something out of the ordinary. He hauled himself
up and examined her desk. Her usual notebooks, sketch pads,
pens. But still he was sure she was gone, and had left through this
new hidden passage.

Another shudder in his belly. Had Clive gone with her? Used
his clever tongue to convince her of Aaron's guilt? That their best
option was to abandon him, the slow one, the still one. Aaron
made a mistake, Mum. He didn't mean to do it. But, you know
Aaron; he blunders. And now our dad is dead. There's no helping
him, Mum. It'll come out at some point. So we just have to cut
him adrift. The best thing is to leave him here. Maybe he'll be fine,
and it won't catch up with him. But we don't want to be here when
it does.

Aaron stabbed at the floor with his crutch. He wanted to deny
that Clive would ever do such a thing. That this fantasy was
impossible. But he couldn't. Clive had shown he was prepared to
let Annette and Christine take the fall. He'd done all he could to

stop Aaron speaking out. And now he'd accused Aaron – to make him, his own brother, his twin, take the fall instead. But why? To absolve himself? But of what?

Aaron did speak out loud now.

—Nothing. We did nothing. We just saw him fall.

His voice seemed to carry along the corridor, tinny, with a minute echo. It made his words weak: a brittle denial. As if he was guilty. As if what he remembered was the wrong version of events. As if Tabitha's version, and now Clive's, was true. And now Zöe knew those versions too. And had left. Because Aaron had lied. Had told her that no one pushed Leonard.

He turned now and bent himself over. He was able to make himself just short enough that he could shuffle through the cupboard and into the corridor. It was dark. The draught here was straight, cool. There was something else open at the other end. He stood up and flung his crutches forwards, moving fast through the grey air, his mind unable to untie the idea that Zöe now thought him a killer from this strange escape through the tower's innards.

There was a door open at the other end of the corridor – to the slide, he thought at first. But no. A staircase. Another one. Another secret Clive and Zöe must have shared.

He missed the narrow steps several times with the feet of his crutches as he climbed through the dark, guided by the cool air that blew from above. He stumbled on, to another opening, again left wide open. When they explored these hidden places, he and Clive were always so careful to close every door behind them. Why had Zöe been so lax?

He was on the service stairs now. He stopped, looked up and down. And the idea came to him that perhaps it wasn't his mother who'd passed through here from the back of the study. Could it have been someone else? Annette and Christine? Zöe said they were back already. But nothing could explain them coming down through the guts of the tower and ... What? – he snorted; it echoed up and down the stairs – kidnapping Zöe? In revenge for

Clive and Aaron's silence. Or did they, too, think Aaron had pushed Leonard? Was this truth that somehow Aaron couldn't recall, wasn't party to, now spreading from one person to another, until it infected everyone and thus became reality?

A chime from above. Like something striking a bowl. It stirred him out of his abstraction. He started to climb the stairs, his quickened heartbeat telling him that this was reality. The reality in which only Zöe could have left all these doors open. In which only Zöe knew the entirety of her plan for the estate. The reality in which he had done nothing wrong. His inner voice sounded unconvinced.

The trap of the hatch to floor thirty-one was open, of course. He climbed through and paused on the landing. Windy light dropped down the flight from the roof. Another chime – a double one now, impatient. The wind wanted to show him what it had found.

On this last flight, it seemed his strength had run down. His arms felt light, and he needed to lean against the wall for the last few steps, the light dazzling him, so he couldn't see what was outside.

Nothing. He propped himself against the doorpost and scanned the roof. Curtains of grey air fell around the sides of the tower, the distant hills and streets all muted colours. The garden was rattling stalks, heaps of leaf dust cast in curves. A climber had collapsed, a dead genuflection.

Zöe wasn't here. No hair flying, a dark sail in the wind.

He paced each side of the roof, his strides and hops becoming more uneven as his panic accelerated. The series of open doors was a trail for him to follow, he was sure now. Zöe meant him to come up here. But what did she intend him to think, to feel, now he was here? Because she wanted him to think something – Zöe never did anything without an intention.

The wind galloped across the roof, picked up a handful of leaves and threw it in the air. A speck pricked his eye. The tremor that had been growing in his throat and belly these last few minutes seemed to travel to his arms and hands, so he couldn't ignore it any more. So he couldn't refuse what Zöe was showing him.

She wanted him to approach the edge, to look over. He couldn't. He kept a yard, two, three, back, but still felt he was about to fall. To follow her over. To meet her thirty-one floors below. A messy embrace.

He stopped, drew himself in, the metal of the crutches close to his bare legs. He almost thought that he should fall.

She had fallen.

No, she had jumped.

It was like an admission. As if he had pushed her too.

His next breath came with a strangled sob.

He made to turn, to get to a phone, to another person. But his hands had forgotten about his crutches, and he was tripping and tangling with them, staggered steps making his knee scream. He was near the pool now, and grabbed at its side to stop himself from hitting the floor. His hand splashed into the water and a slick glob shot up into his face.

His every memory of that day now arrives with the smell of stagnant pond water.

43

Clive wheels himself to the terrace door, pushes the button to open it and rolls outside, all with sharp, expert movements.

The carer calls from inside the apartment that she's leaving now and will see him tonight. He spins round and waves a thank you. When he's heard the lift doors shut he turns again and settles down for a stare.

Today's milky light makes the windows in all the towers shiny grey. He can't even pretend – as he so often does – that he can see miniature cut-out figures, shuttling back and forth across the rooms of Marlowe Tower. Yet Clive is sure Aaron is over there, watching him. Waiting, perhaps. Because now they do need to talk.

The last time Clive even considered this was the day of Zöe's memorial service. The investigation into her disappearance had been short. Clive had discovered that Aaron had alerted the police and that Markham had taken personal charge of the case. He'd called Clive several times to update him. He'd even cajoled him a little. 'You boys need to sort out your differences. You're all you've got now, the two of you.' Clive had replied with silence.

The inquest was brief too. Zöe's personal effects – money, cheque book, passport, keys – were all in her study. The 2CV was still parked at the foot of Marlowe Tower. In the absence of a body, Zöe was presumed to have taken her own life, jumping from the river side of the tower and dropping into the water, her body carried away by the following morning's high tide. Almost the whole estate had been at the party in the town square, so it was no surprise that no one had witnessed her fall.

With no body, there was no funeral. And if it hadn't been for

Aunt Elspeth – Zöe's sister – and some cousins, Clive doubts whether there would have been any event to mark her death. His grandmother, usually a handsome, well-put-together woman, looked as if she'd shed her leaves when he saw her. He'd used his new disabilities as an excuse for doing nothing; he'd heard people on telephones saying he had so much to cope with, it was no wonder. He'd not heard anyone wonder what Aaron's excuse might be.

At the time he'd been certain it was guilt. Guilt over saying Clive had pushed Leonard off the roof. Guilt about the panic that had led him to say it. Clive had lain awake in the hospital, watching the light change behind the curtain, and imagining the breathless thought process Aaron must have rushed through, without Clive there to stay it. For a year Aaron had been desperate to say what had really happened, but Clive had managed to prevent him; Clive's logic had held him back. The logic that said to tell would be to admit guilt, however true it was that they'd done nothing – that Leonard had walked off the edge of the roof unintentionally and unaided. But since the accident, since they'd been so riven, Clive no longer had a hold, and Aaron had panicked. Knowing he couldn't tell the truth, he'd told a lie.

Why couldn't he have chosen silence? He'd chosen it before. They had silently let Annette and Christine take the fall. And they had been acquitted. The harm done to them temporary as far as Clive could see. It had been over. Only Tabitha was in the way now, and she had given her promise. All Aaron had done was traumatise their mother. And it had been too much for her to bear.

Clive stares at the riverside corner of the tower for a moment. Then drops his gaze to the river beneath. There's a stretch of grey-brown beach exposed right now. A falling body would thump into the gravel and sand. Back then, the tide was high, they were told. Zöe would have made an echoing splash. Then floated away, her body now a jumble of bones in the seabed off Sheppey.

Clive didn't attend the memorial. He didn't want to meet

Aaron was the complete and final truth of it. He'd argued with himself elaborately, but in the end that was the reason. He'd been sure Aaron would be there, though. On the day, Clive sat in his room in the rehabilitation centre, and imagined Aaron – sad, doubtful, adrift – in the congregation at the RIBA, where the memorial was held, and he felt a pang; Clive should be there to anchor him, whatever their differences. When Elspeth visited later in the day and told him Aaron hadn't been there either, Clive was first surprised, then resentful. Aaron had betrayed him again; had been happy to allow him to mourn alone.

The wind picks up around the terrace, pots and plants and the open door click and clunk, and then settle. An upward gust and then a hoot – as if an owl has flapped past on an uncharacteristic daytime hunt.

Clive needs to speak to Aaron. Aaron needs to speak to him. If Annette and Christine have returned, then they are all back to 1977, and the intervening years have disappeared, concertinaed away as the pages snap shut.

Physically, the accident put a brake on Clive's life. Nowadays, Clive thinks, with no little begrudgement, it's easier to travel, to get around the place in a wheelchair. Back then, each journey was a complex operation. It made him essentially stationary, the rest of the world flowing around him. He had to make a noise to be heard, throw his hands up to be seen. And he was. People did pay him attention. They came to him, sat to bring themselves to his level, made a special space so he could take a place at the table – and he'd quickly ensured it was the head. And there he remains, watching everyone else sitting and leaving, rising and walking.

He thinks of Aaron, with his legs, which he's used to go nowhere at all. As far as Clive knows, at least.

Since Zöe fell from the top of Marlowe Tower, their only communication has been through lawyers. Initially, it was the same one – Zöe's family lawyer in Blackheath. Clive never visited him there, or at his office. But he knew Aaron went in person. In a call the lawyer might say 'your brother was here yesterday' or 'Aaron dropped into the office'. And Clive had wanted to ask 'Does he limp because of his knee?' and 'Has he cut his hair?' But never 'What does he say about me?'

Zöe's will was rather complex – bequests and instructions for so many different organisations, friends, cousins, a distant uncle. She'd named Elspeth executor. Clive can Zöe her in the meetings with her lawyer, the focus in her eyes, the tip of her nose pointing at her intentions. He's not surprised that her gift to Annette and Christine – outside the will but almost concurrent with it – escaped both his and, he presumes, Aaron's attention.

He stares at floor thirty now. Locates the windows to 304. Squints. Frowns. No one, of course.

He needs to speak to Aaron.

Zöe left Aaron flat 246 and a big lump of money. She left Clive her business.

Clive wonders, not for the first time, about her thinking. He resented Aaron the lump sum at the time. But he wouldn't have given up the business for it. He wanted both. In truth, he wanted Aaron, he now acknowledges, nodding and shivering in the wind on his terrace. He remembers wheeling himself through the gardens of the rehabilitation centre, trying to get himself as far away from the building – from other people – as possible. He was still learning how to manoeuvre his chair, still building up the required strength in his arms. At last he was in the arbour, which looked out over the shallow Surrey valley below. There were sheep a field away. A crow stalked the long grass ahead of him. But otherwise he was alone. He allowed himself to cry in a way he wouldn't in his room, with his books, papers and radio as witnesses. He cried for his druthers. For his brother. It shouldn't have been like this. It should've been how he'd dreamed it. He and Aaron, taking shares in the company. He would have led, of course, Aaron behind, pressed against the back of his arm, murmuring encouragement or caution.

But Zöe had thought herself wiser – or more prejudiced. She had made the will in the year between Leonard's death and her own, reapportioning her estate, now she'd inherited parts of his. And she'd decided what her sons' fates would be.

Clive she'd made work – for great gain, he concedes. Aaron was left to drift. But he'd ended up staying in the same place. Clive she'd judged right. He hadn't failed her confidence in the way he's always felt Aaron has.

After a year out recuperating, learning to live as a paraplegic, Clive returned to university. To ramps and help and friends who would push. And friends who would band together to lift him and hold him high, his wheels spinning and his drink slopping into his lap and into the faces of the gang below. And then had flown, as if they had launched him from above their heads. Into the eighties. It sounds like a song to him now. His architecture was of minor importance to him by then. His real interest was development. The big projects. The big money – it still washes around him now. In the eighties he built several ugly low rises in and around the Isle of Dogs. He had them demolished and rebuilt twenty years later. Taller, slicker, harder. Goldsworthy stopped being an architectural practice early on. He took Thatcher's easy money and turned away from Zöe's worthiness. Estates, social housing, held little interest for him. Not for forty years. Not until the Deptford Strand opportunity presented itself.

It was Kulwant who drew his attention to it. An article in an online industry magazine about Deptford Council gaining permission to rebuild the iconic and prize-winning estate, to make it compete with the luxury apartments lining the river either side of it.

—Isn't this your mother's estate? You lived there, didn't you?

Kulwant had clearly heard Clive giving a speech at a conference or dinner: 'Growing up in a concrete monstrosity as I did...'

Clive knew Aaron still lived there. And Aaron was his first thought when Kulwant turned his laptop towards him to show him the article. At last, Aaron will have to move, he thought. The world had finally caught up with him.

Zöe's money had acted like an anchor on Aaron. Yes, it gave him stability, but he had never seemed able to raise it and sail on. For years Clive thought that Zöe had believed Aaron would find something; she simply had to give him the means to do it. But now, as the cool air penetrates the wool of his jumper and blasts his ears so they ache, he wonders whether she decided that Aaron would do exactly what he has done: spend his life doing nothing. An unobtrusive existence inside flat 246 Marlowe Tower. Did Zöe watch the two of them drifting apart after Leonard's fall, after the heat of the summer had dissolved, and realise that without Clive, Aaron would come to nothing? And that coming to nothing required a little help? Had she changed the will then? How had it read before? A big sum for Clive too?

He laughs out loud, and the wind obliges by dropping for a moment, and not snatching his laugh away. He know he's ridiculous. He owns this penthouse. He owns the whole building beneath it. He built the damned thing. His wealth is large, yet the idea that he may have lost a sum to Aaron when they were nineteen irks him. Irks.

Yes, he does need to speak to Aaron.

It's really too cold now. He turns on the spot – one wheel spun backwards, one forwards, and rolls back into the living room.

44

From above, Clive is a moving vehicle. A hawk, hovering nearby, observes the flicking movements of his pale hands on his wheels. It twitches, adjusts its angle in the air, then moves on, distracted now by the little crests forming on the river. The wind is whipping the surface against the current and the tide is aiding it from below. Their little battle makes foam. The beach on the Deptford shore is slimmer now. Each wave spreads up the shingle, dyes the dun sand dark grey, then retreats, but leaves a millimetre more water than the last.

From the river wall, Aaron stares down at the tangled waters, the paradox of downstream and up, the incoming tide and the flow of the river. From above, he is a smudge, an error on a rough draft. And then he moves, and his random shape organises itself. He strides now, and disappears into the tall building.

Sometime later he re-emerges, and now we see a face. He's gazing upwards. His features are scored, angular. It's only for a moment, and then his long grizzled hair lets the wind wrap it around his ears. Following Aaron's greying head and now-energetic limp, we see him as almost the only mobile object on the whole mess of the estate. He crosses the town square without pause, passing the parade of shops, closed for several years now, and the rubble of the community centre. The broad avenue between the long blocks leading onto Evelyn Street is narrowed to an alley now by long barriers and fences bearing the Clive Goldsworthy logo. Aaron speeds through. A bus is approaching the stop on the other side of the road – near to where he and Clive jumped off one early-summer night in 1976. He runs a stiff-legged, swaying lope across the road, waving a hand. The white-topped bus halts as he crosses in front of it, and he slips inside.

He is briefly in sight again as he crosses into the Tube station at Canada Water, but then he's gone – for however many moments it takes to travel under the river. From above, not everything is in view. There are hidden places. Dark, rattling tunnels.

He appears again, crossing the square at Canary Wharf. We recognise the limp. He stops momentarily and raises his face to the tall buildings surrounding him. He knows where he's going, it seems, yet something about them surprises him.

He enters the DLR station and takes the next train heading for Mudchute. There he takes another bus. A few stops and he hops down. A little stagger as he gets his bearings. We see his hands – one pointing in that direction, then this, the other positioned a little behind him, indicating where's he's come from, perhaps.

Assured, he crosses the road and takes a turning opposite. It's quiet – like the wrecked estate. But here the streets are bricked and clean. Neat trees stand straight, their trunks in cages.

And at the end of the street, the river. He stops by the wall, a thousand feet across the water from where he stood an hour ago. Three hundred limped strides. He should have taken a boat.

He turns. The wind sweeps back his hair. Yes, his features are scored, angular. His eyes stare at the tower reaching up in front of him, Clive at its top.

45

Clive can see on his phone that the call is coming from reception. He shuffles through the possibilities. The carer has come back for something? A physio appointment he's forgotten? Kulwant?

—Mr Goldsworthy, a visitor for you? Not in the book.

—Who is it?

—Aaron Goldsworthy.

There's an unnecessary pause, some muffled words, then:

—Your brother.

Clive wants to stand up. The urge travels through his body. The need to rise. To move. Even to flee. He's still seated, of course, still parked by his desk, the phone still in his hand.

—Shall I send him up?

Not only can Clive not stand; he finds he can't speak. The miniature panic at wanting to move his legs and not being able to was once common. But it became familiar – and then rare. But never has he been unable to speak. The panic roars for a second – perhaps two.

—Mr Goldsworthy?

—Sorry.

A rush of relief. The reflexive apology has unstuck his tongue.

—Sorry, he repeats. Sorry. Sorry.

—Shall I send him up, or will you come down?

—Sorry, says Clive. Send him up. Send him up.

Clive tries to end the call, and clatters his phone onto his desk. He rolls himself to the lift, bumping into a side table on the way. He presses 'unlock lift' two or three times. Wishes he hadn't. He reverses away from the lift, still facing it, staring at the doors.

Could he cancel 'unlock lift'? he wonders. This system doesn't

let you change your mind. Why won't it let him change his mind?
He's allowed to change his mind, in the time it takes a lift to rise
twenty floors. He doesn't want to see Aaron now. He didn't want
to when he said 'send him up'. He said it because he was saying
'sorry'. Because he was stuck with 'sorry' on his tongue, and 'send'
came out because 'no' was too difficult, and his tongue was
threatening to go the way of his legs.

The lift car is nearing. He can hear the change in tone beyond
the doors. He turns the wheels backwards. It seems incredibly
difficult to do something he's done without thinking every day
for forty years. His hands slip off.

The lift has arrived. There's a pause for thought between the lift
mechanism's halt and the door mechanism's start.

The doors open.

◆

Aaron hadn't expected to have to look downwards. Clive is in a
chair. A wheelchair. Aaron knew this, but he's still surprised that
he has to lower his eyes.

The lift doors begin to close. Aaron hasn't moved. Hasn't been
able to move.

Clive instinctively leans forwards. A split second later he
remembers he needs to move his wheels. But it's too late, he's
falling.

The sight makes Aaron move, finally; he tries to squeeze
through the closing gap. But the doors hit his body and for a
second he's trapped. Clive is on the floor. Aaron hears a grunt and
an oof.

The doors reopen and now Aaron is bending down. It hurts his
knee, but he ignores the pain. He's already taking Clive by the
arms, hauling him up.

—I'm OK, I'm OK, Clive is saying, but he feels like he might
be sick.

He thinks he should be struggling out of Aaron's grip. He feels Aaron's hands on his upper arms, then the warmth of his chest as he shuffles him backwards, and despite himself, Clive lets his body weaken. He should stiffen up, help the operation. But he languishes. He closes his eyes. His cheek against Aaron's. Aaron smells of the outside.

Aaron knows he doesn't need to hold Clive so tightly. He could grab him under the arms and swing him into his chair. But he doesn't. He presses Clive to his chest. Clive smells of fresh laundry, a sharp deodorant. His arms, chest, back are solid. But Aaron can feel the droop and lightness of his legs, like the train of a dress.

Clive is in the chair and has to let go. Aaron has to straighten up and stand back.

They can do nothing but hold each other's gaze. Neither knows how long they do this for. Neither knows how to begin, but they both know that they have already begun. They've already embraced.

—That's the first time that's happened, Clive says at last.

—I know, says Aaron.

Clive doesn't ask him how.

—Annette and Christine have come back, says Aaron.

—I know, says Clive.

—I thought you did.

Aaron's hair is the same length it was when Clive last saw him. But now there are shades of grey. In the same places Zöe had them. Clive wonders whether he'd have the same if he grew his hair long. Aaron is wearing jeans and a denim jacket. Clive thinks this is his uniform. He's been wearing the same thing for forty years, Clive is sure.

The thought makes him spin on the spot and shoot himself across the parquet towards his desk. Aaron thinks the skilful manoeuvres are for his benefit.

—Sit down, then. Clive nods at a sofa.

Aaron does as he's told. Comfortable with that.

As he sits, he sees that, straight ahead of him, taking up most of the wall opposite the lift are two vast paintings, hung one next to the other.

—You kept that painting. He points at the one on the right; the one he saw in the flat on the thirty-first floor of Marlowe Tower. He thinks the heavy crust of paint has cracked. Its crevices have collected dust. The whites have a slight yellow tinge.

—Yes, says Clive. And I found its twin.

Aaron glances at him to catch his smirk. The other painting is indeed a twin. The background to both is essentially the same – shades of white with a faint brown vertical strip running down the centre. But whereas the other painting has a vivid red stripe running a fifth of the way from the left, this has a vivid blue stripe a fifth from the right.

Aaron glances around the rest of the room. He's sure there are other items from the thirty-first floor in here. He knows its contents went to Clive at some point in the will negotiations.

—Mum painted them, Clive says. There's a signature on the back.

—Mum did? I didn't know she painted. Sketched yes, but, painted?

—I think Mum did a lot of things we don't know about. I found the twin in a store, with a load of other bits of art she'd made. I don't know whether they were meant to be hung together, but it seems Leonard had one and Zöe had the other.

—When were they painted?

—Before we were born. 1958 and 1959 according to the signatures. I can only think that we must have seen Zöe's one in Blackheath at some point when we were small.

Aaron observes the painting in silence for a moment.

—Have you spoken to them, then? says Clive.

Aaron looks at Clive as if he doesn't know who he's talking about.

—Annette and Christine, Clive prompts.

—No, he says. I suppose ... I suppose I thought I needed to talk to you first.

To Aaron's surprise, and to his own, Clive doesn't have a reply.

—And then, well, I spoke to Tabitha, says Aaron.

—Tabitha?

Clive adjusts the angle of his chair.

—She got a flat in Marlowe Tower years ago, says Aaron. She was moved out with all the other tenants.

Aaron stops. He feels uneasy about how easy they are with each other. He wants to be less comfortable. To stand up, or at least sit in an upright chair. In fact he wants to move away. Go into another room. There's a big terrace outside the big windows. He wants to go out there. Have the glass between them. Look back through it at Clive.

—So Tabitha is angry?

—Of course. Most of them are. Most of us are.

Clive grips the arms of his chair.

—Does she want something?

—She didn't say. But she's spoken to Annette and Christine. She says she's told them—

Clive interrupts:

—She told them what she reckons she saw? Because of a damned rented council flat?

The room is tall and wide. His voice rings off the white walls. The anger in his face makes him younger. His arms are energetic. He looks like he might launch himself out of the chair again, but this time leap across the floor.

—Everything she said she saw that night, she says she's told Annette and Christine, says Aaron.

—Why?

—Why do you think, Clive? She said she kept our secret—

—There *was* no secret—

—She kept our secret all these years, she said, but she didn't expect to be chucked out of her home.

—No one's chucking people out. It's normal in redevelopment. She'll have got a new home.

—No one sees it like that, Clive.

—Oh, it's bullshit. Left-wing bullshit.

—So what if it is? It means she's told Annette and Christine a pack of lies. Who knows what they'll do now.

Aaron wants to add more. Wants to blame Clive more. Wants to load accusation upon accusation.

—How can Tabitha do that? says Clive. She didn't even see what she said she saw. Why lie like that, forty years after the fact?

—You did.

Clive looks like he's been slapped. He pushes his chair forwards. He has the urge to ram his legs into Aaron's. Pin him to the sofa.

—I lied? *I* lied?

—You lied, Clive. How can you say you didn't?

Aaron's throat tautens. It's unfamiliar. He hasn't shouted in years.

—Because you're the one who fucking lied, says Clive. You!

Clive loosens his grip on the wheels and throws both hands up. The chair rolls back a little.

Aaron finds himself standing up, about to speak. But Clive speaks first. As always.

—You told Mum I pushed him, he says.

It's the sentence that was on Aaron's tongue.

And Clive sees in his eyes that it was. And he knows:

—And she told you that *I* said *you* pushed him...

Clive's voice is flat and quiet. The echoey room shrinks; sits listening. Rapt.

Aaron nods. His body is ready to spring. Grab Clive in a hug. But something stops him. The wheelchair. The stoop he'd have to make to reach his brother's body. The rest of the words they need to speak. The years and years of sentences and paragraphs. Zöe. He sits back down.

—When did she tell you that? Aaron manages at last, slumping back into the sofa.

—The night of the Jubilee party. Before she disappeared. It was our last conversation.

Aaron stares at the two paintings.

—She told me that afternoon, he says, before she went to see you.

They study each other's faces with the complete comfort of love. Neither has looked at anyone like that for forty years. Each watches the other's process as if it generates his own.

—She thought we did it together, says Clive.

—Yes.

—She thought she could get the truth out of us by setting us against each other.

—It worked, says Aaron.

—What?

—I told her what happened. Exactly. The real version.

'Real' rings around the room. Hovers above their heads. A flash – a reflection from a window across the river – darts across the room. Spears the word. Dissolves it.

—I thought you'd lied because you couldn't cope, says Clive. I thought you blamed me for stopping you telling the truth, so you were trying to save yourself.

—I did blame you. I hated you for the position you put us in. You put me in. But I'd never have lied like that. Said you'd killed someone to save myself? Never.

—I thought we must've broken something after our fall, says Clive. That was the only way I could explain it.

—I thought for a long time that somehow you believed I had pushed him. That maybe our fall affected your memory or something. You were in a coma for days. I thought that maybe Tabitha's version had become your version, because you couldn't remember what really happened.

Clive wonders for a moment. He had had memory problems when he'd come out of the coma. Names escaped him for a long time after. He recalls once, a week after he woke up, looking at Zöe and struggling for the word 'Mum'. Claws grip his chest. Dig in. He shoots a glance at Aaron. Could what he, Clive, remembers of the party, of Leonard's fall, be false? Had Aaron really pushed him but then blamed Clive. Was he here telling lies again?

Clive reaches inwards, diving deep for those moments. The darkness, the flickering candles and lamps. The heat. The hot wind blowing upwards at the edge of the roof. Leonard turning. Walking. His fall. The white flag of his shirt swallowed into a dark throat. How was it so vivid if it hadn't happened?

And with a twitch, the grip on his chest tightens; he gasps in air. Aaron starts, eyes wide. Alarmed.

—What's wrong, Clive?

—I don't know. It's like I can't remember properly anymore.

Clive feels himself shrinking away from something – some attack. Everything is suddenly unreliable.

—What do you mean, you can't remember? says Aaron.

—Whether what happened that night happened the way it happened, or whether...

Clive needs to move. His brain is firing signals to his legs, telling him to run. He spins himself towards the balcony doors, but his driving skills have abandoned him; he collides with the corner of the sofa. Aaron jerks. Stands. Puts his hands on the wheelchair handles. Manoeuvres the chair to free it.

He stares at the top of Clive's head.

—Whether what? Aaron says, loudly, as if he needs the volume to get the words through Clive's skull, the bone thickened over the injury.

Clive rolls away from him, and Aaron is left holding out his empty hands. If Clive can't remember that night, then Aaron is alone with his memory. Tabitha was there, but what she said she saw was wrong – wasn't it?

For a sliver of a second he wonders if it was right. If she somehow saw Clive push Leonard when Aaron was looking away.

Clive swings his chair round, glaring up at Aaron as if he's heard Aaron's thought.

Aaron grasps the tails of his hair and pulls. It's all so confusing. After a life of miserable peace, his mind – his body – can't manage this onslaught.

—It happened the way it happened, Aaron says, letting go of his hair and chopping the air with both hands.

—Which was? Clive says. He wants to force Aaron to say it. Twin telepathy, twin intuition, won't suffice. He needs words, sounds that bounce off the walls.

—He fell, says Aaron. By himself. By accident. He walked off the edge of the roof. We didn't touch him. Neither of us. I told Mum the truth, says Aaron.

—And she didn't believe you, says Clive.

—No, says Aaron. I don't think she did.

—Which is why...

—Which is why she killed herself.

It doesn't clutch at Aaron's throat, his chest, thinking about Zöe, her death. The events leading up to it still feel recent, open, alive. But her death itself seems long ago. A fossilled bereavement. Tap it and it's hard, durable.

He takes a step towards Clive. He wants to feel his brother's body again. But his own body refuses it. Or the need is not strong enough to move his limbs.

Clive half expects Aaron to bend, but he doesn't. And Clive understands. And is both disappointed and relieved. The reconciliation has a faint stench about it.

—And now they think we pushed him. Clive nods towards the window.

Aaron looks over at Marlowe Tower too.

—We can't know that, he says. They wouldn't take Tabitha's word for it, would they? Aaron grimaces. She said they were angry at us. Like they believed what she told them about seeing us that night. But Tabitha could be lying. She's no different from how she was back then.

Clive lines himself up beside Aaron, so they're both gazing ahead.

—I found out something. Recently. Since the council started offering to buy flats from the owners.

Aaron waits, doesn't look down.

—Mum gave Annette and Christine flat 304.

Aaron does look at Clive now.

—She signed the transfer on the day she disappeared, says Clive. It's documented on the Land Registry. She split the lease in two. Handed flat thirty-one to the council and 304 to them. A gift.

Aaron walks a little circle beside the large window. He comes to a stop beside Clive's wheelchair.

—Tabitha told me Mum gave the flat to them, he says. I guessed they owned it. I even heard them say it ... He stops. He's given himself away.

—You've been eavesdropping?

—Wouldn't you? But I didn't have any idea that Mum gave it to them, not until Tabitha told me. Why would she do that?

—Recompense? says Clive. If she thought we'd really pushed Leonard, maybe she thought they were owed something for their year in prison.

—OK. But does a flat make up for that? And from the mother of the people who let them go through all that...?

—Unless she told them we were the ones who pushed Leonard, they threatened to go to the police and the flat was the price for their silence. But a flat in a council block in Deptford?

—And why fight for it now? says Aaron. I've been in 246 nearly my entire life. They left in 1977 and they've only just moved back in. What's making them dig their heels in now?

—Unless it's a simple message. They want to tell us they think we pushed Leonard.

—It doesn't add up, says Aaron.

He wants to go out on the terrace again. It's big. There are plants and large containers, trembling, fearful in the wind. He reaches for a handle on the door, but can't see one.

—Press the button. Clive nods towards it.

Aaron presses it and the wall of glass trundles open. He steps out and the wind catches his head in its grasp, runs fingers through his hair and then gads off over the river, laughing and looking back. Laughing again.

Clive appears by his side. Edges a little ahead of him. Aaron steps aside, but after a moment shifts back. He finds his thigh beside Clive's arm. He moves one step. They touch. Clive feels the mass – warm, flush against his triceps. Adjacent.

—We have to speak to them, don't we? says Aaron.

—We have to speak to them.

46

Aaron arrives on floor thirty of Marlowe Tower a little breathless from his climb, his knee making its usual complaints. The corridor stretches this way and that. The floor a herringbone – strips of light spreading from the open doors of the empty flats. With one fault, one missing stripe. Flat 304. Its door is closed. He steps silently towards it, holding the letter low and to his side, like a stiletto.

He can hear something now. A ticking. Not a clock. A drum. Bass. They're playing a record. And now he can hear horns – trumpets. He passes what was Mrs Ledbury's flat. He imagines her banging on the wall. And just as he does, the music jumps louder. Someone has turned it up. Annette, not Christine, he thinks. He hears women's voices now. He's right outside the door. They're singing about bringing only love.

Aaron bows slightly, lifts the flap of the letterbox and slips the envelope through the slot.

47

The flap claps, and Aaron is already away – his limp almost a hop. He now has to imagine the letter lying on the doormat. We, however, can follow it, through the letterbox and into the hall.

The record stops abruptly, with a crack. Someone has taken the needle off. Down the hall, in the living room, Annette is sitting on the edge of the sofa, her hand slightly raised, the other flat on the cushion. She has just sat forwards. She's looking at Christine with her mouth open. Christine is still bent over the record player.

Christine straightens up. Makes a move into the corridor, and Annette is up and now ahead of her. She stoops to pick up the envelope, but Christine takes it from her as they walk back to the living room. They are yet to speak. Christine's braids are a little shorter and greyer than Annette's. She was sick for a while, several years ago. Now her hair breaks more easily. Annette puts her sister's braids in bunches for her, but has to make the style different from her own.

Christine opens the envelope, and they each hold a side of the page as they read it. They must read it twice, because they stand immobile for quite some time.

At last, Annette lets go. Christine lets the letter drop to her side. It flaps – it's thick, high-quality paper. Christine sits and places the letter on the coffee table in front of her as Annette sits down opposite. The air is thick with thought. It's hard for us to fly through. Perhaps we haven't earned the right to hear their thoughts. Have Aaron and Clive? Perhaps Annette and Christine are about to decide.

Annette straightens her head, breathes in through her nose and passes her tongue over her top lip – a mannerism she's developed that Christine hasn't.

Christine straightens her head too. They both open their mouths, about to speak.

◆

But before a word is spoken, we are out through the window and falling, lightly, past the empty balconies and grey glass of the vacant flats, down six floors until we arrive outside the balcony of flat 246.

And here is Aaron, entering the living room from the hallway. He stands in the middle of the room, his keys in his hand. He looks straight ahead, out of the balcony window and straight into our eyes. All he sees, of course, is a clear pool of air, filtered of all character so it blends with the gases around it – giving it the sense that it is omniscient.

◆

The flat doesn't seem to be his anymore. It's as if Clive has moved back in. The table has a pale oval patch, where Aaron sits and eats three times a day. The cushion where he leans his head is dark, the pile flattened and matted. The parquet bears a pale trail from the door, to the corridor, to the kitchen. Clive would see all this.

Aaron puts his keys on the table. Puts his hand in his pocket to pull out his phone. Clive put his number into it. Should Aaron phone him and say he won't come back to stay there tonight, after all? Now he's back here, he knows that their rift wasn't fixed in the two or three hours they spent together.

He walks into the kitchen. His mouth is dry. He takes a glass from the cupboard.

But perhaps his home never really was his. Zöe gave it to him along with the money he's lived on all his life, but he's never so much as bought a piece of furniture or painted a wall. He's been a tenant all this time.

He knows that he will go back to Clive's tonight. The thought of sitting here alone – he pictures it briefly, his hand on the tap – scares him now, even though he has done it for thousands of nights.

He turns the tap and it coughs. A splutter of water hits the pan of the sink. Another, then a dribble. And then nothing. A sigh and a clunk somewhere behind the cupboards.

Aaron puts down the dry glass and turns to the light switch. Click, click. Nothing.

He doesn't believe for a second that this is Clive's doing. He doubts even that the council has switched off his utilities. Somehow it seems more likely that Marlowe Tower has at last decided to spit him out. He steps back into the living room and scans it once again. Now he knows the lights don't work, it seems darker, the shadows slovenly, their edges blurring the clarity of Zöe's design.

He heads down the flight of steps and into his bedroom, pulls out his ancient canvas knapsack, its leather straps scaly and stiff, and wanders round the flat, filling it with odd items, not thinking too hard about what he's packing.

At last he makes for the door, but as he approaches it, his foot skids. His groin yelps, and his knee joins in. He's slipped on an envelope. It's now lying a yard down the hall, the tread of his shoe stamped on its white surface.

He hesitates to pick it up. He bends and his knapsack swings off his shoulder and onto the floor, but the envelope is in his hands. It's addressed to him. Mr Aaron Goldsworthy, 246 Marlowe Tower, Deptford Strand Estate. But there is no stamp. *BY HAND* is written in the top right-hand corner.

He almost drops it. Almost stamps on it again.

But he opens it, of course.

The Residents' and Tenants' Trust

2 May 2021

Dear Mr Goldsworthy.

Further to my letter of 3 April, I'd like to invite you to a meeting with members of the trust's team, residents and former residents of Deptford Strand Estate, as well as other parties concerned, to discuss what steps we can take to get a better deal for the estate's residents in light of the ongoing redevelopment project.

Since we last wrote to you, we have been in touch with the other owner-occupiers of Marlowe Tower as well as our legal advisers, and we believe we have a strong case to challenge this specific aspect of the development plan: i.e. the sale of Marlowe Tower to Clive Goldsworthy & Co.

The meeting is planned for Monday, 17 May. Please contact me by email or on the below number to let us know if you'd like to attend.

Kind regards
Sally Perry
Advice Manager

It's dim in the hall. Aaron reaches for the light switch so he can read the letter again, more clearly. A click, and he remembers.

Why didn't Sally Perry post this in the normal way? He turns the envelope over. His name and address are printed on a label. *BY HAND* is handwritten. His footprint crosses the two words, but they still feel like a threat. He can't recall ever seeing Annette and Christine's handwriting, but he's in no doubt they wrote and underlined those two words, then crept down the stairs and slipped the letter through the letterbox, just as he has done with the note to them.

But when did they post it – while he was at Clive's? Or just a moment ago, while he was packing? Which is why he didn't see it when he came in.

He looks at the back of the door, loath to unlock it now, loath to deal with this by himself, now that he doesn't have to.

He shakes himself, stuffs the letter into his knapsack and fumbles himself out of the door, annoyed that Clive is so far away, but just across the water.

48

At seven o'clock on the evening after Aaron posted the invitation, Clive receives a call from reception.

—They're here, he says to Aaron. And on time.

Clive presses 'unlock lift' and they both look at the doors.

Nothing, for what feels like four decades.

Clive breaks the silence:

—Have you had your Covid jab?

The question takes Aaron by surprise. And Clive is surprised that he asked it. And that he's asked it right now. It makes Aaron's throat tighten a little.

—Yes, both, he replies. You?

—The same. Good. So we're both, you know, safe. These are my first visitors in more than a year. Apart from the carers. And work people. And you, of course.

Aaron moves a little closer to Clive and places a hand on one of the wheelchair's handles. Clive feels the gentle pressure.

And then the numbers on the small panel beside the call button move. A tiny hum makes every molecule in the room vibrate. Soft bumps and nudges suggest each floor the car passes up through. And then it stops, with a sound like a sip.

Another forty-year pause. More. Enough to travel back to 1977 and forwards again, to now.

The doors seem to brace. And then they open.

And then two women appear.

Two black women. That is what Aaron and Clive see, before they see that the two black women are Annette and Christine.

Annette steps forwards first; Christine follows a blink after, but her first step is long so they move into the room side by side.

—Annette, Christine, thank you for coming, says Clive, spinning himself round with a flourish. Please sit down. We've laid out some drinks. Help yourselves.

It's Clive's business voice. Kulwant would recognise it. Aaron perhaps doesn't.

—And hello to both of you, says Annette as they sit down.

—Hello, says Christine. Neither she nor Annette have yet smiled.

There's a pause. As if the audience is holding its breath. The stage lights are bright, the actors acting. The director has told them to hold the moment for as long as possible.

Aaron breaks it first.

—We always knew, he says. Then stops.

There are clearly more words stored up, ready to tumble out. But Aaron isn't used to speaking.

Annette and Christine's faces are stretched with confusion. They exchange a quick look. Aaron organises himself.

—We always knew you didn't do it. Push Leonard. Off the roof.

He points upwards. Then tilts his head towards the window, to Marlowe Tower.

Clive has opened his mouth, but instead of speaking he grips the arms of his wheelchair and makes himself more upright. This can't be how he wanted this scene to play. He must be preventing himself from scowling at Aaron.

But we must stop looking at Clive, at Aaron. We've spent so much time with them that we can now, with confidence, imagine their reactions, the track of their thoughts, the ebb and flow of their emotions. We should look instead at Annette and Christine. Because their expressions have shifted. They're staring at each other. It would be an uncomfortably long stare for anyone else – but it doesn't seem so for them. Christine looks quietly thoughtful, her face completely relaxed, a little jowly. Annette's is more taut. But their expressions change at the same time – they've made a decision.

Christine turns away from Annette and speaks:

—We should talk about our mother.

Another pause. Annette and Christine take turns in monitoring Aaron and then Clive, Clive and then Aaron. Finally they look at each other once more. Annette places the tip of her tongue between her lips and tips her head slightly to one side:

—We're guessing you don't know, then. Zöe was our mother too.

—We're your sisters, adds Christine.

This pause fills out the stage, the room, the auditorium. The page. It's precarious. Any one of the four people that hold it could collapse at any time. You may already have known what Annette and Christine have revealed. Perhaps you guessed it long ago – at the beginning of this story, even.

But Aaron and Clive haven't.

Clive's wheelchair rolls backwards. Aaron rubs his face.

Christine looks at Aaron, Annette at Clive. Then they both glance up at the wall facing them, gazing at a painting each.

—You're – Aaron coughs – our sisters.

—Yup.

Aaron stands up. Clive claps then rubs his palms together.

—Well, I need a drink after that.

He rolls forwards to the low table and busies himself with bottles and glasses – it looks like a bit of business in a play.

—She told us it was her that pushed Leonard, says Annette.

Clive's hands freeze – one is still on the cap of a bottle. Aaron steps outside the square of sofas, paces the long wall opposite the window, then re-enters the square from the other side.

Annette and Christine watch their brothers, waiting for them to settle after these first gusts.

Aaron sits down again, but leans forwards, towards his sisters. Clive stops playing with the drinks and angles his chair towards them.

It's as if the lights around the four now fade, and a spot rises on the tableau the sisters form. They're facing their brothers, they're facing us, but their bodies are angled slightly towards each other. Their dark braids and the silver lines pencilled through them, their umber skin and the points of their noses, which we can see now are Zöe's, tell the beginning of their story. Christine picks up the thread:

—She came to see us, on the night of the Jubilee, before she disappeared.

Aaron and Clive's faces are dark now. We can't see their expressions, but we can imagine their thoughts, the chase to catch up with Christine's words.

—She didn't knock at the door. She came down from Leonard's flat. And just walked in.

—Like she owned the place, says Annette. Which she did, of course.

—She said she thought we wouldn't let her in, and that she needed to speak to us, so she used her key. She said sorry – like, a hundred times.

—It was like punctuation, says Annette. Sorry at the end of every sentence.

—She apologised so much, she wasn't making any sense. Annette made her sit down and gave her a drink.

—To be honest we thought there was something wrong with her, you know.

—She asked why we weren't downstairs at the party, says Christine. She said we had every right to be there, that we'd done nothing wrong – people should be apologising to us.

—And then she said we were the victims in all this, says Annette. None of this was our fault, but we'd suffered the most. Sorry, sorry, sorry.

—We should go to the party, she said. Come down to the party, she said. But honestly, there was nothing 'party' about the woman.

—I said, and what kind of reception do you think we'll get down there? The jury might have found us not guilty, but them down there, they still believed we did it. 'Of course it was the black girls.' They didn't see two young women studying at college. No. We were interlopers. Who brought nothing but trouble.

—And then she just came out with it. 'I did it,' she said. 'I pushed him off the roof.'

There are shuffles in the dim fringes of the spotlight. Christine continues:

—For a second we couldn't believe it. But only for a second.

—It made sense, says Annette. The simplest explanation. Occam's whatsit.

—We knew all about her and Leonard. He talked about her constantly. They'd been apart for nearly twenty years, but it was like they'd just split up.

—He had that bitterness, you know? says Annette. When someone chucks you and it feels like the greatest betrayal in history. But you're still in love with them.

—We've always thought he was still in love with her. He had to be to hate her that much.

—We never let on to you what he said about her. You didn't need to know that. You don't need to know it now.

—Suffice to say, it was a surprise that we hadn't suspected it was her before, I suppose, says Christine. He was clearly harassing her – and had been for years.

—After she'd said that, she started up again with all the sorries, again, and I got fed up with it. We get it, I said. You hated your ex. He'd pushed you too far. You shoved him off the roof in an argument or whatever. Then everyone started blaming us, and you let them. You got away with it. You had no reason to own up.

—But we were thinking, why was she owning up now? And to us. If she was that guilty she'd go straight to the police, wouldn't she? And then she said ... And then she said, 'I did have a reason to own up. I do have a reason. I'm your mum. Your birth mother.'

—She kind of struggled over 'birth', says Annette.

Annette and Christine gaze at each other now. It's a rare expression, one few of us see, and none of us sees often. It's of a deep love, but one without passion, and without the memory of passion; and with none of the imbalance of the look of love between a mother and child.

—She just stared at us then, says Annette. It seemed like for days. I couldn't think what to say. Neither could Christine.

—I couldn't think what to say. So we just said nothing.

—Nothing for what seemed like hours.

—The windows were open, says Christine.

—The flat was stale and stuffy...

—...After a year of not being lived in. We could hear the music from the party, says Christine.

—It's a long way from the square to the tower, so either the wind was carrying the sounds, or they were playing their tunes damn loud. I remember thinking that they complained about us all those months, but it was fine for them to play their music, party outside, when everything was dressed up with Union Jacks.

—But Zöe was sitting there, staring at us, says Christine. Not saying anything.

—And then the music stopped. And it was like she'd been waiting for the song to end. Because she started talking.

—She started talking sort of into the air. Not to us particularly.

—I don't think she looked at us once during that whole story, says Annette.

—She met our father in Jamaica. She had a commission to build a hotel, and he was one of the civil engineers. She said things were already difficult with Leonard.

—Zöe's career was taking off, says Annette, and Leonard was doing well. He'd started calling them a 'star couple', but the truth was Zöe was the star. He was a sidekick. And he was not happy with that description.

—So when a handsome engineer on a far-off island caught her eye, and she caught his too, well...

—You met him once. The night we met you. Ronald. He never knew he was our dad. And we didn't either at that point.

—Zöe never told him, says Christine. Leonard, Zöe and Ronald stayed friends for years. Even after Zöe and Leonard split up, they each kept in touch with him. But neither of them ever told him he had twin daughters. And by the time we knew, we'd lost touch with him.

—We traced him years later. He'd gone back to Jamaica and died there.

—Leonard was not happy when he found out she was pregnant, says Christine. And he was even more furious when he discovered it was twins, she said. They'd not planned for children. But there was no pill back then, of course. So they just resigned themselves to the situation.

—She said that it was while she was pregnant that she designed Deptford Strand Estate, says Annette.

—It came out in a big creative rush, she told us. She was sick, sick, sick at first. Morning sickness all day long. But apparently Leonard wouldn't tell anyone she was pregnant. He made up some other illness.

—But then the morning sickness cleared up and she started showing. And she started working again. The firm already had the commission for the estate, and Leonard assigned junior partners to do a lot of the work. He wanted to keep her away from the office, away from the clients, he said. They struggled to take a female architect seriously anyway; a pregnant one would be too much of a challenge. And she accepted it. Agreed with him in fact. He suggested she go and stay with her sister, Elspeth, who was living down in Cornwall somewhere at the time. He'd tell everyone she was convalescing – that she needed some months of rest. No one questioned a woman's illnesses back then.

—But while she was in Cornwall, she just ignored all the stuff the juniors were coming up with and worked on her own, says

Christine. So the entire estate was her vision from the big scheme down to the tiny details. But you know this. You've seen it all.

—The day after she completed the design, she went into labour, says Annette.

—It took two days for us to be born. Leonard never made an appearance, of course.

—And then there we were. Two black babies, says Annette.

—She said she'd always suspected we were Ronald's. The timings fitted. She'd spent the whole pregnancy constructing various plans for what she would do. She told us she wanted to keep us. She said she'd told her sister she wanted to keep us.

—But ... two black babies, says Annette.

—She told us Leonard's first words when he saw us were 'You can't really believe you can keep them, can you?' She didn't tell us how the argument went. How she told him Ronald was our father. But she said that Leonard gave her an ultimatum: they would stay together, as husband and wife, and as partners in the business, and she would give us up for adoption; or she would be a single mother of—

—Two black babies, says Annette.

—She tried to explain it to us, says Christine. The council was raving about the design for the estate already. This was her break-through. It would make her name. Put paid to all the critics. Everyone who said a woman couldn't compete with male architects. Did she want to throw all that away?

—For two black babies?

—No one in her professional life knew she'd even been pregnant; everyone thought she was sick, bedbound. So she would be able to 'make a recovery' and breeze back into work. The new star of architecture. She tried to say it was all Leonard's plan. That she was vulnerable after the birth. That he'd convinced her it was the only way. That keeping us would be suicide.

—Suicide, say Annette. And there's a pause.

—And you can see it, can't you? continues Christine. Late

1950s. An up-and-coming star in her field. Interviewed on TV. Then gives birth to illegitimate twins.

—Black twins.

—Her career would have been over, says Christine. So that was it. She said we were with her for less than a week. Biggest regret of her life, she told us.

—And then she got pregnant again.

—She told us that Leonard blamed her for her carelessness when she fell pregnant the second time. He even suggested she should get rid of you – which was still illegal back then, 1959. She said she couldn't bear the idea of losing two more children. That losing us was too much pain. She couldn't go through it again.

—But, you know – two white babies, says Annette.

—It's difficult not to see the difference. She gives her black babies up for adoption. She keeps her white ones.

—And all the scandal they were trying to avoid by giving us up happened anyway, says Annette.

—She refused to terminate her pregnancy. She told people that designing the estate put an unbearable strain on their marriage; although everyone thought they split because she was hugely successful and didn't need him anymore. She said all that was true, but the real last straw was the fact that he'd asked her to get rid of you.

—She threw him out while she was pregnant, says Annette.

—There was a very public mess over the business. But you know all that.

—And Zöe remained a star.

—Would she have been a star if people knew about us? says Christine.

—You know, two black, illegitimate babies she managed to hide from everyone.

—Perhaps Leonard held that over her all those years, says Christine.

—And then went and found us, and brought us to Marlowe Tower.

—She told us she was terrified when she found out we'd moved in. It was twenty years since she'd buried us. That was the word she used: 'buried'.

—To our faces. But it's difficult to bury live people, says Annette.

—Leonard loved it, of course. We saw him change at the time. He was quite, you know, dour before, when we first knew him at college.

—A misery-guts, I think describes him, says Annette. It was partly why we refused his offer of moving into 304 the first couple of times he asked. But when we accepted he was suddenly so cheerful. Full of the joys. Always up in his garden.

—Zöe knew he'd come back the year before, she said. He'd owned flat 304 forever and had never lived in it. She'd thought he'd kept it empty to make sure she knew he still had a stake in everything she had. Another way of reminding her of her betrayals – that, after everything he'd done for her, she'd thanked him with infidelity, babies he didn't want and then separation and divorce. When he moved back in, she'd hoped it was just a new way of needling her. Never letting her forget what she'd done to him. But she said she was suspicious. She feared he had some new plan. That he'd got bored with simply stalking her, and had something more dangerous in mind. And then she found out about us. She said he was waiting by her car one evening. The blue 2CV she drove. 'I've got new tenants in 304,' he told her.

—She said he flicked his lit cigarette butt at her as he walked away.

—And then Mrs Ledbury filled her in, says Christine.

—'I've got blacks moved in next door to me. Blacks. Two of them. Sisters. Twins. Do they even have twins, blacks?'

—We don't know she said any of that, says Christine. Zöe just said that Mrs Ledbury came to her; 'coloured girls' were the words she used. She was sure straight away who we were. She now knew why Leonard had moved into Marlowe Tower. Bumping into her at conferences wasn't enough for him anymore. Now he was threatening to expose her biggest secret, she was sure. But what she couldn't work out was how he'd found us. So she confronted him about it.

—The truth was, he hadn't been searching for us at all, says Annette. We'd fallen into his lap.

—He told Zöe he knew who we were as soon as he saw us at our first lecture. We'd kept the first names Zöe had given us. So all he had to do was look at our dates of birth on our college files to confirm his suspicions. And then he concocted his little plan.

—Zöe was right: he'd held on to his property in Marlowe Tower to aggravate her, to make sure she knew she'd never be rid of him, says Annette.

—But when he met us, he'd found a new 'line of attack', that's what she called it.

—She said, 'I don't believe in God, a higher power, but the two of you turning up at his university, becoming his students – it was like I was being put in my place. Like I was being told I couldn't control my own destiny.' I've never forgotten those words, says Annette.

—He moved into Marlowe Tower – and invited us to live there with him.

—We turned him down initially – but like we told you at the time, we got a bit obsessed with Zöe's work while we were at college. And the fact he was her ex-husband, and maybe knew stuff about her we couldn't find out in the textbooks...

—It became too much to resist, says Christine.

—She said it worked, Leonard's scheme. Knowing we were living just a few floors above her was agony. She described it as a physical pain. And I can understand that.

—She said her instinct was to come straight upstairs and see us, tell us who she was, says Christine. But of course she couldn't.

—'Imagine what I'd risk if I did,' she said. As if we'd automatically understand.

—We did understand. She'd given us up—

—Her two black babies, says Annette.

—And managed to keep it a secret all those years. Apart from hospital staff and adoption people, only her mother and sister knew she'd given birth to us. Leonard hadn't told us she was our mother, and of course you two didn't know. If she came up and told us 'I'm your mum' – exposed herself like that – who knows what might have happened; who she might have hurt?

—And then we met the two of you, says Annette. And became friends.

—Zöe said she felt sick the whole time, knowing we were together so much. And she did what she could to stop it, she said. But that didn't work.

—Of course we got on, says Annette. We were brothers and sisters, even if we didn't know it.

—There was nothing any of us could see that made us siblings. But in our blood, in our nerve endings, we must have felt it, says Christine. That's why we got on instantly. That's what I think.

—But Zöe saw it differently, says Annette. She said it sitting right there in front of us. 'It's a reckoning, this.' Those were her words.

—She said she came up to the party that night. She came up and found him, and told him she just wanted him to stop. She said that he laughed at her. Told her this was just the start, that he'd introduced us to Ronald and we'd become great mates. That he was going to drop the bomb and tell Ronald we were his kids; he just needed to find the right time. And then it would be time to tell us who our mother was. She asked him what he thought that would do to you two, finding out we were your sisters. She said he laughed again and said he didn't care. He didn't care about you at all. And she said that was when she gave him a push, just to get him out of her way, so she could walk off, she said. She didn't realise how close to the edge of the roof they were, it was so dark up there. She even told us that she'd never designed the roof to be used for anything like a party.

—She said that, like she could control everything that anyone did.

—She said she pushed him, says Christine. That he stepped back, his hands went out, he wobbled for second. And then he was gone.

—And then she started with the sorries again.

—She said she couldn't give us a good reason why she didn't go straight to the police. Why she didn't confess. Why she ran back downstairs to her flat and pretended she'd not been at the party at all. Why she was coming to us now. She was sorry. She couldn't explain it. She couldn't explain why she'd stayed silent for a year.

—Now, if Zöe had just been some neighbour, says Annette, the white woman who designed the estate, who got into a row with her ex and accidentally pushed him off the roof, who then kept her mouth shut when two black girls from upstairs were arrested for it...

—We might have understood. You can see the logic of it can't you? You can see why someone would do that. You might make out you wouldn't do it yourself, but you would, wouldn't you?

—But she was our mother, says Annette. And she told us who she was—

—Who we were—

—In virtually the same breath as she told us she killed Leonard—

—The woman who gave birth to us—

—Who gave up her two little brown babies—

—Killed a man and let us—

—Let her brown babies, her black girls—

—Take the fall for what she'd done—

—And stayed silent about it for a year—

—A year. Silent. Nothing.

—Our mother, your mother, watched on while her children, her daughters—

—Her black twins—

—Went to prison. For a year.

—Can you tell we've had forty years to stew on this? says Annette.

—Maybe she just didn't see herself as our mother for that year. Maybe she suddenly did when we were acquitted. And then she broke her silence.

—We were silent too, I suppose, says Annette. After she told us all this. After she left the flat and went wherever she went.

—She went up the stairs into Leonard's place, and that was the last anyone saw of her, wasn't it?

—We stayed silent. We didn't go to the police. We didn't tell them what she'd told us. We didn't say she was 'our mummy'. We didn't tell them she'd confessed to killing Leonard.

—But was it out of loyalty? Because she was our mother? says Christine. Or was it because we were too scared they'd try and pin something else on us – say that we'd killed her too. Telling them she was our mother would incriminate us.

—Can you imagine that? Thinking that saying someone is your mother would incriminate you?

—We had all these thoughts going through our heads, says Christine. They were all reasons we stayed silent I suppose. But we were never sure we were right to do it.

—So many times I've said to Christine, 'We should've said something. We should say something now. We should tell our story.' It was only, what, four years later that the New Cross fire happened? We knew people who were at the party that night, who died. Burned to death. An accident, the police have always said. Fault of the black kids at the party. 'Sound familiar?' I said to Christine. 'We should say something,' I said. Then the same year there was Brixton. I said to Christine, 'We should say something.' Then Broadwater Farm, Stephen Lawrence, 2011, all these times, I thought, 'We should say something'.

—You know, we didn't even realise we were mixed race until she told us she was our mother. We had two foster families, and then our adoptive family was black. We were no lighter than their other kids, really. We just thought we were black.

—Imagine that, says Annette. Discovering at twenty-two that you're mixed race.

—We'd decided between ourselves years before that we didn't want to find our real mother and father. But we'd never thought one of them was white.

—All those people on the estate who saw us as the outsiders, who thought we were invading their white territory, who were railing against the council because they thought they'd been promised the area would be kept 'British' – what would they have said if they found out the white woman who designed the place was our mother? Every time we discussed it, I said to Christine, 'We should say something.'

—But we didn't. We stayed silent.

—Traps shut. Like we had lockjaw or something.

—Why? asks Christine.

The word hangs in the spotlight. Then Christine continues.

—Because she was our mother and we just couldn't convince ourselves—

—Or maybe wouldn't allow ourselves to think—

—That what she did was racist. She gave us away, because we were black babies, says Christine. Because she couldn't pass us off as Leonard's. But was that because she was racist, or because the world was racist then?—

—Is racist now.

—She didn't acknowledge us when we came to live in Marlowe Tower; but was that because we're black, or because we weren't hers anymore, because admitting her secret would damage her? She didn't admit to pushing Leonard, and instead she let us get arrested and tried for it. Was that because we're black? Or was it simply self-preservation? She could have done all these things for racist reasons. But equally, she might have done them for her own reasons, that had nothing to do with race.

—Or maybe, says Annette, we just couldn't bear to think the woman who gave birth to us could have seen these little brown babies and thought, nope. Not mine. Take them away.

—So maybe we gave her the benefit of the doubt.

—Even after she was long gone.

—But then...

—But then...

—We heard a rumour. About you two, says Christine.

—It was from Tabitha.

—We hadn't seen her for so many years. But we still recognised her, and she recognised us.

—And she said something, says Annette.

—She said something—

—That made it all make sense.

—We'd known you were our brothers for years, says Christine. We lost track of you, though. We left Marlowe Tower, rented out our flat, so we didn't know Aaron still lived there.

—Not until Tabitha told us.

—But we caught up with you, Clive, long ago.

—And long before you were making a big name for yourself.

—We're in housing, you see, says Christine. We ran a housing association for years. Set it up ourselves in the 1980s. We bought one of your schemes, Clive, in the early nineties.

—We wondered if we might come into contact with you.

—We weren't sure what we'd say. What we'd do, says Christine. But of course, you weren't involved in any negotiations. You probably didn't even see our names on the association's board. Since then we've watched your career. Seen you go on to bigger and bigger things.

—Zöe would be proud, wouldn't she? Her baby overcoming disability like that?

—But would she be more proud of her daughters, setting up a social enterprise, giving people good housing, creating communities? We tried to think she would.

—That she'd take as much pride in her black kids' successes as she would in her white kid's ones.

—And then we met Tabitha, says Christine. We resigned from the housing association a few years ago. Now we run the Residents' and Tenants' Trust. Do you know it? We've been following the development of the estate very closely these past couple of years.

—And we have not liked what we've seen, Clive, says Annette. Not at all. Redevelop the estate while you turn Marlowe Tower into luxury flats, cordoned off from the rest? Cover it all in cladding – even after Grenfell? No.

—Tabitha is one of the Trust's clients, says Christine. She told us that you were still in the tower, Aaron. That you were refusing to move out. And then you wrote to the Trust, didn't you? You can't have known that we're on the board, I suppose. You can't have known you were writing to *us*. Sally Perry told us about you, all alone in the tower. She was full of admiration.

—So you gave us the idea yourself, Aaron, says Annette. We thought that if we wanted to make a bit of a problem for Clive and the council, we could move back in. It was in our power as owners. And so we did.

—But it was what Tabitha told us just a few days ago that put a whole different cast on things, says Christine. On what we've been thinking about for forty years.

—We thought we'd moved back into Marlowe Tower to see you off, Clive. To continue the work we've been doing nearly all our lives—

—Giving people a home, basically.

—We thought we knew exactly what happened over there – with Leonard, with Zöe, with you two. We thought we were the only ones that knew all the secrets. But then Tabitha came to visit. And we learned there was another story altogether.

—Something that gets rid of all our doubts, says Christine.

—Because, if you did what Tabitha says you did—

—And if Zöe knew—

—Then she'd saved her white babies by letting her black ones take the fall for them.

—And that's plain racist. Whichever way you look at it.

There's a long pause. The light is still, but there's a sense that it's breathing – heaving as if after a tiring run. Annette and Christine's mouths are slightly open, drawing in air. In the dark penumbra around the spotlight, there is some shuffling. An intake of breath, the preparations for speech, but then a hesitation.

—It explains why Zöe said she didn't know why she'd stayed silent for a year. But she did know. And now we know too. She was protecting you. Hoping we'd go down for Leonard's death. But then, when we didn't, she confessed to it herself. To protect you.

—And then she threw herself off the roof, says Annette. Maybe because it was easier than facing us. Facing you. Or maybe it was simply to make her story more convincing.

—Zöe rarely left anything to chance, did she? That wasn't her style at all.

—She must've felt sure we'd go to the police and tell them what she'd said. To vindicate ourselves. And then you two would be in the clear forever.

—But we stayed silent, didn't we, says Christine.

—Has that been uncomfortable for you, all these years? says Annette.

—If we'd done what she meant us to do: gone to the police, said 'Mum killed Leonard', and then they had found her body, that would have been the whole case, over.

—But we didn't, says Annette. And she didn't kill herself properly. She should've jumped off the same side of the tower as Leonard. Not into the river. She should have left a note – a confession. But she didn't.

—So you've had to live not knowing. Just keeping your mouths shut and hoping.

—You could have finished it all, says Christine. Come out and told everyone what you'd done. You've had years to do that. But you've stayed silent too, like us. Granted, you didn't know we're your sisters. But still.

—But even still.

—You got our letter yesterday, Aaron? Yes.

—It was an ambush, you know, that meeting. Sally had no idea what we were going to do. What we were going to say when she was out of the room.

—But then you wrote to us, says Christine.

—All these letters. Like we're back in the seventies again.

—We thought that maybe you'd confess. Tell the truth about what you'd done, says Christine.

—That you killed your father and stayed silent.

—That you let us take the fall.

◆

Aaron and Clive are silent.

The light falls on them now. Annette and Christine move, rearranging limbs. They each pick up a glass, each take a drink. A sip.

—We didn't kill Leonard, says Aaron.

—Our father, says Clive – an empty clarification.

—He just fell, says Aaron. By accident. He walked off the edge of the roof.

—Just like that? says Annette?

—Just like that, replies Clive.

He sits himself up straighter.

—And Mum didn't think we'd done it for that whole year, says Aaron. So you're wrong: she wasn't protecting us by letting you go to jail.

—She only started to suspect us when you were acquitted, says Clive. She'd never have let you take the blame for something we did. I'm sure of it.

—Are you? says Christine.

—You're sure a mother could never treat her brown babies different from her white ones? Annette's eyebrow is high. High high.

—But when we had our fall, says Aaron. She, well, she...

—She betrayed me to Aaron, and Aaron to me.

Christine puts her glass down. Annette puts hers beside it.

—Hang on, what do you mean?

—She tried to get the truth out of each of us by lying, said Clive.

—She told Clive I'd said he pushed Leonard.

—And she told Aaron I'd said that *he* did it.

—And did you? says Christine.

—Either of you? says Annette.

—No, we just told you, says Aaron. We were talking to him. It wasn't even an argument.

—It was an argument, says Clive. We can't pretend it wasn't.

—We weren't shouting.

—He was.

—Well, then, it didn't come to blows, says Aaron.

—Didn't it?

—Didn't it? says Annette.

—Who pushed him? asks Christine.

—Nobody pushed anybody, says Clive with vigour.

—Neither of us did, says Aaron. He walked off by himself.

—All by himself? says Annette.

—We touched him, I remember, says Aaron. Things were getting overheated. I put a hand on his shoulder ... or, and, well ... he poked Clive, poked him in the chest. And then, and then...

—And then?

—And he pushed us, didn't he? says Clive, as if he's now recalling the moment clearly. Barged past us, rammed into us with his shoulder.

—Yes, yes. That's what happened.

—You seem not exactly sure, says Christine.

—You seem to be making this up as you go along, says Annette.

—We're not.

—We're not!

—We touched him. A hand on his arm.

—On his shoulder. That was all.

—That's all Tabitha saw, says Aaron. And then she saw him walk off the roof. But she said she'd seen us push him. But she can't have.

—He just walked. We didn't touch him, says Clive.

—We touched but we didn't push.

—We didn't push.

—We didn't.

—We didn't kill him.

—And neither did Mum.

—And neither did we, say Christine and Annette.

—So what does that make you? say Annette and Christine.

49

From above, we see a man fall from the top of a tower. A winged seed dropping from a tree.

It is night – a suffocatingly hot night in 1976. From above, the roof of the tower is like the cavern of a candle – a dancing glow at the centre surrounded by crenelated walls. A man falls from the roof. His white shirt a flake of paper sipped into the throat of the night.

How did he come to fall? Did we see what happened?

No. We're too high up here. From our position it looked like a tussle, a little tangle of bodies, two too similar to distinguish one from the other. The arms and hands and angles too quickly placed, too briefly glimpsed to decide where exactly the force came from that propelled him off the edge. Were they steps or staggers he took across those last two yards? Was he facing his sons, or turned away? From above it's impossible to say. He's a figure in black and white, and the lamps and candles dotting the roof, the ambient light from the city around it – so much dimmer back then – make the dance with his sons a confused chiaroscuro – the image abstract and ambiguous.

From above, back then the Isle of Dogs was a wasteland. Now, though, it's a dense plantation, its trees alive with lights as the evening drifts in from downriver.

From above the tower by the river near Mudchute is a dark square rimmed with a glow. Drop down and we see there's a garden up here, lit by spots among the leaves. And here is a head. Long hair. And now legs that move with a stiff, stuttered limp. Aaron has come out of the big living room. Behind him is Christine. Then Annette, with Clive following behind.

As the evening has settled on the river, they have talked, and talked some more. Annette has started sentences with 'All this time', Clive with 'How could we?' Aaron with 'I've always wanted' and Christine with 'From now on'.

Have they reconciled in any way? Is that why they've come out together onto the terrace? Is that why they're staring across the river? Can Annette and Christine forgive Aaron and Clive their silence? Do they even believe their version of Leonard's fall?

◆

From above, Marlowe Tower is now a pale headstone in the greying night. All its windows are dark. It is unoccupied at last, it seems. It's making its habitual noises – the creaks and pops and sighs that are its usual song. But there is no one here to hear it. It is cool concrete, coiled steel rebar and dusty floors now; no body warmth glowing in any of its rooms.

But no. There, on the top floor, is a patch, a denser dark. A movement. A something.

That something – usefully for the purposes of ending a story; usefully for the purposes of ending a story in a certain way – is a someone: Zöe Goldsworthy.

Aaron and Clive, and Annette and Christine are sitting on Clive's terrace – the evening air is cool but comfortable. They are discussing their mother now. At intervals, each of them looks across the river at Marlowe Tower, but none of them sees her. The distance is too great, the evening has become too dim, the story as they know it written in too different a way.

But we, if we choose to, can see her. We can float outside the thirty-first-floor windows and look into her eyes, and admit the possibility that on the evening of the 1977 Jubilee, after she had visited her daughters – and for the first time in twenty-two years, called them her daughters – she climbed the service stairs up to the roof.

She walked to the very edge that night, so close it seemed she might jump. But instead she picked up a plant pot and slipped underneath it the page bearing her confession. Then hurried herself back to the door, and down the service stairs – not to her own flat, but into the basement and out of the tower via one of her most recondite routes.

She surfaced close to the walkway as it crossed Evelyn Street and she leaped onto a passing bus, clutching her bag of money and new papers tightly to her body as she did so. The bus was empty. The conductor barely looked at her when she proffered her ten-pence piece. Told her it was free tonight, on account of the queen and that...

Where she has been for four decades we do not know. She's silent as she stares across the river at the pool of light at the top of Clive's tower – none of her thoughts slips from her lips this time. Perhaps she has been monitoring her children's lives from afar. Perhaps she has been holed up in a distant city – in India, perhaps, in Le Corbusier's Chandigarh, where she would be surrounded by a whole city planned by a single architect. And from there, perhaps she has followed Clive's rise, tutted and frowned at newspaper and magazine articles, but smiled to herself too. And perhaps she has also smiled when she has found mentions of the Mayfield twins – cutting a path in the opposite direction to Clive's, but more in keeping with her own. And maybe – most likely, rather – she has fretted about Aaron, and hoped that no sign or sound from him means he has remained, as she expected he would, safe in Marlowe Tower, content to reside in the perfect little world she created.

Maybe it is the destruction of that little world that has brought her back here – perhaps she read about Clive's redevelopment of Deptford Strand. Perhaps she was the passenger bent into a window seat on the approach to Heathrow at the beginning of our story, seeing London laid below, the tall buildings like standing stones.

And perhaps she has just taken the stairs of Marlowe Tower a flight, a step, at a time, her ninety-year-old legs slow, her ninety-year-old heart straining. It's likely she stopped at flat 246 and found it empty. Stopped at 304 and found it empty too. And has finally found her way up to the thirty-first floor, her head aswim, the cloak of hair a metal grey now.

However and whyever she got here, she now gazes out of the window, across at her four children sitting in a garden on top of a tower on the Isle of Dogs. Can she see them from Marlowe Tower? It doesn't seem possible.

But when she turns away, in the dull-steel light we see a slump of peace in her cheeks, a satisfied sleep in her eyes, as if finally everything is now where she intended it to fall.

Acknowledgements

Unlike my first novel, I flew solo on *Fall* – without the advice and critiques from a writing group or fellow writers. So my first thanks goes to my publisher, Karen Sullivan, who was also my first reader, and reassured me that it hadn't been such a risky decision after all.

My thanks must also go to Karen for allowing me the time and space to write this one. It's taken a while, and the stop-start nature of the pandemic lockdowns didn't help, but Karen was patient with me and understood why I found it so difficult to write at home.

My thanks must therefore also go to the London Library and its staff. When it was open – between lockdowns – I cycled up to St James's Square each and every Friday, and those Fridays piled up and turned into pages, and into the book you have before you.

Thanks too to Mark Swan for his wonderful cover, Elaine for her typesetting, and to the whole Orenda team – Cole, Anne, Sophie, Mary, Liz and Max – for all the work they do getting these books out there. And thanks to the bloggers for their great reviews and support, and for keeping the all-important book social-media machine going.

To my friends and family, for your unwavering support, my thanks.

And finally to the reader: thank you for reading.

—West Camel